Whispers in the Dark

Secrets of Whispering Pines, Volume 1

Holly Bowne

Published by Write Expressions Ink, 2024.

This is a work of fiction. Similarities to real people, places, or events are entirely coincidental.

WHISPERS IN THE DARK

First edition. May 1, 2024.

Copyright © 2024 Holly Bowne.

ISBN: 979-8224077403

Written by Holly Bowne.

PROLOGUE

Pain shot along her jaw. Alex could feel the welt rising on her cheek where she'd been struck. The coppery taste of blood filled her mouth. She wished she could spit it out. The skin around her mouth was raw, pulled taut by the duct tape that permanently muted her cries.

She struggled back up into a sitting position. And in the growing darkness, she watched as her captor paced. Her eyes tracked his movements. The woods were silent now, except for the occasional rustle of trees swaying in the night wind.

She couldn't do anything about her bound ankles. But whenever he turned away from her she worked at the ropes that held her wrists tightly behind her back. They ached. In fact, her entire body ached from fighting against him.

Even now in the dim light, she could still see the marks her nails had clawed into his face before he'd finally subdued her. Her eyes filled in frustration and she squeezed them shut to keep the tears from blurring her vision.

Don't give in to fear.

He paused in front of her as he'd done a moment ago, staring down at her with a maniacal light glowing deep in his eyes. And she stared back at him. Unblinking. Waiting for another blow. But she refused to flinch.

She was scared, yes. Evidenced by how fast and painfully her heart thudded inside her chest. But even more, she was angry. And her blood ran hot with it, her mind raced. All she needed was an opening. Any opening. Something she could turn to her advantage.

Then, her captor's cell phone buzzed.

CHAPTER 1

Alex wandered closer to the water's edge, letting the wet sand ooze between her toes with each step. Her sandals dangled from her fingertips. She tipped her face to the rising sun and reveled in the chill as a frothy wave slipped over her feet. Even at this early hour, the day's heat already warmed her skin.

She inhaled the tangy Lake Michigan air and marveled as always at how much more like an ocean it seemed than a massive lake. She willed the rhythmic pulse of its waves to soothe the corded knot that seemed permanently jammed between her shoulder blades. She'd been in Whispering Pines for a week now in response to her grandmother's unexpected request. And while she usually found visits to the quaint village relaxing, her insomnia and stress were still frustratingly present.

Turning north, she made her way up the shoreline, zigzagging around two small children who shrieked in delight as they played tag with the waves. Hopeful seagulls caterwauled overhead, diving for scraps left from the previous day's picnickers. A few boats dotted the horizon. Sharp, white specks against the lake's deep navy blue. A soft breeze pulled at the shorter wisps of dark hair that escaped her ponytail. They tickled her cheeks and neck, and she brushed them back, tightening the elastic.

Alex knew that in a few hours the beach would be swarming. Families toting coolers and beach toys would stake their claims across the soft, white sand. Groups of teens would fill the volleyball courts, flirting and lying down to bake in the warm June sunshine. But for now, it was blissfully vacant.

She reached for her cell phone to check the time, and suddenly, her legs were swept from beneath her. Alex cried out as her body hit the ground hard, sandals flying from her grip. She was flat on her back, trying to catch her breath, when a cold, wet nose and sloppy tongue assailed her. Twisting her face away, she pushed hard at the offender.

"Rex, *nein*! *Pfui*!"

The panting golden retriever instantly backed away at the command. Alex sat up, glaring at the dog, who didn't appear the least bit repentant, tongue lolling, tail wagging. Instead, he looked expectantly at Alex and barked.

She brushed at the sand which now clung to her arms and clothing. And feeling the sting of it in her eyes, she squeezed them shut, swiping at them with both hands.

"I'm so sorry. He's normally better behaved," said a deep voice nearby.

The dog continued his short, staccato barks.

"What's his problem?" Alex muttered, still brushing sand from her eyes.

"You're sitting on his Frisbee."

Squinting through one eye, Alex looked up to meet the voice's owner. A pair of dark eyes met hers. So dark, in fact, Alex couldn't make out where the pupils ended and the irises began. They were framed with thick, dark lashes—the kind most women would kill for. At the moment, though, the eyes were looking back at her from a masculine face wearing a bemused expression. This irritated Alex even more than the leg sweep from the dog.

The stranger reached down to offer his assistance, but Alex ignored him as she struggled to her feet.

Rex immediately dove for the Frisbee, gripping it between sharp, white teeth. He trotted to his master and dropped the toy, barking once again.

"Okay, boy!" the man said, picking it up. He curled the disk into his chest, then let it sail. In a flash of red-gold fur, Rex was off at a gallop, chasing it down. The stranger bent to retrieve Alex's sandals, handing them to her.

The man was tall and lean. Hard biceps flexed below the sleeves of his faded T-shirt. His well-worn jeans were rolled up several inches to reveal tanned, muscular calves above bare feet.

"Sorry about Rex," he apologized again. "He tends to get kind of energetic when we play. That's why I like to bring him for his beach run early, just so this sort of thing doesn't happen."

"What? Tackling unsuspecting beachcombers?" Alex said, brushing more sand from her shorts.

"Yeah, like that." The man grinned and extended his hand to her. "Jake Riley."

She hesitated an instant before grasping his hand in return. "Alex Fontaine." His grip was warm, encompassing hers.

"I don't recall seeing you here before," he said, still smiling. His gaze was direct. And disconcerting. And he was still holding onto her hand. She felt heat stain her cheeks as she pulled her fingers awkwardly from his.

"Well, it's a public beach. I don't suppose you can keep track of everyone," Alex said drily.

"True. But I do try to keep track of the pretty ones." He winked.

Alex stiffened. "Yes, well…I was just leaving."

Jake's charming grin faded. "Hey, I—"

Rex bounded back, distracting them both. He dropped the Frisbee directly in front of Alex and barked excitedly.

"Looks like he's trying to apologize, too."

Alex looked down at the dog. He was a beautiful animal, his coat shiny and softly curling. If dogs could smile, she'd have sworn that's what Rex was doing now. He gazed up at her with liquid amber eyes that crinkled at the corners. She reached down to scratch his head, which inspired some energetic tail wagging. He gave her palm a lick.

"Pushy little guy, isn't he," Jake said. "Stealing a kiss like that."

Alex shot Jake a sharp look, but his expression remained mild. She picked up the faded green Frisbee. Its edges were peppered with teeth marks, and gritty lakeshore sand clung to it.

She addressed the dog. "All right, buddy, but just one throw, okay?"

Rex barked.

Alex laughed and threw the Frisbee with a snap of her wrist.

"Nice!" Jake said as they watched the disk skim a course parallel to the shoreline.

"Thanks," Alex replied as Rex raced after it. "I thought dogs weren't allowed on the beach."

"He gets special dispensation," Jake said.

Alex looked at him curiously, but Jake didn't explain. Instead, he turned toward her, his expression sincere. "The least you can do is allow me to buy you breakfast after I let Rex knock you over like that."

The light wind coming off the lake played with the loose dark curls covering his head, and the angle of his jaw sported a good day's growth of beard. He noticed her scrutiny and flashed another quick smile, teeth bright against bronzed skin.

Alex dropped her eyes then and mentally gave herself a face slap. *Do not go there, Fontaine.*

Just then, a young woman jogged past, long silky ponytail swishing from side to side as she moved. "Hey, Jakey!" She managed a sexy smile between puffs of oxygen.

"Lookin' good, Vicki!" he called after her.

If Alex had needed something to bolster her resolve, that was it. Taking a deep breath, she said, "Look, I appreciate your apology, Jake. But as far as breakfast goes, I have to pass." She paused, then added, "It was, er, nice meeting you." And turning, she walked as swiftly as the sand allowed back toward the parking lot.

She could feel his eyes on her as she tossed her sandals into the car and climbed in. *Please start. Please start. Please start.* She turned the key in the ignition of her ancient Impala and resisted the urge to hug the steering wheel in relief as the engine hummed to life. She rolled her window down, then stretched across the massive front seat to lower the passenger's side. She sighed with relief as the trapped heat escaped. Rex's excited barks rose above the waves and gulls, but she didn't dare look back as she pulled out of the lot and headed into town.

Driving up Main Street, she snagged an empty parking space directly in front of Fort Stearns, the town's kitschy tourist trap.

She made her way up the sidewalk, silently applauding her confident shutdown of Jake Riley's blatant attempts to flirt. Not so long ago, she would have been flattered to have such a hot guy expressing interest in her. As a matter of fact, she thought grimly, stopping at an intersection, not so long ago, she *had* been flattered.

Despite her daily resolve to keep all unpleasant thoughts at bay, memories pricked at her like shards of seashell underfoot. She found it frustrating that even after nearly six months, the wound was still so raw, and the pain close to the surface.

"Fool," she muttered under her breath. The light changed and she marched through the intersection, sandals slapping hard against the steamy pavement. She cut across a parking lot and flung the Westlake Gas Station's door open with such force that the jangling entrance bell flipped on its wire.

The yeasty smell of baking hit her in the face and Alex inhaled deeply, calming herself. Westlake provided a unique dual role to the citizens of Whispering Pines, serving as a gas station and the village's only bakery.

Alex selected half a dozen donuts from the colorful bounty laid out behind the glass. After completing her purchase, she dug into the white bakery bag and pulled out a Boston Crème. Heading toward the door, she took a huge bite just as it swung wide to admit Jake Riley. She looked up at him, cheek puffed out like a squirrel with a nut.

That same slow grin from earlier spread across his lips and his eyes twinkled down at her. This time, she noticed he had deep dimples on either side of that dazzling smile. Suddenly, his hand shot forward, catching a glob of chocolate icing just as it fell from the corner of her mouth.

"Boston Crème, eh?" he said, popping it into his own mouth and smacking his lips together. "Mmmm. One of my favorites."

Alex felt her face redden in shock.

"Will you look at this, Pat?" Jake said, directing his attention to the woman behind the counter. "I offer to buy the lady breakfast and she chooses one of your Boston Crèmes instead."

"I don't blame her one bit." Pat chuckled, polishing the sparkling glass. "Steering clear of you is probably one of the smartest things a girl could do."

"Ouch." Jake placed both hands over his heart, his features arranged into a pained expression. "Haven't I always been true to you?" He moved past Alex, sidling up to the counter to lean close to the older woman. Alex noticed his pants were no longer cuffed, and he had on work boots.

"Well, I guess you're as true now as you were when you were a donut-loving five-year-old," she laughed.

"Got a couple more of those Boston Crèmes left for me?"

"Don't I always," she replied with a wink.

"Yes, ma'am." Jake reached for her across the counter. "You've always got what I want." Pat slapped his hand away and scurried off, giggling like a teenager. "Jake Riley, you are shameless!"

"And one jelly filled too, please," he called after her.

He's absolutely disgusting! Alex thought.

It was clear, however, that Pat enjoyed Jake's banter. Studying the woman, Alex guessed her to be in her mid-sixties. Her hair was dyed an unnatural burgundy color, pulled back from her round face, and crushed under a hairnet. A white apron covered her ample bosom and dumpling-shaped torso.

"You in town for a while this time, Jakey?" Pat asked, filling the bag.

Alex returned her gaze to Jake to find he was no longer looking at Pat. He lounged with his back to the countertop, eyes resting boldly on Alex. Her mouth tightened, and she spun back toward the door.

"Till the end of summer," he replied, "maybe longer. Hey, Pat, have you met Alex Fontaine?"

Alex had just pushed open the door, but halted in her tracks, shooting Jake a dark look over her shoulder.

Pat returned to the counter to hand Jake his bag. "Nope, sure haven't." Removing the plastic glove she used to handle the food, she extended plump fingers with a smile. Alex was forced to cross back to the counter to shake it.

"Fontaine, eh? You any relation to Tilly Fontaine?" Pat asked, tilting her head.

"She's my grandmother."

"You look like her, especially 'round the eyes."

"You know my grandmother?"

"I sub in a card group with her and a couple of other ladies," Pat explained. "I can't commit to every month what with taking care of Earl, so I just fill in on occasion."

The older woman didn't elaborate, and Alex was too polite to ask who Earl was.

"Well, well..." Jake raised his brows. "Visiting grandma. How nice."

"Yes, it is nice." Alex felt irrationally annoyed that this man now knew even this tiny detail of her life.

Pat turned her attention back to Jake. "And how's your grandpa doing?"

"Ornery as ever." Jake grinned. "Giving me *lots* of input at the site."

Pat snorted. "What does he know about building condominiums?"

"Plenty, from the way he sees it." Jake laughed.

"You're the one building those new waterfront condos?" Alex blurted out before she could stop herself.

His eyes slid back to hers. "You've seen them?"

She looked away, refusing to meet his gaze. "I noticed the building renovation going on down at the beach," she mumbled.

In truth, Alex had studied the huge sign located at the construction site with interest. It announced Riley Development Corporation was converting the old R & B Watchcase factory into some charming, new lakefront condominiums. Alex had suggested her grandmother might consider selling her present home and purchasing one.

Grandma Tilly lived several miles outside of Whispering Pines, in the home she and Alex's grandfather had built for their retirement years ago. When Alex's grandfather passed away, Tilly had insisted on remaining in the home. Tilly would be celebrating her seventieth birthday soon, and though her grandmother's health was good, aside from her recent accident, Alex worried that soon the house and yard would be too much for her.

The sound of Pat's voice brought Alex out of her reverie. "Earl and I will be moving in as soon as they're finished." Pat nudged Jake's elbows off the glass countertop to polish the fresh smudges he'd created. "Did Rita give you the deposit and paperwork we filled out last week?"

"She did," Jake replied, peering into his bag and pulling out one of the Boston Crèmes. "It's a good thing you staked your claim. We've been generating a lot more interest since we finished up the remediation."

"Well, it's a fine idea you had, Jakey. Fixing up that old eyesore and making it into something useful. Of course, Earl and I especially like your idea of including the assisted living section." Pat paused in her polishing. "Have you had any more incidents at the site?"

Jake swallowed the bite he'd taken. "Nope. Everything's running smoothly now and we're kicking it into high gear."

Pat tossed her rag aside and started asking about specific amenities the complex would offer. So Alex was able to slip unnoticed out the door. She'd taken only a step when she heard a soft whine. She turned and saw a pale blue leash stretching from a chipped cement post at the side of the building to the collar on Rex. Alex walked over and squatted down to pet him. "He left you all alone, huh, boy?" she whispered. Rex's tail thudded against the ground and he leaned his head heavily against her palm.

The bakery doorbell jingled. "See you later, Pat. Try not to miss me too much."

"Oh, I'll do my best." Pat chuckled from inside.

Jake was beside them in an instant. Alex watched as he reached into his bag and pulled out the jelly-filled donut. "Here you go, boy," he said, handing it to Rex.

"You're feeding your dog a *donut*?"

Rex held the treat in his mouth, blinked once, then devoured it.

"Sure, it's his breakfast. What's the problem?"

"Have you ever heard of dog food?"

"Yeah, but Rex has more, er, refined tastes."

"Oh right, like—"

"I thought that was you, Jake." A stunning woman with an abundance of wavy, auburn hair approached them, her gaze focused on Jake.

Jake smiled. "Hi there, Christina. How've you been?"

"Much better now," she drawled, curling her fingertips around his upper arm and giving it a squeeze. "I was wondering when you'd be in town again."

"Well, here I am," he said.

The woman's face brightened. She slid a brief glance in Alex's direction, then looked pointedly at Jake, making the universal "call me" sign with her hand before sashaying off.

Alex was on her feet in an instant. *Seriously? Could this guy be any more of a player?*

Jake looked back at Alex. "So, does your grandmother live here in town?

"No."

"Ah, somewhere on the outskirts then?"

"Not exactly."

He arched one brow. "Well, how long will you be visiting?"

"A while."

"Got any special plans for the day?"

"Not really." With a final pat on Rex's furry head, she turned away.

"Hey, wait! Where are you going?"

"Nowhere."

"What a coincidence, me too! Want some company?"

Alex crushed the top of her bakery bag as she turned slowly back. "Look, no offense, but I'm here on—on vacation. *Alone* on vacation," she emphasized. "And I plan to keep it that way." With that, she whirled and walked purposefully back toward her car.

Slamming the door shut, she closed her eyes and whispered her "please start" prayer again, feeling another surge of relief as the engine roared to life. This time, she risked a look back. To her annoyance, Jake and Rex stood right where she'd left them, both wearing bemused expressions on their faces.

CHAPTER 2

Jake watched Alex stalk off and get back into her car.

"Well, I'm sorry to see you go, but I sure do love watching you walk away," he whispered to himself. Then he looked down at Rex. The dog looked back at him accusingly.

"What?"

Rex barked.

"Come on, let's get to the site." He opened the passenger door of his pickup truck and Rex leaped inside.

The watery blue sky of early morning had paled into a cloudless white haze. Despite the heat, Jake rolled down his windows instead of using the air conditioning. He tuned his radio to the local oldies station and "Under the Boardwalk" by The Drifters crooned through his speakers. Jake sang along, loudly and badly, pulling up beside Alex at the intersection and waving. He laughed as she lifted her nose and kept her gaze straight ahead until the light changed.

"She's one tough cookie, isn't she, Rexy." He reached over to pat the dog's panting head. Within minutes, Jake pulled through the chain-link fence that separated the Riley Development construction site from passersby. He jumped out, Rex bounding after him. Pulling his hard hat, black duffle, and a water jug from the truck bed, he headed toward the trailer that served as his on-site office.

The choppy pulse of machinery alternated with the rhythmic clank of metal on metal as Jake wound his way past shrink-wrapped stacks of materials.

"Yo, Jake! A little late, aren't you?"

He looked up to see Cesar Ruiz grinning down at him from the second floor of the structure. Cesar's tool belt was slung low beneath his round belly, and he swung a torpedo level in one hand.

"Yeah, just don't tell the boss, okay?" Jake grinned back.

Cesar laughed. "Too late, bro. She's already in there."

Jake opened the trailer door, letting Rex leap in first.

The dog made a beeline for the woman sitting behind the narrow built-in desk at the far end. A rainbow of file folders and neat stacks of paper were piled on either side of her as she faced the computer screen.

"Hi, Rita," Jake said, tossing everything beside the small, worn loveseat crammed against the back wall.

Rita McCay spun her chair sideways. "Ooooh, come here, lover boy."

"I wish you'd stop calling me that."

Rita laughed, scratching the top of Rex's head with red lacquered fingernails. "You know I'm only talkin' to you, don't ya, boy," she said, cradling the big dog's face between her palms. Although Michigan had been Rita's home for the past thirty years, she still retained her Missouri-born southern twang.

Jake flopped onto the loveseat, grateful for the small air conditioning unit that cooled the tiny space. "It's hot out there," he said, raking his hands through his hair.

Rita looked over at him. "Well, it's about to get even hotter."

"What do you mean?"

She handed him a copy of the local newspaper that was sitting on top of one of the paper piles. While most cities had moved to digital versions of their news, Whispering Pines still put out a print edition of the Whispering Pines Gazette.

"What now?" Jake asked, reaching for it.

Rita's bright red hair was teased into its usual cotton candy-shaped mound. She pulled at one of the green gemstones glittering at her earlobes, a typical sign she was feeling anxious. "Just look at the Opinion section."

Jake flipped to it, his eyes scanning the page, then he groaned. "When will that guy give up!"

He leaned forward, reading aloud. "'No More Condos!' by Frank Farley. If Whispering Pines is to regain its former luster, expensive luxury condos are *not* the answer. What this town needs are jobs, and affordable housing for its year-round citizens. It's a shame to see the fair village of Whispering Pines being ruined, turned into an exclusive, tourism-hungry destination by companies such as Riley Development Corporation."

Jake rolled his eyes and read on.

"It's easy for visitors to compliment the beauty of Whispering Pines and the incredible views of Lake Michigan, while the rest of us watch our own view of the lake being sold off to people who don't live here except for a few weeks each summer. These people don't shop at our local businesses and don't have to live in the poverty that tourism has brought here. Companies like Riley Development are only thinking about their bottom line. They ignore the fact that eighty percent of the local population despises tourists and tourism."

Jake paused, sputtering. "Eighty percent? Does this joker even realize that would be nearly 8,000 people?"

Rita shook her head, gum-snapping in response.

He continued. "Not only has poverty come to Whispering Pines because of tourism, but drugs and crime as well. When will people open their eyes and take back our community? Citizens of Whispering Pines, join with me and stop the condos! Let's bring in some decent paying jobs instead!"

Jake threw the paper aside in disgust. "Poverty? Drugs and crime? Is he kidding? And we *are* creating decent-paying jobs!" Jake leaned forward, ticking off on his fingers. "We've employed local architects, contractors, roofers, painters, carpenters, electricians, plumbers, landscapers, realtors! What the heck does Frank Farley call all that?"

"I know, I know," Rita soothed, toying with the beaded chain of her reading glasses hanging from her neck. "If brains were leather, Farley wouldn't have enough to saddle a June bug. But you're preachin' to the choir here, sugar."

Jake gave a brief snort.

"Besides," she added. "He's only one squeaky wheel."

"Yeah, well, I wish he'd stop squeaking so loud," Jake grumbled, rising.

Rita spun back to face the computer in front of her, gum crackling as she resumed typing on her laptop. Jake grinned at the effect she created with her bright hair, fuchsia Lycra top, and electric blue reading glasses perched at the end of her nose.

Although Rita was around the same age his mother would have been, Jake was pretty sure his mother would never have worn the flamboyant attire and three-inch slingbacks his office manager was wearing. But Jake accepted Rita's unique non-construction-site attire with barely a passing thought. He'd known her since he was five years old. She'd been the first person his father hired after starting Riley Development. Colorful wardrobe aside, he knew her to be intelligent, competent, and loyal, not to mention her well-hidden heart of gold.

Jake moved to the planning table at the opposite end of the small room. He mulled over this latest development with Farley as he spread diagrams of the building's exterior in front of him.

Farley had been dead-set against the watchcase factory renovation even before Riley Development came on the scene. He'd protested vehemently more than a decade earlier when the defunct factory was nearly replaced with a high-rise hotel. When the original developer discovered the grounds were contaminated with arsenic, mercury, and other heavy metals, Michigan's Department of Environmental Conservation and the Federal E.P.A. had swooped in. The remediation process took so long, the hotel deal never came to fruition, much to Farley's satisfaction.

The property sat idle for years until Riley Development came along and bought it, completing the final phases of cleanup and proposing the condominium project.

Now Farley had re-emerged as a thorn in Jake's side, formally protesting to Whispering Pines' City Council and blanketing the surrounding neighborhoods with flyers full of inaccurate information about the project. He even initiated a lawsuit against the company and the village, claiming the Council hadn't followed protocol when filing their environmental impact statement. The courts ultimately ruled against Farley. But nothing seemed to deter the man's quest to halt the project.

Rita broke into Jake's thoughts. "I finished those reports you needed. I'm emailing 'em to you right now."

"Thanks. Have we heard anything about the variances yet?"

"Nope."

Jake frowned. "I wonder what the holdup is."

Rita shrugged, then wheeled around in her chair. "Hey, sugar, mind if I kick off work a little early today?"

He glanced up. "Not a problem. Something special going on?"

She grinned at him. "Oooh, just a hot date."

"Hmmm." He narrowed his eyes. "Do I know him?" Jake and his two brothers took a protective stance where Rita's love life was concerned. His entire family had witnessed her messy divorce and the challenges she'd faced raising her children alone. But now, with her kids grown, Rita's naturally boisterous personality seemed to have gained momentum, and she tended to get a little wild at times.

"Nope. Met him at the Ballroom last weekend when I was out shooting pool after work with some of the guys. He helped me with my backspin." Rita winked.

"I'll just bet he did." Jake looked at her sternly. "Where's he taking you? Not the Captain's Galley, I hope. I don't want a repeat of what happened the last time you—" The trailer door banged open, interrupting him.

"Hi-de-ho folks!" a voice boomed through the open door.

The already tight space was immediately filled to capacity as Jake's grandfather stepped inside.

J.P. Riley was the same height as Jake. But where Jake possessed a lean, sinewy build, his grandfather was more solid with a broad chest. And he retained the commanding presence cultivated during his former career as a U.S. Coast Guard Captain.

"Whew, it's steamy out there!" he said, tossing his bicycle helmet on top of Jake's duffle.

Rex rose from his spot at Rita's feet and trotted over to receive his due attention from J.P., and to investigate the new smells associated with the sweat-stained helmet.

"Pops, you shouldn't be out riding your bike today. It's an Ozone Action Day, and I'm pretty sure the elderly are supposed to remain in cool, air-conditioned places."

J.P. snarled and took a swing at him. Laughing, Jake sidestepped him and knocked over a stack of files from Rita's desk. Rex joined in, barking playfully.

"All right, that's enough outta you boys. No roughhousing in my office!" Rita snapped, but her eyes twinkled as she peered over the top of her frames.

Jake scooped up the files and restacked them.

"Sorry, Rita," J.P. said, dropping his large frame onto the sagging loveseat cushions. "But that grandson of mine needs a good whooping every now and again." He pulled out a handkerchief and mopped the top of his bald head.

Jake reflected that some sixty-eight-year-olds would look ridiculous in the cycling shorts and colorful jersey his grandfather wore. But J.P. was a model of physical fitness. Rarely driving his car between spring and fall, he preferred to cycle his way around town in addition to maintaining a regular jogging schedule.

"What brings you by, Pops?" Jake asked, moving back to the planning table.

"Figured I'd stop in and see how the construction is coming along."

"Not much different from where we were yesterday," Jake replied, smiling.

"Well, I noticed some new plumbing work being started," J.P. said.

Jake laughed. "You got me there."

J.P. leaned back and folded his arms behind his head. "I still can't believe you got Benny to agree to this renovation. I know he'd rather have just demolished the old place. Never had the passion for historical buildings you and I do."

"I still can't believe Dad legally turned the entire project over to me. I just hope I don't blow it," Jake added drily.

J.P. waved the concern away. "The entire village is grateful you're turning this crumbling eyesore into something useful and beautiful."

"Not the *entire* village," Jake said, indicating the paper on the floor.

His grandfather eyed it and gave a derisive snort. "Farley's letter to the editor?"

Jake nodded, not surprised his grandfather was already aware of it. J.P. was active in Whispering Pines politics, even more so since the death of Jake's grandmother three years earlier. He'd even taken over his late wife's role on the Historic Preservation and Architectural Review Board.

"Don't worry about that old fart." J.P. leaned forward, his normally booming voice turning conspiratorial. "Hey, Jakey-boy, I got the inside scoop on those variances you've been asking for."

Jake was instantly alert. "What's the word?"

J.P. smoothed his handlebar mustache, looking like a poker player with an unbeatable hand. "I had coffee this morning with Garrett from the Zoning Board. Let's just say I think you'll be pleasantly surprised at the vote tomorrow night."

"They're approving both of them?"

J.P. grinned.

"Yes!" Jake did a fist pump. "That's great news, Pops!"

"Yessiree," J.P. said. "Benny sure can't complain now. He's got to see you were right all along about this being a good investment."

"It hasn't been easy," Jake said, opening the mini fridge to pull out three water bottles. "All the bizarre accidents and delivery problems haven't helped Dad's impression that this might have been a mistake to take on. Not to mention how tough it's been for him to admit I could possibly be right about anything."

"You're still a wet-behind-the-ears pup in his eyes, sugar," Rita said, not looking up as her fingers tapped away.

Jake set one bottle beside her on the desk and handed another to J.P. "It's like my nearly three years with TCL Environmental don't count for anything."

J.P. unscrewed his lid. "I think it's tough for any parent to admit his kid might be right about something he disagrees with."

"But you're not like that, Pops," Jake protested. "You've been my biggest cheerleader from the start."

A wide grin split J.P.'s lined face. "You're my grandson, not my son. Grandchildren can do no wrong."

"Awww." Jake grinned back.

"Besides, you and I share common interests," J.P. said. "When you worked for TCL, I saw how your concern for the environment and passion for brownfield renovations like this one really grew. I even take credit for bringing this old place to your attention. In a way, you could say this was all really my idea."

Jake laughed. "That's not so far from the truth, Pops."

"Here's to the success of the project," J.P. said, raising his bottle to tap against Jake's before they each took deep swallows.

J.P. smacked his lips, then waved his hand, indicating a change of subject. "So, Jakey-boy, what do you have going on for dinner tonight?"

"Nothing special," Jake said. Even as he said the words, for some absurd reason, a picture of Alex Fontaine's lovely face took shape in his mind. He shook his head, dissolving the image. *If she wouldn't have breakfast with you, she's definitely not going to go for dinner.*

"Good," J.P. said, lively blue eyes sparking as he leaned forward. "I have a little surprise for you. I had a recent brainstorm about your project here, and I've set up a meeting for us this evening."

Jake groaned. "Aw, Pops! What have you done now?" Although Jake appreciated his grandfather's enthusiasm, he was notorious for overstepping boundaries. Like the time Jake caught him holding a meeting regarding traffic flow patterns for an assembled group of project workers.

J.P. held up a thick palm, halting Jake's protests. "Just an idea I've been tossing around, Jakey-boy. I think it will really give the whole project a sort of..." He looked off into space. "What was that 'juno-sake-way' thing your Nana Ellen used to say?"

"*Je ne sais quoi,*" Jake mumbled.

"Yeah, that. Anyway, I booked one of the conference rooms at the library for seven o'clock tonight."

Jake looked doubtful.

"Trust me." J.P. flashed a mirror image of Jake's own charming smile directly at him.

Jake sighed. There was no point in arguing. His grandfather would be relentless until he got his way.

"Fine. Seven o'clock at the library. I'll be there."

"Good." His grandfather rose, settling his helmet back into place. "Well, I'm off." The trailer door banged shut behind him.

Sometimes, just sometimes, Jake wished his grandfather wasn't always quite so supportive.

CHAPTER 3

Annoying, egotistical, arrogant flirt! Alex thought, gunning her car past Jake's truck when he turned into the construction site entrance. And as much as she didn't want to admit it, an incredibly gorgeous one as well, which was probably why she felt angrier than the situation warranted. Seriously, why should she care if a stranger flirted with her a little?

She sighed aloud. She knew darn well why.

Turning right at the final intersection before the lake, her car lumbered north up Lakeshore Drive. Alex gazed out her open window, watching the lake flicker and ignite as sunlight bounced off its rippling waves. She slowed her breathing, letting the breeze cool her.

After a few miles, she turned off, making her way over the back roads to her grandmother's home.

Alex pulled into the driveway, admiring the charming setting as she always did. The log cabin nestled among maple, walnut, and birch trees which formed the edge of Whispering Pines' State Park forestland. Her grandmother's well-tended flowerbeds spilled over their borders. Geraniums, coreopsis, sedum, and petunias surrounded the tiny front porch in a profusion of color. The large windows fronting the A-frame's entrance and loft gleamed in the filtered sunlight.

Alex smiled as she noted the familiar burgundy station wagon parked in front. She grabbed the bag of donuts—minus the three she'd eaten between the bakery and home—and headed for the door.

Her trim figure belied her habit of stress eating. A piece of good fortune, which her mother loved to point out, would not last forever. Alex sighed again, imagining her mother's reaction to her earlier encounter with Jake Riley. *You could have at least smiled and pretended to be friendly.* Ugh! What for? She'd been down that road before and look where it had gotten her.

A cream-colored plaque hung above the doorbell proclaiming the cabin, "The Fontaines: Matilda & Joseph." Alex climbed the front steps and, out of habit, let her fingers trail lovingly over the armrest of the mahogany-wood rocking chair that had once belonged to her grandfather. She imagined him sitting there now. Rich vanilla-cherry pipe smoke forming wispy curls above his head, which was inevitably bent over a book.

Pulling open the front door, she stepped inside.

The home was constructed of thick honey-colored logs. Aside from the windows on the main floor, plenty of light filtered through the large, wedge-shaped windows filling the south wall of the loft area above.

A low oak coffee table strewn with books, magazines, and mail stood in front of a brown, leather loveseat draped with colorful quilts. Two matching recliners sat on either side of it. All the furniture faced the room's focal point, an authentic riverstone fireplace. "Oh, Alex, you're back," her grandmother said. "Did you have a nice walk?"

The ceiling fan whirred softly overhead as Alex crossed to the round oak dining table where Tilly sat with her two visitors. Despite the thick cast covering most of her left forearm, Tilly looked lovely as usual, her ivory skin blooming above the sky-blue top she wore. Her soft, silver hair was swept into the loose French twist Alex had styled for her earlier.

"It was wonderful," Alex said, dropping a kiss onto her grandmother's cheek, then greeting the two women seated with her. Gretchen Sinclair and Margot Reardon were two of her grandmother's closest friends. Each lady had an elegant bone china teacup and saucer in front of her. A plate of homemade sugar cookies arranged on a white doily sat in the center of the table.

"The lake was so peaceful," Alex said, dropping into an empty chair and eyeing the sugar cookies. "I see you've been baking again, Margot. They look delicious."

Margot flushed with pleasure. "Help yourself, dear. I just thought a nice sugar cookie might cheer up your grandmother since she can't work on her pottery right now." Margot's lips formed a delicate moue of sympathy as she looked over at Tilly.

Gretchen took a swallow of tea, then snorted, setting her cup down with a rattle. "For pity's sake, Margot, how're a couple of sugar cookies supposed to make up for Tilly's inability to sculpt pottery?"

"Well, er, I didn't mean—I just—" Margot floundered.

"Margot is just offering me a bit of comfort during a difficult time," Tilly said, reaching across with her good arm to pat Margot's hand. "She knows how stir-crazy I get when I can't work."

Gretchen snorted again and Alex stifled a grin. Whereas Margot was the picture of feminine elegance and grace, Gretchen reminded Alex of a bulldog. Squat and stocky, her hair was dyed a harsh, flat brown and hair-sprayed within an inch of its life. It sat unmoving on her head like a helmet.

Her tiny, beetle-black eyes turned to Alex. "You're out and about early this morning, little miss. Left your grandma all alone again. I thought helping her was your whole point in coming."

Alex wasn't put off by Gretchen's bluntness. Despite her gruff façade, Gretchen was a devoted and loyal friend to her grandmother. She'd been the first to come to Tilly's aid when she fell and broke her arm two weeks ago. Gretchen spent several nights in Tilly's home, helping her adjust to living with the cast on. And it was at Gretchen's urging that Tilly had finally called Alex to ask for help.

Tilly hadn't wanted to pull Alex from her work. But for Alex, the call couldn't have come at a better time. She'd been dragging her feet with regard to marketing for new mural projects, and her summer calendar was depressingly empty.

Before Alex could respond to Gretchen, Tilly cut in smoothly, "She *is* here for me, Gretchen. Didn't you see my lovely hairdo?" She turned her head for their inspection. "And besides," she added. "I'm not a complete invalid, you know. I'm perfectly capable of doing things for myself."

Gretchen harrumphed and took another swallow of tea.

"Since you ladies have those delicious cookies to eat, you probably don't want any of these," Alex said, placing the crumpled white bag on the table.

Tilly's eyes widened in delight and she reached for the bag. "Oh, you stopped at Westlake's. Wonderful!" She pulled out a chocolate glazed donut and passed the bag to Gretchen, who helped herself to a jelly-filled one.

"There's only one left. Didn't you get any for yourself?" Gretchen asked, passing the bag to Margot.

Alex cleared her throat. "I, uh...already ate mine."

"Pat's donuts are the best," Margot said, nibbling on an apple fritter. "Big city bakeries haven't got a thing on her." She looked at Alex. "How's Pat doing?"

"Alex doesn't know Pat," Tilly said, wiping her fingertips on her napkin.

"I do now. We were just introduced."

"Really, by whom?" Tilly looked at Alex curiously.

"Some random guy I met on the beach who happened to be there at the same time."

Her grandmother wasn't fooled by Alex's casual tone. "What random guy?"

Gretchen leaned forward, dark eyes glittering. "Yeah, was he an old guy or a young guy?"

"About my age."

"What's his name?" asked Margot.

"Jake Riley."

Gretchen leaned back and gave a hoot of laughter. "Jake Riley is not some random guy!"

Margot looked thoughtful. "Riley... Is that J.P.'s son?"

"*Grand*son," Gretchen supplied. "And he's *hot*!"

"Gretchen!" Margot looked mortified.

"Well, he is. Didn't you think so?" Gretchen swung her sharp gaze back to Alex.

Alex sniffed. "Not particularly."

Gretchen smacked her hand on the table with another crow of laughter. "Every pretty young thing from here to Grand Haven thinks so, but not you, eh?"

Alex got up from the table, crushing the empty donut bag. "Honestly, I didn't really notice, Gretchen. In any case, I'm not interested in...in any hot guys right now." *Maybe ever.*

"You still mooning after that bozo," Gretchen said.

Alex jammed the bag into the kitchen garbage container. "No!"

"Really, Gretchen," Margot put in sternly. "You can be downright vulgar sometimes."

"Can't help it," Gretchen said, leaning back. "Stuff just comes into my head and out my mouth."

"Maybe we should get you a muzzle," Margot muttered, dusting crumbs off her fingertips and onto her plate.

"Isn't Riley the name of the company building the new lakefront condominiums downtown?" Tilly asked.

"Yup, J.P.'s son Ben owns that company," Gretchen replied. "But Jake is the one handling this project."

"I think it's wonderful he's keeping so much of that old watchcase factory intact," Margot said. "It's such a lovely building."

"How's he keeping it intact?" Alex asked as she cleared the dirty dishes from the table.

Margot looked up at her. "Well, dear, instead of tearing the place down and building something new, he's chosen to renovate."

"Not an easy job," Gretchen said. "That place was a crumbling pile of ivy-covered bricks." She shook her head. "Dangling gutters, broken windows, it's been a mess for twenty years."

"Remember that rumor about it being torn down and replaced with some fancy hotel?" Margot said.

"That was before you and Joe moved here," Gretchen interjected, glancing at Tilly.

Margot's pale eyes grew bright. "Imagine if our quaint, little town had become home to some fancy luxury hotel. Thank goodness nothing ever came of it."

"That was only because of the contamination," Gretchen said.

"Contamination?" Alex asked, settling the dishes into hot, soapy water.

"Arsenic," Margot said.

"Not just arsenic," Gretchen said, swallowing a mouthful of donut. She cradled her teacup, warming to her subject. "That factory was built in the late 1800s. For centuries, cleaning solvents and heavy metals were flushed into its drainage system. The soil and surrounding groundwater were saturated with poisons. The area was sealed off and declared a Toxic Waste Site."

"Toxic waste!" Alex abandoned the dishes, coming back to sit at the table. "Is it still dangerous?"

"Nope. Between the previous owner and Riley Development, the area's all cleaned up now." Gretchen sipped her tea and made a face. "*Psht!* It's cold now." She lifted the tea cozy from the table to replenish her cup.

"That must have been quite a project," Tilly said.

"It seemed to drag on forever," Margot said, her fingertips toying with the dainty lace collar of her dress.

Gretchen nodded, settling back in her chair. "There were all kinds of legal battles that lasted for more than ten years. It was only a few years ago that the property was declared ready to develop. Of course, that's when the fun really started." Gretchen turned to Margot. "Remember all that hullabaloo about who *really* owned the property?"

"I remember that scandal!" Tilly exclaimed. "It was big news in the Whispering Pines Weekly when Joe and I first moved here. Didn't the original buyer already have a contract to sell the property to somebody else?"

Margot nodded. "Some big Chicago developer."

"Weston," said Gretchen.

"Who?" said Tilly.

"Peter Weston, a local businessman, was the original buyer. The paper never said what happened with his deal, but next thing we knew, the property was back on the market again."

Margot sighed. "And there it sat. Again."

"Until Riley Development came along," said Gretchen. "Even with all the setbacks they've had, they're finally making things happen."

"What kind of setbacks?" Alex asked, recalling Pat's earlier discussion with Jake.

"Oh, just some minor problems at the site that slowed down their progress."

"The condos look like they're going to be beautiful," Tilly said. She was struggling to worm a finger inside her cast.

Alex jumped up and grabbed a plastic straw, handing it to her grandmother.

"Thank you, sweetheart." Tilly shoved the straw inside the cast, vigorously scratching it up and down. "I can't wait until I get this blasted thing off!"

"Have you thought any more about what I suggested?" Alex said, eyeing her grandmother meaningfully.

"What?" Gretchen said, her eyes shooting back and forth between them.

"She thinks I should sell this place and buy one of the new condos," Tilly explained.

"But you love this place!" Margot cried.

"Sounds like a good idea to me," Gretchen said simultaneously.

"I do love this place," Tilly said, smiling at Margot. "This is Joe's and my dream home." She sighed wistfully, then straightened. "Let's not talk about that now, all right? We have much more interesting things to discuss." Her eyes sparkled, and the eyes of the other two women turned speculatively toward Alex.

"Why are you guys looking at me like that?" Alex said.

CHAPTER 4

Alex finished lacing up her hiking shoes and slung her camera bag over one shoulder. She walked into the great room, and Tilly looked up from the book she'd started reading after dinner. "You look more like seventeen than twenty-seven with your hair in a ponytail that way," she teased.

"Very funny!" Alex said, giving her a quick farewell kiss.

"Think about what we discussed!" Tilly called as the screen door banged shut behind Alex.

Murmuring her usual engine-start prayer, Old Bessie groaned to life, and Alex backed out of the driveway. She shouldn't have been surprised at the turn the conversation had taken with Tilly and her friends earlier that afternoon. After all, she *was* a muralist, and Tilly was the head of the newly formed Whispering Pines Mural Society.

Her grandmother joked she'd gotten the position because she was the closest thing Whispering Pines had to a professional artist. But Alex knew Tilly was selling herself short. Unlike Alex, who'd recognized her artistic gift at a young age, Tilly had only discovered her talent later in life. Her grandmother's pottery pieces were dramatic. And her work was becoming sought after throughout much of West Michigan.

Alex bumped along a dirt alley, then turned north toward Whispering Pines State Park. Her thoughts drifted back to the earlier discussion.

"Alex, sweetheart," Tilly had said, her good hand clasping Alex's. "We'd like to offer you the honor of painting the city's first official mural."

Then all three ladies started talking at once and it took several minutes for Alex to discern what the project entailed.

The Whispering Pines Mural Society had been set up to promote the village's local business community by painting outdoor murals on the storefronts of different businesses. The murals would depict local history and were to be painted so that local residents, as well as visitors to Whispering Pines, could understand the stories they shared. The Society's plan was for ten murals to be completed within the next three years.

Once the ladies finished their explanation, they'd all peered expectantly at Alex. She'd sat in silence for several moments before eventually telling them she'd think about it.

"Don't think about it too long," Gretchen said, blunt as always. "We want you to attend a meeting with our first client tonight."

"Tonight!" Alex shot Tilly a look. Her grandmother's gaze was sympathetic. She knew the simple request was more complicated than it seemed.

Alex's career as a muralist had taken off quickly. She'd obtained her first commissioned project even before graduating from the Detroit College for Creative Studies. For a couple years after graduation, she'd worked for an insurance company to build up her savings, only doing mural projects on the side. But she'd been able to go full-time a few years ago, having obtained some higher profile projects on both the east and west sides of the state. As a result, word of her talent spread and her client base grew. However, her healthy savings account had dwindled down significantly these past six months.

Writers get Writers Block, but what's it called when an artist can't paint? she thought bitterly.

Speeding past white dunes peppered with spiky clumps of grass, she pulled into the park entrance, slowing just enough for the attendant to see the annual state park sticker on her car window. Giving a wave, she continued along the familiar curves of the park's main road.

Was it really only just over a year ago that Derek Pendleton had strode into the restaurant where she'd been painting a mural?

When his hazel eyes had locked with hers, it had been just like a scene from a cheesy, romantic movie. All outside sounds had faded away, and it was as if she and Derek were suddenly the only two people in the room.

He'd walked over to examine the wall she was working on. She'd created a doodle grid of random letters and numbers on a wall that would serve as reference points for the colorful, patriotic scene she'd planned for a popular Grand Rapids restaurant known as GR Joe's.

But then he'd returned his gaze to hers. "Absolutely stunning," he'd said, his eyes never leaving her face.

"There's nothing to see yet," she'd said, confused.

He leaned close. "I disagree." Then he offered her his hand, accompanied by a brilliant smile. "I'm Derek Pendleton."

Derek, it turned out, worked for a restaurant broker, and he'd been tasked with selling GR Joe's for the owner, Papa Joe. Confident and polished in a tailored suit and sleek leather shoes, he wore his dark blond hair a little long but combed back from his handsome face. He was classically handsome, a heart-stopping blend falling somewhere between Zac Efron and a California surfer.

Even now, Alex could recall the dizzying headrush his presence incited.

She'd extended her hand to shake his before noticing the paint splatters on it, pulling it back with an apology. But Derek had clasped it with a playful grin. Then, rather than shaking it, he'd turned it over and with his eyes locked on hers, had slowly lifted her inner wrist and brushed his lips against it, murmuring, "A pleasure, Alex."

Her stomach had flipped, a rush of warmth radiating from deep inside.

Derek had continued flirting shamelessly with her, pursuing her for weeks until she finally agreed to go out with him. And their romance began, swirling Alex up with the power of a gale force wind.

She shuddered now, shoving the memory away. Hard. It did no good to revisit the past. She looked out the window to distract herself. Tourists drifted their lazy way down the Thornapple River on inner tubes. Maple trees arched overhead, branches lush with deep green leaves that filtered the sunlight to create lacy patterns of light and shadow over the road. Pulling into a campground parking lot, she climbed out and slipped on her camera backpack. She knew her cell phone camera was good, but she always preferred the effects she got using her Minolta.

She glanced at the posted trail map but had already decided to start out on the Lost Lake Trail, which she knew connected to the Ridge Trail. She loved the solitude along this particular route, as well as the rigorousness of the hike.

Although the air was slightly cooler in the woods, she was soon damp with perspiration as she clambered her way up steep inclines and over loose sand. Rising higher, her footfalls fell softly on the path of decayed leaves and rust-colored pine needles. Alex breathed deeply, savoring the scent of damp earth and growing things.

Ever since her grandparents had moved to Whispering Pines, hiking in the state park with her grandfather had been one of Alex's favorite things to do during visits.

Grandpa Joe had been a quiet man, a former college English professor, and knowledgeable in many areas. During their walks, he'd done as good a job as any park ranger explaining the flora and fauna to Alex.

For the past year though, between spending time with Derek and working on her career, Alex hadn't visited as often. Now she realized how much she'd missed the natural beauty of the area, as well as the rich character of the small town. She had to admit that despite her negative interaction with the annoying Jake Riley, she held a grudging respect for the way Riley Development Corporation was preserving the old watchcase factory.

Alex's heartbeat accelerated as she powered her way up one small hill after another. She stopped suddenly and squatted low with her camera. The tiny porcelain-colored balls that decorated the crimson stalks of blooming white baneberry caught her eye, and she couldn't resist taking a few shots. A moment later, she spotted a family of deer, nearly hidden in the lengthening shadows of some giant oaks. They saw her, too, but only gazed back, ears pricked forward–statues against the leafy green backdrop. She snapped several photographs of them as well before moving on.

She came to the base of an old wooden staircase and bounded up the steep steps two at a time. At the top, she caught her breath and admired the glimmering waters of Lost Lake far below. A pair of pristine swans floated gracefully among the creamy waterlilies near the shoreline. Assembling her tripod and switching to a more powerful zoom lens, Alex got some great shots of them, as well as a red-crested pileated woodpecker hard at work on the satiny trunk of a nearby beech tree.

The park's trails emptied during the early evening hours, which was why it was Alex's favorite time of day to hike. She continued her climb, finally emerging at the highest point of the trail. The hills sloped away in a breathtaking tumble of white sand and dune grass, leaving the path exposed to the elements. Upended tree roots threaded between the gnarled trunks of windswept trees, and sunlight sparked off the waves of Lake Michigan in the distance.

She sat down, leaning against the broad trunk of a fallen tree, and lifted her heavy ponytail off her neck. Closing her eyes, she let the sounds of the natural world going about its business thrum around and through her.

After a time, the sun dipped lower, and with a sigh, she rose to begin her descent. Angling southeast, she skirted the edge of a wooded valley, and just beyond a marshy patch, encountered an old stone shelter. Alex took some pictures of the ancient structure before honing in on some of the vibrant purple lupine blossoms which grew beside it. Pausing, she leaned against one wall to review her shots.

Whump! Something solid smacked into her legs from the side and only the shelter kept her from falling.

With a startled exclamation, Alex looked down into the liquid brown eyes and lolling tongue of Rex, his leash trailing behind him.

"What are—" she began.

"Rex!" Jake's deep voice thundered from nearby. He came around the corner of the building and stopped short. "Oh. That explains it."

"Explains what?"

"Why he suddenly took off. He never does that."

"Could have fooled me," Alex grumbled. But she reached down to pat Rex's shaggy golden head as he wagged his tail in appreciation.

She slanted a look at Jake, who was now beside her, bending to retrieve the dog's leash. He still wore his work clothes. "What are you doing? Stalking me?" Alex said.

"Look, lady, I'm just an innocent man trying to walk my dog. No need for a verbal attack."

"Seems like I'm the one who keeps getting attacked."

Jake sighed. "I'm sorry. Again. I don't know what it is about you that's such a draw for Rex. I'll try to do a better job of controlling him, all right?" He looked at the dog, "Rex, *setzen*!"

Rex immediately sat down, and Alex could see Jake looked genuinely troubled.

"It's okay," she relented. "He's a nice, friendly dog. But what's with the weird-sounding command?"

"It's German."

Alex raised a brow in question.

Jake scratched the dog behind his ears. "Rex is a retired police dog. An officer who works with my brother was his handler but couldn't keep him. So, I adopted him."

"Oh, that's, um...pretty cool," Alex said.

"You don't have to sound so surprised," he said, flashing a dimpled smile at her.

She swallowed. He'd just put a chink in the "shallow player type" image she had of him.

"I guess that explains why the local cops allow him those early morning beach privileges?"

Jake gave a grin of affirmation, then said, "So, what are you taking pictures of?"

"Nature shots, lighting effects, wildlife..."

"Can I see?"

Alex was surprised. "Uh...sure." She handed over the camera.

His fingertips brushed hers as he took it from her, and white-hot fire surged through her body at the touch, causing her to involuntarily shiver.

Jake didn't appear to notice. His dark head was bent over the camera as he scrolled slowly through the images. She watched him, struck again by how handsome he was. Not in the polished way of Derek. Jake's was a natural appeal. The hard muscles of his chest and arms belonged to a man used to physical labor as opposed to working out at a gym. She noted how his thick lashes swept against strong cheekbones, then her eyes drifted to his mouth. She liked the way his lips alternately curved into a smile or relaxed as he looked at the pictures. He raised his head and she jerked her eyes back to his.

"Some of these are really good. Like this one." He held it up so she could see the image. "How did you get such a crisp shot in low light like that?"

"Good equipment mostly."

"So, you're a photographer?" He handed the camera back to her.

"No, I'm a—" She stopped.

"A..." he prompted.

She sighed. "I'm an artist." Uttering those words used to fill her with immense pride. Now, she felt like a fraud. *I'm an artist who doesn't paint.*

Jake's eyebrows shot up. "Really? That's different."

"Yeah," she said weakly.

"Pat told me your grandmother is an artist, too?" Jake lounged against the wall of the shelter, his ebony eyes disturbing in their steadiness.

Rex, sensing they weren't going to continue their walk anytime soon, lay down at Alex's feet.

Alex knelt to stow away the camera. "Yes, she's a ceramic artist."

"Did you learn from her?"

"No, I...paint."

"What sorts of things do you paint?"

"Do you mind if we change the subject?" Alex said, zipping her bag and standing up.

"Sure," Jake shrugged. "Let me help you with that." He picked up the camera bag and slung it lightly over his shoulder.

"I don't need any help, thank you," Alex said, trying unsuccessfully to reclaim the bag.

He turned and grasped her wrists gently. She stilled.

"You barely let me apologize about what happened this morning. You wouldn't let me buy you breakfast. And now you're attempting to refuse my assistance. Lady, you're shooting my chivalrous knight act all to pieces."

She stared up at him and he released her. "I'm sorry," she said quietly. "I didn't mean to be unappreciative."

He indicated the path from which she'd come. "You took the Ridge Trail up?"

She nodded.

"Well, it looks like we're both taking the Island Trail back, so why not let Rex and I accompany you for a bit."

Alex eyed him warily.

"I promise I don't bite. And neither does Rex," he added as an afterthought.

He readjusted the backpack and moved forward down the trail, the dog loping at his side. Alex stood still, gnawing at her lower lip.

"You coming?" he called over his shoulder.

She looked skyward, sighed loudly, then followed.

The shadowed coolness of the wood enveloped them, and they walked without speaking for a time. Then Alex abruptly broke the silence. "I'm sorry."

Jake looked over at her. "You already said that."

She continued. "I know I was being rude. I just wasn't interested in...walking with anyone," she finished lamely.

"Well, you're going to have to," Jake said matter-of-factly. "At least until the trails intersect up ahead." He glanced sideways at her. "No offense, but are you always this difficult to talk to?

"I'm not difficult to talk to!"

Jake guffawed, and she pressed her lips together.

"Oh, all right," she acknowledged. "It's just that I'm in Whispering Pines on a sort of sabbatical. I've been creatively burned out lately, and I thought being alone and taking a break from my work might help." She paused before adding, "I'm just not looking to make any new friends right now."

Jake seemed to consider this as he offered his assistance over a sharp decline in the path that was now webbed with tree roots. Every few feet, Rex paused to sniff at something. Now he was investigating a mound of creeping snowberry dotted with dainty yellow wood sorrel. Jake clicked his tongue, urging the dog forward.

"We don't have to be friends," he said finally. "But is it all right if we talk while we walk?"

"I suppose."

"Your enthusiasm is underwhelming."

Alex suppressed a smile.

"So, what do you do with all the pictures you take?" He lifted a low-hanging branch, allowing her to pass beneath.

"Some I put into albums, and some I use to inspire my work."

"Hmmm, but we can't talk about your work." Jake tapped his chin. "Or why you're up here, or where you live. That leaves..."

Alex laughed. "Okay, okay. We can talk about where I live. I'm from Plymouth, a suburb near Metro Detroit. How about yourself?"

"Here."

"Really?"

"Well, no."

Alex looked at him curiously.

He smiled. "My family's from Grand Rapids, but I spent every summer here."

"Every summer?"

"Since I was five."

"Staying with your grandparents?"

Jake looked surprised and Alex's cheeks grew hot. "My, er, grandmother and her friends mentioned your grandfather to me this morning."

A slow smile crept over Jake's lips. "Sooo, you were talking about me, were you?"

Alex rolled her eyes. "Don't get all full of yourself. We were discussing the construction project."

"Uh-huh." He looked away, but his grin held.

Alex ignored it. "So, tell me about the condominiums. It sounds like you're keeping the factory's original appearance."

Jake nodded. "Not just that, we've kept the entire shell of the factory intact. We're just shoring it up where it's crumbled."

He blocked her progress with an outstretched hand, indicating a particularly boggy section of the path. Moving off to the right, they tramped single file through thick patches of wood nettle before resuming their positions side-by-side again.

"My grandmother's friends said the site was full of toxic waste," Alex said.

"It was," Jake agreed. "But we cleaned it up, and barring any more hiccups, construction will be back on schedule soon.

"What kind of hiccups have you had?" Alex asked. They were now level with an inlet of Lost Lake and they paused beside its glassy perimeter, thick with water marigolds.

"Let's just say not everybody in Whispering Pines values what Riley Development is trying to accomplish."

"You make it sound like it's bigger than building condominiums," Alex said. She leaned against a tree with a low branch that touched the water's surface.

Jake raked a hand through his hair, making his curls leap in all directions and making Alex's fingers itch to smooth them. "It is bigger! We're restoring one of the area's most significant historic landmarks, and we're using the highest preservation standards available." His face was flushed, dark eyes glinting. "We're using natural and recycled building materials whenever we can. It would've been a lot easier to buy some piece of undeveloped land and let that chemical cesspool sit there. But instead, we're transforming it. We're turning a brownfield site into an environmentally responsible one!" He expelled a breath and glanced at her, looking sheepish. "Sorry, I tend to get a little worked up about it."

"I can see that." Alex smiled as they resumed walking. "I think what you're doing is admirable."

He smiled back, clearly pleased with the compliment.

"I'm confused, though. Everything you've described sounds really positive. So why would anybody object?"

"Ignorance." Jake gave a frustrated shake of his head. "Some people don't understand the benefits of brownfield remediations."

"Does your company do many of them?"

He shook his head again. "This is our first one. *My* first one," he clarified, kicking at a pinecone in the path. "Riley Development is my father's company, but he's turned this entire project over to me."

"He must have a lot of faith in you," she said.

Jake snorted. "More like he didn't want to risk the entire company if I botched it," he said. "My dad and I don't exactly have the best relationship."

"Oh." Alex felt uncomfortable. Jake was openly sharing bits of his life with her while she refused to share anything of her own.

Studying the tree branches overhead, she searched for a more neutral subject. Her foot caught and she stumbled over a tree root in the path. Before she could catch herself, Jake's arm snaked around her, and she found herself pressed up against him for an instant, long enough for her to appreciate his broad chest and rock-hard abs.

"Are you all right?"

She slowly looked up and met his eyes. Big mistake. Their eyes locked and she felt as though she couldn't look away even if she wanted to. His arm remained wrapped around her waist, and with each passing second, she felt like a magnetic force was drawing them closer. His gaze moved to her lips. Beyond the warmth of the day, heat pulsated from his body and her insides quivered. An unfamiliar heat rose inside her, and she found it difficult to breathe.

"Uh...fine. Good. I'm good, thanks," she said, stumbling over her words. She brought up her palms, pushing gently away from him, and the spell was broken.

As they resumed walking, she desperately tried to ignore the inner turmoil caused by the fact that she'd been certain he'd been about to kiss her. And she wasn't sure if she was relieved or disappointed that nothing had happened.

"Here's where we part company," she said with forced brightness a short time later. She indicated the point where the Island Trail veered southwest off the Lost Lake Trail they were walking on.

Jake opened his mouth to speak, but she said quickly, "I'll take my backpack now."

With a slight frown, he removed it, handing it to her. Rex, who'd been investigating a new smell, trotted back to see what the holdup was.

Alex put on the backpack, and avoiding Jake's eyes, patted Rex's head.

"You realize these trails meet up again on the other end of the lake?" Jake said.

"Yeah, well, I parked over there." She waved her hand vaguely in the opposite direction.

"Uh-huh." He looked amused. "I'll be seeing you again, Alex Fontaine," he called after her as she moved off down the trail.

That annoying flirtatious quality had crept back into his voice, and she tossed back over her shoulder, "Not if I see you first."

Rex whined as they watched Alex walk away. "C'mon, boy." Jake nudged the dog back onto the path.

He couldn't recall ever receiving more mixed signals from a woman in his life.

One minute, she barely agreed to converse with him, and the next, he'd have sworn she wanted him to kiss her. And in that single heartbeat, as she'd stood there looking up at him with those amazing eyes, kissing her was exactly what he'd wanted to do. He'd never before seen eyes quite like hers. Wide set with a slight downward slant at the corners, fringed with thick, dark lashes. Their color seemed to shift with her mood, sometimes sky blue, sometimes sea green. A man could get lost in those eyes.

Rex paused to sniff at a fern and the leash grew slack as Jake stood thinking. What was it about him that seemed to repel her? And what was it about her that drew him in? Because like it or not, he was undeniably attracted to her. She was nothing like the "party girl" type he usually went for. Alex seemed intelligent and mysterious and...beautiful. She wore no makeup, her glossy hair pulled back into a simple ponytail, and yet when he looked at her, his breath went right out of him. He also had to admit, her genuine interest in his project was flattering.

He shook his head. Why waste his time? It was obvious Alex wasn't interested in him. And it wasn't exactly as if he was hard up for female companionship. Besides, this was not the time to start another of his infamous flings. He needed to stay focused on his work.

He tugged at Rex's leash and they began moving again. His long strides brought him to a section of the trail lined with rich, green sedge and bright clusters of wood lilies. He never spotted those large, orange blossoms without thinking of his mother. They'd been her favorite flower.

When she'd died, Jake, the youngest of his brothers, had been only five years old. Each Riley male had dealt with her loss in different ways. His father had attempted to ignore the gaping hole in their lives by throwing himself into making a success of the business they'd started before her death. And he had. But at what cost? Over the years, his father had rarely been home, and the chasm between the father and his three sons ran wide and deep.

Jake increased his pace as he and Rex clambered onto a boardwalk. If it hadn't been for his oldest brother Wade, Jake was certain he and Noah would have ended up in a lot more trouble than they had. As it was, Wade had stepped up to the plate, helping with homework, making dinners, and keeping track of their whereabouts. All three boys learned to rely on one other for support and encouragement, and as a result, were unusually close.

Wade and Noah had both been surprised when he'd accepted the position with Riley Development. But despite his ambivalent feelings toward their father, the chance Ben Riley was giving Jake was too important, and he wasn't about to blow it.

Exiting the boardwalk, Jake realized they'd reached the small lake where the two trails intersected again, but there was no sign of Alex. He smirked, guessing she'd probably run the entire way along her path, just to avoid another encounter.

An egret soared gracefully overhead, and delicate blue dragonflies flitted amongst thick leaves and velvety brown cattail heads. Frog song filled the air along the lake's swampy border. He stood for a moment, admiring the serenity of the wetland. Then he checked his watch and sighed. "Better get to the truck, Rex. We wouldn't want to be late for Pops' meeting now would we?"

CHAPTER 5

Alex tossed her camera bag into her car and leaped in. She was sweating from having jogged so far, but it was just as well. She'd avoided a second run-in with Jake, and she still had plenty of time to clean up before the Mural Society meeting. Turning the key in the ignition, the engine gave a strained cough, then fell silent. Alex felt her heart pump faster. *No, no, no!* She held her breath and tried again. Click. Nothing. She thumped her head against the steering wheel. *This. Is. Not. Happening. Not now!*

Snatching her cell phone from her purse, she dialed her grandmother's house phone. The answering machine greeted her. Of course, Tilly had probably already been picked up by Gretchen to prepare for the meeting. With a growl of frustration, she gathered her things and climbed back out of the car, slamming the door shut hard. Why had she ever decided to wait to get a new car until *after* the wedding? She needed to stop putting her life on hold.

There were no Ubers in Whispering Pines. So there was nothing to do but start walking. With a deep sigh, she began the trek up the winding road leading out of the park. Alex knew Tilly would be disappointed, but there was no way she'd make it back in time for the meeting. In all honesty, she felt a little relieved. She wasn't sure she could have accommodated their request anyway. She paused to shake sand out of one shoe. She hadn't even touched a paintbrush since her dramatic breakup with Derek. It was as if her muse had died along with the relationship.

As she walked along the flattened grass at the side of the road, the words of a famous quote danced at the edges of her mind. Something about closing your eyes to things you don't want to see, but being unable to close your heart to things you don't want to feel. True enough, she thought. If only she could turn a faucet handle and shut off the painful memories. Instead, they rushed through her like roistering rapids in a ceaseless flow.

She'd been aware of Derek's constant need to flirt from the start of their relationship, but hadn't minded. She'd recognized that flirting was as much a part of him as breathing.

He was a charmer.

He was a schmoozer.

He was a cheater.

Alex gazed sightlessly over the spiky clumps of dune grass. It had been her own lack of experience, plus the fact that she'd viewed him through love-colored lenses, that had caused her to miss all the signs of his true character.

White-hot anger burned afresh inside her as she recalled the last time she'd seen him. Her arms full of groceries for the special dinner she'd planned to welcome him home from his business trip, she'd used the key he'd given her to enter his apartment. She'd taken only a few steps in when she'd been startled by muffled sounds coming from the back bedroom.

She'd moved in silence up the carpeted hallway until she stood, frozen, before the open door of Derek's bedroom.

Then everything happened like a movie on fast forward, flickering rapidly through each scene.

Sunlight slanting over tangled white sheets. Long, blond hair splayed across a pillowcase. Derek's bare back angled toward her. Derek's silky voice murmuring into another woman's ear. The hushed tones of the woman's answering giggle.

Alex sucked in air but couldn't breathe. The grocery bag dropped to the floor, and she squeezed her eyes shut. Blocking out the image of Derek. Her Derek. Making love. With a stranger. This was like the plot of some cheesy B-grade film. It could not really be happening.

She opened her eyes then. And her shocked disbelief had quickly morphed into a bubbling rage.

Derek and the woman both jumped when the bag hit the floor. Now they stared at her with stunned expressions. Derek's handsome face had gone pale. And for once, his smooth-talking skills escaped him.

Alex reached for the nearest objects she could find on the dresser beside her and began hurling them, punctuating each throw with language she'd never used before in her life. A hairbrush. His deodorant. His wallet. His keys.

"Alex, stop!" Derek found his voice, lifting an arm in protection.

Ignoring him, she started in on the groceries at her feet. A pasta box. A head of lettuce. She felt a sick sense of gratification as the wine bottle smashed into the wall, spraying shards of dark glass over the bed while blood-red veins of liquid streaked down the creamy wall.

"Alex, please!" Derek cried out. "It's not—"

"Don't you dare say, 'It's not what I think!'" Alex snarled, cutting him off.

Derek clutched at the sheet, a desperate, pleading look on his face. "Please, baby. We need to talk."

The wide, blue eyes of the woman beside him were fixed on Alex in dazed alarm. "You're...married?" she squeaked, turning to him.

"No!" Derek shouted. "She's...a woman I've been seeing."

A part of Alex knew she was out of control, but she couldn't stop herself. Her overwrought emotions boiled over. "Just a woman you've been seeing!" she hissed through taut lips.

She marched over to the bed as the couple cowered beneath the thin sheet. She shoved her left hand at Derek's face. The marquis on the engagement ring glittered in the late afternoon sunlight pouring through the window, making hundreds of tiny rainbows dance across the walls. She heard the woman's sharp intake of breath. Then Alex curled the fingers of her right hand into a fist and let it fly, punching Derek in the face with every bit of strength she possessed.

Sharp pain stabbed through her hand and up her arm, but she didn't care. Derek made a gurgling sound and clutched at his nose, trying to staunch the flow of blood suddenly spurting from it.

She wrenched the ring from her finger and flung it at his head. Then she spun around and strode from the room.

Alex was suddenly snapped back to the present by a loud wolf whistle.

Caught up in the memory, she hadn't noticed a vehicle approaching from behind. Glancing over her shoulder, she groaned as Jake Riley's dusty truck rolled up beside her. Rex's panting face hung out the passenger window.

"A hike in the woods wasn't enough exercise for you?" Jake asked, sliding his sunglasses on top of his head.

Alex didn't answer but kept walking.

He rolled slowly alongside. "You do realize you're walking on the wrong side of the road?"

Alex stopped walking and faced him. "My car died," she said flatly.

"Oh. Well, hop in. I'll give you a ride."

She hesitated.

"Oh for Pete's sake, Alex, get in!" Jake ordered Rex into the back seat and pushed the passenger door wide.

Alex slid in. "Thank you," she said, buckling her seat belt.

"Where are you headed?"

"I'm running late for an appointment."

"Where at?"

"The library."

Jake shot her a strange look but didn't comment.

"I was sort of hoping to go home and change first, though," she murmured.

"Not a problem," Jake said. "I've got time."

"You really don't have to—"

"I know I don't have to, but I'm offering," Jake said, accelerating. "So, what happened to your car?"

Alex looked gloomily out the open window. "Old Bessie's number finally came up, I guess."

"Old Bessie?"

"My car."

"You named your car?"

"Sure, don't you?"

"Uh, no. So how old is Old Bessie?"

"She's an '84."

Jake gave a low whistle. "Yup, Bessie's old all right."

Alex sighed and pulled the rubber band from her hair, combing her fingers through it. "I've been holding out on getting a new car."

"Why?"

Alex leaned back in her seat and closed her eyes. "Lots of reasons."

"Like..."

Alex opened one eye and peered at Jake. "You ask a lot of questions."

"It's called having a conversation. Although with you, it's more like pulling teeth."

Alex suppressed a smile. "Turn here." She pointed to a narrow side street.

Jake's truck bumped over the dirt road.

"So, what do you think I should call my truck?"

"How about Pig Pen?" Alex said, indicating the empty fast food containers scattered on the floor at her feet.

Jake laughed. "It's not normally this trashed. I've been busy the past few days."

She directed him through two more turns, then into her grandmother's driveway.

"Give me fifteen minutes, okay?" she said, hopping out. "Make yourself at home."

She hurried up the front walk.

"This is great," Jake called after her, following at a more leisurely pace. "It's so nice to see an authentic log cabin as opposed to the prefab kind so many summer residents use as cottages."

When Alex returned to the living room, she found Jake standing by the stone fireplace, closely examining the hand-carved wooden mantle that fit to the rocky surface like a puzzle piece. It was decorated with an arrangement of chunky candles, misshapen from frequent use, and an elegant pottery vase sprouting deep purple irises.

"My grandfather made it," Alex said, coming to stand beside him. Her freshly brushed hair was loose now, falling softly to the middle of her back. She'd traded her shorts and T-shirt for a pale pink sundress. Its gathered top gave way to a flared skirt that fell just above her knees. Her hiking boots had been replaced with a pair of low-heeled sandals.

Jake's eyes looked her over appreciatively. "Very nice. You look like a girl."

"Thank you. I think."

Jake grinned and looked back at the mantle. "This is really good," he said. "Your grandfather made it, huh?"

"Yes, after he retired, he started doing woodwork and chip carving as a hobby."

Jake ran his fingertips over the intricate ivy leaf carvings that twined across the mantle's face.

"You rarely see this type of work done by hand anymore. Seems like everybody uses lasers."

"I know," Alex said. "He was a talented man."

"Was?"

"He passed away five years ago."

"Oh. I'm sorry to hear that." Jake said. He glanced up and indicated the vase on the mantle. "Your grandmother's work?"

Alex nodded, smiling with pride.

"She's pretty talented, too."

"That she is." Alex picked up her purse and a large, slim, black case that had been leaning against one of the recliners. "I know you're doing me a huge favor, Jake, but I'd like to get going."

"Oh, right." Jake followed her out the door. As she started down the front steps, he said, "Wait, aren't you going to lock up?"

"My grandmother never locks it."

Jake frowned, following her down the front steps. "Why not?"

"My grandparents lived all their lives in a big city," she said. "When they moved here, they were determined to embrace every aspect of small town life, including knowing your neighbors and never feeling the need to lock your door."

Jake grumbled something about not being very practical as he opened the truck's passenger door and offered her his hand.

Alex stared at the proffered hand. "What are you doing?"

Jake lifted his brows. "Helping you in?"

"Oh." She hesitated for a heartbeat, then placed her hand in his. She tried to ignore the tingling jolt that went through her at his touch. She wondered if he'd felt it, too, as his eyes held hers for the briefest instant. Then he released her fingers and shut the door.

Climbing into the driver's seat, he started the engine. Rex shoved his panting head between them as they pulled onto the road. "You know, Alex," he said. "I can't help but notice you seem taken aback by anything remotely...er, chivalrous. Doesn't your boyfriend find that a little frustrating?"

"I don't have a boyfriend."

He grinned, seemingly unruffled by the sharp note in her voice. "Well, your old boyfriends, then?"

Alex gazed out the window. "I don't have any of those either."

CHAPTER 6

Alex looked anxiously at the truck clock, but true to his word, Jake reappeared from inside his rental home within moments, wearing a fresh shirt and khakis. Rex's face looked out at them from the front picture window. He'd explained that he also had an appointment and needed to change.

"Don't look so worried," he said to her through the truck's window. "I told you I'd get you there on time." He opened the door and grabbed her case.

"What are you doing?" she asked.

"You'll see. Come with me."

Alex tried not to show her impatience as she got out of the truck and watched him lift the single-stall garage door.

"We're switching to my car."

Alex admired the sleek, black sports car parked inside while Jake placed her things in the trunk, then he opened the passenger door for her.

"Sweet ride," she said, getting in.

"Yeah," he grinned. "My one vice."

"Your only one?" she smirked.

He laughed and started the engine, lowering the top. "I figure a woman as lovely as you should really have a more appropriate chariot, and maybe not one filled with fast food trash and dog hair."

"Thank you for the compliment, but it really wasn't necessary, Jake."

"Ah, but it is, milady."

As they drove, Alex contemplated that for all of Derek's smooth sophistication, he'd never shown her the deference that Jake, a man she barely knew, was showing her now. Derek had never held doors for her or helped her in and out of cars. And honestly, until this moment, she hadn't given it a second thought. She was an independent woman, perfectly capable of opening doors for herself. But somewhere deep inside, in a place she hadn't even been aware existed, she felt a tiny thrill at these gestures. They made her feel like...like a lady. She almost giggled at the ridiculous thought.

She snuck a sideways glance at Jake's profile. The white polo shirt he now wore set off his golden tan to perfection. Dark curls brushed his collar and tangled around the curve of his ear. She fought an impulse to reach out and twist one around her finger.

The taut muscles of his arms flexed and relaxed as he turned the wheel. Alex forced her eyes back to the road, straightening in her seat. *Geez, Fontaine. Next thing you know, you'll be drooling!*

She cleared her throat. "I really appreciate this."

Jake smiled. "Like I said, it's no problem. You know, I was just thinking, a friend of my grandfather's owns one of the repair shops in town. I can arrange to have your car towed there if you'd like."

Alex shot him a grateful look.

He made the call as they drove, finishing the arrangements just as they pulled into the library parking lot.

Popping the trunk, he handed over her case. She thanked him again and started toward the entrance, surprised when Jake fell into step beside her.

"What are you—" she began, but a redhead who had just exited the building spotted Jake and squealed, cutting her off.

"Jakey!" she cried, hazel eyes sparkling. She extended both her hands so he could take them.

"Hey, Nora." He gave her a quick kiss on the cheek. "How've you been?"

"Faaaabulous!" Her dazzling smile widened. She pulled her left hand from his to wave a large diamond ring at him.

"Congratulations!" he said, capturing the waggling fingers.

"Well, I couldn't wait for you forever, could I?" she teased, leaning close.

Jake laughed good-naturedly while Alex controlled the urge to roll her eyes. *Seriously? Again?*

She inched away from them as the redhead chattered on, but she didn't get far before Jake bade Nora farewell and hurried to join her on the wide concrete steps.

"Another girlfriend, Jake?"

"Just a friend." He shrugged. "So, are you going to tell me what's in that black case, or do I have to guess?"

"Just some samples of my work."

"Can I see?"

Alex turned to face him at the door. "Maybe another time. Look, I appreciate everything you've done to help me. I really do. But I can take it from here. I can catch a ride home with one of my grandmother's friends."

Jake smiled, reaching for the library door. "Actually, my appointment is here tonight, too."

Alex smirked and placed a hand on her hip. "Uh-huh, sure it is, Jake. Do you really even—"

"Well, well, if it isn't the man responsible for bringing total ruin to our fair village," a crusty voice called from the sidewalk below.

Alex turned to see an elderly man marching up the steps toward them. He stepped with quick, jerky movements and was glaring hard at Jake. Thick tortoise-shell frame glasses magnified his watery blue eyes, making them disproportionately large in his craggy face.

Jake stepped forward slightly, shielding her from the older man. "Good evening, Mr. Farley," he said, his pleasant tone contrasting with the annoyance flickering deep in his eyes.

Thin tufts of white hair fluttered atop the man's head as he waved a file folder in Jake's direction. Alex thought his sagging jowls and the downward turn of his mouth made him look as if he'd just tasted something sour.

"I just had a *very* productive meeting with the Zoning Board," he said with obvious satisfaction. "I'm sure I've convinced them it's not in the village's best interests to approve those absurd variances you want." His thin lips stretched into a humorless smile. "Now you won't be able to meet the renovation requirements and that should put an end to your little condominium scam."

Jake sighed. "It's not a scam, Mr. Farley."

Farley snorted. "Sure, it's not. And I suppose all your catering to the tourists isn't bringing more squalor to Whispering Pines either, right?

"I've told you before, sir, the condos will be a positive addition to this community. And as for your ideas regarding tourism, they make absolutely no sense. If not for tourism, there would be less money coming into local restaurants, hotels, and downtown shops. The businesses of Whispering Pines *depend* on tourism."

"And I've told *you* before," Farley said, bushy eyebrows snapping up to meet his vanishing hairline. "Tourists come from big cities. And big city folks only bring drugs and crime with them. You are single-handedly destroying this town!"

Jake took a deep breath. "It's unfortunate you feel that way. Now, if you'll excuse us, Mr. Farley, we have appointments we need to get to." He turned, placing his palm lightly on Alex's back to usher her through the door.

Alex felt Jake pull away and turned to see that Farley had grabbed his arm.

"I won't excuse you!" the old man shouted, jabbing the folder into Jake's chest.

Jake snagged Farley's wrist in one large hand and tossed it aside. He didn't raise his voice, but the tightly checked power behind his words was evident. "We are through talking, Mr. Farley. Good evening."

Farley seemed to notice Alex for the first time and turned his myopic gaze on her. "Who's this? Another one of your women?" His lips twisted sardonically. "You're just like your grandfather, boy. You Rileys are all about taking whatever you want and"—his eyes swept meaningfully over Alex—"having a good time."

Jake's tight control burst, and he lunged forward, his face inches from Farley's. "You listen to me, old man. You will never disparage my grandfather, or my family, in my presence again. And since you have not yet been introduced to this young lady, you will address her with respect."

Farley lost some of his bravado, backing down a step. But his faded eyes still glittered with dislike. "I will not give up, boy. I won't stop until your project is permanently halted. You may not care about this town, but I do!" Then he turned on his heel and stomped back down the library steps.

Jake's cheeks were flushed and the small muscle of his jaw worked, and he stood staring blindly for several long seconds as the old man disappeared from view.

"Well," Alex finally murmured. "That was fun."

He looked at her in surprise, as if he'd forgotten she was there.

"I'm sorry you had to hear that," he said.

"Who was that guy?"

He hesitated. "Aren't you going to be late?"

"Oh, right!" The confrontation had distracted Alex from her purpose. She walked swiftly into the library. It was nearly empty, with only a handful of people spread among the old wooden tables working on laptops and reading books.

The utilitarian carpet muted Alex's footsteps as she approached the main reception desk. The woman behind it directed her to one of the conference rooms bordering the reference section.

She started walking and then her steps slowed. She willed herself to breathe. It was ridiculous to be nervous. She'd had loads of client meetings in the past. And she'd worked with everyone from corporate executives to homeowners. This would be no different. *Except that you haven't held a paintbrush in almost six months.*

She hesitated outside the floor-to-ceiling glass window of the meeting room. Her grandmother, Gretchen, Margot, and another woman were seated on one side of a rectangular conference table. On the other side sat an older man with close-cropped gray hair encircling the bald crown of his head. He sported a waxed handlebar mustache and exuded authority, even from the small, molded plastic chair in which he sat.

Beside him sat a gentleman in a suit who, despite his salt-and-pepper hair, appeared much younger than the first.

Alex took a deep breath and swung the door wide. The conversation in the room broke off as all heads turned toward her.

"Oh, thank goodness! Tilly exclaimed. "I was getting worried, Alex."

Alex was about to respond when she sensed movement beside her. She turned in surprise as Jake slipped past her into the room.

"What—"

"Jakey-boy!" the man with the handlebar mustache boomed. "Get your butt in here. You're late! Course, I can see why." He grinned at Alex and winked.

Alex frowned in confusion as Jake greeted the mustached man. "Sorry, Pops," he said. "Hey, Markham." Jake reached across to shake the suit's outstretched hand.

"Jake," the suit replied, smiling. "Cutting it a little close, aren't you?"

"We ran into some interference on the way in," Jake said grimly, settling himself into a chair beside the man he'd called Pops.

"What interference?" Pops asked.

"Our old Op-Ed friend," Jake replied.

"*Psshht!* I ran into that old fart earlier today and gave him a piece of my mind," Pops said.

Tilly cleared her throat delicately.

Jake looked amused as Pop's face turned bright red. "Sorry, ma'am," he said. "I meant to say I ran into Farley earlier—"

"Farley?" Gretchen cut in. "Oh, for pity's sake, Tilly, he *is* an old fart!"

"Perhaps we should get started," Margot said diplomatically, organizing some papers in front of her. "Alex, dear, why don't you come sit here beside Tilly."

Alex had remained at the room's entrance, feeling like the only person missing the punchline of a joke. All eyes turned to look at her again, and flushing slightly, she moved to the empty chair.

"Tilly, would you like to call the meeting to order?" Margot suggested.

"Oh, I don't think we need to make this too formal," Tilly smiled. "Why don't we just start with some introductions?"

First Tilly, then the other members of the Whispering Pines Mural Society stated their names. Alex nodded politely to the one member she hadn't met before, Susan Carlson.

There was no mistaking the pride in Tilly's voice as she touched Alex's shoulder. "And this is the artist, my granddaughter, Alex Fontaine."

Jake's midnight eyes glittered at her from across the table, making it difficult to concentrate. She recalled their conversation in the woods earlier and regretted that she'd mentioned her creative burnout troubles to him. She prayed Jake wouldn't say anything. Averting her eyes, she murmured, "Hello, everyone."

"And I'm Jacob Riley, Sr., a.k.a. J.P. or Pops, depending on who's talking," said the man with the handlebar mustache. "This here's my grandson and namesake, Jake." He pounded Jake's back. "And this," J.P. jerked his thumb in the direction of the man in the suit, "is Keith Markham. He's Riley Development Corporation's attorney for this project. I invited him along for an extra set of eyes and for any legal perspective that may be required."

The greetings taken care of, Tilly took charge. "Now, let's clarify the purpose of our meeting. Mr. Riley, Sr. here has requested that the Whispering Pines Mural Society paint a mural on one exterior wall of the new watchcase factory condominiums."

Alex saw Jake's eyebrows shoot up.

"So, what do you think of my big surprise, Jakey-boy?" J.P. exclaimed, elbowing Jake in the ribs and looking pleased with himself.

Jake leaned back in his chair and folded his arms. His eyes studied Alex's face. "Where exactly would we put it?" he finally asked.

"I was thinking on the east side, so you'd see it as you approached from town," J.P. said.

"Hmmm...that's a pretty prominent location, Pops. The artwork would have to be a real showcase piece. It would need to match the tone of the entire facility. How do we know this artist's work is..." He swept his hand in Alex's direction. "How can I say this diplomatically, er, up to such high standards?"

Alex felt her face grow hot. But before she could open her mouth, Tilly jumped in. "I'm quite certain you'll find my granddaughter's work to be of the highest caliber. She's extremely gifted and has received commissions from a variety of clients, ranging from individuals to small businesses to major corporations."

"Show 'em your stuff!" Gretchen ordered.

"Yes, why don't you show us your stuff?" Jake said, leaning forward, his voice filled with barely concealed amusement.

Her cheeks burned even hotter, but Alex chose not to look at him. Slipping her black portfolio onto the table, she focused her attention on the other two men in the room. "These are some of my larger projects," she explained, unzipping the case and spinning it around to face them.

The first image was one of her personal favorites. "I completed this mural for a client who had a passion for the Riviera Liguria."

Three pairs of eyes looked up at her, questioning.

"It's a specific area on the Italian Riveria," she explained.

Sounds of acknowledgment issued from the group, and Alex was gratified to note Jake leaned in for a closer look.

The mural depicted the small harbor town of Portofino, one of the glittering jewels of the di Levante region. She'd enjoyed contrasting the rugged beauty of its coastline with the smooth, sun-drenched hues of the buildings clustered at the harbor's edge. The water reflected the colors of the buildings and was home to a multitude of tiny, bobbing fishing boats. Verdant hills created a lush backdrop for the entire scene.

"The colors are so vibrant," Keith Markham said, looking up at Alex with admiration. "I like the touch you added here, with the clothes flapping in the breeze on the clothesline above the street like that. It makes it seem like you were really there."

"I was," Alex said as she turned the page. She felt rather than saw Jake's eyes look at her in surprise.

"This next picture is a detail of a mural covering the walls of a Greek restaurant in my hometown, inspired by my travels to the Greek Island of Santorini."

Curved buildings capped with blue domes filled the bottom corner of the painting. Shadows created by Romanesque window openings and myriad staircases formed a cool contrast to the snowy white of the buildings. The undulating turquoise and emerald sea drew the eye out and up toward gray volcanic rock forming the island's famous caldera.

Murmurs of appreciation came from around the table as Alex again turned the page.

"I was hired to paint this piece for one of the vineyards on the Leelanau peninsula," she explained.

This time, they were treated to ribbons of orderly grapevines running over dusky, purple hills set against a pale cloudless sky. In the foreground, a fieldstone walkway led to a rustic arbor and fence serving as an entryway to the vineyard. The small, wooden gate was thrown wide, as if welcoming the observer to enter. The arbor itself was ensconced in fan-shaped leaves and twining vines laden with ripe fruit. A single tree branch hung artfully from the upper corner of the mural.

"So beautiful," Margot whispered, her fingers skimming the plastic-covered image of Alex's work.

Jake looked up. "You said this is the Leelanau peninsula? As in up north?"

Alex met his eyes and immediately wished she hadn't. She grew warm under the directness of his gaze. She hoped nobody noticed. "No, I said

I painted it *for* a vineyard in the Leelanau peninsula. It was inspired by a vineyard in Tuscany.

"I suppose you've been there too," he muttered.

"Actually, I have," she said lightly and turned the page.

She led them through the remainder of her portfolio and when she finished, the room was silent.

Alex looked around at their faces, her nervousness returning with a vengeance, stomach clenched like a fist. "I can...I have more samples online that I could show you if—"

"I don't believe that will be necessary, do you, Jake?" said Keith Markham, leaning to peer at him across J.P.'s broad chest.

"Are you kidding?" J.P. cut in. "This girl's got talent comin' out her eyeballs!"

"Your work is truly remarkable, Alex," Keith said, smiling, his gentle brown eyes crinkled at the corners. "You are obviously quite gifted."

"Thank you," Alex said, feeling uncomfortable as she always did when people praised her work directly to her face.

"Well, it sounds like you're hired." Jake folded his arms again. "So what's all this going to cost me?"

J.P. waved a hand dismissively. "That's not something you need to worry about, Jakey-boy. Part of the cost is covered by mural society funding and the rest is a gift from me...and Nana." His boisterous tone softened. "It's something I *know* she'd have wanted to do." J.P. cleared his throat. "Alex can give us a quote. And Markham here can handle the contract or whatever Alex needs to get started."

"This is wonderful," Tilly said, looking pleased. "Well, ladies, we have our first commission!"

The four mural society members began chattering at once, and Jake's voice broke through the milieu. "Um, excuse me, ladies, but what exactly is she going to paint a mural of?"

Margot leaned forward. "That still needs to be decided. The purpose of our murals is to help promote business activity in the village, as well as share some local history. Through the murals, we want to capture the distinct character of Whispering Pines. With those points in mind, it's up to you, Captain Riley, and Alex to develop a mutually agreed-upon idea. The Whispering Pines Mural Society will approve the final design, of course."

"Captain?" Alex asked, looking at J.P.

J.P. grinned. "Retired captain of the U.S. Coast Guard at your service, Miss Artist."

Alex couldn't resist smiling back at him as she closed her portfolio and sat down. "I'll need to learn more about the area's history. Any suggestions on where I might start?"

"You won't find a better source of local history than Captain Riley here," Gretchen said.

Tilly cleared her throat. "Perhaps, with the condominiums being located right on the water, and with Captain Riley being so intimately involved with the project"—J.P.'s broad chest puffed up even larger—"you might consider something involving the U.S. Coast Guard activities, or maybe the lighthouse?" Tilly suggested.

Alex nodded, considering. "I'll need to take a look around the site to get a feel for the location," she said.

"Of course," Susan Carlson agreed, glancing at her watch. "It's not too late. There's still some light left, maybe you could go right now."

"Well, I would, except…" Alex turned to Tilly. "I didn't get a chance to tell you why I was late for the meeting. Bessie died this afternoon."

"Oh no!" her grandmother exclaimed.

"Criminy, girl! Why didn't you tell us a friend of yours had passed away today?" J.P. leaned forward, looking concerned. "We'd have arranged the meeting for another day."

Jake smirked. "Bessie is her *car*."

"Her car has a name?" J.P. said.

"I knew it was only a matter of time before that beast bit the dust," Gretchen put in matter-of-factly.

"Gretchen!" Margot frowned. She looked at Alex. "I don't normally drive after dark, dear, but I could—"

"That won't be necessary," Jake cut in. "I brought Alex here. I'll be happy to swing her by the site and then take her home."

"Oh, wonderful." Margot looked relieved, oblivious to Alex's dismayed expression. "Well, are we finished then?"

"There are a few details I'd like to discuss with Miss Tilly," J.P. said, turning in Tilly's direction. "If you don't mind staying for a bit, I can give you a ride home myself."

"That would be fine," Tilly said, then scanned the room. "I guess our first meeting is adjourned."

"Sounds good," Keith Markham said. Everybody rose to leave.

Alex refused to make eye contact with Jake as she picked up her purse and portfolio. She was frustrated to have to rely on him for a ride again. She knew the less time she spent with him the better.

Alex led the way as the small group cleared out of the room, leaving Tilly behind to speak with J.P. The rest of the group fell behind as the three women chatted with Keith Markham and Jake. Alex strode from the building and down the sidewalk. She was waiting at the car, tapping her foot, and hugging her portfolio to her chest like a shield when Jake strolled up a moment later. He popped the trunk and she shoved her things into it before climbing into the car, ignoring his proffered hand this time.

He rested one hand on top of the open door frame and gazed down at her. "Did I do something to offend you?"

"Not at all," Alex said, staring straight ahead.

He continued standing there while an uncomfortable silence grew. Finally, she looked up at him. The twilight sky glowed behind him, highlighting his skin wherever the sun touched it. She took a breath. "I just don't like having to rely on you again." She folded her arms. "Also, you didn't exactly sound thrilled about me painting this mural for your project. I'm sure you're probably doubting my abilities since I told you about my creative troubles and—""

Jake ducked his head into the car, bringing it level with her own. Startled, Alex stopped talking. A heady combination of woodsy notes and the natural musk of his skin filled her nose. "I apologize for my reaction," he said, looking directly at her from much too close. "Despite your creative troubles, I have no doubt about your abilities. I was just caught by surprise with this entire project."

Alex squirmed in her seat, averting her eyes and dusting imaginary lint from the hem of her dress. "Yeah, well, I guess I could tell you were kind of clueless."

"Pops tends to get a bit..." he paused, "...enthusiastic about things. When that happens, he moves full-steam ahead and never looks back."

Alex smiled, thinking of J.P. "He's obviously proud of you. I think it's nice he's so supportive of your work."

"Yeah, he is that," Jake agreed. "So, am I forgiven for my initial lack of enthusiasm then?"

"I suppose," Alex said.

He laughed at her show of nonchalance. "Okay then, let's go see the site."

Jake drove toward the lake. The clear blue sky of the day had been transformed. Now it was alive with the warm hues of the setting sun in shimmering streaks of pinks, purples, and tangerine. Above the water, dusky blue clouds were painted along the horizon, each one edged in golden ribbons of fire.

Jake stopped his car outside the chain-link fence encircling the site.

"You know," Alex said, looking around. "I probably should have said something sooner, but I think it's really too dark for me to see well enough to do anything constructive."

"Yeah, I see that now. How about if we just take a walk around the perimeter so you can at least get a feel for the location?"

Alex shrugged. "All right."

Together, they skirted the six-foot high protective fence decorated with bright orange signs proclaiming safety regulations and warning off trespassers.

Alex hooked her fingers through the wire fence frame and peered in.

Massive, shrink-wrapped pallets bordered the edge of the site. Bright yellow machinery sat dormant amid mounds and valleys of dark earth, crisscrossed with tire marks. Thick ivy twined up portions of the impressive red brick structure, which rose four stories at the center. Two-story wings extended from either side. Elegant curve-topped windows lined the façade in neat rows, exposing glimpses of a rich, timber interior and the shiny metal of new duct work.

"Beautiful, isn't it," Jake said, coming to stand beside her. It wasn't a question.

"It is," Alex agreed. "Renovating isn't easy though, is it?"

"Definitely not as easy as starting fresh after a demo job." Jake smiled. "But worth it. It's probably the most historic building in Whispering Pines, and it's just been sitting here deteriorating for decades."

"And you're really keeping the original structure?" Alex asked, recalling their earlier conversation.

"When we're finished, the building exterior will look almost exactly like it did when it was built in 1881...with the exception of one historic-themed mural," he added with a smile.

Alex swallowed, pushing negative thoughts away. "That's very cool. Of course, you'll have to make big changes to the interior, right?"

Jake nodded. "We've already taken out all the old electrical and plumbing and pulled up the flooring. We're also shoring up damaged sections of the walls."

"You can tell the brick was really lovely at one time," Alex said, her gaze roving over the exterior.

"It will be again," Jake said, then sighed. "It would be so much easier if we could just pressure wash the brick to restore it. But doing that could blow the old mortar right off. In fact, we've had to implement a lot of safety precautions just so we don't damage it."

"Sounds time consuming."

"And then some. It's going to take the right tools and the right people. But I love having the opportunity to bring it back to life."

She noted the glow in Jake's eyes as he spoke. "So, tell me about the interior."

"In the center, we're going to have forty-eight loft-style condos, and the first floor will hold a lobby, dining room, kitchen, and exercise area." He pointed at the two wings of the building. "Those sections will be set up for assisted living apartments."

Alex tilted her head toward the site entrance. "I noticed one of the signs said something about this being a green residential project. What does that mean?"

"It means that besides renovating the building, we're also making this project as environmentally responsible as possible," Jake said, turning to face her and leaning against the fence.

"In what ways?"

"Well, for one thing, we're recycling and reusing any salvageable building materials from the site, like the brick masonry and timber framing." He indicated the items as he spoke. "We're going to use geothermal heat pumps, as well as rooftop solar panels."

Alex nodded, impressed.

Jake grew silent and Alex glanced at him. The light had faded, but she could have sworn his face was flushed. "Is something wrong?"

"I did it again, didn't I?"

"Did what?"

"I'm completely monopolizing the conversation."

"Honestly, I find it fascinating. Anyway, that's why we're here, isn't it?"

Jake straightened and looked out over the water. The dune grass surrounding the site barely moved in the soft breeze coming off the lake. "The view they'll have across Lake Michigan is spectacular," he said. "Want to take a short walk?"

Despite her earlier tension, Alex now felt completely relaxed. Perhaps it was Jake's animated discussion of the project or the hint of humility he'd just shown over talking so much. Or maybe she was just getting loopy from her own lack of sleep. But she found herself agreeing.

Jake cuffed his pants and they both removed their shoes, tossing them into his car before stepping onto the soft sand.

They strolled along the water's edge. The only sound the rhythmic whisper of waves slipping up and back along the shore. The beach was nearly as vacant as it had been that morning. Only the occasional couple or small group was there to watch the sunset, clustered on the benches that edged the beach.

Every so often, Jake would pick up a rock and skim it out over the lake, where it would skip several times before sinking beneath the surface.

"I've never been able to do that."

Jake looked startled that she'd broken the silence. "What?"

"I've never been able to skip rocks like that."

"It's not hard."

"Thanks."

He laughed. "You need to start with a nice, flat rock." Searching the ground, he reached down. "Like this one," he said, holding out a smooth, white stone.

"Now, the secret to successful skipping," he continued in a conspiratorial tone, "is that it's all in the wrist." He demonstrated the motion, keeping his arm parallel to the ground and snapping his wrist. "Now you try." He dropped the stone into her open palm.

Alex threw it, and even she could tell her motion was awkward.

The corner of Jake's mouth twitched. "You're throwing like a baseball." He reached for her hand, then hesitated, looking her in the eye. "May I?"

Her heart flipped in her chest, but she nodded, keeping her expression neutral.

Stepping behind her, he gently gripped her right hand in his own. Goose flesh rippled up her arm in response to the contact. But she forced herself to concentrate.

"More like this." He moved her hand and wrist in rhythm with his own. "It's sort of a reverse of the way you threw the Frisbee." Stepping back, he said, "Okay, try again."

Gnawing at the corner of her lower lip, she focused and threw. The rock skimmed the surface perfectly, bouncing twice off the waves before sinking. "I did it!"

"Awesome!" He was looking down at her with an unreadable expression, and her heart rate sped up again.

"What time is it?" she asked suddenly.

Jake glanced at his watch. "Almost nine. Why?"

"I need to get home."

He grinned. "Grandma gave you a curfew?"

"No, it's just…I don't want her to worry."

Then, as if she hadn't spoken, he dropped onto the sand and patted the space beside him.

"She knows you're with me. Besides, she had that meeting-after-the-meeting with my grandfather. She probably hasn't even missed you yet. C'mon, take a load off. Let's watch the grand finale." With a sweep of his arm, he indicated the brilliant sky and glowing orange ball hovering just above the water line.

Warning bells clanged like crazy inside her head. She knew she was in dangerous territory. Jake was worming his way past her defenses with his blasted charm and dimpled smile.

He gazed up at her now, brows raised expectantly. "I told you I don't bite." He flashed white teeth. "At least not today."

Alex sighed and sank down onto the sand beside him, curling her legs off to one side. She looked out over the lake, marveling at how the sky had transformed yet again. It was now swathed in deep fuchsia pink, the setting sun blazing a path of molten light across the dark, undulating water.

Jake leaned back, resting on his elbows. Without looking at her, he said, "Your work is pretty spectacular, you know."

"Thank you." She was surprised at the sincerity in his voice.

"Where did you learn to paint like that?"

She smoothed her hands over her skirt and shrugged. "I've messed around with painting as far back as I can remember. But I guess my skills developed most while I was at Detroit's College for Creative Studies. My professors there really challenged me. Studying abroad helped, too.

"Is that when you traveled to Tuscany and Greece?"

"Tuscany, yes, but Greece was during summer vacations when I was growing up."

Jake looked at her curiously.

"My dad worked for an automotive supplier and traveled a lot for work. He felt it was important for me to have..." Alex made air quotes with her fingers, "global experiences."

Jake whistled softly. "I've never been outside of the U.S." He grinned. "Well, except for Canada. Does Canada count?"

"Depends. Were you there long enough to eat a meal?"

"Definitely."

"Okay then, I'll allow it."

He laughed, and the sound of it washed over her like a scintillating wave.

They sat in companionable silence for a while, watching the heavenly brushstrokes of color mutate overhead.

"You know, you're much nicer to be around now than you were earlier today," Jake observed, straightening up to brush the sand from his forearms.

"Maybe that's because you are," she responded lightly.

"Lady, I'm *always* nice to be around."

Alex angled her head, peering sideways at him. "Always?"

He leaned close and whispered, "Always."

His warm breath whispered against her cheek, and his enigmatic gaze seemed to look right through her, making her feel too exposed. He leaned even closer and the world tilted. Her breath caught in her throat, and she felt locked in the moment. It was like there was a magnetic pull between them that kept drawing her in. The heat between them was palpable, and she knew without a doubt that he was about to kiss her.

She gave herself a mental shake and abruptly stood. "Can you please take me home now?" She stood stiffly, her arms wrapped around her middle as if the evening was chilly instead of the balmy eighty degrees it was.

Jake sighed, shaking his head, but he didn't get up. "Is the idea of kissing me that frightening?"

"I have no intention of kissing you!"

He looked up at her then, but she averted her eyes, looking toward the darkening horizon instead.

The tiny lights of a distant fishing boat bobbed against the skyline. A couple strolled past, holding hands, their quiet conversation lost in the sound of the waves.

"Somebody must have done a real number on you."

She pressed her lips together.

"Want to talk about it?"

"Not really."

"Oookay." He sighed again and started to rise.

"I'm engaged," she blurted out, surprising herself.

He stopped moving. "Didn't see that one coming."

"I mean, I *was* engaged."

Jake was silent, waiting for her to continue.

"I—he—we broke it off a few months ago."

"Ahhh." Jake nodded as if he'd just solved the mystery of the ages.

Alex frowned. "What's that supposed to mean?"

He stood now, brushing off the remaining sand. "You're still in love with him."

Anger roiled up inside her. "I am not! I'm over him. I'm *so* over him."

"Sure you are."

"I am!"

"Prove it."

"How am I supposed to do that?"

"Kiss me."

She crossed her arms. "Jake, I am not kissing you."

"Scared?"

"No!"

"Then..."

"Then, nothing. I'm not kissing you!"

"Knew you were scared."

"I'm not scared!"

He arched a brow.

"For crying out loud, Jake, we just met. I don't kiss total strangers!"

"We're not strangers. And technically, this is our third date."

She threw up her arms. "What are you talking about?"

"Our first date was our walk on the beach with Rex this morning," he said, ticking off his fingers as he spoke, "when you fell hard for me." He smirked and Alex rolled her eyes. "Our second date was the hike in the woods this afternoon. So, that makes this our third date. A lovely beach stroll at sunset."

He leaned toward her, closed his eyes, and pursed his lips expectantly.

Alex stared at him, emotions fluctuating between rage, annoyance, and the ridiculous desire to laugh. The latter won out, and his eyes flew open. "You're laughing at me? I'm hurt."

She shoved him hard in the chest and he pretended to lose his balance before straightening with a grin. "Come on, I'll race you back to the car."

CHAPTER 7

She surprised Jake by nearly beating him.

"I suppose you're a marathon runner, too," he panted when they reached the car. He was bent over at the waist, trying to catch his breath.

"Nah, just a former high school sprinter." Alex grinned. "You should really keep your head above your heart."

Jake grunted and opened her door.

One by one, stars glimmered into view as they drove. Jake lowered the windows, letting in the cooler evening air. He flipped the radio to the local jazz station and sultry saxophone music drifted between them.

"It's so pretty here," Alex said, resting her chin on her arm, which was crooked over the open window ledge. Her long, dark hair whipped back from her face and Jake studied her graceful profile in the fading light. Then she turned those extraordinary opal-colored eyes in his direction and he swallowed, forcing his attention back to the road.

"You were fortunate to spend so many summers here," she said.

"Fortunate?" Jake gave a mirthless laugh.

Jake turned a corner and the wind whipped her hair across her face. Brushing it away, she frowned. "I thought you and your grandfather were close?"

"We are. It's not that. It's...complicated."

"Oh. Want to talk about it?"

"Not really." He smiled, tossing her own words back at her.

Jake was grateful she didn't press the issue. His mind drifted back to their conversation at the beach. He was curious to know what had happened with her engagement, as well as why she remained so frustratingly closed off.

He was accustomed to charming his way into the good graces of any lady he chose. Alex not only seemed immune to his appeal but was repelled by it. Sure, he'd finagled some genuine conversation out of her today, but the instant he got physically close, or made any overt gesture of interest toward her, she shut down. Or, he corrected himself, she'd give off a reciprocal vibe of interest, and *then* she'd shut down. He was still puzzling over this when they turned into her grandmother's driveway. "Hmmm…that's weird."

"What?" Alex asked.

"Pops' car is here," he said, pointing at the parked car glinting in the beam of his headlights. "He's an early riser and never normally out this late."

Dozens of moths flitted around the yellow porch light as they climbed the front steps. Jake batted them away and they rushed through the door together.

The overhead chandelier cast a soft radiance over the center of the main floor, with the room's perimeter fading into shadow. J.P. and Tilly sat at one end of the dining room table, deep in conversation, they turned as Jake and Alex entered. Jake smirked as he noted the steam curling from the delicate, floral teacup in front of his grandfather.

"Took you long enough, Jakey-boy!" J.P. boomed. "Wasn't it a bit too dark out there to explore the site all this time?" His grandfather winked, and out of the corner of his eye, Jake saw Alex stiffen.

He decided to ignore the blatant gest. "Yes, it was, so we took a walk along the beachfront to give Alex a feel for the view instead."

"I'll take a closer look at the site tomorrow during daylight hours," Alex said, her tone all business.

"That must have been a nice walk, dear." Tilly turned in her chair. "I noticed the sky was gorgeous tonight. If I could capture those color transformations in my pieces, I'd be a happy woman."

"Tilly was showing me some of her work," J.P. said, indicating a small cluster of vases, dishes, and bowls at the opposite side of the table. "She's as good with her pottery as you are with your painting, Miss Artist."

Tilly blushed. "Oh, stop it, J.P. It's just something I enjoy doing."

"I was serious about buying one of your pieces, Tilly. I'd like to come back another time and see more of your work, if that's all right."

"That would be lovely," Tilly said with a bright smile.

J.P. rose from the table. "Well, it's late. We both ought to be going, Jakey-boy."

"Can you give me a ride home, Pops?" Jake asked.

"But your car is here," Alex protested.

Jake faced her. "How were you planning to get to the site tomorrow?"

"Well, I...I hadn't thought that far ahead yet."

Tilly rose, looking concerned. "Oh dear! I'm sorry now that I got rid of your grandfather's car."

"Don't be silly, Grandma. You don't even drive. It would have been ridiculous for you to keep it."

"I've got the company truck back at my place. Just use my car until yours is fixed," Jake said reasonably.

"I can't take your car!" Alex exclaimed.

"Sure you can. I trust you." Jake smiled at her. She gave a vague smile in return, then quickly looked away.

"Great idea," J.P. put in. "C'mon, boy, let's let these beautiful ladies get some rest."

Jake dangled the keys in front of Alex. "What time should I expect you tomorrow?"

She didn't reach for them, so he lifted her hand and pressed the keys into her palm.

"How about ten o'clock?"

"All right," she relented. "And thank you. *Again.*"

Jake sighed with satisfaction. "That's right, princess. You're indebted to me once more."

"Yeah, yeah."

He spun and followed J.P. out the door, his deep laughter floating behind him on the night air.

CHAPTER 8

Alex helped Tilly clear the cups and saucers from the table. "I know he's helping me, but Jake Riley can be the most arrogant, infuriating man!"

"Mhm."

"And I know you're just trying to help me get my mojo back with this mural job, Grandma, but I don't know if it's such a good idea for me to spend a lot of time with him."

"Mhm."

"He has this frustrating way of..." Alex's words trailed off as she realized her grandmother wasn't even listening.

"Yo, Grandma! You with me?" Alex set the dishes on the counter and waved her hands in front of Tilly's glassy gaze.

She blinked. "Oh, I'm sorry, dear. What were you saying?"

Alex's eyes narrowed. "I knew it! You're tired. You're not usually up this late."

Tilly laughed. "I'm not tired. I was just thinking."

"About..."

"Oh, lots of things. About this project," she added, her expression transforming into a look of concern. She seated herself on one of the breakfast bar stools facing the kitchen sink. "Alex, sweetheart, am I pushing you too hard?"

Alex dried one of the fine china teacups she'd just washed and sighed. "No, I suppose it's the kick in the pants I need right now. Nothing else seems to be working." She raised her head from her task, feeling suddenly vulnerable. "But what if I really can't do it, Grandma?"

Tilly reached across the short distance separating them and patted Alex's damp hand. "You will do it," she said with confidence. "We'll just take it one step at a time."

Alex wished she shared Tilly's optimism, but it had been so long since she'd painted anything. She loved her work too much to give it up without a fight, though. Tilly was right. Taking the project one baby step at a time was the way to go, starting with her survey of the site the next day. And as far as Jake was concerned, she would just learn to control or ignore any feelings he roused in her. This was a business arrangement. Pure and simple.

"That was certainly sweet of Jake to loan you his car," Tilly said.

"I suppose." Alex hung the towel on the oven door handle to dry. "I'm sure I could have figured out something else, though."

"I don't know about that, dear. Particularly with me having nothing here for you to drive." Tilly's expression was rueful.

Alex often wondered if Tilly regretted never learning to drive. She'd been raised in Chicago, marrying Joe Fontaine right after high school. They started their family, remaining in the city where Grandpa Joe worked as an English professor at North Park University. As a result, Tilly's driving had never been an issue. Even after Grandpa Joe's death, here in Whispering Pines, she had plenty of friends she could count on for rides.

Alex walked into the great room and flopped onto the loveseat, switching on the lamp nearest her. "How did your meeting with J.P. go?"

Tilly followed, sitting down in a recliner beside her. "Just fine, dear. I'm certain he'll pay a fair price for your work. He seems very flexible and easy to work with."

"That's not what I meant. It looked like you two were deep in discussion when Jake and I came in."

"Did we?" Tilly looked startled. "I suppose that's because he was telling me about tomorrow's City Planning Committee meeting."

"What about it?"

"Apparently, an issue with Riley Development's construction project is on the agenda." Tilly was having difficulty getting comfortable, so Alex adjusted the pillow at her back and was rewarded with a grateful smile.

"What sort of issue?"

"It's that gentleman Jake and J.P. referred to earlier, Frank Farley."

Alex shuddered. "He's an angry little man. I met him with Jake outside the library this evening. How's he involved?"

"Apparently, Mr. Farley spoke to the Zoning Board, urging them to deny approval for some crucial variances required for the project. The chimney and water tower are too tall to meet Whispering Pines' height restriction code."

"Jake told me it's important to maintain the original structure for funding purposes. I wonder why Mr. Farley is so against this project," Alex said.

Tilly made a cluck of annoyance, then spoke with uncharacteristic vehemence. "Frank Farley fights against anything and everything that causes the slightest change in Whispering Pines. He even tried to stop the formation of the mural society! He simply doesn't understand the advantages of progress or change of any kind. You know, I have a good mind to go and speak before the commission tomorrow."

"Go for it, Grandma," Alex said and yawned. "I think I'm gonna turn in. It's been a long day. Maybe I'll finally sleep tonight."

After getting Tilly settled for bed, Alex padded into the bathroom. As she washed her face and brushed her teeth, her thoughts drifted to Jake. He was such an intriguing mix. On the one hand, he was this shameless flirt, completely aware of his appeal and the effect it had on the women around him. At the same time, though, he displayed a surprising depth and an old-fashioned charm. Opening doors, gallantly offering assistance and protection, even his fondness for that weird, old jazz music.

Alex splashed her face with cold water and patted it dry with a hand towel. She considered herself strong and independent. And as much as her feminist soul objected to his seemingly sexist treatment of her, she had to admit, she sort of liked it.

Pulling on her favorite butter-soft sleep tee and boxers, she wriggled between the sheets, fluffing the lightweight quilt on top. She closed her eyes and relaxed her body, willing sleep to come. She was exhausted, but as usual, her brain was a live wire, snapping with flashes of memory. She flipped onto her side and punched at the pillow, groaning in the darkness as, once again, sleep eluded her. Tonight was different. This time, she wasn't battling against thoughts of Derek. Instead, the images flitting through her mind made her pulse race and triggered a warmth that radiated from deep within her core. Because every image involved the inscrutable Jake Riley.

At some point in the early morning hours, she must have drifted off, because she woke with a jolt, sunlight blazing through her window. Kicking herself free of the tangled covers, she got up and found Tilly gone. A note explained Gretchen and Margot had picked her up for their weekly breakfast date.

Alex threw on a pair of jeans and a tank top and ran a comb through her hair. She gulped down some lukewarm herbal tea that was left in the pot, grabbed an apple, the keys, and her small sketchbook before dashing out the door.

Sliding behind the wheel of the sleek automobile, she couldn't resist caressing the soft leather seats. Alex always thought of cars as a mere convenience, a way to get from point A to point B. She'd never thought of a car as sexy. Until now. The comfortable bucket seat cradled her body and she breathed in the mingled scent of Jake and leather interior. When she started the engine, it purred so quietly in comparison to Old Bessie that she rolled down the window to make sure the motor was running.

Warm sunshine beamed down, so she opened the sunroof before taking off. Pulling out of the driveway, she jerked in surprise as a clipped, feminine voice informed her she was heading west on Cherry Street.

"Uh...thanks, Lola," she muttered to the glowing GPS unit built into the dashboard. She turned on the radio and huffed in annoyance to find it was still tuned to the jazz station from the night before. She punched buttons until she located an alternative rock station and cranked the bass as she sped up the road.

Pulling into the site with a minute to spare, she saw Jake immediately step out of the office trailer, as if he'd been watching for her.

"Here," he said, extending a pair of clunky work boots and a sunny, yellow hard hat toward her as she got out of the car.

"No way!" she protested. "I'll get hat hair!"

"Nobody enters the site without a hard hat on," he said, plunking it down on her head. As he adjusted it, his fingers brushed her cheek, and Alex's heart skipped a beat in response. She closed her eyes, quelling her thoughts.

"Still tired from yesterday? Jake asked, misinterpreting her reaction.

Her eyes flew open. "Uh...yeah. I mean, no!"

He grinned at her, then pointed at the boots. "Now you just need the right shoes to complete your ensemble."

Alex eyed the grubby boots sitting on the ground in front of her. "First of all, how do you know they'll fit? And second of all, are you positive I won't get a foot disease from them?"

Jake laughed, his dimples deepening. "You're a size seven, right?"

"How could you possibly know that?"

"I'm just that good," he said with a wink. Then he knelt down in front of her and opened up the laces on one boot. "Okay, princess, give me your foot."

Jake's hands felt warm as he lifted her right ankle and gently slid it into the boot. She felt a quiver deep inside as his calloused fingers lightly trailed along the exposed skin of her leg while he secured the laces and adjusted them for a snug fit. He performed the same process with the other boot, and the sensation of his touch sent further sparks through Alex.

With both boots firmly tied, Jake stood and grinned down at her. "Ready for the official guided tour?"

"Absolutely," Alex said, collecting herself and following him toward the center of the site.

The air hummed and clanged with activity as construction traffic and workers crawled over the property. Huge backhoes spread dark earth around the perimeter, and Alex recalled what Gretchen and Margot had said about the contamination left behind by the watchcase factory.

"So how did you get all the contamination out of the ground?" she asked Jake, raising her voice above the commotion.

Jake leaned close so she could hear. "The original owner started the cleanup using something called a vapor extraction system. When we took over the project, we got the remainder out through soil sparging."

"Soil sparging. Of course," Alex said drily as they started moving again.

Jake laughed. "We forced air into the groundwater to make it bubble, and that released the toxic gases. We did that until the air quality of the building reached a safe level."

"And you're finished now?" Alex asked.

Jake nodded. "The site was officially declared clean and Superfund de-listed a few months ago. That's when we could finally begin construction."

"I understand you've got a big meeting tonight about the chimney and water tower variances?"

Jake raised his brows. "How did you know that?"

"Hey, I do my research. I'm not just a paintbrush," Alex said, lifting her chin.

"No, you're definitely not just a paintbrush," Jake agreed, eyes gliding over her with a mischievous glint.

Alex pretended not to notice as they skirted the towering stacks of building materials she'd seen the day before. He led her inside the east end of the structure. "We're building three new stair and elevator cores," he explained, indicating different sections of the interior as he spoke. "And each condo will have an exposed brick wall and three large windows to create a light-filled, airy feel."

Alex remarked on the beauty of the elegant arched window openings that lined the walls. Jake agreed, explaining that the original seven hundred windows had contained asbestos glazing putty. "It was brutal work, but we removed it all. Next, we'll install thermally efficient double-hung windows that duplicate the frame profiles and mounting divisions of the originals. But we'll put in casings to make them standard size."

He placed a palm almost lovingly against one of the standing walls. "We'll build a new raised floor system so all the piping and ductwork can run underneath it. And we'll showcase the original heavy timber ceiling framework in each condo interior."

He opened his phone and showed her photographs of the decorative Victorian wood cornice and scroll brackets that had once crowned the building's brick facade. Although they'd been removed years ago, he was having replicas made based on the original design. Alex was admiring the images when a shout interrupted them.

"Yo, Jake! Can you come take a look at—" A short, thickset man topped with a scuffed orange hard hat appeared from around a corner. He stopped mid-sentence when he saw Alex. "Oops, sorry, boss. Didn't realize you had a guest."

The man grinned wide, extending a beefy hand to Alex. "Cesar Ruiz, plumbing guru," he said, brown eyes twinkling. He spoke with a slight Mexican accent.

Alex smiled and introduced herself, shaking his hand in return.

"Cesar is our plumbing sub-contractor for this project," Jake said. "In fact, I've been lucky enough to nab Cesar for several of our past projects."

Cesar leaned toward Alex and spoke out of the corner of his mouth. "I've got him totally snowed. He thinks I actually know what I'm doing."

Alex laughed.

"Alex is our newly hired muralist."

Cesar's thick brows lifted. "Muralist? Like as in an artist?"

"A new development as of yesterday evening," Jake said. "Compliment of Pops."

"Ahhh." Cesar nodded with apparent understanding.

"I'm just giving her a feel for the place," Jake said.

"Mhm." Cesar shot Jake a knowing look before turning back to Alex. "If he gets outta line at all, you come find Cesar. I'll keep you safe," he said with a wink. "But for now, Alex, do you mind if I borrow him for a minute?"

"Not at all," she said.

At a small nearby drafting table, Cesar unrolled an oversized sheet of paper covered in diagrams. The two men were soon deep in discussion, so Alex wandered away, admiring the eloquent beauty of the building's interior.

Drawing close to one wall, she gazed up. Large portions of the structure had been exposed to the elements for over two decades, and she watched as workers, balancing expertly on the wide beams overhead, worked at removing damaged sections of the building's upper level.

Jake had explained that the deteriorating roof would be replaced with a new "green" roof, which would be extensively landscaped and made accessible to the building's occupants. It would be a sustainable design feature to reduce rainwater runoff and make the entire building more energy efficient.

She turned to watch the activity rolling through the first floor. She imagined what the transformed factory would look like when the project was finally completed. Through an open section of the building, she saw the office trailer door swing wide and Keith Markham stepped out, briefcase in hand. She crossed to the open space and called out to him in greeting. He had just reached his car and was looking around the dust-filled lot in confusion when he spotted her. He smiled and raised his hand in return. Suddenly, his friendly expression morphed into a look of shock. Alex had no time to think before there was a sharp cry overhead and something slammed her body hard to the ground.

CHAPTER 9

Alex was smothered in darkness and she couldn't breathe. An instant later, a resounding crash reverberated through her body. As her ability to suck in air returned, she registered the smell of sawdust overlayed by a rich, earthy fragrance.

The darkness vanished as Jake lifted his head to look down at her. "Are you all right?" he rasped.

"I'm...fine." Alex frowned up at him, bewildered. "What happened?" His face was inches away and she was uncomfortably aware of his hard, muscular body protectively encasing her own.

Jake took a steadying breath and rolled off to one side. He ran a hand over his face, then rose to his feet, offering a hand to help her up.

"Ay, caramba!" she heard Cesar whisper. "She could have been killed!"

Once Jake no longer blocked her view, Alex saw multiple large bricks scattered in cracked hunks on the floor in the precise spot where she'd been standing.

Her mouth fell open, but before she uttered a word, Keith Markham raced into the building. His face was white and strained as he looked at Alex. "Are you all right?" he asked, grabbing her hand.

"I'm fine," she said again, giving him a shaky smile. Then she looked at Jake. The concern she'd seen on his face mere seconds ago had been replaced with a thunderous expression. His dark eyes snapped as he looked up at the stunned faces on the scaffolding overhead. "What in the blazes just happened?" he bellowed.

"I don't know, boss!" a man with a boyish face called down. "Those bricks weren't even supposed to be up here. I know they weren't there yesterday."

"Hank Miller! Where are you?"

"Here, Jake." An older man wearing a low-slung tool belt beneath his protruding belly stepped up beside the first man who'd spoken.

"You're supposed to be managing the removal of the damaged bricks. I want to know who put that stack in such a dangerous position, and I want that person in my office. Now!"

"Yes, sir," Hank replied.

Jake raked his hands through his hair as he eyed the pile of broken bricks. "This could have been the worst one yet," he said, looking at Keith.

Keith nodded.

"The worst one what?" Alex asked.

"Accident," Keith said. "We've had more than our fair share of them since this project started."

"What else has happened?"

"Nothing as bad as this," Cesar said, stacking broken chunks of brick up against the wall. "Just annoying inconveniences for the most part. Like machines breaking down, deliveries getting messed up, paperwork going missing, stuff like that."

"The only truly dangerous incidents occurred before Riley Development was ever involved," Keith said. "The site had deteriorated to the point where crumbling bricks would randomly fall onto the sidewalk. The city had to fence the property in so it no longer posed a threat to passersby. But Jake has been meticulous about following safety procedures and keeping the structure clear of loose debris."

"Until today." Jake looked grim. "I'm going to get to the bottom of this." He turned to Keith. "You're leaving?"

Keith nodded.

"Do you have time to meet with me later today on a separate issue?"

"Sure." Keith looked at his watch. "I'm late for an appointment right now, but what time were you thinking?"

"How about three o'clock?"

"That should work," Keith said. He looked at Alex once again. "You sure you're all right? Do you want to file a report or anything?"

"No." Alex smiled, holding up her hands. "I promise not to sue."

Keith clasped his hands in mock prayer. "Thank heavens!"

"Cesar, you don't have to do that," Jake said when he noticed the man was still stacking the broken brick pieces in a pile. "It's not your responsibility."

"Hey, we're all on the same team." Cesar grinned.

"I'll be back to help just as soon as I see Alex off."

"But our tour wasn't finished!" Alex protested.

Jake took her hand and towed her out of the structure. "It's finished. Come on." As she allowed herself to be pulled toward the car, she tried to ignore how nice his hand felt wrapped around hers the way it was.

He released it once they reached the driver's side door.

"Look, Jake, I can tell you're a bit shaken up by what just happened, but I'd really like to—" she began.

"Are you going to unlock the door, or should I?"

"I think you're overreacting."

"Alex, you could have been seriously hurt. Or worse!"

"I had my hard hat on!"

He gave her a pained look.

Instead of opening the door as requested, she removed the hard hat and studied her reflection in the car's glossy window. "Great. I knew it!" She handed him the hat, then flipped her hair back and forth several times before looking again. She groaned. "Now I'm going to walk around Whispering Pines looking like *this* all day."

"Lucky Whispering Pines," Jake said.

"Funny," she said, hitting the key fob's unlock button.

"I am funny, aren't I?" He opened the car door and stood looking down at her.

She waited a moment, then crossed her arms. "Since you're so anxious for me to leave, would you mind moving so I can get in?"

Instead, he narrowed his eyes and took a step toward her. Alex instinctively backed away. His earlier anger had dissipated, and now there was an intensity to his gaze that was having a strange effect on her breathing.

"What's the magic word?" he said softly.

"Knock it off, Jake." To her annoyance, her voice wobbled.

"Wrong. Try again."

She sighed. "Please?" She hated how breathy her voice sounded.

He flashed one of his lady-killer grins and leaned even closer, his intent clear. Alex turned her head abruptly.

"You're welcome," he whispered. Then his lips brushed the skin just beneath her ear, making her insides quiver.

He stepped back and allowed her to escape behind the wheel of the car. "I guess that will have to do," he said, laughter suffusing his voice. "Even though this is our fourth date."

"You are crazy," Alex said, finding her voice again.

"Don't I know it," he said, resting his hand on top of the doorframe. "So, what are your plans now?"

She restacked her sketchpad and pencils on the passenger seat to calm herself before answering. "I'm going to check on my car, and then I'm going to see if I can connect with your grandfather to get some historical information about Whispering Pines."

"Pops will love that. You'll need his phone number and address." He reached across her and pushed the ignition button. "If you give me your cell, I'll sync it to the car, too." He tapped some buttons on the dashboard and her phone while Alex surreptitiously breathed in his heady scent.

He finished, then pointed at the glowing GPS screen. "It's programmed to guide you to Thompson's Auto Shop, then to Pops' house."

"How convenient. Thanks, Lola," Alex said.

"Did you just call me Lola?"

"The GPS unit."

"You named my GPS unit?"

"Um, yeah."

His lips twitched as he shut the door.

She grabbed her sunglasses and jammed them on her face before waving an airy farewell. As she pulled out, she couldn't resist sneaking a peek at him through the rearview mirror. He stood watching her, arms folded across his well-formed chest, dark curls ruffling in the breeze. Her heart somersaulted. And the memory of his lips against her skin made her tingle. *Why did he have to be so flippin' charming?* She jerked her eyes back to the road. Entirely too charming for her own good.

Twenty minutes later, she'd forgotten all about Jake as she sat in front of the repair shop, thunking her head against the steering wheel. The news about her car had been discouraging. Apparently, Old Bessie truly was Deceased Bessie. The repair costs were more than the value of the car. Taking deep breaths, she leaned back and gazed sightlessly at the plush ceiling.

It wasn't like she hadn't expected this to happen at some point. Bessie was ancient and she'd had every intention of replacing her after the wedding. In fact, Derek had promised to take her car shopping once they'd returned from their honeymoon. She fought against the stab of pain that twisted at her insides every time she thought of Derek's betrayal. How could she have been so ignorant? Although she wanted to lay the blame for their failed relationship entirely at Derek's feet, she couldn't discount the niggling feeling that she'd somehow caused the entire situation through her own lack of romantic experience.

Throughout high school, she'd been painfully shy. Unlike a typical teen, she'd only had a couple of friends. Aside from track, she'd rarely done social things, preferring to stay home and read or paint. Her social skills improved a bit in college. But because she hadn't dated at all in high school, she still felt extremely insecure in that area. And so, she'd simply avoided it, making excuses whenever anyone did ask her out. It was much easier to focus on perfecting her skills as an artist than putting herself in nerve-wracking dating situations.

When she shared all this with Derek, he'd told her he understood. He'd said he respected her decision to hold off on taking their relationship to the next level. But she still struggled over how their relationship had ended. Had it been unfair for her to neglect his need for intimacy?

Alex shook her head to free it from this endless cycle of frustrated anger. Starting the car again, she followed Lola's directions to J.P.'s home.

Located only a few blocks from the lake, the charming bungalow was tucked on a small lot like every other house on the street. But unlike its neighbors, the tiny home was dwarfed by a generous wraparound porch. The slate blue clapboard exterior was accented with white trim, giving the home a classic lakehouse look. Thriving ferns hung from the porch roof at evenly spaced intervals. Edging the front and sides of the home were fluffy white snowball bushes, fronted by shorter explosions of colorful petunias and impatiens.

Alex paused to inhale the fragrance of a climbing rosebush that twined around the wrought-iron railing of the porch staircase.

She climbed the remaining steps. The front door of the house was flung wide, with only a screen door separating her from the home's interior. "Hello?" she called, cupping a hand around her eyes to peer inside.

"That you, Miss Artist?" a voice boomed from deep within.

"It is," Alex answered.

"Come on in and make yourself at home. I'll be right out," J.P. called.

She entered and the screen door banged shut behind her, making her jump. She stood blinking as her eyes adjusted from the bright summer sunshine to the shady interior of the home. The tiny living room was claustrophobic, filled to capacity with chunky pieces of walnut furniture. The rich mocha paneling and blue shag carpet evoked visions of the 70s. The home was tidy, however, and decorated in a decidedly nautical theme.

J.P. was nowhere to be seen. A navy blue sofa, draped with a sailboat-pattern quilt, sat beneath the room's large picture window. Alex crossed the floor to study the bookshelf standing beside it. Scanning the titles, she noted classics were intermingled with books on history, gardening, and several autobiographies. She smiled to see two entire shelves devoted to paperback romance novels while a third was filled with well-worn cookbooks. Her scan halted at a set of framed pictures clustered onto one of the higher shelves.

One photograph in particular drew her attention. Three boys posed around a massive sandcastle. The oldest boy's expression was serious as he stood behind the creation. Another knelt in front of it, an easy grin splitting his face, arms thrown wide to display their work. She smiled as she recognized the features of the youngest boy. Jake Riley stood ramrod straight to one side of the castle and was apparently the only one mouthing the requisite "cheese" as the photograph was snapped.

Next to the picture of the boys was a photograph of J.P. His cheek was pressed up against that of a bespectacled woman with fluffy white curls that framed a genial, round face.

Alex spotted a third picture tucked behind the first two. She reached to lift it out. Squinting at the sun-faded colors, she viewed a young couple. Their arms wrapped around each other as they faced the photographer. Cropped brown waves swept back from the man's high forehead and his gentle eyes crinkled at the corners.

The young woman in the photograph was absolutely stunning. Long, dark hair hung in corkscrewed curls to her waist. Her oval face glowed, framing thick-lashed eyes that radiated vitality. She had a dazzling smile and deep dimples, reminding her distinctly of—

"That's Jakey-boy's mama." Alex started in surprise as J.P. came to stand beside her. His voice was uncharacteristically gentle.

"She's beautiful," Alex said.

J.P. set the water bottle he was holding onto the rope-handled boat chest in front of the sofa. He took the picture from her, staring at it for several long seconds before replacing it on the shelf. "That she was."

Was? Alex felt guilty, as if she'd been prying by scrutinizing the photographs. J.P. didn't seem to mind, though. He picked up the photograph of the boys. "This here's Jakey-boy," he said, jabbing his thick finger at the smallest child, just as Alex had suspected. "And his two brothers. Wade," he pointed at the oldest boy, "he's a police officer now, and this is Noah," he pointed at the gregarious middle child.

"Is Noah a policeman, too?"

"Nope, he's a businessman. Handles marketing or some such. Just like his mama used to do."

Settling the picture back on the shelf, he pointed at the photograph of himself and the smiling woman. "That was my Ellen," he said proudly.

"You have a lovely family, J.P."

"I do," he agreed, his expression wistful. But he quickly regained his usual joviality. "Come on and take a load off, Miss Artist," he said, moving to the sofa. A towel hung from his neck. He wore an old gray T-shirt emblazoned with "U.S. Coast Guard" and a pair of athletic shorts. The ancient sofa creaked under his weight as he settled onto it. "I apologize for my appearance," he said. "I just finished up my weight workout."

Alex couldn't hide her surprise as she sank onto one of the two wing-back chairs across from him. J.P. caught the look and frowned. "What? You think an old fart like me can't lift weights anymore?"

"No, no! I..." She blushed.

J.P. chuckled and waved a hand dismissively. "Just messin' with you, girl! Heck, it's true. I can't do everything I did a few decades ago. But I do what I can. I'm a big believer in exercise for maintaining quality of life." He dabbed fresh sweat from his forehead and wrinkled his nose. "It's probably a good thing you're not sitting too close to me. I'm not my usual fresh-as-a-daisy self at the moment." Then he guffawed at his own joke, making Alex grin.

J.P. took a swig from his water bottle, wiping his mouth with the end of the towel. "Pardon my manners. Can I get you something to drink?"

"I'm fine, thanks."

Although he presented an imposing figure, J.P. somehow managed to exude a receptive warmth. Alex cleared her throat and risked asking the question that had troubled her ever since his comment about Jake's mother. "I couldn't help but notice you said 'was' when you referred to Jake's mother."

"Yep." He took another swing. "She was killed in a car accident."

Alex was surprised at the bluntness of his response. "I'm so sorry," she breathed.

"It was a long time ago," J.P. said.

Alex remained silent. Great. Now she felt guilty again. She knew she was being overly inquisitive regarding Jake's family life. What was the matter with her? She tried to think of a graceful way to segue into Whispering Pines' history and the mural project. But J.P., who was unaware of her discomfort, continued. "She was hit by a drunk driver on her way to pick up the boys after school." Alex was shocked to see tears form in the big man's eyes. "It was three-thirty in the afternoon for cripe's sake. Who gets drunk at three-thirty in the afternoon?" It was a rhetorical question, and Alex realized it was one he must have asked himself repeatedly over the years. "Anyway, that's why none of the boys touch the stuff."

"Stuff?"

"Alcohol," J.P. clarified.

"Oh." Alex nodded in understanding. She tried to imagine what Jake's mother would have been like. "She was your daughter, then?"

J.P. set down his water bottle and leaned forward, massaging his kneecaps. "Daughter-in-law. Jakey-boy's daddy is my son," he said. "But we couldn't have loved Kat any less if she'd been our own flesh and blood. She was a ball of energy, always laughing and making us laugh, too. And she knew how to keep those boys in line. Every one of 'em, including my Ben.

"They met in college. Got married right after graduation. Ellen and I thought she was the perfect complement to Benny. He was always the quiet, studious type. Nothing like me!" J.P. barked a laugh. "Kat breathed such a spark of life into him. Ellen and I'd never seen him as happy as he was with her." J.P. sighed and leaned back. "When she died, it was like that spark left with her."

Alex didn't speak, sensing his need to go on.

"They'd had a dream of one day starting a business together. After she died, Ben poured everything into making Riley Development a reality. It was like by focusing on their dream, he was keeping a part of her with him..." J.P.'s voice trailed off and they sat in silence for a long moment.

Alex cleared her throat. "Jake told me he's spent all his summers here since he was five."

J.P. refocused on her. "Yes, ma'am. They used to come up for family vacations now and then. But when Kat died, Ellen insisted the boys come for that entire summer. They stayed with us every single summer after that. Ellen said it was better to have them here with us old folks than to be home alone while their daddy worked so hard." Something flashed in the depths of his eyes. "We did our best to provide as much stability and love as we could manage while they were here." J.P.'s eyes clouded briefly, but an instant later, he sighed and tipped his water bottle into his mouth, emptying it. "But you didn't come over to hear *my* history did you, Miss Artist?"

Alex smiled at the nickname he appeared to have developed for her. "Nope, you're right," she said. "I understand you're the man to teach me all about Whispering Pines' history, or at least enough to help me figure out what type of mural I should create for you."

J.P. leaned back, folding his hands behind his head and staring up at the ceiling. "Let's see, where to begin..." He cocked a brow at her. "Have you been out to the state park?"

"Many times."

"Good. Then you can imagine what this entire area was like centuries ago. All rich, forested land full of wildlife like deer, black bears, cougars, wolverine, eagles, fish..." He sat up, warming to his subject.

"French missionaries and explorers arrived first. They connected with the Native Americans in the area and learned the skills they needed to work the land. In the mid-1800s, an English businessman named Caswell Robinson settled here with his family. He took advantage of the towering white pines that grew here and started a lumber business.

"It thrived, and this area became a key shipping port of the Great Lakes. In 1897, the Pere Marquette Railroad built a fleet of car ferries to transport the lumber across Lake Michigan to Chicago, Milwaukee, and other port cities. It wasn't long before Whispering Pines was one of the largest car ferry ports in the world. Today, we've only got the S.S. Wolverine left." J.P.'s expression displayed regret. "She's the last and largest coal-fired car ferry ever constructed."

"She's huge," Alex commented. "I've stood at the waterfront to watch her departure."

"An impressive sight, all right," J.P. agreed. "But now she's purely for leisure passengers and their automobiles, as opposed to lumber and railroad freight."

"Did the U.S. Coast Guard interact with the car ferries much?" Alex asked, her eyes flicking to the wording on his shirt.

"Not really," he said. "Unless they had trouble, of course."

"You were a captain?"

"That's right." He saluted. "Lake Michigan sector commander for the last twelve years of my thirty-year career. I retired after Ellen got sick."

J.P. didn't expand, and Alex didn't want to pry any more than she already had.

He continued. "Our station's main responsibility was rescue missions, covering more than 1,000 square miles of coastline between Big Sable Point and Stoney Lake. We handled about a hundred Search and Rescue cases every year," he added proudly.

"That sounds like such challenging work," Alex said.

"Definitely had its moments." J.P. nodded. "I miss it sometimes." His eyes took on a faraway gleam, then he grinned. "You're getting me off topic again, little miss."

"Sorry!"

He settled back against the sofa cushions. "Now, as the waterfront grew, so did downtown businesses, and the village flourished." He held up a thick finger. "Let me back up a bit. Around the turn of the century, just as Whispering Pines was experiencing its economic boom, Caswell Robinson's oldest son, Russell, along with his good friend Fritz Baumgartner, started a watchcase company here."

"The R & B Watchcase Company!" Alex exclaimed.

"Bingo!" J.P. said, aiming his pointer finger at her. "Fritz happened to be an excellent watchcase designer and engraver who'd emigrated from Switzerland."

J.P. paused and placed a hand on his stomach. "You know what, Miss Artist? I'm starving. C'mon, and I'll whip us up a couple of sandwiches while we finish this conversation."

Alex followed him through a narrow passageway that led to the kitchen at the back of the house. She marveled at J.P.'s thorough knowledge of the area's history. She would never have been able to recite such detailed facts about the suburban town in which she'd grown up.

The kitchen was a sunny contrast to the heavy, dark furnishings in the living room. Its walls were painted a pale yellow. The cupboards were white and shiny ceramic tiling covered the wall behind the stove and sink. The round kitchen table stood in front of a large bay window overlooking a colorful backyard flower garden.

"What would you like to drink?" He stood, peering into the open refrigerator door. "I've got orange juice, apple juice, and some fresh-made sun tea."

Alex turned from the window view. "Tea would be great, thanks."

He moved comfortably about the kitchen, pouring drinks and piling large slices of turkey and cheese onto slices of whole wheat bread.

Alex sat down at the table, gratefully sipping the ice-cold tea he presented to her. "Mmm. This is really good." Alex took another swallow. "Is that mint I taste?"

J.P. winked at her as he rinsed clusters of red grapes at the sink. "Yep." He lowered his voice conspiratorially. "It's my secret recipe. I use green tea bags, but I float some fresh mint leaves from the herb garden in it while it's steeping in the sunshine."

Alex couldn't help but smile. Here was this larger-than-life, ex-military man sharing recipes with her in his kitchen.

He carried the food-laden plates to the table and sat down beside her. "When my Ellen was alive, she did all the cooking. But it's been several years, and I've learned to do a lot of things I never did before. I've found I actually like cooking."

Alex hadn't realized how hungry she was until that moment. She'd only eaten the apple for breakfast, and that had been hours ago. She took a bite of her sandwich, chewing with gusto.

They ate in companionable silence for a few minutes, then J.P. turned his bright, blue gaze on her. "Now, where were we?"

"You were starting to tell me about the R & B Watchcase Company," Alex said, popping a grape into her mouth.

"Ahhh, that's right," J.P. said after taking a swallow of his tea. "The factory was built in 1881. They manufactured gold cases for pocket watches. Took care of all the metal stamping, plating, cleaning, and polishing processes. For decades, they were a huge success. Then, in 1936, Robinson and Baumgartner wanted out, so they sold the business to DaviSmit Corporation."

"*The* DaviSmit?" Alex asked, surprised. "That huge international conglomerate?"

"That's the one." J.P. chuckled, stretching out his long legs beneath the table. "And they ran it until the early eighties before finally stopping production."

"Why did they stop?"

"There was a deep recession around that time. Businesses were struggling and making cuts wherever they could. The factory sat idle for a few years, then DaviSmit sold the right to purchase the property to a local businessman named Peter Weston." J.P. shook his head. "At the time Weston acquired the rights to the factory, he already owned a strip mall and restaurant that weren't exactly thriving."

Alex pushed her empty plate forward and rested her chin in her palms. "If he was already struggling with the properties he had, why would he take on the challenge of another project like that?"

J.P. snorted. "Guaranteed profit. Or so he thought."

Alex frowned. "I don't get it."

J.P. polished off his last bite of sandwich, smacking his lips in satisfaction. "Weston didn't plan to hold onto the property. He'd already put the wheels in motion to re-sell it to this big Chicago developer named Roberts.

"But before that happened, Weston discovered the contamination." J.P. gazed out the kitchen window as he recalled the story. "He reported it like he was supposed to. But typical government red tape; it took them more than a decade to figure out who had jurisdiction, who was responsible for the cleanup, and even exactly how to clean it up. By then, Weston had lost his strip mall and his restaurant, and real estate prices had skyrocketed.

"He had all his eggs riding in one basket, so to speak. He tried renegotiating, hoping to sell the property for more money. But Roberts wouldn't play. Said they were sticking with the original agreement." J.P. turned his brilliant blue gaze on Alex. "The other piece of this was that Roberts was going to flatten the old factory and put up a luxury hotel."

Alex grimaced. "I heard about that from my grandmother and her friends. It sounds like that didn't go over well with the Whispering Pines community."

J.P. chuckled. "Probably the one and only time I've ever agreed with that ol' geezer, Farley. To destroy that wonderful old building would have been a terrible loss to Whispering Pines' history.

"Weston took Roberts to court. But he not only lost that fight, he ended up losing his financing as well, and the whole contract became null and void. With all the legal hassles and community complaints, Roberts decided to move on. And there the factory sat.

"Eventually, DaviSmit put it back on the market, and that's when Ben and my Jakey-boy entered the picture." J.P. rose from the table, taking their empty plates and glasses to the sink.

"What happened to Weston?" Alex twisted in her chair to face J.P. at the kitchen sink.

He frowned slightly as he rinsed their dishes and loaded them into the dishwasher. "I don't really know. I heard he'd passed away several years back."

J.P. put the iced tea pitcher back into the refrigerator, and when he turned, his gaze moved off her face, his attention captured by something behind her. In an uncharacteristic whisper, he said, "C'mon, Miss Artist, I want to show you something."

Intrigued, Alex rose from her chair to follow him out of the kitchen and into an adjacent sitting room, where double-wide French doors led to the backyard.

He motioned for her to stand beside him as he peered through one of the small glass panes in the door.

"Oh!" she breathed, following his gaze.

There was a cluster of flowers off to one side of the steps leading from the small wooden deck into the backyard. An iridescent emerald hummingbird hovered in view, its slender bill sipping nectar from a lush red blossom.

The tiny bird hung there for several seconds, delicate wings an invisible blur. But before Alex could exhale, it was gone.

"That was amazing!"

"Yep," J.P. agreed with a wide grin. "This was my Ellen's pride and joy." He swung the doors wide, and they both stepped onto the deck. "Her butterfly & hummingbird garden."

After the stuffy warmth of the small house, Alex inhaled the fragrant air appreciatively and looked over the well-tended flowerbeds. "You've obviously maintained it."

"Not me. Jakey-boy."

Alex was surprised. "Jake?"

For the first time since she'd met him, J.P. looked slightly uncomfortable. "Well, ah, it was something special he shared with Ellen. Started when he was real young. The older boys weren't as interested, but every summer, Jake and his nana planted a different type of garden together. They always had a theme." He smiled in memory. "Over the years, they had a pizza garden, salsa garden, herb garden, salad garden, and once they even had an edible-flowers-only garden. Even after Jakey-boy was grown, they kept up the tradition. This was the last garden Ellen was able to do with him." J.P.'s voice broke, and Alex looked away, allowing him to compose himself.

"By the middle of her last summer, she was real weak from the chemotherapy and radiation, so Jakey-boy did most of the work." His smile returned. "She loved sitting out here to watch the hummingbirds and keep Jake company."

Alex studied the big man as he looked out over the garden. It was clear J.P. had deeply loved his wife. Alex could hear it in the subtle way his voice changed whenever he spoke of her. And it was obvious that he loved his grandsons with an equal passion.

"So, Ellen enjoyed gardening," Alex said, resting her elbows on the deck railing. "But what sorts of things did you do with the boys when they stayed here?"

"Oh, the usual grandfather-grandson kinds of things, I suppose," he said. "Taught the boys to spit watermelon seeds, chop wood, get dirty. We fished and hiked a lot. Sometimes, I'd bring them down to the station to visit."

"That must have been exciting for them," Alex said.

J.P. laughed. "For my men, too. They loved sharing their rescue stories just as much as the boys loved hearing them."

Then J.P. regaled her with some of his own rescue stories until Alex was shocked to hear the grandfather clock inside the house chime four o'clock.

"Tell Tilly I'll expect her at the meeting tonight," he called as she hurried to the car.

"Will do!"

She tossed the books J.P. had loaned her onto the passenger seat and slipped inside. The engine purred to life. "Time to get home and make Grandma's dinner, Lola," she announced to the glowing GPS screen.

CHAPTER 10

Alex walked through the front door and was met with a resounding silence. "Grandma?" she called.

"I'm in the studio, dear," came the faint reply.

Alex cut across the great room and down a short hallway to step inside the art studio at the back of the home. Grandpa Joe had added it on after Tilly started getting serious about making pottery. Alex loved the airy, open space. The three exterior walls had floor-to-ceiling windows, letting in plenty of natural light, as well as an immersive view of the surrounding woods. It made Alex feel as if she had just stepped back outside. There was a gleaming, wide wooden worktable and beside it, shelving was filled with neat rows of bowls, vases, and dishes.

Tilly was seated on a low red stool in front of her dormant potter's wheel. Her back was turned to it, however, as she watched a blue jay hop about the bird feeder, which hung from a tree branch nearby.

"What are you doing in here?" Alex asked, sliding another stool across the floor so she could sit down beside Tilly.

"Wishing."

Alex reached out to smooth back a stray wisp of Tilly's silver hair. "It's hard, huh?"

Her grandmother's expression was wistful. "Which part?"

Alex looked rueful. "I guess that was a loaded question."

Tilly's lips curved into a faint smile. "I try not to focus on negative thoughts, but, darling, sometimes..." She sighed. "Sometimes I just miss your Grandpa Joe so much."

Alex leaned forward and put an arm around Tilly, laying her head on her grandmother's shoulder. "I know, Grandma. I miss him, too. I can't believe it's been five years." They sat in silence for a bit, watching as the blue jay chased off a couple of curious chickadees. "I can still smell his pipe smoke whenever I sit in his favorite chair."

Tilly nodded, smiling. "That's the reason I've kept some of his old coats and flannel shirts." She reached up and patted Alex's cheek. "But life marches on, dragging us along with it."

Alex lifted her head and Tilly lifted her casted arm, eyes glinting playfully. "And, yes, Alex, I do miss my pottery! You know, I doubt I'd have ever discovered my skill if your grandfather hadn't encouraged me—inspired me, really—to overcome my fears and just try."

Alex nodded. "I remember."

"And you." Tilly's eyes met Alex's. Her grandmother's eyes seemed more gray than blue in the early evening light.

"What about me?"

"You inspire me too, Alex."

Alex snorted. "What are you talking about?"

"I waited until I was well over fifty years old to pursue my dream. But you..." Tilly gazed at her steadily. "You not only recognized your talent but pursued it with single-minded passion. I still think about the confidence you showed, standing up to both of your parents when they tried talking you out of attending that creative college. That sort of self-assurance is rare in one so young." Looking back toward the window, her eyes took on a dreamy quality.

"When I'm in the middle of creating a new piece, I get this feeling of...of coming alive. It's invigorating! And addicting." She looked at Alex again. "And to think I missed out on that feeling for so many years of my life, just because I was afraid. And I'm not even sure what I was afraid of. Success? Or failure?"

Alex laughed. "For me, it's both."

Tilly looked surprised. "You've felt afraid?"

Alex's eyes widened. "Loads of times! I try to ignore it, though. Just shove the fear into the background of my mind, force it to shut up."

"And that works?"

"Usually." Then she added glumly, "Except now, of course. This is...different."

"How so?"

"I don't know. It's hard to put into words. I suppose the best way to describe it is to say that my inspiration, my muse, has abandoned me."

"Hmmm." Tilly looked thoughtful. "I once read a profound quote for writers, but it could apply to artists as well."

"What is it?"

"I only write when I'm inspired, and I make sure I'm inspired every morning at nine o'clock.'"

They both laughed.

Then Alex grew serious. "I don't know what to do, Grandma. When I even think about going back to my home studio to start work on this, I get sick to my stomach. What if I can't paint this mural?"

Tilly patted Alex's arm. "You will. I know you will." She said the words with a confidence Alex wished she shared. Then suddenly, Tilly's eyes widened. "I have an idea."

"What?"

Tilly waved her good arm in an expansive gesture, encompassing the entire room. "Use my studio."

"I can't do that!"

"Of course you can! I certainly can't use it right now. We'll just move my things out of the way, and you'll have plenty of room."

"I can't—"

"Oh pish posh!" her grandmother said in a rare flash of anger. "You most certainly can. And you will," she added emphatically.

Alex looked around the room with new eyes, taking in the open space, high ceiling, and natural light. She had to admit, using the studio and remaining in Whispering Pines held an appeal. "But all my supplies are back at home," Alex demurred.

"There's a wonderful art supply store in Pentwater. Let me gift you the funds to get whatever you need there."

"But–"

Tilly laid a finger on Alex's lips. "No buts. It's a perfect idea and you know it. Maybe the new setting will shake you out of your funk. Besides, my studio has been pining for an artist in residence for too long as it is."

Alex laughed. "Oh, all right. I'll *try*."

Rising from her stool, she wandered over to the west-facing window. The sky glowed like candlelight above the scruffy tops of the pines. She doubted the change of location would make a difference and gnawed at her lower lip.

"Don't underestimate yourself, dear," Tilly said softly, as if she could hear Alex's anxious thoughts.

Alex turned and clapped her hands together, abruptly changing the subject. "Are you hungry?"

"Starved." Tilly smiled.

"Come on, I'll make us something to eat.

They walked back to the kitchen side by side as Tilly asked, "How did everything go today? Did you get a good tour of the site?"

As Alex pulled chicken breasts from the refrigerator, she shared the day's events. Tilly expressed concern over the accident at the site, but Alex dismissed it with a shrug. She told Tilly about her informative interview with J.P. "He's so knowledgeable. And a very...paradoxical man," Alex concluded.

"How so?" Tilly sat on a high stool at the breakfast counter, watching Alex work.

"Well, he's this larger-than-life, tough-talking sailor. A real man's man, right?" Alex said, putting away the spices she'd just used to season the chicken. "At the same time, though, he's able to appreciate the serenity of his late wife's flower garden and share his deepest feelings. Alex pulled a bag of snowflake rolls from the pantry. "It's strange, but even though he arranged for this mural, he just doesn't seem like the artsy type, you know?"

Tilly came around the counter to pull out plates and silverware. "His late wife was very involved in the community. She was particularly passionate about the arts. The Whispering Pines Mural Society was originally Ellen Riley's idea. I think J.P. hopes to carry on her work this way."

Alex placed the chicken into the preheated oven. "Oh, that reminds me, he told me he'd see you at the Planning Committee meeting tonight."

Tilly nodded, then looked speculatively at Alex. "Maybe you should attend it with me, darling."

"Me?"

"Yes." Tilly arranged their two place settings. "The vote tonight concerns you as much as Riley Development Corporation."

"How do you mean?"

"If those variances don't get approved, the project will be halted yet again. I don't know if they can afford any more delays. No project means no mural."

"And that would be bad because..." Alex said.

Tilly frowned, pursing her lips.

"I'm sorry." Alex was instantly apologetic. "I'll stop being negative."

"Thank you!"

Alex was quiet as she tore lettuce, dropping it into a glass bowl.

"Jake is extremely lucky nobody was hurt in that accident today," Tilly said, returning to their earlier topic.

"Yeah, he was so over the top about it," Alex said with a shake of her head.

"He most certainly should have been over the top about it!" Tilly exclaimed. She reached out her good arm to touch Alex's cheek. "You're one of my most precious blessings and I don't want anything happening to you."

"Oh, Grandmaaaaaaa." Alex feigned a whine. She finished slicing cucumber for the salad just as the timer for the chicken went off.

They sat down together, and Alex dished some sliced up chicken breast onto Tilly's plate. "If I go to the meeting with you, do you mind if we don't sit anywhere near Jake?" Alex asked.

Tilly looked startled. "Why ever not, dear? Does he make you uncomfortable?"

"Absolutely," Alex said.

CHAPTER 11

Alex and Tilly entered the Whispering Pines Community Center a few minutes before seven o'clock. Small clusters of people engaged in quiet conversations milled around the lobby, which was warm with body heat. In contrast, as they walked into the meeting room, frigid air blasted through the vents, and Alex shivered.

At the front of the room was a long table with a row of seven chairs behind it. Opposite the table, several neat rows of padded spectator chairs were filling with people. A video camera on a tripod was set up against the back wall of the room. A young man lounged beside it, head bowed over his cell phone. Tilly explained the meetings were always recorded and broadcast on the city council website.

The low murmur of voices, and occasional bursts of laughter, hummed pleasantly throughout the room, yet Alex felt an undercurrent of energy charging the small space. She spotted Jake immediately and ignored the excited leap of her heart, forcing herself to breathe normally. He was seated in the front row beside Keith Markham and another man. Their three heads were bent toward each other as they spoke quietly together.

Instead of his usual work clothes, Jake wore a suit of midnight blue with a striped red tie. His dark curls were combed back from his face, brushing the crisp, white collar that circled his neck. His tan skin glowed.

It figured only somebody like Jake could look good in this hideous fluorescent lighting, Alex thought sourly.

As if her thoughts created some sort of radar, he turned suddenly and spotted them where they stood at the room's entrance. He rose with a smile and began weaving his way toward them. He moved with unusual poise for such a tall man, and Alex was instantly reminded of a black panther, all elegance and restrained power.

He reached out and gently squeezed Tilly's hand in welcome, his gaze taking them both in. "I'm grateful you came," he murmured. "I'm not certain how this is going to go." Jake tilted his head toward a small group of people surrounding Frank Farley in one corner of the room. His usual mischievous twinkle was absent, and his dark eyes looked flat. "I can use all the reinforcements I can get."

"You got me, Jakey-boy!" a voice exploded from behind them, making Alex jump and every head in the room turn. "What more do you need?" J.P. laughed uproariously at his own joke and thumped Jake on the back.

"Hello there, Miss Artist." J.P. laid a meaty hand on her shoulder. "And good evening to you as well, Miss Tilly," he added, looking down at her grandmother, his voice softening slightly.

Tilly greeted him, then turned to pat Jake's arm. "It will all work out fine, Jake. Don't you worry one bit."

"I hope you're right, Tilly," Jake replied.

Alex surveyed the room, looking for a place to sit. She noted Frank Farley and his cohorts were now seating themselves in the last row of chairs. Farley's white-tufted head bent low as he frowned over some papers gripped in his bony hand.

Jake excused himself, and they selected seats near the room's entrance. A moment later, Margot and Gretchen slipped into two chairs behind them.

"What took you so long?" Tilly asked.

"Margot couldn't decide which dress to wear for the occasion," Gretchen grunted with an eye roll.

Margot's face flushed. "That is not the reason at all and you know it, Gretchen Sinclair! She—"

Margot was interrupted as the meeting was called to order. The chairman did roll call and everybody stood for the pledge of allegiance. Then recent correspondence and committee reports were all taken care of before the topic of Riley Development finally arose on the agenda.

Alex watched Jake rise from his seat and step over to the microphone and podium, which faced the board. He stood straight as an oak, his gaze sweeping over the faces of each board member. "Good evening." His voice through the microphone was low and formal. "My name is Jake Riley, and

I'm representing Riley Development Corporation. I'm here to present our request for a site variance."

There was a derisive grunt from somewhere in the back of the room. No big guess as to where it came from, and Alex refused to look around.

Jake's voice remained calm and clear as he spoke. "As you are all aware, Riley Development Corporation completed site remediation on the former DaviSmit Watchcase Factory grounds. We're hoping to proceed with our original plan to renovate the property and create a forty-eight condominium facility featuring a combination of independent and assisted living. As much as possible, it's our desire to preserve the character of the building. In order to maintain our tax benefits..."

This time, a loud coughing fit issued from the back of the room.

Jake ignored the interruption. "...it is essential that we reconstruct the building façade as close as possible to its original form. To do this, we're requesting a variance for the chimney and water tower, which will exceed Whispering Pines' current height code."

One board member, seated at the far end of the table, was a stout woman in her late fifties wearing a chic, cream-colored suit. Her platinum hair curved around her jawline in a stylish bob. She smiled at Jake. "You've been working hard on the site, haven't you, Mr. Riley?" She glanced down the row of her fellow board members. "I attended the architectural review several months ago, and it looks like the condo complex is going to be just fabulous."

Now there was murmuring coming from the audience. Alex couldn't tell if they were sounds of agreement or dissent.

Another board member, seated directly beside the chairman, frowned slightly. "I've reviewed your plans very carefully, Mr. Riley," he said. He folded his hands on the table and leaned forward to peer at Jake over the top of his readers. "I still have some concerns. Would you be willing to answer a few questions for us?"

"Certainly," Jake responded, looking remarkably relaxed given the circumstances, Alex thought.

"With respect to the parking you have planned. That area around the marina already suffers from traffic congestion, and it looks to me as if your plans will only exacerbate the problem."

"What the heck does that have to do with the water tower and chimney?" Gretchen whispered loudly. Margot shushed her.

The man Alex didn't know, who had been seated beside Jake, rose and handed Jake a piece of paper, conferring with him briefly.

Jake nodded and turned back to the microphone. "Clay Williams is our project architect," he indicated the man who had just resumed his seat. "According to our plan, access to the parking lot will be from Loon Street and Sea Gull Lane, so we'll avoid contributing to any traffic congestion along the main road.

The man who'd asked the question nodded in satisfaction, but then other board members started asking questions and making comments about the project. Alex sensed that in addition to the blond woman, at least two others appeared favorable toward the variances. Not quite a majority, she thought grimly.

Once they'd finished their questions, Jake resumed his seat and the floor was opened up for audience participation before the voting took place.

There was a bustle of movement from the back of the room and Frank Farley scuttled up to the podium. Rumbles of anticipation issued from the crowd. Farley's worn, button-front shirt was tucked into a pair of brown pants pulled high and bunched tight around his skinny midsection with a matching belt. He reached up to smooth his hair and cleared his throat.

"Ladies and gentlemen of the board," he intoned. "My name is Frank Farley and I've lived in Whispering Pines all my life. I represent a constituency—" J.P. snorted loudly at this, earning him a glare from Farley before he continued. "A *large* constituency of our village," he continued, "who feel that it would be wrong to allow any exceptions to Whispering Pines' height restriction code. Whispering Pines is a quaint, historic village which has been around for hundreds of years. There are those who would like to forget that in the name of progress."

"Is the man daft?" Tilly murmured quietly. "How does maintaining the façade of a 19th-century factory *detract* from the town's historicity?" Alex shrugged.

"Over the past few years, Whispering Pines has seen a decline in population. This is due to projects precisely like this one being handled by Riley Development Corporation. Whispering Pines does not need condos!"

Farley thumped his bony fist on the podium as he spoke. "What we need are more jobs. All these condos will do is attract tourists. It's a known fact that eighty percent of Whispering Pines' citizens despise the manner in which tourists and tourism invade our little village. Tourism is ruining this town, leading our community to apathy, drugs, and crime!" Farley's voice rose. "Expensive condominium projects such as this one cause nothing but trouble. With their uppity attitude, Whispering Pines will end up becoming a plutocracy!"

"That guy is whacked!" Gretchen muttered.

"And then there is the danger to innocent lives as well. All the problems with the site's remediation and the freak accidents. The company would pretend that these are all issues in the past, but as I understand it, just today, one visitor to the site nearly lost her life!"

There was a unified intake of breath from the small audience, and Alex started. *How could Farley have known about that?*

Jake's face darkened and Keith Markham started to rise from his seat but was surreptitiously waved back by the chairman. "Your three minutes are almost up, Mr. Farley," he said smoothly.

Farley leaned closer to the microphone, his milky eyes gleaming behind his glasses. "I urge the board to deny this variance request! And, in fact, I once again implore you to put a stop to this entire project. Riley Development has already finagled their way out of getting a proper environmental impact statement." He peered pointedly at several board members. "These condos should not even be built, let alone be allowed any special exceptions. Thank you." He restacked his pages and walked jerkily back to his seat while every eye in the room followed him.

Alex looked at Jake, and it was clear from his expression he was keeping a tight rein on his anger. The volume of the room increased as many held whispered conversations with their neighbors, but she still couldn't get a clear read on the mood of the crowd. Tilly leaned over and whispered, "He hopes that if this variance doesn't get approved, Jake will be unable to meet the tax credit requirements and lose his funding."

"He's such a hateful little man," Margot hissed.

The chairman tapped his gavel, causing the room to fall quiet once again. "Are there any other members of the audience with something to say?"

"Why that measly little *blivit*—" J.P. started rising to his feet, but Tilly placed a restraining hand on his arm. He looked befuddled but sat back down again.

"What's a *blivit*?" Margot whispered.

"Shhhh!" Gretchen waved her to silence as Tilly rose gracefully to her feet. Alex watched in surprise as her grandmother straightened the soft blue cardigan she wore and approached the podium. She stood before the microphone, her clear, gentle voice addressing the members of the board.

"Good evening, my name is Matilda Fontaine, and I've been a member of the Whispering Pines community for over a decade now. Although I cannot claim to have lived here all my life, as Mr. Farley has, I've grown to love Whispering Pines and think of it as my own hometown."

J.P. rested his elbows on his knees, straining forward to better hear Tilly's words.

"First of all, I would like to say I agree with Mr. Farley that Whispering Pines could use more jobs." Alex heard a choked sound come from deep in Gretchen's throat. "Which is why it's wonderful that Riley Development has made a point to hire local talent to handle the sub-contracted construction elements, such as painting, landscaping, electrical needs, and more."

Alex noted several members of the audience nodding their heads.

"As to the rest of what Mr. Farley shared, I must adamantly disagree." Tilly gripped the podium with her good hand. "If my husband and I hadn't first been tourists in this wonderful community, I doubt we would have chosen to move here for our retirement. Part of what drew us is the quaint historic charm of the area. That very historic charm that Riley Development is trying to preserve.

"I would like to see where Mr. Farley found his statistic claiming that eighty percent of our population despises tourists. I find it hard to believe that there are eight thousand people in Whispering Pines who are against tourism and the development of these condominiums." Tilly shook her head. "Isn't it a fact that tourism brings money into Whispering Pines? If not for summer tourists drawn to Lake Michigan and our wonderful state park, there would be far less people frequenting local restaurants and downtown shops. And as far as apathy, drugs, and crime...come now!" she chided, shaking her head again. "Drugs and crime are not exclusive to Whispering

Pines. They are unfortunately in every community in the country to a greater or lesser degree, and it's absurd to claim they're being brought to our village by city dwellers.

"I would also like to point out that not only has Riley Development Corporation taken on the difficult challenge of restoring a previously contaminated and collapsing historic icon, but they are utilizing green technology as well. I hope most people in this community recognize positive change when they see it. And that's what Riley Development is bringing us: positive change. Thank you."

Tilly slowly made her way back to her seat amid a smattering of applause from the audience and Gretchen let loose a "Woot!" as she and Margot applauded louder than anyone. Jake and Clay were both grinning broadly in Tilly's direction and Keith Markham's mouth literally hung open.

"Grandma, you totally rocked!" Alex said proudly, squeezing her grandmother in a sideways hug as Tilly reclaimed her chair.

The chairman was once again asking for comments from the audience.

"Well said, Tilly," Margot whispered. "But be careful. If looks could kill..." She tilted her head, indicating Farley seated in the back row shooting daggers at Tilly with his eyes.

"I'm not worried about him," Tilly said dismissively.

"You don't have to be." J.P. was looking at Tilly with an indescribable light in his pale eyes. "If he says one word to you, I'll adjust his jaw for him right quick."

Tilly covered a laugh behind a cough. "I'm sure that won't be necessary, J.P."

Their attention went to the front of the room as the chairman's voice rang out. "If there are no more comments from the audience, it's time for the board to vote." He pushed his thick tortoiseshell glasses up on his nose and ran a hand over his shiny bald head before stating, "The applicant, Riley Development Corporation, is proposing..."

Alex tuned out the chairman's legalistic description of the proposal as she studied Jake's profile. His entire body was tense, and she was once again reminded of a lithe jungle cat, this time poised to spring.

"I motion to approve the requested variances for the chimney and water tower and grant full approval of the project site plan," the stout blond woman chimed.

"I second the motion," said the chairman, his head swiveling around the table. "All those in favor, please respond by saying "aye." All seven board members' voices resounded in a unified "Aye."

"None opposing?" The head swiveled again. "Then motion carries."

Alex could hear the collective sigh of relief coming from several people in the room, including herself. She hadn't even realized she was holding her breath.

The chairman looked at Jake. "Congratulations, Mr. Riley."

"Thank you, sir!"

The room quieted once again as he led the board through the remainder of the agenda. The meeting finally adjourned, board and audience members rose, immediately breaking apart into small clusters of conversation.

"So that's it?" Alex asked. "It's a done deal?"

"It's a done deal, Miss Artist," J.P. responded with a wide grin.

Jake, Clay, and Peter started toward their little group, but Jake was stopped repeatedly to shake hands and respond to people's well wishes.

Alex turned away, pretending to watch the video camera operator disassemble his equipment and wishing Tilly would stop talking so they could leave.

Jake finally reached them and bent down to wrap her grandmother in a warm hug. His face was flushed, his dark eyes brilliant. "Thank you so much, Tilly."

"Oh, pish posh!" she said with a blush. "I didn't say anything everyone else in the room wasn't already thinking."

"*Almost* everyone," Margot said, her eyes following the angry progress of Farley as he stalked from the room without a backward glance.

"Oh, who cares? He's a moron!" Gretchen said.

"Gretchen!"

"Well, he is!" Gretchen looked at Margot. "I'm not saying anything everyone else in the room isn't already thinking." She smiled smugly as the rest of the group laughed. "He's been that way since he was a boy," she added.

"You knew him as a child?" Clay asked.

"You bet," Gretchen said. "He was a killjoy back then, too. Probably why he's never married. No woman could stand that sour disposition for long."

"He was engaged once though, wasn't he?" Margot said, frowning in memory.

J.P. snorted. "That was a lifetime ago." He turned, laying his hand on Jake's shoulder. "So what's next, Jakey-boy?"

"Keith and I worked all afternoon, and we've got the paperwork set to submit to the building department tomorrow, then we can really get the ball rolling."

"Everything here is copacetic," Keith said, patting his briefcase. He turned to shake hands with Jake and Clay. "Well, guys, it's late and I've got some other work to finish up. I'll see you in the morning." He bade everyone goodnight.

"I can't believe we've finally got a full green light," Clay said, shaking his head.

Jake thumped him on the back. "Believe it, buddy. And thank you. You've worked as hard as anyone to convince the good citizens of Whispering Pines that this is a worthy project. How many presentations have you done now?"

"Let's see," Clay rubbed his jaw, "there were about five public forums, the Historic Preservations Committee, Architectural Review Board, Whispering Pines Beautification Committee, Ladies' Gardening Society, the—"

Jake held up his hand with a laugh. "Okay, okay, I get it. We should be paying you more."

Clay laughed. "Why don't you just introduce me to this lovely lady who leaped to our defense."

"This is Tilly Fontaine," he said, turning to face her. "She's also president of the Whispering Pines Mural Society."

Tilly shook Clay's hand. "Sorry about the southpaw handshake." She held up her casted right arm. "I'm hoping to get this thing off tomorrow."

Tilly turned to her friends. "These are my partners in crime, Margot Reardon and Gretchen Sinclair." Everyone exchanged greetings, then Tilly twisted around. "Now, where did Alex get to?"

Alex had successfully inched her way to the door, but upon hearing her grandmother say her name, she sighed and rejoined the group. "I'm right here, Grandma."

"Oh," Tilly smiled with pride. "And this is my granddaughter, Alex Fontaine."

Clay shook Alex's hand, his eyebrows raised. "*The* Alex Fontaine?" he asked.

"Excuse me?"

"The Alex Fontaine who is an amazingly talented muralist, and who's planning to join our renegade crew?"

Alex blushed. "Well, I—um..."

"Yep, it's her," Jake said, a playful glint in his eyes. "By the way, how's your history research going, Alex? Did Pops give you everything you needed?"

"'Course I did," J.P. cut in.

"His knowledge of the area's history is wonderful," Alex said with a smile, and J.P. beamed.

"What happens after you've finished your research?" Clay asked.

"Well," Alex tilted her head. "I'll take some photographs; get a better feel of the site. Then I'll make some sketches, and we'll decide on one." Alex smiled at Tilly. "Grandma's letting me work from her studio, which is great." She sighed. "But, I suppose I'll have to go car shopping before I do anything else."

"You heard back on your car?" Jake asked with interest.

"Yes, unfortunately, Bessie's long life is over."

"That's too bad," Jake said with concern. "You know, I have to wait for all our paperwork to be processed before I get really busy. I'll only be working a few hours tomorrow. Would you like me to take you car shopping?"

"Thank you, but that won't be necessary. I'm sure I can handle it on my own," Alex said, lifting her nose slightly.

J.P. laughed heartily. "Looks like you've been shot down pretty good, Jakey-boy!"

Jake grinned wide, unperturbed.

Alex ignored him and turned to Tilly. "Are you ready to go, Grandma?"

"Whenever you are, dear."

J.P. stepped forward to clasp Tilly's hand. "As always, it's a pleasure, Tilly."

Her eyes shone. "Why, thank you, J.P."

"Thanks again, Tilly," Jake said, then his gaze swept the group. "And I truly appreciate all of your support."

"I'm glad we could help," Tilly called as Alex practically dragged her from the room, Gretchen and Margot trailing in their wake.

CHAPTER 12

Tilly relaxed in the passenger seat and closed her eyes as Alex started to drive. She jolted upright a moment later when the GPS unit spoke. "In point two miles, turn right."

Alex turned down the volume. "Did she think I'd accidentally drive into the lake?" she muttered.

"So strange having your car talk to you, isn't it?" Tilly commented, settling back again.

"Mhm." Alex glanced over at her grandmother's serene face, awash in the glow of the fading evening light. She still couldn't believe her quiet, reserved grandmother had been such a confident and vocal speaker at the meeting. Alex had never heard Tilly speak publicly before. Yet she'd delivered her points with eloquence and class, her voice never quavering.

Perhaps that confidence had always been there, lurking just beneath the surface. There were glimpses of it when she began pursuing her pottery. And it had blossomed further when she'd stepped up to handle situations that arose after Grandpa Joe's death. It seemed her grandmother was finally coming into her own. And it was an incredible thing to witness. Alex kissed her fingertips and laid them gently against her grandmother's cheek. Tilly's eyes flew open again. "What was that for, dear?"

Alex smiled. "Because you're you."

Tilly gave a soft answering smile.

"That was some speech tonight, Grandma."

"Mmm," Tilly responded, her eyes closed again.

"Where did it come from?"

"What do you mean?"

"I mean, I've never heard you so...I don't know, passionate, I guess, is the word I'm looking for, about anything."

"Well..." Tilly sat up and gazed thoughtfully out the window as they drove along a curve that echoed the water's edge. The pure colors of twilight undulated gently on its surface. "For years, I suppose I simply accepted things. I never liked to rock the boat, and I always let your grandfather handle our major decisions." She shrugged. "I'm not sure why. Maybe it was because he was ten years my senior. I was so young when we married ..." she trailed off.

Alex turned off the main road. "Were you frustrated all those years?"

"Oh, no! I loved your Grandpa Joe with heart and soul. He just wanted to take care of me, and I let him. We had a good marriage and I suppose I just got comfortable. But looking back now, I see I never really thought enough about my own passions and dreams. Like my art," she added.

Alex nodded in understanding.

"And lately," she sighed in resignation. "I've particularly regretted never having learned to drive." She glanced over at Alex. "I wish I could help you now with this whole car situation, darling."

"It's all right, Grandma," Alex assured her. "I've bought my own car before. I can handle it."

"Why don't you want that nice Jake Riley to help you? It's good to have a second opinion when you're purchasing something as important as a car."

"If I need a second opinion, I'm not getting it from Jake Riley!"

Her grandmother raised her brows in surprise. "But he seems like such a nice, intelligent young man."

Alex gave a short, mirthless laugh. "Oh, he's nice, all right."

"Ahhh, I see." Tilly smiled.

"You do?"

"You're uncomfortable because you find him...hot, as Gretchen would say."

"I do *not* think he's hot!"

Tilly shot her a knowing look.

"Oh, fine," Alex conceded grudgingly. "He's hot. But I've said it before, and I'll say it again, I'm not interested in any romantic entanglements right now. Maybe ever." She glanced at Tilly, suddenly curious. "What are you doing paying attention to how hot some guy is anyway?"

Tilly pressed her lips together, looking prim. "I've been married, but I'm not buried. Of course, I noticed! His grandfather's not so bad either."

Alex made a face. "Grandma! Ewww!" She shuddered and started repeating, "Happy place, happy place. Go to your happy place."

Alex arose early the next morning.

Showering quickly, she threw on one of her old T-shirts and a pair of jean shorts.

She padded into the living room and grinned when she spotted Tilly on the floor in the final relaxation pose of her morning yoga routine. She was breathing deeply and quietly as Alex tiptoed past her into the kitchen to prepare their breakfast.

Tilly joined her just as Alex was scooping hot oatmeal into a bowl. "How was your workout?"

"A little frustrating," Tilly sighed. "I'm so glad to be getting this blasted thing off today." The sleeve of her loose white top fell back as she shook her cast. "It's cramping my style."

"Is Gretchen taking you?"

Tilly nodded, readjusting her sleeve.

Alex took a deep swallow of her coffee and sat down on the stool beside Tilly, who wrinkled her nose. "I don't know how you can stand that stuff," she said, taking a sip of the green tea that Alex had prepared for her.

"Hey, don't knock it. It's my motivation in a cup," Alex said. "I need it today. I've got a lot to accomplish, and I was up late skimming J.P.'s books and working on sketches."

"How did they turn out?"

"Pretty good, I think. J.P. really inspired me. He's a great storyteller."

"He certainly is," Tilly remarked, taking a spoonful of oatmeal. "So, what's on your agenda for today?"

"I'm going to get the supplies I'll need, and then I'm going to do a little car shopping." Alex polished off the last of her toast, licking jelly from her fingertips. "What about you?"

"After I get this cast off, Gretchen, Margot, Susan, and I are meeting to work on our marketing plan. We need to get more downtown businesses on board."

"One mural down, nine more to go, right?"

Tilly lifted her good arm and made a fist.

Alex fist-bumped it with her own and grinned. "You go, Grandma!"

Leaving Tilly on the sofa reading a copy of the Whispering Pines Gazette, Alex tossed her armload of books, notes, and sketchpad onto the passenger seat and slipped behind the wheel. "First stop, J.P.'s," she said to herself. She didn't need Lola for this anymore, so she turned the GPS off and turned on the music of an alternative rock station. The day was sunny and bright, so she opened the sunroof, taking deep breaths of the fragrant air as she drove.

At J.P.'s little bungalow, she peered through his screen door and smiled to see him sitting in the same position in which she'd left Tilly. Black-framed reading glasses were perched on the end of his nose as he flipped a page of the newspaper. He looked up at her knock.

"Come on in, Miss Artist!" he boomed.

Alex entered and set the books down on the coffee table in front of him. "Thanks so much for the loan, J.P."

"Glad to be of service, m'dear." He set the paper down, smiling at her. "Think you're ready to start painting our mural?"

Her stomach lurched at his words, but she pasted on an answering smile. "Almost."

J.P. sat back and shook his head. "Oh, to have talent like yours," he said. "And your grandmother's."

"Uh-huh." She'd been working hard to keep her paralyzing fears at bay, but J.P.'s words brought everything straight to the surface.

He leaned forward. "What are your ideas in terms of a subject?"

"Well, I definitely want to keep with the lake orientation we discussed, but I'm still...um, considering options," she said, suddenly feeling insecure again.

He pounded his hand on the tabletop and laughed. "You creative types!"

She started inching her way back toward the door. "I should get going. Lots to prepare before I can start," she said.

He picked his newspaper up. "Be careful driving around today, Miss Artist. We're in for a doozy of a storm."

"Really?" Alex said, surprised, and peered out the screen door. She'd noticed some broad, fluffy clouds over the lake, but hadn't considered much beyond their beauty.

"Can't you smell the change in the air? Storms come up pretty quickly around here," he said.

Alex pushed open the door with a wave and promised to be careful.

He grunted a response and returned his nose to the paper.

She climbed into the car and as if on cue, fat drops spattered randomly against the windshield. She quickly closed the sunroof, then idled for a bit in front of J.P.'s home while she punched the address of the art supply store into Lola.

Alex sped off, following Lola's directions. Since she didn't need to focus on directions, she started daydreaming and nearly missed a turn and had to swerve quickly into the left lane. A few seconds later, a blaring horn drew her attention. She glanced into her rearview mirror and realized it hadn't been her erratic swerve, but rather a black Expedition that had suddenly swung into the lane behind her that had annoyed the honking driver.

Rain fell harder and the windshield wipers pulsed rhythmically. She wound her way over several dirt roads before realizing Lola was routing her through some back way. "You'd better not get me lost," she muttered to the unit.

Frowning, she reached over and fumbled through the papers on the passenger seat, pulling out the directions she'd printed off from the Internet the evening before. Quickly scanning the page, she realized the included map wasn't sufficient. So, she tossed it aside and stretched across the seat to pop open the glove box, hoping for a map of the area.

Her searching hand patted around the interior and pulled out a slim, plastic file case with the car's registration and insurance information, a pair of sunglasses, and a small flashlight.

She put her hand inside again, but the box was now empty. "Is this guy for real?" she said aloud. "Where's the junk? The gum wrappers, old ketchup packets, and used napkins? And where the heck does he keep his maps?" She shoved everything back inside and slammed it shut.

Straightening in her seat, she was surprised to see the black Expedition she'd noticed earlier was still behind her, following more closely than she'd have liked.

Aside from their two cars, the road was empty in both directions. She slowed down, allowing room for it to pass, but the Expedition slowed down as well.

"In point three miles, turn right," Lola chimed.

She made the turn. And so did the Expedition. Maybe the rain was making the driver hesitant, Alex thought. So, she tapped her brakes, motioning for the vehicle to pass. Instead of doing so, however, it drew even closer. She sighed. "Dude, what's your prob—"

Suddenly, the SUV shot forward, hitting her rear bumper.

Alex jolted in her seat.

In shock, she took her foot off the accelerator, and the car smacked into her again. Harder this time.

Fear and adrenaline began coursing through her. With trembling fingers, Alex tightened her grip on the wheel, knuckles turning white as her mind raced. What was happening? The first hit could have been an accident, but the second? No way. As unbelievable as it seemed, whoever was driving that car had hit her on purpose!

Cold sweat beaded on her forehead. Thinking it must be some type of road rage situation, she knew she needed to get away from this lunatic fast. Jamming the accelerator to the floor, the sports car leaped forward. She raced to the next intersection. Hitting her brakes, she spun the wheel to the left, tires spitting gravel as she fishtailed into a hard turn.

She switched back to the accelerator and shot forward again. The rain was falling hard now and she flicked the wiper dial, increasing its speed.

"Recalculating," Lola said.

"Shut up!" Alex growled. She glanced into the rearview mirror and saw the SUV make the same turn.

Heart thudding in her chest, she sucked in huge gulps of air, trying to breathe and think.

Still accelerating, she groped blindly for her purse, then emptied its contents onto the seat beside her. With shaking hands, she scattered the mess on the seat and located her phone.

The car was close enough to hit her from behind again, and Alex slipped the phone under one thigh, bracing herself. This time, however, the other driver moved into the oncoming lane to come up alongside her.

She looked over at it. But the windows were tinted just like hers, plus they were too high up to see inside. Without warning, the SUV swerved, this time slamming into the side of her car. The steering wheel jerked from beneath her fingers and the car wobbled wildly.

Alex clutched at the wheel, regaining control. Completely panicked, she didn't try dialing 9-1-1 but jabbed her finger on the redial button.

The Expedition, unaffected by the impact, was already beside her again as the two cars raced up the empty road. Some instinct made Alex slam on her brakes. Not expecting this, the other driver attempted to sideswipe her again but only glanced off the nose of her car.

Still, it was enough to wrench the wheel and Alex fought to stay on the road.

"Drive point three miles, then make a U-turn," said the GPS unit.

"Hey, you letting Lola make phone calls for you now?" Jake's teasing voice came through the car's speaker system.

"Jake!" she cried. "Help me!"

"What's the matter?" His joking manner dissolved instantly.

The Expedition was backing up, so Alex started accelerating again. A deep ravine yawned off on the right side of the road, and the car skidded sluggishly as her tires rolled over the wet sand on the shoulder.

"Somebody's trying to kill me!"

"What? What do you—"

The car was beside her again. She was trapped between it and the ditch. "I'm driving north on–"

There was a screech of metal on metal as the Expedition smashed hard into her side. This time, the tiny car was no match for the power of the SUV. Alex screamed as her car went airborne and pitched off the side of the road.

CHAPTER 13

Alex was drifting through a murky darkness. There was a persistent high-pitched whine coming from somewhere far off. And somewhat closer, the sound of someone calling her name.

She wondered vaguely why her shoulder hurt. Something was covering her face and she tried batting it away.

"Alex! Alex, can you hear me?" It was a familiar voice, tight with concern.

She moaned and blinked, her eyes focusing. Jake's dark curls were plastered to his head by the rain. His hands were pressed to the glass of the passenger-side car window.

"Thank God." The relief in his voice was palpable. "Unlock the doors, Alex."

Confused, she lifted her head and looked around blankly for a moment.

"Right here!" Jake pointed to the controls on the door.

Alex pressed the button, releasing the car's locks.

The distant wailing grew louder. She realized now that it was sirens.

The car was tipped at a sharp angle and Jake forced the door open, shoving the deflated airbag out of the way. He climbed inside, scanning her quickly, running a light hand over her shoulders and arms, checking for broken bones. "Are you okay?" he asked. "Does it hurt anywhere?"

"No." Her voice sounded more like a croak to her ears. She started to move and winced. "Well, maybe my shoulder..."

Jake unbuckled the seatbelt, gently releasing her. And Alex rubbed the spot on her shoulder where the seatbelt had been pulled taut against it.

The sirens stopped, and she heard car doors slamming.

Red lights pulsed over them from the road above. And suddenly everything came back to her in a rush. She looked around. "Where's the Expedition?"

"What Expedition?"

Two emergency workers were making their way into the ravine with a gurney and medical bag. A police officer trailed behind them. "Sir, I need you to—oh, hey, Jake," said one of the emergency workers. Jake stepped back from the car door to make room for the men. "Russ," he acknowledged the dark-haired young man. He pointed his chin toward Alex. "This is Alex Fontaine."

The man Jake called Russ stuck his head into the car. "Hello, Alex. Can you tell me if you're hurt anywhere?"

"My shoulder hurts a little, but I don't feel pain anywhere else. I think I passed out, though."

Russ pulled out a tiny light and had Alex stare at his index finger while he flicked the light back and forth between her eyes. She could hear the police officer questioning Jake.

After Russ performed a swift exam, he said, "You don't appear to have suffered any serious injuries, but you'll probably have a nice bruise across your shoulder and upper chest from the seat belt locking. Because you blacked out though, we'll need to transport you to the hospital."

Alex started to protest, but Jake overrode her, and before she knew it, she was strapped onto the gurney and being carried up the slope of the ravine. Jake climbed alongside, his hand gripping hers.

When the gurney reached the road, she blinked through the rain, looking down at the little sports car. Although the windshield was still intact, the front of the vehicle was a crushed mass of metal. She shuddered to think what could have happened to her if the impact had been any harder.

Jake followed her gaze, then looked down at her, his dark eyes serious. "This is the second time in two days you've scared me nearly to death."

"Yeah, well…" Alex sighed. "We can only hope the third time will be the charm."

Jake didn't smile at the joke, and the paramedics slid the gurney into the back of the ambulance. Inside, Alex struggled to sit up. "Hey," she called to Jake through the open door. "How did you find me?"

Jake winked. "It's that magnetic personality of yours. You're irresistible." Before Alex could respond to this enigmatic statement, Russ clambered inside and shut the ambulance doors.

Peering through one of the tiny windows, Alex admired the retreating view of Jake as he jogged away. She sighed and leaned back against the gurney pillow. She'd just been in a major car accident. Somebody clearly had tried to kill her, and here she was checking out a cute guy's butt. Yeah, she needed her head examined all right.

Jake dropped Alex's things from the car into his truck and drove straight to the hospital. He entered the emergency room and headed for the reception desk.

"May I help you?" A matronly receptionist looked up at his approach.

"A young woman was just admitted, Alex Fontaine?"

"Are you family?"

"No, I'm a—friend," he stumbled over the last word. He wasn't so sure Alex would consider him a friend.

She smiled and indicated the waiting room filled with chairs and low tables. "Have a seat right over there and someone will update you."

Jake moved to the indicated area but didn't sit down. He was too tense. He paced back and forth, running his hands through his damp hair and making the curls flip wildly in all directions.

He replayed Alex's phone call in his mind. Had he misunderstood her? It sounded like she'd said someone was trying to kill her. But that made absolutely no sense. He hadn't shared that part of the conversation with the police officer because it sounded so nuts. Why would anybody want to kill Alex? A disgruntled art lover ticked off by a mural she'd painted? He smirked at the ridiculous thought.

There were no other vehicles around when he'd found her, but clearly, something had caused the accident. Was it the rainy conditions combined with her unfamiliarity with the car? And what about the Expedition she'd mentioned?

Thank heavens for the car's security tracking system, he thought. It had taken only a few clicks on his cell phone app to find her.

A chill ran up his spine as he recalled the raw, tearing echo of her scream and the cold fear that had curdled in his gut when the connection went dead.

Jake paused in his pacing and closed his eyes, remembering how his thudding heart had nearly stopped when he'd spotted the tail end of the car skewed at a forty-five-degree angle off the side of Lincoln Road. When he'd reached the car and saw her head lolled to the side, eyes sightless, staring straight ahead, he'd thought for an instant she was dead. He'd been about to shatter the car window when her lashes had fluttered and he realized she could see him.

Jake opened his own eyes now and ran a hand over his face. He was surprised at the ferocity of his feelings concerning Alex. He knew the trauma of witnessing anybody in such a situation would evoke strong emotions. But it was more than that. Even though Jake had known her only a couple of days, there was something about her. His joking claim concerning Alex's irresistibility had not been far from the truth. Despite her apparent aversion to him, Alexandra Fontaine intrigued him more than any woman he'd ever known—and he'd known quite a few. She also frustrated him more.

He didn't want to admit it to himself, but when he wasn't with her, he was thinking about her. And much to his chagrin, dreaming about her as well. He wanted to know what made her tick. And what was it about her former relationship that made her so reticent with men? Or was it just him?

He shook his head. He knew, despite her protests, that she felt the growing attraction between them, just as he had. He'd read it in her eyes.

The hospital's automatic entrance doors slid open, and Tilly rushed in with J.P. close behind. The soft lines of Tilly's face were etched in worry. She spotted Jake and hurried over to him. "Where is she?"

He took her outstretched hands and squeezed them reassuringly. "She seems all right. They're examining her now." He tilted his head toward the receptionist. "You'll probably get more information from her than I did because you're family."

Tilly walked straight over to the reception desk.

J.P. rested his hand on Jake's shoulder in an unusually gentle gesture. "You okay, son?"

Jake nodded. "It was pretty scary, Pops."

"Your phone call was a bit jumbled, Jakey-boy. You only said Alex was in an accident and that I should bring Tilly to the hospital right away. But you didn't give any details about what happened."

Jake started pacing again. "That's because I'm not sure what happened!"

J.P. frowned. "What do you mean?"

Tilly walked back to them. "We'll be able to go in and see her in a few minutes," she said. Her gaze flickered between the two men. "Is anything else wrong?"

Jake stopped pacing and looked down at her. "Yes, I'm just not sure what it is."

Tilly looked confused.

J.P. said, "Was there another car involved? Was anybody else hurt?"

"That's the thing," Jake said slowly. "I didn't see another car, but Alex said something that made no sense just before the phone went dead." He hesitated, looking at Tilly again. "I think we'll just have to wait until we can ask her ourselves."

Not satisfied with this, Tilly forced him to sit in one of the molded plastic chairs, then plied him with questions. He answered to the best of his ability until a dark-haired woman wearing navy blue scrubs approached them. "You're here for Alex Fontaine?"

"Yes," Tilly and Jake responded simultaneously.

The woman smiled. "Hello, I'm Megan. The doctor has finished his exam, and you can all come back to see her now."

Megan swiped a card through a reader, and double doors swung wide to admit them. They followed her down a main aisle lined with examination rooms; the sharp tang of disinfectant hung in the air. Muffled hums and beeps from monitoring equipment issued from occupied rooms they passed.

Midway down the hall, Megan stepped to the side of one doorway. "Here she is."

Jake and J.P. followed Tilly inside. Alex sat on one of the examination tables, her long legs bouncing lightly against the base of it. She looked up, then hopped down as they entered.

"Alex!" Tilly rushed forward and gathered her granddaughter into her arms. "Are you all right?"

"I'm fine," Alex responded, hugging her back.

"Aside from a bruise caused by the seat belt, and some muscle soreness, Alex will be fine," Megan explained. "We're preparing her release papers now."

Tilly cupped Alex's face. "What happened, darling?"

"That GPS unit is super bossy, Grandma. She kept nagging me to make a U-turn, so I did," Alex quipped.

Tilly released Alex's face and dropped into the room's only chair. "I was terrified you were seriously hurt," she said, not smiling at the joke. "What really happened, Alex? What caused you to go off the road?"

Alex wrapped her arms around her slender form and hesitated. She scanned all their faces. "I'm not positive," she said slowly, "but I think this accident may have been intentional."

Jake heard Tilly's sharp intake of breath and saw J.P. frown.

"What makes you think so?" J.P. asked.

Alex relayed everything that had happened from the moment she'd turned off the main road until she'd awakened to Jake looking at her through the car's window.

"So, that's why you were asking me about the Expedition," Jake said.

Tilly looked stunned. "But, why would anybody do such a thing?"

Jake started pacing again. "Do you think this black Expedition followed you all the way from town?"

Alex nodded. "I'm almost sure of it."

"Did you get a look at the driver?" Jake asked.

She shook her head. "The windows were tinted just like your car's, plus it was raining, remember? I could see a little through my rearview mirror, but whoever the driver was wore a hat pulled low and dark sunglasses, which was odd with the rain, now that I think about it. But I never got a good look at the face. She rubbed her hands against her thighs and glanced at Tilly's pale face. "Look, the more I think about it, the more ridiculous this whole thing seems. It was probably just a really bad case of road rage. Maybe I accidentally cut the driver off earlier or something."

"Road rage?" Tilly's voice was faint.

Alex stood straighter, ready to change the subject. "I'm sorry about your car, Jake."

"Don't be ridiculous, Alex!" he responded sharply. When she looked taken aback, he softened his tone. "I'm just grateful you're all right."

She looked directly at him then and his gut tightened. Right now, her black-lashed eyes appeared more gray than blue. He clenched his jaw and shoved his hands into his pockets to stop himself from grabbing her and crushing her in an embrace.

"Whispering Pines is such a nice, safe town. But this makes twice in one week you've barely escaped being seriously injured," Tilly said. There was a concerned light in her own blue-gray eyes. "I'm starting to wish I'd never asked you for help this summer."

"Twice?" Alex frowned, confused.

"First, there was that construction site accident and now this. You could have...could have been—" She choked on the words, and her eyes filled with tears.

"Oh, Grandma!" Alex squatted down in front of Tilly's chair and put her hands on her grandmother's shoulders. "Please don't worry. These were just freak accidents."

"It does seem a strange coincidence to have two life-threatening things happen so close together," J.P. interjected.

Alex shook her head. "You guys, we're blowing this out of proportion. The construction site situation was definitely an accident. And this, well, the driver of that Expedition was a psycho! But I really believe it was road rage."

"Still, you should let the police know," Tilly said firmly. "You need to file a report."

"I'll take her," Jake said quickly. "I know the officer who was at the scene."

"Jake, I don't need you to take me," Alex said, rising. "I'll take myself, and then I still plan to run my errands."

"And what are you going to run your errands in?" Jake asked, arching a brow.

"I—" Alex's face fell.

"That's two cars in one week. I'm out of wheels for you to use. You'll have to let me drive you wherever you need to go," Jake said, folding his arms in triumph.

"Alex, you should come home and rest," Tilly protested.

"The doctor says I'm fine, Grandma," Alex said gently.

As if on cue, Megan entered with Alex's release papers and instructions on what to do if the muscle soreness bothered her. Then the little party trouped out.

At the hospital exit, Tilly hugged and kissed Alex once more before they parted. "Take good care of my girl," she said to Jake.

"I will," he assured her. Then, he turned to Alex with an evil grin. "You're in my hands now."

CHAPTER 14

The rain had stopped and the dark clouds were dissipating, allowing dazzling bursts of sunlight to peek through. Alex followed Jake to his truck. When he opened the passenger door for her, she saw her lists and notebooks all neatly stacked on the seat. Suppressing a smile, she scooped them up and climbed in.

After a stop at the police station to file her report, Jake started the engine. "Where to now, m'lady?"

She gave him the art supply shop address, which was thirty miles away, then leaned back and closed her eyes. She hadn't realized she'd fallen asleep until she heard Jake say, "We're here."

She sat up, feeling fuzzy. "I can't believe I fell asleep!"

"You had a pretty eventful morning," Jake replied.

She yawned and stretched, then rifled through the papers in her lap for her shopping list. "You can wait here if you want."

"Ooooh, no. Tilly said I'm responsible for you."

Alex sighed. "Fine. Just don't get in my way."

"Your gratitude for my protection is overwhelming."

They entered the store and Alex paused to orient herself in the close little shop. She breathed in the familiar blend of charcoal pencils, canvas, and paints. The aisles were narrow but neat. Colorful tubes, bottles, and brushes lined the shelves in orderly rows.

Grabbing a cart, she walked up the first aisle with Jake following close behind. She paused to consult her list.

"How about this?" Jake asked, holding up a tube of blue oil paint. "I like this color. It reminds me of the lake."

Alex took the tube from his hand and put it back on the shelf. "No, dear, that's not the right blue. Besides, I need acrylics." She moved up the aisle.

"Why not?" Jake asked, still trailing close.

"Why not what?"

"Why wasn't that the right blue?"

Alex took a deep breath and turned to face him. "Certain colors are more lightfast, which makes them better than others for outdoor murals. I also have to consider the building's proximity to the lake, as well as the weather conditions when I'm choosing my materials." She tilted her head. "Make sense?"

"I suppose," he acquiesced. "But I still liked that blue."

She returned to the papers in her hand and flipped through marked-up sketches. Then she moved forward to put cans of primer and topcoat into the cart. These were followed by an array of different sized brushes. Within minutes, she was completely absorbed, muttering to herself as they stood in front of the acrylic paint section. Her sketches were strewn across the aisle floor, tubes of color scattered over the pages. She moved the paints around. Arranging, rearranging, removing, and replacing until, satisfied, she dropped her final selections into the cart.

Despite her apprehension about being able to complete this mural, Alex couldn't deny a growing feeling of exhilaration. It was something she always experienced at the start of a new project. That heady feeling of possibility.

She turned up the next aisle with Jake shadowing so tightly, he stepped on her heel.

"Oops, sorry."

She knew he was sticking close because he was still concerned about what had happened to her earlier. She found his attention sweet and a little annoying. Once she'd calmed down and thought about everything objectively, she realized it was ridiculous to be concerned. The two events were unrelated freak accidents, nothing more.

She placed two large containers into the cart.

"Um...those aren't paint."

She glanced up at him, her eyes unfocused. "What?"

He pointed at the tubs. "Those aren't paint."

She followed the direction of his finger, then smiled and spoke in the tone one uses when explaining something to a small child. "That's gel extender. It extends the volume of the paints I'm using."

"Oh."

They moved into the next aisle.

"What do you need this for?" Jake picked up the packet of sandpaper she'd just tossed into the cart.

"I use a sander to prep the aluminum panels before I paint them."

"Ah." He paused a beat, then frowned. "But I thought you were painting the wall of my building."

She made an exasperated sound. "I'll explain later, all right? I need to focus."

He mimed zipping his mouth and tossing out the key, and with great effort, she hid a smile.

He stayed quiet as they moved up and down the remaining aisles. It was only after she'd stood in one place for several long minutes, mulling over panel materials, that she heard him yawn loudly. She turned to see his long body draped over the cart, fingers drumming against his broad cheekbones.

"Hey, you're the one who wanted to come with me," she said.

"Actually, I said I would take you," he corrected.

"Same thing."

"Not exactly."

"You could have just loaned me your truck." She smiled sweetly.

"Uh...not with your track record, angel. Two cars destroyed in less than a week."

"It's not my fault! I've been a victim of circumstance."

"Call it whatever you want, but after yesterday and today, I'm not letting you drive or out of my sight. Besides," he added, disentangling himself from the cart. "My truck is too much machine for you."

"Oh yeah?" she taunted, putting a hand on her hip.

"Yeah." He leaned toward her, matching her playful attitude.

Their eyes held, and his mischievous smirk slipped a little. They were standing close together. The heat of his body radiated through his shirt, and like a homing pigeon, she drew in even closer.

Suddenly, a husky voice made them both jump. "Can I help you find something?"

They turned in tandem to face the wispy figure before them. The speaker was dressed completely in black. Spiky jet hair with a streak of electric blue in the center topped the head of the young store clerk who'd asked the question. Thick kohl lined the teenager's eyes and black rimmed tunnels filled gauged earlobes. The husky voice made it difficult to tell if it was a boy or a girl talking. Upon closer examination, Alex noted the pale, fine-boned hands and delicate planes of the face and concluded she must be a female.

The girl sighed and raised a pierced brow. "I said, do you need anything?" She looked utterly bored.

"We're fine," Alex said. The girl turned away and she added, "On second thought, I was wondering about the different aluminum composites you have here. Do you have any info sheets on them?"

"Sure." She moved up the aisle, tossing over her shoulder, "Follow me."

"I'm scared," Jake hissed in Alex's ear. She elbowed him hard in the ribs, making him double over and stifle a laugh.

The girl led them to the front of the store and started digging beneath the counter under the register. "What are you working on?" the girl asked.

"An outdoor mural," Alex replied.

"Really?" The girl paused in her rummaging, her expression showing signs of life. "I paint murals."

Alex studied the girl more closely. Although covered in harsh makeup, Alex could see the marked interest shining in her bright blue eyes. Alex extended her hand. "I'm Alex Fontaine. What sort of murals have you done?"

The girl extended her own ring-filled fingers to shake Alex's hand. "I'm Zoe Forester. And, well..." She flicked a tiny wrist decorated with twined yarn and black leather. She looked suddenly shy. "I haven't painted anything major yet. I did one mural for my friend's family's rec room." She resumed digging behind the counter. "And a lady I babysit for wants me to paint a mural on the wall of her kid's bedroom." She looked down with a frown. "The folder you need isn't here. Just a sec."

She moved to some low shelves further away and Jake muttered, "Somebody lets *her* babysit?"

Alex cut him a stern look just as Zoe returned with a thick black binder.

"That's exactly how I started," Alex said as Zoe placed it on the counter in front of her.

"Really?"

Jake was draped over the cart again, looking bored.

"Sure. I did a few murals for friends when I was still in high school. That's when I knew it's what I wanted to do with my life. After high school, I went to the Detroit College of Creative Studies and got formal training."

"I applied there! Got accepted too," Zoe's features darkened, "but I can't attend."

"Why not?"

She sighed. "My parents are making me enroll in community college first. They don't want me wasting money on an art degree. They want me to choose something more practical." She made air quotations on the last word.

"Ahhh." Alex nodded sympathetically. "Been there, done that."

Zoe gaped. "Seriously?"

"Seriously."

"How did you end up getting to go to CCS then?"

"I'm really, er—stubborn, I guess."

Jake snorted, then winced as Alex pressed her foot down hard on his own. He yanked it from beneath hers and started piling items into the cart as Zoe rang them up. "I'm stubborn, too," she sighed. "But my parents seem to be more stubborn than I am."

Alex flipped through the binder and found what she was looking for. She read Zoe the appropriate codes and the girl punched them in.

"They're just worried about your future," Alex said, closing the book.

"Yeah, they say I won't be able to support myself. There's no future in it. Blah, blah, blah," Zoe said in a nasal singsong tone, an obvious impression of her parents' voices. "It doesn't help that both my parents are C.P.A.s, my older brother is a C.P.A., and my annoying little brother is a member of some future American business executives club at school."

Alex laughed.

"Besides, if I go against them, they'll refuse to pay for my college." Zoe sighed again.

"Have you thought about scholarships, or work-study programs, or even loans?" Alex asked as she handed Zoe her credit card.

"Not really."

"Well, that's how I managed it, at least, at first. I got a small local scholarship, plus, I marketed myself all over the place and got a few decent paying mural jobs the summer before my first year. Then I got a job on campus. By the following summer, I had more gigs lined up, and my parents started to see that maybe art could be a real career. You don't *have* to be a stereotypical starving artist."

Zoe was listening to Alex with rapt attention. "I wish I could have *you* to talk with my parents."

Alex laughed again.

They made arrangements to have the aluminum panels delivered while Jake gathered up the purchases and rolled the cart to the door.

Alex trailed behind, feeling true empathy for the girl. At the door, she suddenly stopped and turned. "Listen, Zoe, I'm starting this project pretty soon. Why don't you give me your name and number? Once I'm set up, you can come over and take a look at what I'm doing. Ask me more questions if you'd like."

"That would totally rock!" Zoe replied, her black-rimmed eyes dancing. She scribbled her information onto a scrap of paper and took it to Alex, who was holding the door open for Jake. "Thanks so much, Alex. It was great meeting you!" she gushed.

"We'll talk soon," Alex replied with a wave.

Jake and Alex worked together to load the items into his truck. "She's still watching us," Jake murmured without moving his lips.

"She's just excited," Alex said.

"She's freakin' me out." Jake cast a sidelong look at the shop window while he opened her door, and Alex grinned.

"Where to now?" he asked, slamming his own door shut.

She was about to answer him when the rumble of her stomach filled the truck's cabin.

"I thought you'd never ask," he said, starting the engine. "I'm starving, too."

Alex laughed. It was late afternoon and she'd eaten nothing since before the accident.

Jake drove a short distance before turning onto a side street to park.

"What are you doing?" Alex asked.

"This is it," he replied, pointing across the street. "Best burgers in town!"

Gull Landing was a single-story restaurant of rough-hewn timber. Fish netting hung between low wooden posts at the entrance, and a sign boasted an open-air deck and live jazz music in the evenings.

Since it was in between lunch and dinnertime, the restaurant was nearly empty, and a sign at the hostess stand indicated guests should seat themselves. Alex followed Jake out onto the deck, where he chose a table overlooking a river.

Resting her elbows on the table, she admired the sparkling view. Spiky dune grass and small ornamental trees surrounded the deck. Tubs of colorful impatiens, geraniums, and yellow daisies were spaced between the tables. Giant holes had been cut through the flooring to allow graceful white birch trees to grow unencumbered. Branches arched over the deck, their small, green leaves filtering the sunlight.

Alex closed her eyes and inhaled the pungent tang coming off the water, enjoying the light breeze that cooled her skin and caused tendrils of her hair to brush against her cheeks. She sighed with contentment and opened her eyes to find Jake studying her. She was grateful for the distraction of the waitress' arrival with menus and iced water. They placed their drink orders and Alex studied the menu selections, finally deciding upon a bacon and Swiss burger. She closed the menu to once again find Jake's disconcerting gaze on her. "What?" she said, exasperated.

"That was pretty cool what you did back there."

"What?" She frowned.

"Encouraging that kid to pursue her dream. Giving her practical advice like that." Jake was gazing at her with obvious admiration in his dark eyes, and Alex felt heat creep up her neck.

"It's no big deal," she mumbled. "I just remember how I felt. I wish somebody had been there to advise me when I was her age."

"So, your parents didn't want you to be an artist?" he said.

"Not one bit." Alex folded her arms on the table. "My situation was a lot like Zoe's. My mom's a bank V.P., and, as I mentioned, my dad's an automotive company executive. My interest in art was viewed as..." She gazed out over the water, searching for the right words. "A charming, little hobby, I suppose," she said.

"It sounds like they eventually understood," Jake said.

"I'm not so sure," Alex replied, grinning. "I think it's more that they just accepted it. The same way they've been forced to accept a lot of my decisions."

"Now there's an enigmatic statement." He leaned forward, dark eyes dancing.

Alex dropped her gaze. "I frustrated my parents a lot when I was in high school," she said.

Jake laughed. "Didn't we all?"

She smiled. "I don't think I mean it in the same way you do."

He motioned for her to go on.

She gazed back out over the water. "I wasn't into the usual high school stuff. I was extremely shy and didn't have many friends. I didn't go to parties, or football games, or dances. My parents were constantly nagging me to be more social, telling me I'd regret it later."

"Do you?"

She swung her eyes back to his. "I don't regret one second I've poured into my art."

"You must have been pretty determined to stand in the face of all that pressure from your parents." There was a note in his voice Alex didn't understand.

"I suppose I was," she said. "Of course, I always had Grandma in my corner."

"She seems a lady of strong convictions."

"She is that," Alex agreed.

The waitress returned with their drinks and took their lunch orders.

Jake downed half his glass of lemonade, smacking his lips in satisfaction. "Didn't your father understand your passion for art since his own mother is an artist?"

Alex sipped her Coke. "Grandma didn't start doing pottery until she and my Grandpa Joe moved to Whispering Pines."

Jake's eyebrows shot up.

"She regrets not having started sooner, and that's why she encourages me so much."

Jake nodded in understanding. "Sometimes the hardest part of pursuing a dream is taking those first steps."

That note was in his voice again. She studied him curiously. "What about you?"

He cocked his head. "What about me?"

She set her glass down and looked him square in the face. "It's obvious you have great passion for your work. And even though you say you and your father have, or had, a difficult relationship, at least he's encouraged your dreams and made you part of his company."

Jake tilted his head in acknowledgment, then leaned back in his chair, turning his attention to some nearby ducks who were dipping their heads underwater to nibble waterweed. "You know," he said after a moment, "it's kind of ironic I work for Riley Development at all, considering how much I used to hate the company."

"Hate?" Alex said in surprise.

Jake didn't respond for so long, the silence grew awkward, and Alex shifted uncomfortably in her seat.

"My mother died when I was five," he finally blurted.

Alex started at the sudden confession, uncertain how it connected to his previous comment. And although she'd already learned this fact from J.P., she kept quiet, letting him talk.

"I don't remember her much. Mostly fragments." His voice was husky and he cleared his throat. "And I can't remember what my relationship with my dad was like before she died. I only know that afterward, he withdrew from my brothers and me. He started working really long hours and we were left on our own a lot. We all grew up resenting the business." The muscle of his jaw tightened.

"Now that I'm working with him, though, I think I understand a little more about why he acted the way he did. We all handle grief differently. That doesn't mean I agree with what he did. But I get it. Our relationship isn't totally there yet, but we're trying."

Then Jake shook his dark head like a dog flinging off water and slapped both hands on the tabletop, his natural good humor restored. "Bah, what do I know? I'm no shrink. I only play one on lunch dates." He winked and the pain etched behind his eyes slipped away.

The waitress arrived with their food and they dug in.

Alex swallowed a large bite and closed her eyes. "Mmmm, you're right. This burger is awesome!"

Jake squirted a large blob of ketchup beside his fries, then doused his burger with it. "You know, it was Pops who talked me into taking the job in the first place."

Alex smiled as she took another bite. "I'm not surprised. Your grandfather can be most...um, persuasive when he wants to be."

Jake grinned. "Got that right."

"Where did you work before joining your dad?"

Jake swallowed a mouthful of ketchup-drenched fries. "I got hired by a remediation consulting firm straight out of college. It was a great job, but after a couple of years, I knew I wanted to do more. I wanted to use what I'd learned to flip brownfields. Pops knew the best way for me to get started on that route was through my dad's company. So, he encouraged me to bite the bullet and ask. I was surprised how happy my dad seemed about the idea. He took me on right away." Jake paused a beat. "I think he regretted it soon after, though."

"Why?"

Jake smirked. "I agreed to work for him, but not in the position he offered me."

"And that was because..."

Jake's smile curved wider. "He wanted me to be his second-in-command. But no way was I coming in as the privileged boss' son, set up in some cushy spot right off the bat. I wanted to learn the business from the ground up. I knew if I wanted the respect of the staff, I needed to get my hands dirty."

Alex felt a glimmer of respect for the man seated across from her. Perhaps there was more to Jake Riley than her initial first impression had indicated. Not that it mattered, she reminded herself sternly.

"I've legitimately worked my way up over the past few years. But honestly, this is the biggest project I've had since coming to Riley Development." He went on, "I admit, I'm a little nervous about it going well, especially considering my dad wanted nothing to do with renovating that place."

"But why? It's such a great idea in an ideal location."

"Oh, he thought the location was great," Jake agreed, taking a sip from his lemonade. "But he'd have torn the whole thing down and started from scratch.

"But the building is so magnificent!" Alex exclaimed. "Why tear it down?"

"The cost difference between renovating versus building is pretty big." Jake shook his head. "I argued with him for weeks. I love the historic beauty of that old place. I finally got him to agree to the renovation instead. But," he added, "he would only do it if I agreed to be the one solely responsible, so he drew up paperwork and created a subsidiary turning everything officially over to me."

Alex smiled. "So this condominium project really is *your* baby."

Jake nodded. "Whether it fails or succeeds, it's all on me." He swallowed another bite of hamburger. "Money was a big issue. I hunted down every source of funding I could find. I actually got pretty creative." He looked smug.

Alex waited curiously, but when he didn't continue, she said, "Okay fine, I'll bite. What was so creative?"

Jake grinned. "Well, there was all this residual gold and silver dust covering the factory interior. I had it collected and sold," he said. "That, plus some government grants, helped significantly offset the costs of the renovation. Pops joked to my dad that, 'Only Jakey-boy could've figured out a way to spin dust into gold.'"

Alex couldn't resist smiling back. "That was definitely creative."

He swirled a last handful of fries around in the ketchup and popped them into his mouth. At that moment, the waitress glided in with the check. Alex snatched it up before Jake could lift a finger.

"What are you doing?"

"Look," she pulled bills from her purse, "you're doing me a huge favor by driving me all over the place today. The least I can do is feed you."

Jake grumbled a bit and insisted on leaving the tip. "Promise me you won't tell J.P. I let you pay," he said as they made their way back through the restaurant interior.

Alex sighed dramatically. "I cannot believe how old-fashioned you are." Once they were on the sidewalk, she paused and clasped her hands under her chin, batting her eyes up at him. "Goodness!" she drawled. "Whatever you do, don't let the poor, defenseless woman fend for herself out here in the cold, cruel world." She dropped her pose and narrowed her eyes in mock suspicion. "You're not really a time traveler from the eighteenthcentury, are you?"

Jake grinned as they reached the truck, and leaning close, he whispered, "Uh, yeah. But could you keep it down? Nobody's supposed to know." He shut the door on her laughter.

As they drove to the town's only used car dealership, Alex flipped on the radio, surfing until a heavy metal tune blasted from the speakers.

Jake immediately reached over and switched it to the jazz station.

Alex flopped back in her seat with a groan.

"Sorry to disappoint you, but I don't do screamo. Maybe you could hang out with Zoe later and listen to some," he added in a polite voice. "I'm guessing she may have similar taste in music."

"Don't be a hater," Alex said, folding her arms. She gazed out the window as they drove, thinking about the young girl they'd met earlier. Although she had no idea if she and Zoe shared the same taste in music, Alex had recognized the raw hunger in the girl's eyes. The same hunger she'd had at the same age. The desire to take blank canvas and shape it into something tangible and fresh and unique. Would she ever experience those feelings again?"

Sultry saxophone music drifted from the speakers and she slid a sidelong glance at Jake as he negotiated a left turn. He was another enigma. The man was an obvious player, yet he had all these paradoxical qualities that didn't fit the mold.

Alex surmised the old-fashioned manners came from him spending so much time in the company of his grandparents, especially his grandfather. She wondered if the jazz music was a result of J.P.'s influence as well.

If she was being totally honest with herself, she had to admit she found the whole gallant gentleman thing sort of charming, if somewhat annoying. But when they arrived at the car dealership, the annoying part took a giant leap to the forefront.

"What do you mean let *you* do the talking?" She stood at the entrance of the dealership, hands on hips, glaring up at him.

"Look, angel, I'm only trying to help. This gu—"

Alex's brows crashed together. "Angel? Seriously, you did not just call me angel again," she stormed. "Look, I appreciate you driving me around. But this is my car. My situation. I'll handle it."

She flung open the door and marched inside, head high, dark hair swinging. "Oh, and please speak only when spoken to during my negotiations," she flung over her shoulder.

She approached the first desk in a row of three, where a young man sat. He had cropped red hair and a face spattered with freckles. He glanced up as she drew near and his expression morphed into one of such eager anticipation that he reminded her of a new puppy.

"Hello," she said as he rose from his chair to greet her. She shook his hand, then braced her fingertips on his desktop. "I'm looking to do a little car shopping today."

"Certainly, miss. Is there anything in particular—" His voice faded as his attention was diverted to something behind her. "Hey, Jake! How's it goin', buddy?" The young man stepped around her to grip Jake's hand and they were soon thumping each other's backs in traditional man-hug style.

Alex rolled her eyes.

"What've you been up to? How's Pops?"

Alex sighed and crossed her arms, foot tapping a rapid staccato on the tile floor.

"He's great, just great," Jake replied. They exchanged more pleasantries until Jake finally said, "Toby, I'd like to introduce you to my good friend, Alex." He threw an arm around her shoulder, pulling her up close against his side. "She's in the market for a car, and I said to her, Toby is the man to see. Didn't I, angel?" He beamed down at her.

The young man's face flushed nearly the color of his hair in response to Jake's praise.

"Yes, that's what he said all right." Alex smiled beatifically, slipping her own arm around Jake's waist and pinching his side. She was gratified to feel him wince.

"Gee, thanks, Jake. I sure appreciate that." Toby turned back to Alex. "Did you have something specific in mind?"

A little over an hour later, they climbed back into Jake's truck. Alex tossed the paperwork for her new car onto the floor, still annoyed. "Is there anybody around here you *don't* know?"

Jake grinned and pretended to look thoughtful. "Well, there's...hmmm. Now that you mention it, no, I don't think there is anybody I don't know. Well, except for you, that is. You, my girl, remain a compelling mystery."

She lifted a brow.

"I'm serious," he replied, slipping his key into the ignition. "Somehow, you managed to get me to spill my guts during lunch today, but I still know next to nothing about you."

"That's not true," she said, dropping the attitude. She ticked items on her fingers. "You know about my parents. You've met my grandmother. You know what I do for a living. You know I'm an only child."

Jake clasped her gesturing hands to still them. "That's not the stuff I want to know," he said softly.

His eyes held hers.

"I want to know what makes Alex tick. What excites her. I want to know why it's like pulling teeth to get her to spend time alone with me." He paused, then added with a faint smile, "I haven't had this much trouble getting to know a girl since I was in the fifth grade and Amanda Thompson clobbered me on the head with her backpack, then threatened to sic her big brother on me. And she didn't even have a big brother."

Alex laughed, then said drily, "Smart girl." Her voice was calm, but she couldn't quite suppress the happy dance the butterflies were doing inside her belly at the touch of his hands on hers.

He leaned in closer. "You do realize this is our seventh date."

"You're crazy," her voice wavered.

"Am I?" He dropped his head and whispered close to her ear. "We've had a beach walk and breakfast..." His lips were nearly touching the sensitive skin of her neck beneath her jaw and she shivered. "...a hike in the woods, a trip to the library together..." Now white-hot sparks were shooting through her. "A second beach walk, a construction site tour, and now an entire day together, plus lunch." He paused a beat, then said softly, "Has anyone ever told you that you smell like—"

"A paint store?" she finished for him. Her voice sounded breathless to her ears. And she closed her eyes, swaying toward him.

She felt him pull back a few inches and her eyes flew open. He was gazing down at her, and her hands were still captured in his, but she made no move to pull them away.

"Ketchup," he said without smiling. His hematite eyes glittered.

She licked her lips nervously and his gaze dropped to her mouth.

"You know what I think?" he said.

"What?"

"I think you should let me kiss you now," he said.

He bent his head slowly toward her. She didn't move, and he gently touched his lips to hers, soft and sweet. She felt her own lips yield beneath the gentle caress.

One kiss. Then he released her mouth, his lips hovering a breath away in an unspoken question.

Alex let out a small sigh and, slipping her hands from his, she tangled them in his dark curls as his head dipped to hers once more. His mouth moved deliciously against her own, his own hands coming up to cradle her face.

Her earlier admonitions against getting involved with Jake Riley were chased away by her racing heart. And she kissed him back with abandon, pressing against him as much as the awkward angle of the seats allowed.

On some level, "Sensible Alex," the one who still had a functioning brain, was screaming at her to stop. But Sensible Alex was completely ignored by Wanton Alex, the one who was at this moment reveling in the feel, the smell, and the taste of beautiful Jake Riley.

When they finally drew apart, they were both breathing hard. "You have no idea how much I've wanted to do that," he murmured.

Through a reeling haze of sensation, Alex heard a low humming vibration and Jake groaned.

He eased himself from her embrace and pulled out his cell phone, studying it. Then he frowned, tapping the screen and putting it to his ear.

Alex straightened, trying to pull herself together. What was wrong with her? Did she have some sort of self-destructive desire where men were concerned? She'd be a fool to put herself in the exact same position she'd been in with Derek.

"When?" Jake's tone was suddenly terse. He ran a hand through his hair in the agitated manner to which Alex was growing accustomed.

She couldn't hear the speaker on the other end but saw Jake's body tense. "How is he?"

Somebody was hurt. His grandfather?

"I'll be right there," he snapped, looking straight at her. Although, Alex had the distinct impression he wasn't seeing her.

He put down the phone.

"What is it?"

His dark eyes sparked dangerously. "Another accident at the site. And this time someone was hurt."

He started the engine.

"Who?"

"Keith Markham."

CHAPTER 15

Jake peeled out of the parking lot. Neither of them spoke as he sped back toward Whispering Pines. He softly cursed a moment later when he found himself trapped behind a line of slow-moving cars. He gripped the wheel more tightly and swerved into the opposing lane, gunning it past a row of four cars before tucking back into the right lane in one neat move.

Accelerating again, he spared a sideways glance at Alex, but her expression remained calm as she gazed straight ahead. He wondered what she was thinking. Did she regret the kiss? Judging from the depth of her response to him in that too-brief moment, he didn't think so. But she confused him. She'd been adamant about not getting involved with him, yet she'd kissed him back with a passion that matched his own.

Now she appeared totally composed. Long legs crossed and dark hair swept over one shoulder, leaving the side of her neck exposed. Heat surged through him as he recalled the scent of her skin and the soft feel of her lips beneath his. He gnawed at his lower lip, forcing his thoughts away from Alex and back to the pressing issue of Cesar's call.

Jake couldn't believe there'd been another accident. If he didn't know better, he'd swear the site was cursed. The first issues had been minor, but now, things seemed to have escalated. Nobody had ever been injured. Until now. Although he had yet to find the culprit behind the falling bricks incident with Alex, he'd increased safety precautions even further. But apparently, they still weren't enough. And Cesar told him Keith was stubbornly refusing to be taken to the hospital.

A short time later, dust and gravel spewed from the back tires as Jake cut a sharp left into the site entrance. He parked, leaped out, and was running to the office trailer before Alex had unbuckled her seat belt.

Yanking open the trailer door, he bounded inside, surveying the scene before him. Keith sat on the loveseat. His face was pale, head resting against the wall behind him. His suit jacket, shirt, and tie hung over the armrest beside him. Jake noticed red stains on one sleeve of his crumpled white dress shirt.

Rita was seated beside Keith. The bright frames of her reading glasses were perched on the end of her nose as she snapped her gum and worked on Keith's arm.

Cesar had rolled Rita's desk chair over beside them both and was leaning in to look. He jumped to his feet when Jake entered. "Bro, you got here quick!"

Keith looked up in surprise. "What are you doing here?"

"I called him," Cesar said.

Keith groaned. "You didn't need to do that!"

"Yes, he did," Jake responded, moving to Keith's side. "How bad is it?"

"I think he might need stitches," Rita said.

"I'm fine," Keith said at the same time, trying unsuccessfully to withdraw his arm from Rita's ministrations.

She wore rubber gloves and was pressing fresh gauze to the gash on Keith's forearm. The first aid kit contents were scattered across her desk and several blood-soaked wads of gauze lay in a small dish.

"You should at least have it looked at by a doctor." Four heads swiveled toward the doorway in surprise as Alex stepped into the crowded room.

"It's just a scratch," Keith said. "If I go to the hospital, I'll end up having to claim worker's comp and we'll have to file a bunch of paperwork. It will be a huge pain, and trust me, you don't need that right now." He shook his head. "Especially on top of whatever Farley is cooking up."

"What's Farley got to do with this?" Jake asked.

Rita, Cesar, and Keith all exchanged looks. Jake folded his arms. "Talk."

Cesar cleared his throat. "Farley showed up at the site this afternoon."

"He *what?*" Jake bellowed.

Rita sighed as she secured fresh gauze onto Keith's arm with medical tape. Cesar held up a hand to forestall any further eruption from Jake. "He was passing out flyers in neighborhoods again and—"

"Wanted to be thoughtful and let us know what he was doing," Rita finished drily, dumping all the soiled gauze into a plastic bag that she sealed and tossed into the trashcan.

Cesar took a fluorescent piece of paper from Rita's desk and handed it to Jake, who scanned it, then crumpled it into a ball. "Now he's claiming we used improper procedures during the asbestos removal," he growled. "I've had it!" He slammed his fist on top of the desk, making Alex jump. "I'm suing that guy for libel this time."

"You might want to re-think that," Keith said. His features were pale and drawn. "I wasn't the only one hurt today."

Jake looked at him in surprise.

"I went out to tell him to leave when I saw he was on the site, and he handed me that." He pointed his chin toward the crumpled page. "While we were discussing his semi-illegal marketing tactics, I..." Keith cleared his throat, looking sheepish, "sort of lost my temper. I started shouting at him. It was completely unprofessional of me, and I apologize."

Jake put a hand on Keith's shoulder. "You've done a better job than I have at maintaining your cool with that guy."

Cesar picked up the story. "I was inside the building working when I heard Keith shouting. I looked out and saw the two of them up in each other's grills. Then I saw Keith throw up his hands and turn away. But the old man grabbed Keith's arm and jerked him back around.

"Doug was working the Bobcat, moving a truss not far from where they were standing. All of a sudden, it started slipping, like the clasp holding it wasn't locked or something. I shouted, but it was too late." Cesar looked grim.

"I don't know if I heard Cesar's shout or caught it out of the corner of my eye," Keith said. "But I moved forward and it hit the ground first before tipping into me. The next thing I knew, I was on the ground and Farley was, too. He was holding his foot and howling."

"Where is Farley now?" Alex asked.

"He took off right after it happened," Rita said grimly, repacking the first aid kit.

Keith started to rise, but Rita put a manicured hand on each shoulder and pressed him back onto the couch. She peered sternly over the top of her glasses. "You're staying put till I tell you to get up, mister."

Keith's brows shot up, and Alex made a choked sound. Jake glanced over his shoulder to see her struggling to keep a straight face.

"Look, Keith," Jake said, turning back. "Rita and Alex are right. You need to have those cuts looked at by a doctor."

"But—"

Jake held up a hand to silence him. "I don't know how this happened, considering all the precautions we've taken. But I will not risk your health, or compromise ethics, just to avoid potential legal repercussions." He turned to Cesar. "Can you write up an accident report?"

"Sure thing, Jake."

"Technically, wasn't Farley on the site without permission?" Alex asked. "I mean, you've got no trespassing signs posted all over the fence."

Jake smiled at her. "Good point." He sighed. "Do you think Farley was hurt badly?"

Cesar shook his head. "I don't think so. He didn't get hit straight on because Keith's arm deflected it some. And he was able to hobble back to his car." Cesar grinned. "Sure didn't hurt his vocal cords any."

"Rita, can you file a trespassing report with the police? I'll take Keith to the hospital, then follow up on Farley."

"All right, sugar," Rita said, moving to the phone.

Just then, Jake looked at Alex. She must have read his face because she waved a hand dismissively. "Don't sweat it. I'll have one of my grandmother's friends come get me. You can swing by with my supplies whenever you're finished.

Jake's face cleared. "Thanks, Alex. You're a—"

"Yeah, yeah, I know. I'm an angel."

Jake grinned and leaned to brush his lips against the soft curve of her cheek, enjoying the rosy blush that stained them in response. "I'm looking forward to continuing our earlier discussion," he said. And her color deepened.

She pointed an imperious finger at the door. "Go! Keith could die at the rate you're moving." Keith grunted in annoyance at her words but preceded Jake out of the trailer.

Alex placed a quick call to Tilly while Cesar pulled paperwork from the filing cabinet. "I'll fill this out and bring it back. I want to check on my guys first, though," Cesar said, moving toward the door himself. "Good seeing you, Alex." The trailer door banged shut behind him.

"I guess that leaves you and me, Alex," Rita said, pulling off the rubber gloves and tossing them into the garbage. "I'm Rita McKay, Jake's office manager." She extended her hand in greeting.

"Nice to meet you, Rita. I won't be in your hair too long. My ride should be here shortly," Alex said.

"May as well make yourself comfy while you wait then." Rita indicated the loveseat with a wave of her hand.

Alex sank onto the soft, lumpy cushions, studying the older woman with interest. Rita had bright red hair teased into a high pile on top of her head. Alex surmised the electric blue spandex dress she wore wasn't typical construction site attire. A chunky white bead necklace hung around her throat, with matching earrings bobbing at her earlobes. Rita sat down and swiveled in her chair to face Alex, her blue gaze appraising but not offensive.

"It seems you and I have had more than our share of excitement today, haven't we?" Her eyes widened with concern. "Especially you, sugar. I was here when Jake got your phone call this morning."

Alex nodded. "I've definitely filled my quota today." She folded her legs beneath her, "Please don't feel you need to entertain me, Rita. I don't want to interrupt your work."

Rita waved an airy hand. "I'm nearly done anyway."

"How long have you worked for Riley Development?" Alex asked.

Rita leaned back, snapping her gum, frowning in thought. "Let's see now, I started with Jake's daddy when my own kids were..." She counted on her fingers. "It's been over twenty years now," she said. "I can't believe it's been that long already." She shook her head, earrings thumping against her cheeks.

"You must have been with the company since it started."

"Just about," Rita said. "Ben Riley hired me as his very first office assistant. He's a good man, and I've loved every minute working for him.

He and the company have stuck by me through good times and hard. Death of my parents…death of my marriage," she added with a vicious crack of her gum. "I count all the Rileys as family."

Alex found herself taking an instant liking to the woman. She could tell a warm and sincere heart beat beneath that flashy exterior.

Rita leaned toward her and lowered her voice. "I love all my Riley boys, but Jake's my favorite." Her blue gaze was steady. "I'm happy he's started seeing you."

Alex laughed nervously. "We're not *seeing* each other."

Rita smirked.

"I'm serious!" Alex protested. "We're not dating, if that's what you mean. We've just been sort of, er, forced into each other's company for the past few days."

"Forced?" Rita lifted artfully sculpted brows. "Hmmm…"

"What?"

"Nothing."

"Rita!"

"It's just," she paused, considering. "It's clear Jake seems real sweet on you."

"Sweet on me!" Alex was shocked. "He hardly knows me."

Rita let out a hoot of laughter, swiveling to and fro in her chair. "Honey, I've known Jakey since he was a skinny little tyke of about six years old." She jabbed a lacquered nail in Alex's direction. "I know what I'm seein'."

Alex squirmed uncomfortably.

The tiny air conditioner suddenly hummed to life and cool air began filling the small space. "Dang, I meant to turn that thing off." Rita hopped up from her chair, punching buttons on the unit before sitting back down again.

Alex used the time to compose herself. She sat forward now, feet on the floor, hands folded primly in her lap. "I think you've misunderstood my relationship with Jake, Rita. He's hired me to do a mural for the condominium project."

"If you say so, sugar."

Alex was disconcerted but couldn't resist asking, "What gave you the impression Jake was interested in me…*that* way?"

"Well," she paused, staring into space. "It's only, he gets this sort of look in his eyes when he talks about you. It's hard to explain." Then she looked directly at Alex. "But it's a look I've never seen before."

"No offense," Alex scoffed. "But that doesn't sound like a very accurate way to measure. Besides, in the three days I've known him, we've run into at least a half dozen of his, er, lady friends."

Rita smiled. "I'm not talking about random casual dating. What I'm seeing here seems to be the start of a real relationship." She emphasized the last word.

Alex stiffened. "Listen, Jake seems like a great guy, but I have no interest in a relationship with anybody at this point. Especially not with a…" She hesitated, not wanting to offend Rita, but decided to finish her thought. "…a player like Jake."

Rita gave her a knowing look. "Been burned in that area, have you, sugar?"

"To a crisp," Alex said. And unable to remain seated any longer, she rose to pace around the tiny space.

Rita turned back to her computer screen and began to type. A few moments passed before she spoke again. "You know," she said, her expression turning rueful. "Now, I'm not referring to Jakey, mind you, but there are certain fine-lookin' men out there that are about as good for you as a screen door on a submarine."

Alex smiled. "Sounds like you're thinking of someone in particular."

"Got that right," Rita said, heat edging her voice. "I went out with this guy over the weekend. Promised he'd call. But didn't. I just hate that! Why do they say they're gonna call and then they don't?"

Alex lifted her shoulders helplessly.

The two women were deep in conversation when Gretchen poked her head inside the trailer door fifteen minutes later."

"Ready, kiddo?"

"Yes!" Alex jumped to her feet and bade farewell to Rita.

"Nice meetin' you, Alex. I'm sure I'll see you around again."

Gretchen dropped Alex off at the end of Tilly's winding drive. She started walking and was surprised to glimpse J.P.'s car through the trees.

As she drew near, his car suddenly leaped forward, then stopped abruptly and stalled. Alex halted in astonishment. She heard the grind of the key turning in the ignition for far too long. Then the car sprang to life again, moving forward in stutterous bursts. Sunlight filtered through the pines, dappling the windshield in light and shadow. Alex couldn't get a clear view of the car's interior. Confused, she veered off the driveway and made a wide arc around the vehicle through a small grove of trees. She came up along the passenger side of the now inert but idling vehicle and peered cautiously through the window. Tilly sat behind the wheel, J.P. beside her.

Tilly's eyes were wide and intent on the dashboard where J.P. was now pointing to explain something. Neither of them noticed her, so they both jumped when Alex tapped lightly on the window.

J.P. lowered it. "Hey there, Miss Artist!" he boomed.

"Hello, dear. How did your shopping trip go?" Tilly asked.

"Never mind that! What are you doing?"

"J.P.'s teaching me how to drive!" Tilly said. Her cheeks were flushed, and her blue-gray eyes shone with excitement, making her seem more like a young girl than her grandmother.

Alex blinked. She opened her mouth to speak but was forestalled by Tilly's raised hand.

"I don't want to hear any negativity right now, Alex. J.P. has kindly offered to teach me to drive, and I'm taking him up on it. Besides," she slid a sideways glance at J.P., who had remained uncharacteristically silent during the exchange, "he's doing a marvelous job with lesson number one so far."

J.P.'s normally ruddy complexion turned even rosier in response to the praise.

Tilly continued. "Ever since the situation with your car, I've been frustrated about not knowing how to drive. And then today, well, it's just awful to feel so helpless, Alex."

Alex folded her arms, her gaze moving back and forth between them. "So that's it? You think learning to drive will make you feel less helpless the next time I'm in an accident?"

"Maybe."

"Grandma, I don't—"

"Why don't you go inside and have some dinner," Tilly cut in quickly. "J.P. brought over a bucket of fried chicken and coleslaw for us."

Alex started to say something more, but J.P. was already rolling the window back up. Tilly gave Alex a little wave, then gnawed her lower lip in concentration as she shifted the gear back into drive.

Alex shook her head and watched the car jerk its way slowly up the driveway.

"I hope they both make it back alive," she mumbled, turning to stalk into the house. She saw the remains of Tilly and J.P.'s meal on the dining room table. Grabbing a plate and napkin, she sat down and served herself.

Chewing slowly, she thought about Tilly and J.P. Ever since the Mural Society meeting, they seemed to be spending a lot of time together. Alex recalled Tilly mentioning J.P. planned to try Tai Chi with her one morning next week. And now J.P. was teaching her to drive. Wasn't sixty-nine too old to be learning something like that?

Tilly's talk of regrets replayed in her mind. Maybe learning to drive was like her sculpting, and this was just another case of her finally coming into her own. Alex couldn't help but smile. Tilly's seemingly gentle and compliant nature sheathed an iron will, which was not to be reckoned with. Her thoughts were interrupted when her cell phone rang. She snatched it up. "Hi Jake, how's Keith?"

"He ended up getting stitches, but the doc said it should heal fine."

"That's good," Alex replied. "What about Farley?"

"He won't answer my call, but I checked and he never came to the hospital after it happened, so I'm hoping he didn't suffer any serious injury."

Alex agreed.

"I can bring your stuff out to the cabin now if you'd like."

"That'd be great. And thanks again for—"

"Knock it off, will ya'. I told you it was no trouble. Besides," Alex could hear the laughter in his voice, "you're dangerous on your own. I'll be there in ten."

She was just scooping the last bite of coleslaw from her plate when there was a tap at the door.

"Come in," she called.

Jake's broad frame filled the entrance. He jerked a thumb toward the driveway. "What's going on out there?"

Alex grinned. "Apparently, your grandfather is teaching my grandmother how to drive."

Jake arched his brows. "Really? Well, ah, that's not what it *looked* like they were doing."

"What do you—" Alex's smile slipped. "No. Way."

Jake's dimples deepened at her reaction.

She leaped from the table and hurried to peek through the window overlooking the driveway. Blast it, they were too far from the house! She could barely make out the shadowy forms of two heads inside the car.

"I can show you what it looked like they were doing," Jake said, coming up behind her and standing far too close. Alex closed her eyes and focused on breathing evenly. The effect this man had on her pulse was not healthy.

She opened her eyes again and spun around. "Never mind. I don't want to know." She stepped around him and marched back to the table. "Would you like some fried chicken?" she asked politely.

The corner of Jake's mouth twitched, but he only said, "Sure," and followed her back to the table, angling his lean form into a chair opposite from where she'd been sitting.

She went into the kitchen and returned with a full plate and a glass of lemonade.

"Thanks." He dug in while Alex returned to her seat.

"So, Keith's all right?"

"He'll be fine. It was only a couple of stitches." Jake swallowed and frowned. "The whole thing doesn't make any sense, though."

"What whole thing?"

"How the beam ever broke free to begin with. Because of our earlier issues, my entire team has been overly diligent with every safety precaution. There's no logical way..." His voice trailed off and Alex watched his dark eyes widen. "Of course! I can't believe I never considered it before."

"Considered what?"

He refocused on her. "Can I borrow your camera?"

"Wh–What for?" Alex was taken aback by the sudden change of topic.

"I noticed you had some good night photography shots."

"Yes," Alex said slowly, not following where he was going with this.

"Then I'd like to borrow it."

"Why?"

"Um," he hedged. "I'd just like to take a few pictures at night."

Alex narrowed her eyes. "C'mon, Jake, what's going on?"

"Nothing, I—just really liked some of those shots you took and figured I'd try some."

"Uh-huh." She crossed her arms and leaned back in her chair, studying him. "Suddenly, you're interested in taking night shots? I don't think so. Besides, it's not something you can just go out and do, Jake. You'd need to consider different factors, like the ambient light and time of night. You'd need to understand how to use the manual focus, too. You'll probably want to set it up on the tripod and use the shutter remote, you'll also—"

"Can't you just show me?"

Alex frowned. "How about you show me what you want a picture of and I'll—"

"I promise to be careful with it."

She shook her head stubbornly. "It's not that simple, Jake."

"Don't you trust me with it?" He was beginning to sound angry. "May I remind you, I trusted you with a *car*, and look what happened?"

Alex's mouth fell open. She felt as if she'd been punched.

His tone was immediately contrite. "I'm sorry. That was cruel." He reached across the table to grip her fingers.

She didn't pull them away but kept her eyes on the tabletop. "It's not that I don't trust you with it, Jake," she said. "It's just that there's—"

The cabin door suddenly swung wide, startling them both. Tilly entered with J.P. close behind. Their faces were flushed, and Alex noticed a few silver wisps had escaped the pearl clip holding back Tilly's hair.

Distracted from their discussion, she and Jake exchanged quick, meaningful looks. Alex pressed her lips together hard to keep from giggling.

"And what are you two up to?" Tilly said. Her voice sounded unnaturally high and breathless, as if she'd been running.

"Just talking," Jake said.

Alex realized her hands were still beneath his and withdrew them quickly. "How did the driving lesson go?" she asked.

"Your grandmother is a natural," J.P. enthused. "She's got accelerating and braking down pat now. Our next lesson will be turning corners."

Alex watched Tilly's face as she beamed up at J.P. It had been a long time since she'd seen her grandmother so joyful.

Tilly and J.P. joined them at the table, and in between mouthfuls of food, Jake brought them both up to speed on what had transpired at the site that afternoon.

"I don't understand," J.P. said, shaking his head. "You've been so safety conscious, Jakey-boy."

"Even worse, why did it have to be in front of Farley!" Tilly massaged her now uncast arm, flexing and unflexing her fingers. "As if that angry little man needed more fuel added to his fire."

Jake pushed his empty plate away and leaned back, stretching his long legs out in front of him. "I'm stuffed," he said, patting his washboard stomach. "Thanks, Alex."

"Thank your grandfather, he's the one who brought it," Alex said.

"Oh. Well, thanks, Pops!"

J.P. grunted, but his attention had moved back to Tilly. He'd taken over massaging her forearm and they were looking at each other in a way that made Alex feel like an intruder.

Jake rose to his feet, stretching his arms over his head, apparently unperturbed by the romantic scene playing out in front of them. "Well, Alex, I guess I'll unload your supplies from the back of my truck."

Alex jumped up, grateful for an excuse to escape. "I'll help," she mumbled, tailgating him out the front door.

"The studio's open," Tilly's voice floated after them.

The minute she and Jake were out of earshot of the house, Alex hissed, "What the heck is going on with them?"

Jake opened the back of the truck and waggled his brows. "I'm not certain, Dr. Watson, but something is definitely afoot."

Despite herself, Alex grinned.

They each grabbed bags and carried them around to the back of the house, setting everything just inside the studio's sliding glass door. Alex frowned in thought and Jake whistled while they trudged back for another load.

After the final load, Alex started pulling things from bags and arranging her supplies. Jake stood gazing through the window wall, hands in his pockets, admiring the sky's glow above the scrubby pine silhouettes.

Alex finally broke the serenity. "I don't like it."

Jake continued looking out the window. "Why not, it's an amazing view."

Alex looked over at him. The entire room was swathed in the setting sun's radiance, and the lines of his body and dark curls were limned in warm golden light. Alex swallowed. Oh yeah. An amazing view, all right. As if he didn't already look like enough of a Greek god without nature adding her special effects.

Unaware of her thoughts, he turned and twinkled mischievously at her. "Just kidding, angel. What don't you like?"

Alex forced her gaze away and resumed unwrapping her brushes. With a sniff, she said, "I'm just wondering what your grandfather's intentions are toward my grandmother. How do I know they're honorable?"

Jake laughed out loud. Crossing the room in three long strides, he caught Alex by the shoulders and spun her to face him. "If they're anything like mine, they're not."

"That's what I'm afraid of," she grumbled, refusing to meet his eyes. She knew if she gave him the slightest encouragement, he'd kiss her again, and she wasn't prepared for that. "She's sixty-nine and hasn't dated anyone besides my Grandpa Joe. And she met him when she was sixteen!"

"Sixty-nine?" Jake snorted, releasing her shoulders. "I should be the one worried then. Pops is only sixty-eight. Doesn't that make Tilly a cougar?"

Alex took a swing at him, but he ducked, laughing.

"Careful, angel." He rubbed a hand along the angle of his jaw, then patted his cheek. "Not the face."

Alex tried to maintain her stern look but failed miserably and began laughing along with him.

Jake sat down on a stool beside her and she turned away to continue unpacking. "Are you going to tell me what you need *me* to take a picture of tonight?" she asked, changing the subject.

Jake's smile faded and he rubbed both palms against the knees of his jeans, clearly struggling with some internal debate. Finally, with a heavy sigh, he said, "I want to stakeout the site tonight."

Alex's eyes widened. "Stakeout? As in cops-and-robber type stuff?"

He nodded.

She tilted her head. "Why? What do you think is going on?"

Jake got up from the stool and moved restlessly around the room. He ran both his hands through his hair, messing up his curls as usual. To distract herself from the urge to smooth them, she busied her hands rearranging the paints she'd already organized.

"It was already driving me nuts that such weird things were happening at the site. But then the incident with you and what happened today have really topped it. Like Pops said, if anything, I've been overly safety conscious, and my team is excellent. They know what this project means to the company and for their own jobs." He paused in his pacing, eyes glittering. "Doug couldn't—wouldn't—have made such a basic mistake as not securing that load. I'm wondering now if somebody may have tampered with it. Maybe even been behind some of our other issues. And if that's the case, it may be a person from the outside. Somebody like—"

"Farley," Alex breathed, sitting down hard on the stool Jake had vacated.

He nodded with a humorless smile.

Alex pondered this for a moment. "Why not just call the police?"

Jake threw up his hands. "And tell them what? I think a little old man has been sneaking onto my property during the dark of night and sabotaging my project? Plus, knowing all the animosity that exists between Farley and me, even I wouldn't believe me. They'll chalk it up to sour grapes. And what if I'm wrong?" He shook his head. "No, I need proof."

"Just tell the cops you suspect *someone;* you don't have to say who. Then maybe they'll patrol the area more often."

"Yeah, in their nice, big, black-and-white police car. I may as well put a billboard in front telling the vandals to lay low for a little while. Besides, this project is my baby and I want to find out for myself who's behind it."

Alex was silent for a moment, thinking. Then she said with decision, "I'm coming with you."

"Oh no, you're not."

"Oh yes, I am."

"Look, Alex—"

"Look yourself, Jake. Do you want to use my camera or not!"

"Well, yes, but—"

"No buts. You have no idea how to take pictures in low light. You'd be wasting your time," she said, flipping her hair back. "We'll need to get there before it's completely dark so I can figure out the optimal focal length. I'll take some test shots to determine the best aperture and shutter speed, and try to minimize any optical aberrations—"

Jake stepped close and pressed a finger to her lips.

She stopped talking, blinking up at him.

"Okay, you win. I don't even know what language you were just speaking."

Alex's lips formed a smile beneath his finger.

"You can come, but I have some conditions." He removed his finger.

"Such as?"

"Such as, I'm in charge, okay? This is my operation, no questions asked."

Alex opened her mouth to say something, but Jake cut in. "I mean it, Alex. You've given me enough heart trouble for one day."

"Heart trouble?"

Alex was surprised to see the skin beneath Jake's tan redden, and the tips of his ears turned pink. He cleared his throat. "I was just...concerned," he said, looking uncomfortable. She studied him, fascinated by this unusual show of emotion. He stepped backward, tripping over a box which still lay on the floor. He caught himself before he fell. "I've got to go," he said abruptly and headed for the door.

"Wait! What time will we be doing this stakeout?" Alex asked.

He paused at the slider, took a breath, and turned. "I'll be back to pick you up at around nine," he said, voice steady. And then he was gone.

Alex smiled to herself. Had the mighty flirt been embarrassed to let it show he actually cared? Her smile widened and she hummed the tune he'd been whistling earlier as she finished organizing her supplies.

CHAPTER 16

Jake shifted uncomfortably on the seat of his grandfather's old Buick. He pulled out his cell phone and checked the time. Ten-forty. He glanced over at Alex, who was messing around with the camera again, making adjustments and muttering to herself. She'd brought along the full-size tripod, but once they arrived, she decided against setting it up outside the car. The location was too exposed. He'd parked the car a short way up the street with the passenger side facing the site. Alex had collapsed the legs of the tripod to create a miniature version, which was now set up on the seat beside her, the camera pointed out the open window. This forced them to sit unusually close on the wide bench seat and was the cause behind Jake's discomfort.

Due to the fading light, Alex was continually readjusting the camera's settings and taking test shots. Her long, glossy hair was pulled back into a high ponytail, which brushed his arm as she moved. Jake gritted his teeth. He wanted to yank out the rubber band and bury his fingers in those silky strands. Maybe this hadn't been such a good idea. How was he supposed to concentrate on the job at hand with this distracting creature next to him?

The streetlight's soft luminescence lit the side of her face as she turned to him now, and he sucked in a breath. Every time she turned the power of those eyes directly at him, he felt like he'd been blasted with a laser beam.

"I think we're set," she said with a satisfied smile. She rubbed her bare arms vigorously. "It's colder than I thought it would be." She'd changed into jeans but wore a black sleeveless tank top. Ever since the rain, the air had cooled down considerably.

"Here." He reached into the back seat and handed her a worn gray hoodie. "I put this in the car before I left."

Rex took Jake's hand in the back seat as invitation and stuck his huge head over the front seat, panting softly.

"It's okay, boy." Jake scratched the red-gold head. Rex gave his hand a lick and settled back down onto the seat.

"Are you sure it was a good idea to bring the dog?" Alex asked, eyeing Rex with concern. "Aren't you worried he'll bark or something and scare off any would-be trespassers?"

"Nah." Jake waved away her concern. "I told you, he's a trained professional. You can take the dog out of the cops, but you can't take the cop out of the dog." He smiled back at Rex, whose gentle brown gaze moved between them. "We may need his assistance."

"If you say so." Alex shrugged, slipping the sweatshirt over her head. It was big on her. The sleeves covered her hands and the neck opening left her delicate collarbones exposed. She looked small and vulnerable in it. Jake gripped the steering wheel, fighting the urge to pull her protectively against him.

"When do you think something will happen?" Alex asked, peering out the window. He released the wheel and ducked his head beside hers to view the street. "An excellent question. When do criminals normally carry out their dastardly deeds?"

She giggled and replied in a very poor Vincent Price impression, "I believe it's during the witching hour, when the clock strikes midnight. Bwahaha!"

"If that's the case, we'll be sitting here a while." He grinned down at her. She was so close, gazing up at him again, her lips curved in a faint smile. Electricity jolted through him, and before his brain could form a coherent thought, his mouth was on hers.

Caught off guard, her lips were stiff, but she didn't resist.

His own lips moved gently, coaxing, compelling, and he felt her tremble. An answering shiver rippled up from his core, and her mouth became warm and pliant, molding to his.

Their kiss deepened and his passion grew. Her intensity matched his own. Tiny sounds of contentment escaped her as he pulled her close and began to trail soft, nibbling kisses down the side of her neck. He nuzzled the soft curve between shoulder and throat and she sighed softly.

Suddenly, Rex shoved his wet nose between them, whining softly and forcing them apart. "I—I think he needs to go out," he said.

Alex's eyes were unfocused. "I think we need to reevaluate this whole sitting in parked cars together thing," she whispered. "It's getting dangerous." She struggled upright, snatching Rex's leash and a poop bag from the floor. "I'll take him," she said and stumbled quickly out of the car before Jake could respond.

"C'mon, boy." She flung open the back door, attached Rex's leash, and was gone.

Jake ran a hand through his hair, trying to compose himself. He watched the two of them as Rex pulled her in the direction of the lake.

What was he thinking? Alex had been perfectly clear she wasn't interested in a romantic relationship with him. But then, why had she let him kiss her like that? And why had her answering kiss held a heat equal to his own? He knew he should just drop it, but he couldn't.

What had changed?

Alex was asking herself the same question. A pool of light from the streetlamp overhead illuminated Rex as he sniffed a grassy patch around the empty intersection.

Why had she caved in and let him kiss her? Twice! She snuck a sidelong glance back at Jake through the rear car window. He was still the same over-the-top flirt he'd been at their initial meeting. An incredibly good-looking one. But so what? She'd been down this road before. What was the matter with her?

She felt a tug on the leash as Rex sought new territory, and she let him lead her further from the car. She was certain from Jake's expression that he'd been as shocked by her response as she'd been. But in the moment...Oh, mama. In that moment, it had felt so natural. So...right. As if she'd been starved her entire life and was now being offered a gourmet banquet to feast on.

She straightened her shoulders and took several deep, cleansing breaths. *This will not happen again. It will not. You are not screwing up again,*

Alexandra Fontaine. No boys, no boys, no boys. She repeated the mantra over and over as she walked Rex slowly back to the car.

When they were still a few feet away, the dog abruptly stopped, ears cocked. A rumble rose from deep inside his throat. His gaze was intent on the site across the street. Alex looked but didn't see anything. "What is it, Rexy?" She squatted beside him, trying to determine his exact angle of vision in the darkness. "Something there, boy?"

Suddenly, Rex bolted, taking off at a run, his leash slipped free from Alex's slack grasp. "Rex!" She jumped up.

Jake was out of the car in an instant, racing after the dog. Alex stood helplessly watching, then suddenly caught movement in the shadows at the edge of the site. A figure appeared near the far corner of the brick structure, carrying a large bundle.

She ran around to the driver's side and hopped inside. She slid across the seat to line up the camera's viewfinder and started firing off shots. Rex was barking now, and the figure hesitated, apparently spotting the dog with Jake in pursuit. The figure dropped the bundle and cut across the front of the building, running awkwardly away from them.

Releasing the camera from the tripod, Alex leaped from the car and dashed across the street. Once she was close enough, she pulled up short and raised her camera, focusing.

"Gotcha!" she murmured, depressing the shutter button. A split second later, something hit her square in the back and sent her sprawling. The camera flew from her hands, tumbling across the grassy area that abutted the sidewalk. A large, black-clothed figure bolted past, cutting along the construction site's fence.

"Hey!" she shouted, springing back to her feet. Her palms and chin stung from scraping against the rough sidewalk, but she raced after the fleeing figure. She followed it through the yard of a home that backed up to the site, but the runner was too far ahead and quickly disappeared around the corner of the house.

Alex's heart was pumping, and her legs felt like rubber, but adrenalin pushed her on. She rounded the same corner and stopped short, searching. Old trees lined the street and mature bushes clustered around each home. Not a single leafy branch moved to indicate anybody had recently passed.

The street was silent, except for her own heavy breathing. She stood still, listening intently. The hairs on the back of her neck rose, and somehow, she knew someone was watching her. She whirled in a tight circle but spotted nothing. Moments later, she heard the jangle of Rex's chain and Jake's voice calling her name.

"Here," she called out, returning the way she'd come. She followed the fence and emerged back on the sidewalk to see Jake and Rex coming toward her from the street.

"Alex!" Jake jogged the last few feet to meet her, the relief in his voice apparent. "What happened? Where did you go?"

She relayed what had occurred and his dark brows crashed over eyes that flashed with anger. "What were you thinking going after him like that, Alex? Did you think you could take him down single handedly?"

"I guess, I didn't really think," she admitted.

"No, you didn't," he snapped. Then, sighing, he pulled her close. "I swear, you're going to be the death of me."

"Yeah, I really thought this third time would be the charm, yet you're still here." Her voice was muffled against his chest. "Oof!" She winced as he squeezed her tighter.

He finally released her, tipping her chin to examine the wound on her face in the lamplight. "Hmm…" He looked grim. "Nice soul patch."

"Gee, thanks," she said and held up her palms to show him as well.

He looked at them closely, then announced, "I think you'll live."

"Of course, I'll live," she said, snatching her hands back.

He dropped the bantering tone. "Next time I let you accompany me on a stakeout, please let me handle the chasing.

Rex snuffled his nose against Alex's leg.

Jake looked down. "Oh, and Rex, too."

His expression changed, growing thoughtful. "You know, this means there were two of them."

"Yeah." Alex looked surprised. "What happened to the other guy?"

Jake shook his head. "He had a car stashed in the neighborhood behind the site. By the time Rex and I caught up to him he was driving away."

Alex opened her mouth to ask something else when a metallic glint on the ground caught her eye. "My camera!" She rushed over to scoop it up.

"Is it broken?" Jake came up beside her.

She touched a button and the viewing screen lit up. "Doesn't appear to be."

"Did you get a picture?" he asked hopefully.

She scrolled quickly through the images. "Yes, but it's so dark, and I didn't use my tripod for the last few."

"Maybe some clues I uncovered will help," Jake said.

She looked up at him. "What clues?"

"Oh, just the make and model of the car the dude took off in." Jake looked smug.

"Make and model is good," Alex agreed.

"I also got a partial license plate number, and of course, we have that." Jake pointed at the large, dark bundle the person had dropped after he and Rex had given chase.

"What is it?"

"I'm not sure."

"Well, let's find out." Alex started toward it, but Jake gripped her upper arm, hauling her back. "Ah no, angel."

She frowned at him. "Why not?"

"Because we have no idea what's in that!" Jake's tone was exasperated. "I'm calling the cops."

A ripple of shock ran through her. "Do you think it's a bomb or something?"

"I don't know. But I'm letting the professionals handle this one," he said, pulling out his cell phone.

Alex was suddenly drained. She sank down onto the grass while he made the call. Rex came over and licked her face. "S'okay, boy," she whispered. She sat cross-legged, and Rex tried to squeeze his large body onto her lap while she scratched him behind his ears.

Jake ended the call and sat down beside her. "I can't believe I let you get hurt again," he grumbled.

"You didn't," Alex said. "The jerk who shoved me from behind did."

Rex, thrilled at now having two people at his level, moved his attention to Jake, who patted him absently.

Alex lifted the camera again, going more slowly through the images and magnifying each one on the tiny screen.

"Bummer." She sighed, turning it off.

"What?"

"I doubt any of them are clear enough." She frowned. "That last one I took would have been perfect if I hadn't moved, or been forced to move," she corrected.

"Well, the police are on their way. Hopefully, between the two of us, they'll have enough information to figure this out."

CHAPTER 17

Alex was roused from sleep by the sound of her favorite song playing. She opened one eye and realized it was coming from her nightstand. Her cell was ringing. She tapped the screen. "Hullo."

"Guess what it was?" Jake said without preamble.

Alex yawned and stretched, squinting in the bright morning sunshine that filtered through the bedroom's sheer curtains. "What time is it?"

"I dunno...uh, ten-thirty. C'mon, guess!"

She was shocked to have slept so late. But she and Jake had stayed and answered all the officers' questions the previous night before being ordered to leave the scene when the bomb squad showed up to investigate the mysterious package.

She yawned again, struggling up in bed. "Um...a bomb with only seconds left until detonation?"

"Close," Jake said.

"Seriously?" She shoved her hair out of her eyes.

"It wasn't about to detonate, but it *was* a homemade bomb. It seems we interrupted him before he could hook it up and activate it."

"Oh my gosh!" Alex was fully alert now. "Do they have any information about the car?"

"Not yet."

He hesitated, and Alex sensed there was more he wanted to say. "Anything else?"

"There is one other thing I want to talk with you about." He hesitated again.

"Yeah?" she prompted.

"Are you available for lunch today?"

Alex's stomach lurched. "Uh...sure."

"Great, we'll discuss it then. I'll pick you up at noon."

They disconnected and Alex flopped back onto the bed, covering her face with her pillow.

"I thought I heard you talking. Are you all right?" Tilly poked her head around the door. Alex lifted the pillow slightly, peeking out at her grandmother. Tilly's soft femininity was enhanced by the pale pink top she wore over her cream capris. Her silver hair was swept up in its customary twist.

"Fine, Grandma. I'm just an idiot."

Tilly chuckled and came to sit on the edge of the bed. "No granddaughter of mine is an idiot," she said, smoothing Alex's dark hair back from her face. Then she flexed her fingers experimentally, holding it up to compare with her left hand. "It feels so good to have that bothersome cast off. I can't wait until I've regained all my dexterity so I can work on my pottery again."

"You'll be good as new in no time." Alex reached out to clasp Tilly's hand in both of hers. She studied its still slightly shrunken shape and traced the pale blue veins on the back of it.

"Grandma, what do you think of Jake?"

Tilly looked thoughtful. "He seems like a nice young man. Good head on his shoulders. He clearly cares about the Whispering Pines community." She looked pointedly at Alex. "But I don't suppose it really matters what *I* think of him?"

Alex released Tilly's hand and sighed. She folded her own hands behind her head and stared up at the ceiling. "I think he's a player," she said firmly.

"And?" her grandmother said when Alex didn't continue.

Alex sighed again. "A kind-hearted, generous, strong, intelligent man."

Tilly smiled. "And..."

Alex gave her a sidelong glance. "And a total hottie, as Margot would say."

"Yes, he does seem to be all those things," Tilly agreed. "But why do you sound so depressed about it?"

"Because, Grandma," she scooted back into a sitting position, "I cannot—will not—get involved with another Derek!"

"Darling, what makes you think Jake is another Derek?"

Alex's eyes met Tilly's. "Because they're the same, Grandma. They're both charming flirts!" Alex spat out the last word. "They don't know the first thing about commitment or honesty. Men like that are out for a good time and that's all. I will never allow myself to be hurt the way Derek hurt me. Ever again," she added vehemently.

"I believe you!" Tilly raised both palms in mock terror.

Alex's intense expression eased, and she gave a short laugh. "Sorry. I guess I'm still dealing with my issues, huh?"

"It takes time, Alex. All healing takes time. It's not something you can rush your way through."

Alex eyed Tilly. "And what about you?"

"What about me?"

Alex arched a brow. "Don't play coy with me, Matilda Fontaine! I've noticed how much time you're spending with J.P."

Alex was amused to see her grandmother blush. "Well…" Her hands fluttered in her lap. "J.P. is a very nice man," she said primly. "And that's all I'm going to say about that right now."

"Mhm." Alex grinned.

Tilly rose from the bed, obviously ready for a change of subject. "Would you like me to get you some breakfast?"

"No, that's okay. I'll just have coffee. Jake is picking me up for lunch. He wants to talk about something. I suppose it's the perfect opportunity for me to clarify our relationship as just friends," she emphasized.

"Mhm." Tilly grinned back at her.

"I promise to take better care of her this time, Tilly," Jake said with a cheerful wink. His dimples flashed as he smiled and Alex could see her grandmother melting under the force of his obvious charm. *Yeesh, did the man's power have no generational boundaries?*

Inside the truck, Jake started the engine while Alex punched in her favorite station.

"Nuh-uh, angel," he said, switching from the loud, pulsing beat to his usual jazz.

Alex flopped back in her seat. "I don't get it! How can you stand listening to this stuff? It's sooo slow."

Jake just smirked at her, and one curl fell forward over his brow. Alex swallowed and looked out her window.

The sun shone bright and hot. Small clouds drifted lazily across the sky, their reflections rippling on the waves as they drove past the lake.

"Did you sleep all right after what happened last night?"

Her cheeks burned in memory of their kiss.

He caught her expression and his dimples flashed again. "I meant the *other* thing that happened."

"As a matter of fact, I did," she said, lifting her nose. "It was one of the best night's sleep I've had in a long while."

He carefully passed a car of slow-moving tourists who kept stopping their vehicle to look at the lake. Finally reaching Main Street, they folded into the stop-and-go traffic caused by all the pedestrians clogging the crosswalks.

It was the start of the Fourth of July week, and as happened every year, the population of Whispering Pines tripled. Clusters of teens loitered outside the Dairy House, eating ice cream cones and flirting. Bathing-suit-clad children bounced alongside parents who made their way toward the beach, toting umbrellas and bags stuffed with sand toys.

Jake swung into a newly vacated parking spot in front of the Lakeside Café.

"Hey, Jake!" Welcoming cries arose from several of the restaurant staff as they entered.

Alex shook her head. "Have you ever considered running for mayor?"

"I don't officially live here, remember?"

"You may as well."

He laughed. "It's really only because of Pops and having spent so many summers here."

A curvaceous waitress with glowing green eyes approached their table. "Where have you been, Jakey?" Her lilting voice held the hint of a Greek accent.

"I've been around. How's it going, Marina?" He gave her a warm smile.

"Good! We've missed you!"

"Of course you have," Alex muttered under her breath, hiding behind the menu she was handed as Marina and Jake continued chatting.

Once Marina left, Jake's index finger appeared at the top of her menu, pulling it down so he could see her. "This place has the best burgers in town."

"I thought Gull Landing had the best burgers in town."

"Different town," he grinned.

"You must come here often." She tipped her head in Marina's direction.

"It's one of Pop's favorites."

Alex set down her menu and gazed around the room. Colorful Tiffany lamps hung low over distressed wooden tables that were scattered across the gleaming floor. There were a couple of pool tables in use at the back of the restaurant, and the walls were filled with an eclectic mix of old photographs and memorabilia.

Marina returned with glasses of water and took their order. After she'd gone, Jake folded his hands in front of him and looked directly at Alex. "Sooo," his voice was low and soft, "I mentioned there was something I wanted to talk with you about."

Alex felt her insides quiver but managed to keep her expression neutral. Resting her chin on linked fingers, she said, "Okay, and when you're done, I have something I'd like to discuss with you."

He nodded and took a deep breath. "Look, about yesterday, I was out of line. I should never have kissed you like that."

Alex felt her cheeks flush again. She knew, and she knew Jake knew, his kisses were only half of the problem. It was her uninhibited response that was of greater concern.

"You made it clear from the first time we met that you weren't interested in that kind of relationship with me," he said. "I—well, I just wanted to apologize. It won't happen again." His dark eyes took on an almost pleading look. "Will you forgive me?"

Taken aback by this unexpected apology, she didn't speak for a moment. She hadn't anticipated him being so forthright about what had occurred between them. She knew she ought to feel grateful he'd brought it up. And relief that he was offering her such a graceful way out of the awkwardness. So why had a hard ball of disappointment just settled in the pit of her stomach?

She finally found her voice. "I...appreciate your apology, Jake. And, of course, I forgive you." He smiled wide and the shadowed look in his eyes was replaced with their usual sparkle. She swallowed. "You've really been nothing but kind to me since we met. Helping with my car situation and...well, I appreciate everything you've done."

He leaned back in his chair, running a hand over his face. "I'm so relieved you feel this way, Alex. Because I've come to value our growing friendship. I wouldn't want to do anything to jeopardize it."

"I value our growing friendship too, Jake." The moment the words were spoken, she realized with a shock they were true. For all his flirtatious behavior, Jake was genuinely a great guy. He was clearly well-liked in the community, and regardless of how he tried to pass it off as his grandfather's legacy, it said something about his character as well.

He looked pleased as Marina arrived with their food, setting before each of them a plate with a giant burger and a heaping pile of waffle fries. "I'm glad we cleared the air. Now, what did you want to talk with me about?" he said, taking a big bite of his burger.

"Uh...the exact same thing, actually," Alex said, and Jake grinned.

Throughout the rest of the meal, their conversation flowed companionably. They discussed the condominium project in light of the recent sabotage attempt, then somehow segued into humorous escapades from Jake's childhood summers in Whispering Pines. She, in turn, entertained him by relating some of her more unusual and occasionally disastrous mural projects. By the time they left the restaurant, Alex realized she was having a great time. She was surprised by how relaxed and lighthearted she felt with Jake now that he'd stopped his hardcore flirting and was just being real with her. By removing the threat of any romantic involvement, she felt free to be herself.

They were on the sidewalk heading toward Jake's truck when her phone buzzed. She excused herself and took the call.

Hands in his pockets, Jake leaned against the restaurant's red brick exterior, out of the way of the roaming crowds. With his deep tan, white polo shirt, and dark curls ruffling in the breeze, he painted a very GQ picture, which, Alex noted, did not go unappreciated by several of the women strolling by. He, on the other hand, was oblivious to the admiring stares. His own gaze remained on Alex while she spoke into the phone.

She ended the call and walked over to him, grinning broadly. "My new car is ready!"

He pushed himself off the wall. "Great!" He glanced at his watch. "If you want, I can take you by there right now before I head back to work."

"Awesome!"

A short time later, they sat idling in the dealership's lot while he gave her final instructions before going in. "I don't think he will, but don't let Toby pull any last-minute figure switching on you," he admonished. "He's my friend, but he's also a used car salesman, if you know what I mean."

Alex smiled. "Don't worry. I may be an artist, but I do know how to add and subtract. I can even read, too," she teased. She opened the truck door and he reached over to lightly touch her forearm. She turned back to him, ignoring the tingle that rippled through her at the contact. "One more thing—" Just then, Jake's cell rang. He looked at the screen and frowned, pressing the speaker button. "Jake Riley."

"Mr. Riley, this is Chief Roland with the Whispering Pines Police Department. We've made an arrest in the case you filed last night and we'd like you to come down to the station if you're available."

"Who've you arrested?"

"We'd rather discuss that in person," the officer replied.

"I'll be right there." Jake ended the call and looked excitedly at Alex, who was looking back at him with wide eyes.

"I wonder who it is?" she said.

"Guess I'll find out."

"I want a full report when you're done!" she said as she jumped out.

"Will do," he replied before racing off.

CHAPTER 18

Alex smiled in satisfaction as her silver Cavalier made the smooth turn off Lakeshore Drive. Although the car was five years old, it was in excellent condition. She'd opened the sunroof and a light breeze played over her skin as she bopped to the heavy base pulsing from her speakers. Pulling into the driveway, she spotted Gretchen's car.

She skipped up the front porch steps and swung the door wide. "I'm home!" she called gaily, letting the screen door bang shut behind her.

The three women sat at the dining room table with their customary teacups.

"And how are you lovely ladies this afternoon?" Alex said, gliding to the table and planting a kiss on Tilly's cheek.

Gretchen's helmet of hair shifted with her head as she turned to study Alex with suspicion. "What're you actin' all happy for?"

"Gretchen!" Margot admonished. "You said that like she's not normally a happy person."

"Well, she's not," Gretchen said flatly. "Leastways, she hasn't been. Ever since she got to Whispering Pines, she's been sulking around looking like she's sucking on a lemon." She pursed her lips and sucked in her leathery cheeks in demonstration.

Margot started in on another reprimand, so Alex cut in. "It's okay, Margot, she's right. I have been a crab."

"With good reason!" Tilly defended her, blue-green eyes flashing.

Alex reached over and patted Tilly's arm. "Thanks, Grandma, but Gretchen has a valid point. I've been busier feeling sorry for myself than I have been taking care of you."

"Pshaw!" Her grandmother dismissed her remark with an airy wave of her hand. "You've taken fine care of me, darling. And you have not been a crab."

"Yes, she has," Gretchen said.

Both Margot and Tilly glared at Gretchen.

"What?" Gretchen said.

"Never mind," Alex said. "All that's going to change. I've decided to be more positive from now on."

Gretchen grunted, taking a cookie from the dish at the center of the table.

"What brought this about, Alex?" Margot asked, taking a dainty sip of her tea.

Alex rested her elbows on the table and clasped her hands. "I've come to the realization I have a lot to be grateful for."

"Oh really." Tilly twinkled at her. "Like what?"

"For one thing, I've got a car again. For another, I've got a great new mural commission, thanks to you ladies." She nodded at them. "Grandma's arm is all healed. And...well, it's just a beautiful day!" She opened her arms wide, embracing the sunlight streaming in through the log cabin's large windows.

Margot tittered behind her napkin. "You sound like you're in love."

Gretchen narrowed her eyes, taking in Alex's flushed cheeks and irrepressible smile. She thumped her fist on the table. "You're right, Margot! That's exactly what it sounds like. What'd ya do?" She leaned forward, eyes glittering. "Hook up with Mr. Hot Body?"

"What? Who?"

"Jake!"

"No!" Alex was appalled.

"He really is quite good looking, isn't he?" Margot nodded, disregarding Alex's shocked expression. "He reminds me a lot of J.P. when he was younger."

"Only better," Gretchen said, rubbing her hands together. "Jake's got more of a long, lean look and those curls. Makes you want to run your hands through—"

"Gretchen!"

"Well, it does."

"I am *not* in love," Alex said emphatically. "Jake and I are just friends."

"You realize men and women can't be friends," Gretchen said.

"Would you *please* stop quoting *When Harry Met Sally*, Gretchen!" Tilly groaned while Gretchen guffawed over her own joke.

"It may be a line from a movie, but it's true," Gretchen said.

"Of course, it's not true," Margot said. "Men and women can be friends."

"Prove it," Gretchen said, stirring a heaping teaspoon of sugar into her teacup.

"What do you mean, prove it?" Margot asked.

"Name one."

"I—well, I don't happen to have any gentlemen friends right now. But I have had some in the past."

"Who?" Gretchen took a sip, beady eyes fastened on Margot.

"Dwight Willoughby."

"Dwight Willoughby!" Gretchen smacked the table and laughed. "That was grammar school, Margot! I'm surprised you can remember back that far."

Margot's face turned a deep shade of crimson. "Fine, then." She paused, thinking. "I know. Danny Hanover!" She smiled triumphantly.

"Doesn't count."

"Why not?"

"Danny Hanover now goes by the name of Daniella Hanover, if you know what I mean."

"He does?" Margot looked taken aback. "Well..." her voice wavered. "Jasper Oldham?" This one came out as more of a question.

Gretchen harrumphed. "He was in love with you."

"He was?" Margot breathed.

"For years."

Margot sat looking stunned while Gretchen turned her attention back to Alex. "You see, kiddo, men don't know how to just be friends with a woman. They always want more...or less.

"More or less?" Alex said.

"Sure." Gretchen leaned in, palms flat on the table. "If you're the kind of girl who smothers a guy, they want less. They want out. Men don't like feeling smothered. But," she took a breath, "if you act like you're not all that interested," she winked with a knowing nod. "Well, now, that makes you a challenge. And every man loves a challenge."

"But I'm not acting! I'm really not interested," Alex argued.

"Doesn't matter."

"But we've discussed it, and he knows I'm not interested in him that way."

"You've been spending a lot of time together?"

"Yes, but—"

"Talking on the phone?"

"Yes, but—"

"Has he kissed you?"

Alex blushed furiously.

Gretchen sat back, looking smug. "Like I said...more."

Suddenly, Alex didn't feel so good.

CHAPTER 19

Jake pulled into a visitor space in front of the police station. He bounded up the wide staircase of the tan brick building and entered the lobby and reception area.

The station hummed with activity, busier than he would have expected for a town the size of Whispering Pines. A quick look around, however, led him to conclude that the majority of people in the waiting area were a large group of tourists.

A stocky, middle-aged officer with cropped salt-and-pepper hair sat behind a small reception desk. He was bent over paperwork but looked up as Jake approached. "May I help you, sir?"

"I'm Jake Riley. Chief Roland requested I come in regarding a complaint I filed yesterday."

Frowning, the officer picked up the phone and punched in some numbers. "Hey, it's Hugo. Did you want to talk with a Jake Riley?" He was quiet a moment, then his expression cleared. "Yes, sir."

The officer had Jake accompany him past the stark row of desks that were equally spaced along the gray tile floor, lining each side of the broad room's walls. Some desks were vacant, while others held uniformed officers tapping away at keyboards. At the very back of the room was a glass-walled office; the interior blinds were closed, blocking any view of the interior. The officer rapped on the door.

"Come on in," a voice called out.

Officer Hugo opened the door wide and Jake's first thought was about how much the interior room contrasted with the somewhat sterile feel of the room beyond it. Instead of tile, plush blue carpeting covered the floor. Two windows at the back of the room let in plenty of golden sunshine. Centered between the windows was a filled walnut bookshelf with a matching desk in front of it. A bear of a man with black hair slicked back with gel rose from behind it to shake Jake's hand. A suit jacket was slung over the back of his chair, and he wore the knot of his necktie loose at his throat. The chief's expression was good natured, but his small, brown eyes were alert as he looked Jake over in a manner born from years of practice.

"Thanks, Hugo." He dismissed the officer and waved Jake to a seat opposite as he sat down again. "Thanks for coming in, Mr. Riley. I'm Dave Roland."

"Call me Jake," he said. "You mentioned on the phone you've made an arrest?"

"We have." He flipped through some papers on his desk. "Based on the information you provided at the scene last night, we've placed Frank Farley under arrest."

Jake slapped his thigh. "I knew it!"

The chief looked up sharply. "You knew it?"

Jake grinned sheepishly. "Well, I suspected," he corrected.

"I see." The man's jowls wobbled as he nodded his head. "In addition to the circumstantial evidence, he doesn't appear to have an alibi for the time of the occurrence."

Jake set his mouth in a grim line. "What happens now?"

The chief slipped on a pair of small, black-framed reading glasses and scanned one of the pages. "We've interviewed him, but he's not saying much. He refuses to exercise his right to an attorney either." He looked up at Jake. "We were hoping, given your history with him, that you might be willing to talk with him. Shake things up a bit."

"Isn't it enough I saw him at the site with the bomb?" Jake asked.

The chief laid down the papers and leaned back in his chair, hands folded over his ample belly. "The trouble is you didn't see him." He held up his hand at Jake's sound of protest. "You can't confirm it was Mr. Farley you saw at the site," he continued. "And although we've dusted the contents of the backpack for fingerprints, we've come up empty. Short of Mr. Farley confessing, we may not have enough evidence to keep him here."

"Aw, come on!" Jake slammed back against his chair in anger. "You know he did it!"

"What I suspect and what I can prove are two different things," the chief said. "And what about the other individual who attacked your friend, Ms. Fontaine? Was that person working with the bomber? Was it a separate issue entirely? There are just too many unanswered questions."

Jake ran his hands through his hair, then sighed heavily. He leaned forward, resting his elbows on his knees. "Well then, what's next?"

The chief took off his glasses, rubbing them with a cloth as he spoke. "I'd like to set you up in one of our interview rooms with Mr. Farley. Just talk with him. Don't straight out accuse him, but ask him about last night. We'll be observing in another room to see how he reacts."

"Okay," Jake said. "Let's do it."

Chief Roland rose from his chair and Jake followed suit. He put his hand on the knob, then paused, looking back at Jake. "One more thing."

Jake lifted his brows in question.

"This isn't television. It's just a conversation, not an interrogation, Jake. And it's important that no matter what Farley says or does, you keep your cool."

"I'll do my best."

Jake paced the floor of the windowless interview room. It was sparsely furnished. Only a small wooden table with two molded plastic chairs at either side of it. The walls were a bland beige and the same fluorescent lighting used in the hallway illuminated the eight-by-ten-foot space.

Jake glanced at the fake thermostat hiding the closed-circuit camera that the chief had pointed out when they'd entered. He'd explained the camera was angled for a view of the chair where Farley would sit so they could not only hear him but read his facial expressions and body language.

The room had only one door and it was closed, making Jake claustrophobic and making him wonder how it might affect a guilty party brought in for questioning. Jake had no idea yet what he would say to Farley, but he was curious to see the other man's reaction to his presence. Would he be surprised? Embarrassed? Angry? Why was he so intent on destroying the condominium project?

Until last night, Farley's involvement had been more of an annoyance than anything else. His letters to the editor, protests at village planning meetings, and lawsuits had been a hassle. But a bomb? Jake's rage rose to the surface again as he contemplated what might have happened if Farley had been successful with his plan.

The door opened and Farley was ushered in. The old man's brows lifted sharply at the sight of Jake. Remembering Chief Roland's words, Jake took deep, calming breaths as Farley shuffled to the chair the officer directed him to. He sat down, hunching forward. His thin white hair stuck out in unkempt tufts all over his head.

The officer retreated to a back corner while Farley kept his eyes focused on the tabletop. Jake took the chair opposite him. They sat in silence for several moments as Jake marshaled his thoughts, deciding how best to proceed.

Startling him, Farley broke the silence first. "You gonna waste all your time staring at my pretty face, Riley?" He raised bloodshot eyes to Jake's, and something flickered in their depths.

The corner of Jake's mouth quirked, but he didn't reply, just tilted his head, studying the man. He had to hand it to the old codger. Farley wasn't acting the least bit intimidated by the situation. Despite his outward bravado, though, he seemed older than usual. The lines of his face were sharply etched and paunchy bags sagged low beneath his eyes. It may have been the fluorescent lighting, but Farley's skin seemed to hold a grayish cast.

Jake folded his hands on top of the table and said without preamble, "Enjoy your midnight stroll last night, Farley?"

"What stroll?" the old man shot back.

Jake gave him a patronizing look. "Don't play stupid, Farley. I know it was you I chased last night."

Farley's lips tightened, but he said nothing.

"You won't get away with it," Jake continued, leaning back in his chair.

Farley gave a derisive snort.

"This wasn't just another one of your stupid flyers, Farley." He paused a beat. "You had a bomb."

The remaining color drained from the old man's face, but he still didn't speak.

Jake felt his calm demeanor slip. Smacking his hands hard on the tabletop, he made Farley jump. "Do you have any idea how many people you could have hurt? Or killed?"

Farley shifted uneasily.

Leaning forward, Jake said with emphasis. "I. Saw. You."

At this, the old man's back went ramrod straight. "You can't prove a thing!"

Jake sighed, exasperated. "I saw you drop the backpack. We know it had the bomb in it. I saw you run back to your car. And you have no alibi for last night."

"You can't prove a thing," he muttered again.

Jake tried a different tack. "Who are you working with?"

At this, Farley looked up sharply. "What're you talking about?"

Jake waved his hand impatiently. "Stop wasting time, Farley. I know you're working with someone. Maybe if you tell me who it is, I can get them to reduce the charges against you or something."

Farley's stony demeanor returned.

Jake tried cajoling, logic, and anger. But Farley refused to say another word.

Finally, the door opened and Chief Roland entered the room. The officer in the corner came over to help Farley to his feet. Jake watched as he moved slowly to the door. So full of fire and brimstone when dealing with Jake, he now walked with his head bent low, a defeated old man.

Farley paused at the door, turning back to Jake, his lips twisted sardonically. "You know what, I will tell you one thing, Riley."

"What's that?"

"It ain't over."

"What do you mean?"

"Just what I said. You can keep me locked up here as long as you want," he glanced at the chief, "but the fact is, I'm not the one who's a threat to you and your precious condominium project. I never really was."

CHAPTER 20

Alex stood before the blank panel, anxiety coursing through her as she willed herself to breathe.

She'd washed the aluminum panels thoroughly with soap and water. Abraded them with sandpaper. Carefully primed them in white, and measured out the light gridlines that would act as guides. Her paints were mixed to perfection and placed in orderly rows. She sighed. She'd stalled with every bit of prep work she could. It was time to paint.

From the roughs she'd created, everyone agreed to go with her idea of focusing on Whispering Pines' waterways. A montage spanning the area's former logging days to its present-day recreational uses. The focal point of the piece was a dramatic Coast Guard rescue scene she'd based on a story J.P. had shared during their afternoon together.

She knew the concept was unique and the finished piece would be magnificent. If she could pull it off. And at this moment, it was a huge "if."

Whenever she started a new project, she'd feel a nervous energy. She knew from experience this was normal. As soon as she would start a piece, however, those initial jitters would disappear. And eventually, she'd lose herself. Get to that place where the wellspring of creativity flowed through her, to the brush in her hand, and onto the blank white space before her.

She often felt like a fraud taking credit for her work. She'd once read an account of Mozart's music where he described it as having always existed. A part of the universe's inner beauty, simply waiting until he came along and revealed it. That perfectly captured how she felt about her own pieces. As if the scenes she painted had been there, waiting all along, and she was merely a conduit. Her job was simply to be present.

At least, that's how it used to be.

Now, she stood before the glaring whiteness, completely frozen. Overwhelmed to the point of trembling at the thought of touching brush to panel. With a frustrated sound, she sat down hard on the stool behind her, paintbrush clattering among the paint pots as she tossed it aside. She bent over and covered her face with her hands.

"Kind of tough to paint without looking, isn't it?" said a voice from the doorway.

Alex jerked around, then relaxed, spotting Zoe Forester lounging in the door frame. The girl had been visiting regularly for the past couple of weeks to lend a hand with the mural prep work, and a genuine friendship had begun to blossom.

Zoe sauntered into the room now, her spiky black hair sporting a new purple streak on one side. She pulled up a stool beside Alex and sat, her kohl-rimmed eyes filled with concern. "You still blocked?"

Alex nodded wordlessly.

"My high school art teacher was this super old dude, covered in wrinkles, you know?" Zoe said. "And he had this gravelly voice," she smirked, "like maybe he'd smoked cigarettes for the entire hundred years he'd been alive. I'd already been painting for years before I took his class. I'd developed my own style, sort of an abstract expressionist blend."

She sighed and gripped the stool, stretching her black jean-clad legs out in front of her. "We were doing a basic drawing unit where we had to do all this boring still life stuff, which I hated. Plus, I was ticked off the stupid class was a prereq for the painting class I really wanted. I thought the old guy was a lousy teacher with no imagination, and he was stifling my creativity. He kept telling me I needed to walk before I could run," she said, making air quotes with her fingers. "I totally rebelled against everything he tried to get me to do."

Zoe tipped her head toward the ceiling and closed her eyes. "I started skipping a lot, and by mid-semester, I was failing. I knew I couldn't take the painting class without passing, which just ticked me off even more. Eventually, I just gave up. One day, he caught me in the hall and told me to stop by after school. I thought about blowing him off, but for some reason I decided to go." She opened her eyes and sighed. "And you know what he did?"

Alex shook her head.

"He sat me down, handed me charcoal and a sketchpad, arranged his wrinkled self in a chair across from me, and said, 'Draw.' I just sat there, staring at the guy like he was nuts. Finally, he growls, 'What's the problem?' In that moment, I hated the guy even more."

"Why?"

The corner of Zoe's mouth lifted. "Because he forced me to face the real reason I wasn't doing the work." She glanced at Alex, then back at the blank panel. "It's not that I didn't want to, it's that I couldn't draw realistic stuff the way the other kids did. When I told him that, he threw up his hands and said, 'Of course you can't, Forester!' Then he got right in my face and said, 'You will never draw the way the other kids do. You will only draw the way you do.' Then he said, 'If you draw me, right here, right now, what's the worst that can happen?' I said, 'It'll look like garbage.' And he said, 'So you draw something that looks like garbage. Big deal. It's just paper and a pencil, Forester. You can toss it later if you want, but sometimes you gotta draw a little garbage before you get to the good stuff.'

Zoe turned to Alex. "So maybe you paint some garbage. And it sucks. So you paint on another coat of primer and start again. What's the worst that can happen?"

They sat in silence for several minutes.

Finally, Alex said, "So what happened?"

"When?"

"When you drew him?"

Zoe grinned. "It totally sucked."

Alex groaned. "Was that supposed to be a helpful story?"

"Wasn't it?"

Alex gave her a playful push causing her to fall off her stool.

"How're you girls doing?" Tilly asked, balancing a tray filled with glasses of lemonade and fresh molasses cookies.

"Tilly, you rock!" Zoe jumped up to take the tray and set it down on Tilly's worktable.

"How are your college preparations coming along, dear?" Tilly asked, sipping from the cup Zoe handed her.

"Better, thanks to Alex's advice. I held firm and my 'rents have resigned themselves to the fact that this is what I want to do with my life. Now they're making me search out every possible scholarship. And I had to promise to get a business minor as a backup. But, hey, I can live with that," she said, munching on a cookie.

While Tilly and Zoe's conversation flowed around her, Alex stared at the blank panel, trying to ignore the images of Derek that seemed to fill it. His handsome, laughing face. The look in his eyes as he admired her work. When he told her he loved her.

She felt her fury rise anew. Why was she letting that loser have any power over her now? He wasn't worth ruining everything she'd worked so hard for.

Leaping up, she stomped across the floor to flick on her floodlights, aiming them carefully at the panel. She snatched up a wide brush, dipped it into the blue she'd created as a base for the sky, and with broad strokes, she began to paint.

"Woo-hoo! You go, girlfriend," Zoe cheered from behind, clapping her hands.

Alex flashed her a quick grin, then shooed them both from the studio. "Out, you two. I have work to do."

CHAPTER 21

Alex was in the studio working when her cell rang. She thought about ignoring it, but a quick glance at the screen had her wiping her paint-stained fingertips on her jeans. Smiling, she tapped the speakerphone button. "Hey, Jake."

She could hear the answering smile in his voice. "Somebody's in a good mood."

"Yup." She dropped onto her stool.

"Must be my manly voice. It has that effect on many women, you know."

"Yeah, yeah." She laughed, reveling in how comfortable she'd become with him. Only a short time ago, his flirtatious joking would have caused her to shut down.

"How's everything going at the site?"

"Great! Things are really coming along." They chatted for a bit, then he asked, "What about you, what've you been up to today?"

"Well...I started painting the mural," Alex said with uncharacteristic shyness. Since they'd begun spending more time together, she'd eventually shared more about her creative block with him, although not the reason behind it.

"Alex, that's great!" Jake exclaimed. "I knew you could do it."

"Yeah, well..." She twisted a loose strand of hair around one finger.

"It'll be great, Alex, I just know it. You have an amazing talent."

She grew warm from his words of praise.

"Not to change the subject, but I was calling to ask you something," he said.

"What?"

"I was wondering if you'd like to go to the fireworks tomorrow night with J.P., Tilly, and me?"

"Oh—"

"It was J.P.'s idea. We'd just go as friends, it's not a date or anything," he added in a rush.

Alex smiled. "Sure, that sounds fun."

"Great!"

They disconnected and Alex picked up her paintbrush again. And as hard as she tried, she couldn't seem to wipe the stupid grin off her face as she went back to work.

"Do I look all right?" Tilly fiddled with the buttons of her cherry-red cardigan embroidered with navy blue and white sailboats.

"You look beautiful, Grandma," Alex said. "You're practically glowing." It was true. Tilly's customary twist was held in place by a cloisonné hair comb. A red, white, and blue scarf was knotted at her neck, and she wore jeans in anticipation of the cool evening air.

"You're glowing yourself," her grandmother observed. Alex peeked at her own reflection in the mirror beside the front door. Her dark hair hung loose and shining past sun-kissed cheeks. She wore a white long-sleeve tee and jeans like Tilly, except her belt loops were threaded through with a shiny, star-spangled belt.

"Don't you want warmer shoes, dear? And a sweater?" Her grandmother looked at Alex's flip-flops with concern. "It gets chilly beside the water at night."

"I'll be fine," Alex said. "Besides, I still have this." She held up the sweatshirt she'd borrowed from Jake the night of their stakeout. The tantalizing scent of him still clung to the soft fabric, and she didn't want to admit how many times she'd put it to her face to breathe it in. "I need to return it to Jake, but I'm sure he'll let me use it tonight if I get cold."

As if on cue, the doorbell rang, quite unnecessarily, since the front door was wide open as usual. The two women could easily see the grinning faces of J.P. and Jake through the screen door.

Tilly pulled it open and the two men stepped inside. Alex was struck afresh with how large both men were; their tall, straight frames filled the tiny entry.

"You pretty young things ready?" J.P. boomed.

"I believe so," Tilly answered, smiling up at him.

"Well then, shall we?" He offered his arm to Tilly, which she accepted, leaving Jake and Alex to trail behind.

Alex muffled a giggle as Jake mimicked his grandfather, offering her his arm and whispering, "Shall we, my dear?"

"Oh, we most definitely shall," Alex whispered back, secretly appreciating his firm bicep as her fingertips curled around it. He pulled the door shut behind them, frowning. "I still don't like the fact that your grandmother doesn't lock her door," he said as they walked slowly down the steps.

"Hmm?" Alex was momentarily distracted, admiring the line of his jaw and the way his hair curled at the nape of his neck.

She caught his concerned look and glanced back at the door. "What can I say, Jake," she shrugged. "Old habits die hard."

"Are you saying you can't teach an old dog new tricks?"

"Are you calling my grandmother old?"

"She's an oldie but a goodie." This made Alex chuckle as she climbed into the back seat of J.P.'s Buick. But her chuckle was quickly replaced by an expression of shock. "Grandma, what are you doing?"

As Jake settled himself beside Alex, Tilly glanced at her in the rearview mirror. "What does it look like I'm doing? I'm driving."

"But—but," Alex sputtered. "Don't you need a permit or something?"

"Nah," J.P. said. "If you're over eighteen, you just need some driving time under your belt before you can take the test. And although some may mistake Tilly for a schoolgirl, she is definitely over eighteen."

"Oh, J.P.!" her grandmother tittered, sounding much like the schoolgirl he'd just described.

"She's one hundred percent legal," J.P. said, buckling his seat belt. "Besides, she could use some nighttime driving practice."

Alex saw Jake make the sign of the cross out of the corner of her eye.

"I don't know—"

"It'll be fine," J.P. assured them. "Let's go! I want to buy you all an ice cream cone before it gets too crowded."

Tilly inched her way up the driveway and they drove slowly down the road. Rex lay between Alex and Jake, his head resting in Alex's lap. She smoothed her fingers over his glossy coat as she watched her grandmother, thinking again about how much she'd changed since Grandpa Joe had died.

As they neared town, Tilly faltered a few times in the face of the oncoming traffic, but J.P. kept his tone calm, issuing instructions in a gentle, reassuring manner. Alex had to admit he was a perfect teacher. He had Tilly pull into his driveway, thereby avoiding the need to parallel park in the bumper-to-bumper cars lining the side streets.

"Great job," he said, throwing an arm around Tilly's slender shoulders and giving her a squeeze. Tilly beamed, her face flushed with pleasure.

"I had my doubts, Grandma. But you did it," Alex said while the men pulled blankets from the trunk.

"We all got here alive and everything!" Tilly said in good humor.

"Pops is the best teacher," Jake said, slamming the trunk shut. The four of them walked toward Main Street. "He taught Noah, Wade, and me how to drive, too."

"Wow, I had no idea you were a professional, J.P.," Alex said as they turned the corner.

"Hmm…never thought of it that way," he said, tapping his chin and looking thoughtful. "Maybe I should spend my retirement teaching folks how to drive."

"Aren't you busy enough managing the condominium project?" Jake said with a snort, and they all laughed.

"Speaking of the condominium project, what's happened with Frank Farley?" Tilly asked, twisting around to look at Jake.

"He hasn't been released yet, as far as I know," Jake said. "We haven't had any more incidents at the site since he's been out of the picture. So, despite the fact that he had an accomplice, I think it's pretty clear Farley must have been behind everything."

They reached the Dairy House ice cream shop. The line snaked a long way up the sidewalk, but J.P. insisted on waiting in it. "It's tradition," he said.

Jake explained that every summer when he and his brothers came to Whispering Pines, they adhered to a strict set of Fourth of July traditions. "First, we'd get up ridiculously early to lay claim to our favorite parade viewing spot right in front of the post office."

"What d'you mean, 'ridiculously early?'" J.P. interrupted. "Six-thirty is a perfectly normal time to get up."

"For a Coast Guard captain, maybe," Jake said, rolling his eyes.

J.P. grunted.

"Then we'd head back home where Nana would have breakfast waiting for us. Fresh strawberries with blueberries and pancakes sprinkled with powdered sugar."

"Always the same breakfast?" Alex asked.

"Red, white, and blue," Jake explained.

"Ah."

"Nana always bought us matching patriotic shirts to wear. After breakfast, we'd put them on."

"Awww, you must have looked adorable!"

"When we were under ten, maybe. But in our teens? Not so much. But none of us had the heart to hurt Nana's feelings, so we always wore them."

"You boys looked great!" J.P. interjected. "We have an album of pictures to prove it."

"Then," Jake continued with a pointed look at J.P., "we'd get out our earplugs and head to the parade."

"Earplugs?" Tilly asked.

"Have you been to the parade?" Jake asked.

Tilly shook her head as they inched forward in the line. "I'm embarrassed to admit it, but I've lived in this town for over a decade and I've never attended the Fourth of July parade."

"We'll have to remedy that next year," J.P. said, smiling at her.

Tilly blushed, smiling back. And Alex had that uncomfortable feeling again, as if she and Jake were intruding somehow.

Unperturbed by the older couple making goo-goo eyes at each other, Jake continued. "With the exception of a couple of performers, like the Scottville Clown Band and the high school marching band, Whispering Pines' parades tend to run a bit short on, er, true entertainment."

"What do you mean?" Tilly pulled her attention from J.P. back to Jake.

"We don't exactly have a lot of acts; we mostly have a lot of trucks."

"Trucks?"

"Yeah, semi-trucks. And they like to blow their horns really loud. Used to scare the heck out of me when I was little."

"Cried like a baby the first time we took him to the parade." J.P. grinned.

"Thanks, Pops," Jake said drily.

Alex laughed. They'd finally reached the cashier to place their order, and licking their cones, they meandered slowly toward the beach.

The setting sun flamed at the horizon. Behind it, the sky glowed in rich, burnished ochre.

They wove their way through throngs of people and picked their way across the sand in search of an empty space to spread their blankets.

"We might have to separate," Jake said, scanning the crowded beach. He handed his grandfather half the blankets and pointed to an open space several yards up the beach. "Alex and I will set up camp over there," he said.

"Don't let Alex get lost in the crush when it's over," J.P. warned as they moved away.

"Yessir, cap'n." Jake gave him a mock salute. Taking Alex's hand, he pulled her along to the spot he'd noticed. Spreading one of the blankets on top of the sand, he plunked down in the center.

She kicked off her flip-flops, sinking her toes into the cool, silky sand.

"Bet we won't even need those." Alex indicated the extra blankets Jake had left sitting on one corner.

"We will later." He reached up and tugged her belt loop, pulling her down beside him. "The temperature always drops."

"But I have this!" She waved his sweatshirt under his nose.

"I noticed." He grinned, dimples flashing.

Children raced past with sparklers in their hands, and a strolling hawker drew their attention. Jake called him over and bought a glow-in-the-dark necklace. "For you." He held it up. "May I?"

"You really shouldn't have. It's too much!" she joked, lifting the hair from the back of her neck so he could put it on.

"You're worth it," he said softly. His fingertips grazed her skin as he fastened it, and she trembled at the contact.

Mistaking her reaction for cold, he picked up the discarded sweatshirt and handed it to her. "Maybe you should put this on now."

She let her hair fall back and accepted it, slipping the soft, worn material over her head.

He was seated closest to the water and gazed out at it now, arms draped over his bent knees. The gentle breeze coming off the water played with his hair.

He turned to face her then, his dark eyes reflecting the luminescence of the sky, and her breath caught in her throat. He looked absolutely delicious.

"So, the painting is coming along?" he asked, unaware of her train of thought.

"Yes." She looked away, hoping her expression hadn't revealed anything. "I think between Grandma, Zoe, and you, I've successfully battled my way out of the evil artist's block."

"I knew you would, Alex. You have too much talent and perseverance to let anything like that stop you for long."

She smiled down at her twined fingers. "Thanks." She braved a glance at his face. "Your encouragement means a lot."

He gave her arm a quick squeeze, then released it. She could tell he was working to keep things casual between them. Careful not to cross any physical lines with her, just as he'd promised.

However, she was unreasonably annoyed with this. She knew she should be happy he was respecting her boundaries. But instead, disappointment tickled at the edge of her consciousness. She was further frustrated to find herself savoring any contact she had with him, no matter how small. These lingering romantic notions were stupid and self-destructive, and she needed to get them out of her head.

She cleared her throat. "I—I never told you why I had the block."

"Nope," Jake acknowledged, searching her face with curiosity.

She plucked at the front pocket of the sweatshirt, then glanced sideways at him. The sun was below the horizon now, and the sky had transformed to a dusky blue with the first stars beginning to emerge. "I told you I was engaged."

He nodded.

She looked past him to the dark, undulating waves, suddenly aware of how much she wanted him to know the whole story. It might help him understand her better. And just maybe he wouldn't think she was completely nuts for the way she'd been treating him. Taking a deep breath, she said, "A few months before our wedding, I...found out he was cheating on me."

She glanced at his face again, but he just waited, listening.

She hugged her knees to her chest. "I think it devastated me more than..." she hesitated, "...maybe I should back up. See, I had a total of one date in high school," she said, holding up her index finger in emphasis. "And it didn't even really qualify as a date."

"Why not?" Jake asked.

"He was my best friend's older brother, and it was for senior prom."

"Did he kiss you good night?"

"No!" She was aghast.

"Nope, doesn't count." Jake smiled, then grew serious. "That's almost unbelievable."

"Why?"

"Well...look at you." He swept a hand, taking in her appearance. "How could you not have had guys knocking down your door night and day?"

"Cut it out."

"I'm serious!'

"Well, I didn't," she said shortly. "Partly due to my own shyness and lack of confidence, partly because I've always been wrapped up with my art, and..." She splayed both palms in a helpless gesture. "And, also, I guess I just never met the right person."

Except for an occasional burst of laughter, the hum of conversation around them took on a hushed quality that melded with the advancing darkness. She rested her chin on her knees. "Then I met Derek. He was handsome and sophisticated." She shot Jake a sharp look. "And a total flirt."

Catching her look, Jake put both hands over his heart and arranged his features into a pained expression. "Madam, are you implying I'm a flirt?"

She arched an eyebrow, and his teeth flashed in the darkness.

She continued. "I'd never met anyone like Derek. From the very beginning, he made me feel so special. He was always flattering me and giving me compliments, bringing me gifts and admiring my art. Admiring me. He literally swept me off my feet." She closed her eyes. "And all those loving feelings, that magic of first love, the passion that he evoked in me, I channeled it all into my work. My pieces became more exciting, had more depth. Derek was my muse. When he proposed after we'd only been dating a few months, it was like I was living in a dream."

She paused, hunching her shoulders. But Jake didn't touch her or break the silence, just waited patiently for her to continue.

"He was always flirting with other women, but I didn't think anything of it. I mean, it seemed harmless. It was just...Derek." She shrugged. "I knew I was the one he loved." Her chin dipped below her knees, her voice grew quieter. "One afternoon, when I knew he wasn't due back from a business trip until that evening, I decided to surprise him with a homemade dinner."

Alex balled her hands into fists. "I was barely through his door when I...heard them. At first, I thought I imagined the sounds or that it was a thief or something. I have no idea why I didn't go for help. Maybe it was intuition." She shrugged again. "All I know is I followed the sounds and he was there. In bed with some—" Her voice broke.

Jake put a hand on her shoulder, squeezing gently. "You don't have to tell me any more, Alex," he said, his voice soft.

She lifted her head. The expansive sky was completely dark now, glittering with pinpoints of light. "No, I want to. I need to."

"All right."

"It was unreal. Like some sort of joke. I thought, this can't really be happening." Her voice grew stronger. "I stood there frozen for a moment, then something exploded inside me."

"What did you do?"

"I killed him."

Jake's hand froze on her shoulder, and he carefully removed it, making her smile. "I didn't *really* kill him. Although if I'd had a knife in my hand at the time..."

"But you didn't."

"No, I didn't. But I did have the bag of groceries for our dinner."

"Uh-oh."

"Yeah, I went sort of nuts. I just started screaming at him. And throwing things. I threw every piece of food from that grocery bag at them. A head of Romaine lettuce, raw steaks, salad dressing, everything. I even threw the expensive bottle of red wine I'd selected."

"Oooh." Jake looked pained. "Please tell me it wasn't a Cabernet?"

She shook her head. "Pinot Noir."

"Bet that made a nice weapon."

She nodded, her chin bumping against her kneecaps. "Made a sweet stain on his stupid bedroom wall, too."

Jake laughed, then sobered. They sat in silence until the first shower of gold sparkles exploded overhead followed by the crowd's enthusiastic applause.

"I'm sorry you went through that, Alex."

She nodded in acknowledgment. "I'm grateful for one thing, though."

"That you didn't end up marrying the jerk?"

She smiled faintly. "Yes, that and..." She swallowed. "And the fact that catching him like that stopped me from making a really big mistake that night." Alex turned her head sideways to face Jake, her cheek resting where her chin had been. "See, um...we'd never..." She cleared her throat. "I'd decided not to..." Her voice trailed off as she realized she hadn't originally intended to share this part. Why had she kept talking? It was like once the faucet was turned on, there was no off switch.

"Decided not to what?" Jake was clearly confused.

"Oooooh!" The crowd cheered as a quick succession of colorful lights rained down, one after another.

Alex hugged her knees even tighter. "I'd made a decision about...taking our relationship to the next level."

Jake's face was in shadow, but his voice held surprise. "You mean, you hadn't..."

Alex sighed. "I'd made a promise to myself long ago that I wasn't going to...you know. I planned to wait until I was married." She smiled wryly, "Of course, until I met Derek, it wasn't exactly a huge sacrifice or anything. But even after Derek and I were engaged, he always said he respected that about me. He was so patient and understanding with me, never pushed." She gave a short, humorless laugh. "Turns out he was probably so understanding because he was just getting it somewhere else."

Another series of explosions filled the air, and somewhere in the distance, a small child began to cry.

"I was such an idiot," she whispered.

"No, you weren't." Jake's voice was intense, lacking its usual playfulness. "He's the idiot, Alex."

"On some level, I know that. But, once I realized how he'd betrayed me, that our love had meant nothing to him, it was like something in me died. And my muse died along with it. I couldn't paint, I couldn't—" The sparkling lights of the fireworks blurred before her eyes. With a shock, she felt hot tears slip down her cheeks.

She hadn't cried since it happened, retreating behind a protective shell of cold anger. She'd worked to keep herself safe and hidden away, where nobody could crush her the way Derek had ever again. But now, that tight rein on her emotions had slipped.

She brushed roughly at the tears with the sleeve of the sweatshirt. She was trembling and felt ridiculous for baring her soul to Jake this way—a man who'd been a stranger to her only weeks ago. But somehow, in his presence, the overwhelming mass of emotion bubbled to the surface, and she was powerless to staunch its flow.

Giving up the fight, she bent her head and sobbed freely. She felt Jake's arms slide around her, pulling her to him. He smoothed her hair and made small sounds of comfort, barely discernible over the crowd's awe-filled gasps at the whistling, popping fireworks overhead.

She wasn't sure how long they stayed like that, but after a while, her crying eased and her breathing calmed. She permitted herself to relax in the soothing circle of his arms.

Eventually, she lifted her head to look up at him, face swollen, eyes aching from the salt of her tears. Her words scraped from her raw throat, "Jake, I'm—"

"Do not say you're sorry." Jake looked steadily into her eyes. "You have nothing to be sorry about." Keeping one arm curled around her, he fished in his jeans pocket and pulled out a handkerchief. "It's clean, scout's honor," he said, handing it to her.

She held up the square of white material and couldn't help but laugh, though her cheeks and lips felt stiff from crying. "You do *not* carry a handkerchief in your pocket!"

"Always."

"J.P.?"

"J.P."

She blew her nose loudly into it, then balled it up to dab at her eyes. "I'll bet you weren't even a Boy Scout?"

"Well, no," he admitted sheepishly. "I wanted to be one, though."

She managed another smile. "I can't believe I just did that."

"What happened to you cut deep, Alex. Deep cuts take time to heal. A lot of time," he said. "And unfortunately, there's no escaping the pain that accompanies the healing either."

She looked at him, barely making out his features in the darkness. "You sound like you're speaking from experience."

He was silent a moment, then said, "Let's just say I've been cut deep before, too."

He didn't say any more and she didn't press.

They both looked up as the explosions overhead increased in intensity. Multicolor bursts spurted in every direction, filling the sky with ceaseless, shimmering curtains of light. The crowd shouted and whistled at this grand finale. Then the sky went dark and people slowly rose, gathering their things, folding up chairs and blankets.

Jake's arm was still around her, and with his free hand, he turned her face, lifting her chin. "I want to clarify one thing, Alex."

"What's that?"

Moving his hand from her chin, he lifted her hand and tapped her pinkie finger. "You have more character and class right here than Derek will ever have," he stated. "You said you appreciated his patience with you? It should never have been a matter of his patience, Alex. He should have simply respected your commitment to wait. He lacked honor. He lacked integrity." Jake leaned in close, making certain she could hear him over the sounds of the crowd. "He didn't deserve you."

Alex felt a warm glow radiating from deep within, and she smiled fully now, meeting his eyes. The murmurs of the crowd were dissipating as people left the beach. But they remained. He hadn't let go of her hand, and the intensity of his gaze blazed through her, even in the darkness. Finally, she dropped her eyes, and disentangling herself, rose. Jake stood too and shook out the blanket they'd been sitting on. She waited, hugging the other blanket close to her body and staring at the ground.

"Ready?" he asked.

She looked up. "Thanks, Jake."

He reached out a hand to cup her tear-stained cheek in his warm palm. "Any time, angel."

CHAPTER 22

Alex stood barefoot in the kitchen, sipping her coffee and contemplating the contents of the refrigerator, when the front door opened and Tilly walked in. Her skin was flushed and her eyes glowed.

"I can't even begin to describe how wonderful that was, Alex," she said, stripping off her earth-covered gardening gloves and dropping them onto the low bench behind the door.

Alex smiled and took another sip. "Did your flowers miss you?"

"I'm sure they did!" Tilly said. "Come look."

Alex closed the refrigerator and indulged her grandmother, trailing her back outside for a garden tour, complete with in-depth explanations of each flower type. They were heading back inside when Tilly spotted some weeds she'd missed earlier. She bent down to pull them out. Alex waited for her, soaking up the warm sunshine and taking in the brilliant array of color her grandmother's flower beds created.

A sudden exclamation from Tilly made Alex glance down. Tilly was studying the small diamond-studded watch she wore, a gift from Grandpa Joe for their thirty-fifth wedding anniversary. "Oh my goodness! I need to hurry and eat lunch. I didn't realize it was this late!"

"Do you have plans?"

"J.P. is taking me for a pontoon boat ride."

"Oh reeeally?" Alex smirked, waggling her brows.

Tilly flushed, brushing crumbs of dirt from her hands as she rose. "It's just a boat ride."

Alex followed Tilly back into the house. "You two have been spending quite a lot of time together," she said.

"I enjoy J.P.'s company," Tilly replied, then quickly changed the subject. "Do you have plans today?"

"Painting," Alex said.

"You're putting in a lot of hours," her grandmother said, sounding concerned. "Make sure you take breaks."

"It just feels so good to be painting again," she said. "But don't worry. Jake mentioned hanging out later today."

"Oh reeeally?" her grandmother teased, waggling her own eyebrows in an imitation of Alex.

"You know it's not like that." Alex dismissed her with a wave. "We're just friends."

"I do not understand you at all, Alexandra Matilda Fontaine!" Using her full name was a sure sign her grandmother was frustrated with her.

"What do you mean?" Alex frowned, slipping onto one of the stools at the kitchen counter.

Tilly began slicing the fresh strawberries she'd washed earlier. "Don't play naïve with me, young lady. Jake is a nice, intelligent, handsome young man. You clearly enjoy his company. Why won't you admit you like him as more than a friend?"

"Because I don't," Alex replied flatly.

"Then why have you two been spending so much time together?"

Alex sniffed. "I enjoy his company," she said in an imitation of her grandmother's response.

Tilly huffed in exasperation.

Alex would never admit it aloud, but she knew there was some truth to her grandmother's observations. She'd been spending nearly all her free time with Jake and enjoyed every minute of it. She'd grown to appreciate many of his qualities and recognized there was more depth to him than she'd first believed. Occasionally, she'd catch herself daydreaming about what it might be like if they moved beyond friendship. But then she'd give herself a mental smackdown and remind herself things were fun just as they were.

Over the past few weeks, Jake had introduced her to some of the lesser-known treasures of the area. Besides boating, they'd taken dune rides, enjoyed picnic lunches in quiet coves, and explored some of the quaint surrounding towns. Jake proved a knowledgeable companion, well-versed in the area's history thanks to J.P., and their verbal banter always made her laugh.

As expected, they often ran into people Jake knew, including a disproportionate number of attractive women. Alex was secretly gratified to note that although he was always friendly, he never appeared romantically interested in any of them. He'd also completely backed off from his previous flirtations with her. And she appreciated this. Mostly. Refusing to consciously acknowledge the niggling feeling that she sort of missed it. Or his kisses...

"Could you grab the poppy seed dressing for me, Alex?" Tilly drew her from her thoughts as she tossed the strawberries with almond slices, crumbled bacon, and salad greens. "And two bowls," she added. Alex set the dressing beside her. "Only one bowl, Grandma," she grinned. "I haven't had breakfast yet."

They chatted amicably while Tilly ate the salad and Alex munched on toast with jam. As they were cleaning up, Tilly said, "I forgot to tell you, it's my turn to host my card group tonight. We'll have a house full."

"That's okay, I'll be in the studio. I'll just shut the door if you guys get too rowdy."

Tilly laughed and kissed her cheek. "Would you do me a favor, sweetheart?"

"Sure," replied Alex, placing the last dish on the drain board.

"I don't think I'll have time to pick up the pastries I ordered from Westlake before they close, and—"

"No problem," Alex said before she finished. "I'll go now."

Tilly thanked her, heading to her bedroom to change.

"Have fun with J.P.," she called, walking out the door. "Don't do anything I wouldn't do!" She tripped down the front steps, laughing at Tilly's flustered sputters that followed the bang of the screen door behind her.

Slipping behind the wheel of her car, she inhaled deeply. *Aaah. That new car smell!*

Alex felt giddy sailing up the street with her radio blaring. The sun was shining, the waves were sparkling, and she'd gotten her muse back! She was once again doing what she loved and was filled with gratitude, for Zoe, for her grandmother, and for Jake, who was becoming a wonderful friend.

Sharing what had happened between her and Derek had lifted a huge burden from her. It was liberating. She gazed up through her open sunroof, feeling as light as the seagulls soaring overhead.

In the little bakery shop, she enjoyed a quick exchange of gossip with Pat before leaving with Tilly's order. Loaded down with two large bags, Alex pushed the bakery door open with her foot and walked the short distance to her car.

She had just straightened from settling the packages on the car floor when she caught sight of a familiar form exiting the restaurant across the street.

Mouthwatering as ever, Jake's dark hair and golden skin were perfectly set off by the pale blue polo shirt and khakis he wore. Alex lifted her hand in a wave, about to call out to him, when she noticed the woman. She was tall and elegant in a sleeveless white dress and heels. The two of them were strolling together from the restaurant, deep in conversation. They paused in front of Jake's truck. A sudden breeze whipped the woman's golden hair into her face. She swiped it back and laughed at something Jake said; he answered with his own dazzling, dimpled grin.

Then Alex watched in shock as the woman wrapped herself around Jake in a long hug, pulling back for a quick kiss before he opened the passenger door and helped her in.

The truck had already sped off before Alex realized her hand was still frozen in mid-wave. She used it to slam her car door shut. Marching to the driver's side, she tried to analyze the torrent of emotions whirling through her. Logically, she knew this was none of her business, and she had no reason to feel hurt. What was it to her if Jake had a lunch date? Or even a girlfriend, for that matter? She'd made it clear she wasn't interested in any of that. And Jake was an attractive, red-blooded guy. Naturally, he'd have a normal dating life.

Alex backed out of the parking space.

Curious he hadn't mentioned the young woman before, though. But then again, they'd only known each other a short time. She couldn't possibly know everything about his, life just as he didn't know everything about hers.

She pulled into the traffic of Main Street and shrugged. So. Now she knew. Apparently, he had a girlfriend. Fine. *We're just friends,* she reminded herself. Lifting her chin, she punched the radio on, blaring it out of the speakers.

But the sweet joy she'd felt earlier had soured.

She wished the bowling ball that had formed in the pit of her stomach would go away. And she wished her hammering heart would slow down. And she really, really wished the whiny voice inside her head would shut up.

CHAPTER 23

"Here you go." Jake handed the papers he'd finished signing back to Rita.

She glanced up and took them from him. She flipped through the stack, gum snapping. "Thanks, darlin.'"

Jake checked his cell. Blast! It was nearly seven o'clock. Too bad. He'd planned to ask Alex out for dinner, but it was too late now. He couldn't believe he'd lost track of time and was disappointed. He looked forward to the time they spent together every day. Despite the rocky start to their relationship, Alex turned out to be great company. She was bright and beautiful, with a quick wit. Not his usual girlfriend fare. Of course, he reminded himself for the hundredth time, she was not a girlfriend. He rose to his feet and stretched.

"Is Jordan all set to start tomorrow?" Rita asked, filing the pages he'd just handed her.

"Yup, we're good to go."

Rita nodded, turning in her chair to face him. "You headin' out?"

"Yeah." He slid some files into the pocket of his worn leather briefcase, then gave her a stern look. "You need to get out of here, too. It's late. I was thinking about stopping by Pops' place on my way home. Wanna come with?"

Rita removed her glasses and nibbled on one earpiece, the beaded chain glinted in the light from her desk lamp. "Thanks for the offer, sugar, but I have plans." She cocked her head to one side. "No Alex tonight?"

Jake snapped the briefcase shut. "It's a bit late for a dinner date, don't you think?"

"I dunno." Rita swiveled back and forth in her chair, grinning like the Cheshire Cat. "I'll bet she'd eat dinner this late if it was *you* doin' the askin.'"

"Well, I'm not asking."

"How 'bout drinks then? I think it's Margarita Night at Mitchell's."

"You know I don't drink, Rita."

"I ain't talkin' about you!"

Jake narrowed his eyes at her. "What's with the big push to take Alex out?"

Rita's eyes widened in mock innocence. "Who's pushin'? I'm not pushin'."

"Rita."

"Aw, heck." Rita dropped her glasses, letting them dangle as she leaned forward and propped her elbows on the desk. "It's just that you've been different lately—happy."

"Aren't I generally a happy kind of guy?"

"I sure like that Alex," she said, ignoring his comment. "She's good people. And since you've been hanging out with her, you've seemed, I dunno, more at peace or somethin'." Her blue eyes glittered. "You two make a great—"

"Don't say it! We're *not* a couple, Rita. I've explained this to you. We're just friends. I like Alex, she's great. But she isn't looking for a relationship, and for that matter, neither am I. I've got to focus on this project."

"Just friends," Rita muttered. "Youth is wasted on the young."

Jake pretended not to hear her, and Rex, recognizing Jake was preparing to leave, ambled over to his side. He scratched the dog's head and pointedly changed the subject. "What are your plans tonight?"

"I'm subbing in a ladies' BUNCO group."

"Hanging with ladies is good," Jake said. "You get in less trouble that way."

"Don't be so sure, sugar." Rita winked. Closing her laptop, she pulled her purse from her desk drawer and rummaged through it. "I'm gonna try and talk 'em into heading over to this new Salsa Club in Grand Haven when we're done." She held up a compact mirror and examined her reflection critically. "I think this hottie I met a couple of weeks ago might be there tonight."

Jake shook his head and left with Rex, Rita's raucous laughter trailing after them.

Jake and Rex rolled into J.P.'s driveway a short time later. The two clambered out, and Jake opened the front door with his key. "Hey, Pops," he called out.

"That you, Jakey boy?" J.P.'s voice came from the back of the house.

"Yes, sir! "Got any leftovers from dinner?"

"Hang on, I'm just getting fancied up."

Rex, having finished his thorough investigation of all smells, hopped onto the sofa and circled three times before folding himself into a surprisingly small ball of fluff on the far cushion.

Jake flopped down beside him and rested his feet on the boat chest coffee table. "What's he getting fancied up for?" he muttered to Rex, whose brown eyes peeked up at him from his prone position.

J.P. entered the living room. The silver fringe surrounding his bald pate was carefully combed. He wore a full suit and tie and seemed to be glowing from the inside out.

Jake whistled. "Who're you trying to impress, pretty boy?"

Uncharacteristically, J.P. didn't take the bait. He just smiled beneath his freshly trimmed and waxed mustache. "I'm just making sure everything fits. I'm wearing it tomorrow when I take a lovely lady out for a fancy dinner."

"Again?"

"Yep."

"I swear, you guys have gone out every night since you met!"

"Every night but four. But who's counting." J.P. grinned. "Tomorrow night, though, is going to be more special than usual."

Something in J.P.'s expression halted Jake's quick comeback. He pulled his feet off the chest and straightened, eyes wide. "What's going on, Pops?"

J.P. didn't reply but reached into the pocket of his pants and withdrew a small, blue velvet box.

A feeling of unreality swept over Jake as he watched his grandfather open the box to reveal a brilliant marquis diamond surrounded by three tiny sapphires on each side.

"No. Flippin'. Way!" Jake leaped to his feet, whacking his shin against the chest. "Ouch!"

"Yes, way, Jakey-boy. I'm asking Tilly to marry me."

Jake dropped back onto the sofa, rubbing his shin, eyes never leaving the ring. His mouth hung open, but no words came out.

J.P. snapped the case shut and slipped it back into his pocket. "Better close your mouth, son, or you'll catch flies." J.P. turned and walked down the hallway to the kitchen, whistling as he went.

Jake got back up and followed him. He sat down in a kitchen chair, watching his grandfather pour himself a glass of iced tea.

Finally finding his voice, he said, "You're...getting married again?"

J.P. took several deep swallows and put the glass down, smacking his lips. "I sure needed that. Feeling a bit dehydrated."

"Pops, c'mon. Talk to me!"

His grandfather's jovial face took on a serious expression. "Yes, Jake. I'm getting married again." His voice grew quiet. "If she'll have me."

Jake dropped his forehead into his hands. "Wow."

The room was silent for several long moments as neither man spoke. Jake could not wrap his brain around this. Pops had adored Nana Ellen. Theirs had been a rich marriage full of love, life, and plenty of laughter. Much like the fainter memories he had of his parents before his mother died.

His mother and Nana Ellen. Memories of them mingled and rushed through his mind like a fast-flowing river. His mother's vibrant energy. The scent of her perfume. The comfort of burrowing into her lap. Her off-key voice singing made-up lullaby verses because she couldn't remember the real ones. And then she was gone. And the loss was like a gaping black hole in his family's life.

But there had been Nana. With her grandmotherly love and warmth, she'd partially filled that empty space.

And the summers. So many of them running together in his mind. On top of the fishing and hiking with Pops, there'd been endless days at the beach with Nana, hunting for treasures, feasting on her baked goods, listening to her teach Noah to play the piano, and the hours he'd spent with her working in the garden.

Then came the agonizing sickness. Nana fought against the cancer as hard as she could, but ultimately, death won, stealing her from them as well.

And Jake's heart broke all over again. A fresh wound atop the old.

He lifted his head and looked out the window. Against the pink twilight backdrop, the well-tended flowerbeds were awash in color. He had loved two women in his life. He'd lost them both. And he'd vowed never to let himself experience that sort of pain again. Yet here was J.P., willing to risk it. Putting his heart on the line again at sixty-eight years old. The knowledge left Jake speechless.

J.P. sat down beside him and put his hand on Jake's shoulder. "You gonna be all right, son?"

Jake's vision blurred and he blinked.

"Jakey-boy, I had no idea you'd react this way or I'd have given you more warning." J.P. looked at him with concern. "I sort of thought you'd be happy for me."

Jake straightened. "I am, Pops. Truly. You just caught me off guard, that's all. I had no idea you were thinking along those lines."

J.P.'s hand slipped from Jake's shoulder. "You think I'm too old?"

"No. No! It's not that. It's..." He let his voice trail off, not knowing exactly how to continue.

J.P. leaned back, studying Jake, and his next words shocked Jake still further. "When are *you* going to start living again, Jakey-boy?"

"What do you mean?"

"You've played the field an awful long time now. Have you ever considered getting serious with one woman?"

Jake frowned and crossed his arms. Pops never spoke to him about his love life except to joke about it. "Playing the field is a perfectly acceptable occupation at my age, Pops."

J.P. sighed. "Don't think I haven't noticed how much time you're spending with Alex lately. Haven't you ever thought about—"

Jake shook his head, not letting him finish. "No!"

His grandfather waved a hand. "C'mon, it's me you're talking to. I've watched you play the field, and I've seen the way you are with Alex." He leaned forward again. "You're different with her. What's more, I've seen the way she looks at you. I may be old and need my glasses for reading fine print, but I'm not blind."

"I like my freedom, Pops," Jake said stiffly. "I have no interest in diving in that deep with Alex or any woman. We're just friends, Pops. That's all. When will everybody get that through their heads?"

"Friends." J.P. scoffed. "Whether you admit it or not, you both have feelings for each other that go beyond simple friendship."

Jake was growing angry; he fought to control his voice as he leaned forward, emphasizing his next words. "Maybe I'm not being clear, Pops. I. Will. Never. Marry."

J.P. shook his head. "Never is a long time."

Jake couldn't take the pitiful look his grandfather was giving him now. He shoved back his chair and stood. "I'm leaving."

He strode from the room, but J.P.'s voice followed him down the hall. "Love's a funny thing, Jakey-boy. Sneaks up on a man, even when he's not looking for it."

Jake stormed out of the house, Rex at his heels. He yanked open the truck door, fuming. Pops was wrong. Overbearing and always pushing his opinions on people. He was clearly projecting his own feelings about Tilly onto Jake. Why couldn't he see marriage wasn't for everybody?

Jake sat behind the wheel, staring into space until Rex whined softly at him from the passenger seat. "Yeah, we're leaving, buddy," he mumbled. He started the engine and pulled away from the bungalow. Turning on the radio, he winced as Iron Maiden blasted from the speakers. He reached automatically to switch the station, his finger hovering over the button. Then he slowly withdrew it and let the music play. And despite his anger over the conversation with J.P., his mind filled with the image of a beautiful, dark-haired woman who had the most amazing blue-green eyes.

CHAPTER 24

Alex nibbled the end of her paintbrush and debated adding more green shading to the section she was working on.

The right side of her neck had a kink. She set the brush in the cup of water beside her and stretched her arms behind her back to release the tension. It was a good time for a break anyway, she thought. Opening the sliding glass door, she stepped outside and walked toward the edge of the property. She listened to the pine needles abrading one another in the gentle breeze. Unbidden, the scene she'd witnessed yesterday entered her thoughts. Long blond hair floating around the pretty, laughing face that was angled toward Jake's. She guessed Jake hadn't called yesterday because he'd been busy with the blond.

She growled out loud, annoyed with herself. So what if Jake was dating the blond? She had no claim on him. She threaded her way through the trees bordering Tilly's property.

She needed to get all these stupid romantic notions of Jake out of her head. Stop noticing the way his hair formed ringlets at the nape of his neck. Or the way his lean, muscular body moved with such surprising grace. Or how his fathomless eyes could quickly shift from amusement to something far more primal, making her heart beat painfully fast.

What you need, Alexandra Fontaine, is to focus on your work. She turned and marched back to the house with fresh resolve. Entering the studio, she pulled up her favorite playlist on her cellphone and cranked the volume. Then, with a deep breath, she started to paint.

She was soon so lost in her work that when something moved at the corner of her eye a while later, she shrieked, nearly knocking over her table of paint pots.

She put a hand over her heart and closed her eyes. *Awesome. How was she supposed to get him out of her head when he was standing there grinning at her from the studio doorway?*

"Sorry, I do tend to have that effect on people," Jake said, strolling into the room.

"What are you doing here?" Alex asked once she was breathing normally again.

He crossed over to her phone and tapped the pause function. "I thought I'd stop by and see how you're doing." He circled around behind her to face the panel she was working on. He held his thumb up, squinting one eye at it. "I did warn you about leaving the front door unlocked like that."

"Yeah," she grumbled. "Any sort of freak could just come walking in."

Jake laughed and lightly squeezed her shoulders in a sort of half hug. She resisted the urge to lean back against the broad chest.

He dropped onto her stool. "I felt bad we didn't get together yesterday."

Alex licked her lips, keeping her voice light. "That's sweet. I just figured you had a busy day." She dropped her brush into the water cup and turned to look at him. But he was still studying her work-in-progress, his eyes reflecting open admiration. "You're incredible," he said.

Despite the ambiguity of her feelings toward him, she couldn't suppress the flush of pleasure at his words. "Thanks," she murmured. "I'm having a hard time with the shading here." She pointed to the spot she'd been working on.

He squinted at it, but eventually shrugged. "Looks good to me." He rose from the stool. "I shouldn't be interrupting you." He waved a hand at the panel, indicating she should resume painting.

She picked up her brush but watched from the corner of her eye as he wandered restlessly around the room, picking up pieces of pottery, examining them, and putting them down again.

"So, were you busy with some big plans yesterday?" she said casually.

Jake frowned, turning one of her grandmother's sculpting tools over in his hands. "Nope."

He didn't elaborate, and with a sigh, she turned her attention back to the panel.

He sat down at Tilly's potter's wheel, watching Alex work in silence for several long minutes.

She eventually became engrossed again, and when he finally spoke, she jumped.

"Sooo, Tilly's out with J.P. tonight, huh?"

"Yup," Alex said, pausing to study the effect of the section she'd just finished. "Just like every night now, pretty much."

"Uh-huh."

More silence.

He got up and started pacing. "Has Tilly said anything to you about their relationship?"

"Such as?" *Maybe a bit more brown,* she thought, tilting her head.

"Such as maybe she and J.P. are planning to take their relationship to the next level?"

The brush clattered from Alex's hand as she turned to look at him. "What do you mean 'the next level?'"

"The. Next. Level." Jake enunciated each word.

Alex frowned. "Are you talking about sex?"

"No! I—why are you being so dense?" he flared, halting his pacing.

She looked shocked, and he was immediately contrite. "I'm sorry. I didn't mean—"

The blaring sound of a heavy metal song filled the room. Jake looked at her phone, confused. But Alex picked it up and studied the screen. "It's a phone call, but I don't recognize this number," she muttered, sliding the phone into her back pocket. "Sorry." She smiled sweetly at him. "I believe you were apologizing?" Her teasing grin faded when she realized he seemed genuinely upset. "Jake, what's wrong?"

He started pacing again, running his hands through his hair. "Doesn't it bother you that—"

Alex's phone burst into song again. "Oh, come on!" Frustrated, she wrenched it from her pocket and answered it. "Yes?"

The person on the other end spoke and she felt the color drain from her face. "Why are you calling?"

Jake had stopped pacing and was now staring at her curiously.

She stood listening for several long minutes, then sat on her stool and looked at Jake, mouthing the word, "Sorry."

Jake hesitated, as if uncertain what to do. Then, giving a brief wave, he crossed the floor and left the room.

She heard the front door bang shut as Derek Pendleton said into her ear, "Alex, are you still there?"

Adrenalin was coursing through her, and she took several deep, calming breaths before answering. "I'm here." Her hands might be trembling, but at least her voice sounded steady.

"You haven't responded to anything I just said."

"I'm...thinking." She rose from her stool. "Derek, now is really not the best time to—"

"I'm here," he blurted. "In Whispering Pines."

Shocked into silence, she sat down again. He was here. Now?

"I need to see you," he continued. His voice held a pleading note. If she hadn't known him so well, she'd have sworn the emotion was genuine.

Drawing herself up, she said coolly, "That's unfortunate, Derek. Because I don't need to see you."

"Alex, I—please. I don't want to do this over the phone."

"Do what?" she snapped.

"I've been an idiot. An unforgivably stupid, pig-headed, selfish idiot."

"Keep going," she said.

His voice broke. "Please, Alex. Your parents told me where you were. I just need to talk with you."

Her parents! She gritted her teeth. "*You* need? Honestly, Derek, I couldn't care less about what you need."

"That's not what I meant, Alex. This is coming out all wrong. Look, I understand you want nothing to do with me. But I came to Whispering Pines tonight because I need to speak with you, in person. I'm asking, no, I'm begging. Please, would you meet me tonight?"

She was torn. On the one hand, she was finally moving past the damage wrought by their broken relationship and his infidelity. And she never wanted to go back into that place of cold emptiness she'd existed in for so long. But no matter how irrational it was, she couldn't deny she still had feelings for the man.

She still hadn't spoken when Derek's whispered word filled the silence between them. "Please." He sounded meek. Broken.

She closed her eyes. "I just don't know, Derek."

She heard him sigh. "I'll be at the Boathouse tonight around eight o'clock. Waiting. I...I hope you'll come." He disconnected.

Alex didn't immediately try to stand, her legs were like rubber. She put down her phone and covered her face with her hands. A tangled web of emotion and memories raged inside her. She didn't know if she wanted to cry or scream or laugh hysterically. She'd truly thought she'd never see Derek again. Yet here he was. In Whispering Pines. And he *needed* to see her.

Alex sighed. Whether she chose to go or not, she knew she'd get no more work accomplished. To release the pent-up energy surging through her, she started cleaning up. She covered the paints and carried her brushes to the small sink in the corner. What would she say if she did meet the scumball anyway? Idly she wondered if he'd picked a public place as protection against another potential display of her anger. Maybe she should just slug him this time and get it over with. The thought made her smirk despite her ambivalence.

Warm water ran over her hands as she gently massaged soap into the brush bristles. And what was the deal with Jake tonight? All that pacing and talk about Tilly, J.P., and "the next level." But he'd left before she'd gotten to the bottom of whatever was bothering him.

She set the brushes to dry and glanced at the tiny clock on the studio wall. Straightening her shoulders with decision, she turned out the studio lights and headed to the bathroom. She had just enough time to grab a shower and clean up. She tossed her hair. Yes, she'd meet Derek, all right. But she'd make darn sure she looked amazing when she did. She wanted Derek Pendleton to know precisely what he'd lost.

CHAPTER 25

Jake sat at a table in the back corner booth of the restaurant.

"You gonna eat that, bro," said a voice. Jake looked up to see Cesar's stocky frame sliding into the booth opposite him.

"Have some." Jake shoved the plate toward his friend. He'd hardly touched the burger he'd ordered, and the seasoned curly fries now sat cold and soggy looking.

Cesar wrinkled his nose. "Maybe an hour ago, I'd have taken you up on that."

A waitress appeared. "Can I get you something?"

"What've you got on draft?" Cesar asked.

Once he'd placed his order, the waitress turned to Jake. "You need anything else?"

Cesar looked at Jake, who stared glumly at the top of the table. "Just bring him another iced tea," he said, spying Jake's empty glass. The waitress nodded and left.

Jake eyed Cesar. His friend had cleaned up after work. He wore a colorful button-down shirt over black jeans. His short, thick hair was spiked with gel. "You got a date or something?" Jake muttered.

Cesar grinned wide. "Yeah, with my wife. Her mom's watching the kids tonight. I promised to take her dancing here."

Jake looked around at the people filtering into the spacious dark paneled room. Chair and table legs scraped against the wooden floor as groups rearranged the furniture around the dance floor to suit their needs. "Where is Eliana?"

Cesar shrugged. "She wasn't ready, so she sent me ahead to get a table. She thinks it'll be packed tonight." He angled his chin toward the small stage. "The Rhythm Rebels are playing."

Jake nodded. The waitress arrived with their drinks and Cesar took a deep swallow of his beer, then sighed in appreciation. "Man, I needed that! Long day. We're making good progress though, eh?"

"Huh?" Jake blinked. "Oh...yeah."

Cesar frowned, setting down the frosty mug. *"Cuál es tu problema?"*

"I don't have a problem."

"Don't play me, amigo. I've known you too long." Cesar squinted at him. "You got lady troubles with Alex." It wasn't a question.

"Why does everyone keep talking to me about Alex?" Jake snapped. "She's got nothing to do with my mood."

Cesar held up his hands in mock defense. "Sorry, bro. It's just that you two seem sort of, er, into each other lately."

"If you know me at all," Jake said, leaning toward Cesar. "You know I have no intention of getting serious. With anybody."

"Okay, okay." Cesar curled a thick hand around his glass again. "I know you've always said that. It's just with Alex, you seem different." He shrugged.

Jake sat back and folded his arms across his chest. "How?"

Cesar looked thoughtful. "Well, not to get all Oprah on you, but you seem happier when you're with her, I guess."

Jake scowled.

Cesar took another deep swallow of his beer, undeterred by Jake's reaction. "You both light up like fireflies when you're around each other. Plus, you spend more time with Alex than you ever did with your old girlfriends." Cesar looked Jake in the eye. "Seriously, bro, you see her, like, every day! And how many times have I come looking for you, only to find you on the phone with her, giggling like a teenager."

"I do *not* giggle," Jake said.

Cesar raised his voice into a mocking falsetto. "You hang up. No, you. You first. No, you first." He ducked to avoid the wadded-up napkin Jake pitched at his head.

"Play nice, boys," said Eliana, coming up and planting a loud kiss on her husband's cheek. *"¿De qué estás hablando, cariño?"*

"Nothing," Cesar grinned, sliding over to make room for his wife.

"Sorry I took so long. But you know Mamá, once she gets talking," Eliana said, rolling her large, brown eyes. She planted a second kiss on Jake's cheek before claiming the spot beside her husband. A scoop-neck red top and floral print skirt hugged Eliana's plump curves, and the sides of her dark hair were clipped back from her round face.

"Come on, *gordito*. Tell me, what are you boys talking about?"

"Girls. Ow!" Cesar laughed as Eliana punched him in the arm. He jokingly rubbed the opposite one. "Girls for Jake, *ángel*," he clarified. "I've already got my best girl."

Looking appeased, she snuggled closer to him. Then she flashed her lipstick-red smile in Jake's direction. "Cesar's right. We need to find you a nice girl, Jake." Eliana's accent was more pronounced than Cesar's and whenever she said his name, it sounded like "hake."

"He's already found one, he just won't admit it," Cesar said.

Jake moved uncomfortably. "Look, guys, don't let me interfere with your date night. You two run along and grab a nice table by the dance floor before they're all gone."

Just then, the door to the restaurant swung open. Cesar's eyes widened and he let out a low whistle. "Speak of the devil..."

Jake spun around in his seat and froze. Alex stood at the entrance, scanning the crowd. The pale green dress she wore highlighted her golden skin and brought out the green in her eyes. Her hair hung loose and a glint of topaz and gold dangled from her ears. A moment later, she crossed to the opposite side of the room with a graceful stride, the skirt of her dress swishing against her elegant thighs as she moved.

"Ooooh, she's lovely." Eliana cooed. "Ask her to join us, Jake."

"She appears to already have a table," Jake said, frowning as Alex paused at a table for two near the dance floor. A well-dressed man with sun-bleached hair rose to greet her. He bent to kiss her and she quickly sat, avoiding the embrace. Alex looked especially stunning tonight, glowing, in fact. Jake felt an uncomfortable fluttering deep inside as he watched her talking with the man who leaned toward her with apparent intensity. Alex on the other hand sat back in her chair, her expression calm and reserved.

Jake wondered who the man was. Alex had been adamant about not dating anyone, yet this held all the signs of a bonafide date. Jake felt a flash of envy ripple over him. Then he did a mental shrug, suppressing it. No skin off him. If she wanted to start dating now, that was her business.

The band was setting up, and the Boathouse was nearly full, so Eliana and Cesar remained at Jake's table. They tried to cajole him out of his bad mood, joking and sharing funny stories about their kids. Jake spent plenty of time with Cesar and his family, he always enjoyed their company. But hard as he tried, he couldn't keep his focus on their conversation. His thoughts kept returning to Alex and the blond man. He wondered what was going on behind him.

The band started to play. The Rhythm Rebels were a popular local group known for their unique mixture of reggae riffs and original Latin-flavor pieces.

The lighting dimmed and the band started a number with a fast beat. Cesar and Eliana left to go dance as the floor filled with couples. Jake took the opportunity to slip to the other side of the booth. Sipping his iced tea, he watched the drama unfold from his shadowed corner.

Alex's reserved expression had changed. Her cheeks were flushed now and she was leaning forward, too, speaking with as much intensity as her dinner partner. Jake would have given anything to hear their conversation.

He was surprised when the man suddenly clasped Alex's hand between his own. Even more surprising was the fact that she didn't pull hers away. She listened intently as the man spoke, his face had taken on a pleading look.

Suddenly, releasing her hand, he reached into his jacket pocket and pulled out a cell phone. He studied the screen, said something quickly to her, then made his way out of the restaurant.

Alex remained seated, watching the dancers, one finger idly tracing patterns in the condensation of her glass.

Jake set his own glass down with decision. Slipping from the booth, he crossed the room to her table.

Alex watched Derek exit the building, his golden hair reflecting the shimmering blue and red lights that swept the walls, ceiling, and floor. He slipped among the writhing bodies with his characteristic poise, tossing his head to flick hair from his eyes as he held the phone to his ear. She couldn't help but smile at the familiar gesture. Sighing, she took another sip of her drink.

What was she doing? All her fierce anger toward him, her firm resolve never to see him again, had melted with the touch of his hands, at the sound of his voice, and the look in those earnest hazel eyes. He had begged for her forgiveness. And as much as she didn't want to admit it, his repentance seemed genuine. Derek was a broken man.

With Alex gone, and refusing contact with him, he'd sunk into a deep depression. He'd gone on drinking binges, which ultimately cost him his job, and then his apartment. He'd been forced to move in with his mother. She'd permitted it with the stipulation he got counseling. So he did.

Derek told Alex that until she'd left him, he hadn't realized how the lack of dealing with his feelings over his parents' divorce had fueled his unhealthy, hedonistic lifestyle. Slowly though, over months of therapy, he'd been forced to face the ugly truth of who he really was. And now he'd made real progress in resolving the deeper issues that caused him to act out through sex and alcohol. He'd come to Whispering Pines tonight, he told her, not only to beg her forgiveness, but because he was determined to win her back.

Her emotions were in turmoil. Every stormy word and nasty action she'd dreamt of tossing at him on the way to the Boathouse now drifted from her mind like dandelion seeds in the summer wind. The debonair, charming man she'd fallen in love with was begging her for another chance.

She had no idea how she felt or what to say to him. Thank goodness he'd gotten that phone call, buying her some time. Now she sat lost in thought.

The upbeat dance music changed to a slower number and a shadow fell across her table. "Would you like to dance?"

She looked up, shocked to see Jake extending his hand to her, his dark eyes glittering.

Her mouth fell open. "What are you doing here?"

He flashed that dazzling, dimpled grin at her, making her insides flutter as usual. "Would you believe a complete coincidence?"

She narrowed her eyes.

"Is that a 'no,' then?"

She lifted one brow.

He put his left hand over his heart and lifted his right in the classic "I swear to tell the truth" gesture. "I came in for dinner, saw you sitting here, so I decided to come over." He extended his hand again.

She glanced at the doorway, but Derek was nowhere in sight. So, this time, she accepted it and rose, heat searing a path to her core at his touch. Her mind automatically contrasted the familiar warmth of Derek's touch to this unsettling electricity she felt now.

He led her out onto the floor and, with a light half spin, drew her in, his right hand settling at the small of her back. Jake's shoulders were broader than Derek's and he was several inches taller. His lower jaw brushed her temple, and she fought the urge to rest her cheek against the curve of his neck.

She could feel the hard muscles of Jake's thigh brushing against her own as he began a rhythmic sway to the music.

A few moments later, though, he stopped moving after she stumbled over his feet for the second time. "What are you doing?" she asked.

"I thought we were dancing," he said. "The problem is, you aren't letting me lead. You need to relax."

She met his eyes. "Lead? What is this, *Dancing with the Stars*?"

His chest rumbled against her as he laughed.

"I don't think this music is made for ballroom dancing anyway, Grandpa," she said.

He laughed again. "Not ballroom, Latin. It works better with this music."

"We're doing a Latin dance?"

"A nice basic merengue."

"Ah," Alex said, trying to focus on letting him lead her around the floor.

"So, do you come here often?" He spoke close to her ear, sending shivers down her spine. She felt like a pinball game where the different targets lit up every time the little ball bounced off one of them.

"Is that a line, Riley?" She tipped her head up to look at him, the rainbow lights skipping over his shirt and face.

"Maybe." He grinned down at her.

"You know I'm here with somebody, right?" she asked.

"It looked like you were all alone to me." His dark eyes were inscrutable, as always.

"He...stepped out."

"A date?"

She sighed. "Not exactly." She felt a slight release of tension in the hand holding hers, and she looked at him curiously. "I figured you might have had a date tonight yourself," she said, keeping her tone as noncommittal as possible.

He abruptly stopped moving. "With whom?" He looked bewildered.

"With...oh, never mind," she said. "Keep dancing or we'll get stepped on."

He squinted at her for another second, then pulled her even closer than before, making her gasp. He led her into a turn and she marveled at how confidently he moved on the dance floor. She also couldn't help but notice how perfectly they seemed to fit together.

She forced herself to relax as he'd suggested, and their movements began to flow effortlessly. Closing her eyes, she let herself drift. It was sort of intoxicating. Breathing his delicious sun-drenched scent, feeling the heat of his body against her own. The reggae rhythms washed over her, making her wish she could stay in his arms like this for the rest of the night. All her tension, her confusion, drifted away in a current of sensation.

Too soon, the song ended, and the band struck up a livelier number. Jake didn't immediately release her though, they continued to sway gently, even as the floor filled with gyrating couples. She sighed softly against his neck and imagined she felt a light shudder ripple over him.

She tilted her chin to look up at him again. "Thanks for the dance, Jake."

He gazed down at her, their faces inches apart. And this time, there was no mistaking the look in his eyes. Desire. And something deeper.

She cleared her throat. "Um, Jake?"

He looked about to speak when Alex saw a hand appear and squeeze Jake's left shoulder.

"Hey, buddy. You want to give me back my fiancée?"

Alex saw Jake's eyes grow wide, then harden as he turned to face Derek. Alex noted Derek wore his classic sales smile. The one he used when trying to appear accommodating but was inwardly seething.

People generally couldn't tell the difference, but Alex always could. Jake's own tone was deceptively mild. "Fiancée?"

Alex opened her mouth, but Derek spoke first. Removing his hand from Jake's shoulder, he extended it. "The name's Derek Pendleton."

Jake hesitated an instant before accepting the handshake. "Jake Riley."

"Hey, bro, you're blocking my smooth moves with my lady," Cesar called as he and Eliana sashayed past. "Either get your groove on with Alex or get out of the way!" Cesar gave Alex a broad grin and a wink, and she couldn't resist grinning back.

"We'd better get off the floor," she said, leading the way through the dancing bodies.

When they reached the table, she turned and stumbled, finding both men close behind. Jake stood studying Derek while Derek looked questioningly at her.

She felt suddenly awkward, though she wasn't certain why. "I didn't see you come back in, Derek, or I'd have stopped dancing to introduce you," she said lamely.

Jake glanced back to Alex, his face impassive. "It's fine. Now we've met. Thanks for the dance, Alex. See you tomorrow." And he was gone.

She faced Derek, who looked confused and maybe a little angry. "Tomorrow? Who is that guy?"

"He's a...business associate," she said.

"You two looked like a lot more than business associates when I walked in," he grumbled.

Righteous anger bloomed inside her, and Derek must have noticed the thunderous change in her expression because he instantly backed down. "I'm sorry." He reached for her hands, squeezing them gently before planting a kiss on each one. "I didn't mean it. I hated interrupting our conversation like that, sweetheart, but like I said, it was an important call about a job." His voice held a whiny quality that grated on her. "Can we sit back down?" He indicated their table. "I want to know what you think about everything I shared."

Alex was a jumble of confused feelings. She needed time to think. She also wished Jake hadn't left so quickly, giving her no time to explain. She took a deep breath and returned her attention to Derek, who was looking at her with a hopeful expression. Looking him in the eye, she spoke the truth. "Derek, I do still love you."

He smiled triumphantly.

"But."

His smile slipped. "But what, Alex?"

"I need time to process all this." She pulled her hands from his grasp. "You betrayed me. And you hurt me more deeply than anybody in my life."

He dropped his head. "I know." His voice was a whisper. "I'm sorry, Alex. I'm so—"

She covered his mouth with her fingertips, regarding him steadily. "I just need time."

Derek sighed, resigned. "I understand. I've had weeks of therapy to figure all this out, to realize how messed up I was and how much you mean to me." He gave her one of his most devastating smiles. "I suppose I can give you the time to realize I really am the right man for you."

"Need anything else?" The waitress was at their table again, twirling the end of her ponytail, her attention focused on Derek.

Derek gave her one of his mega-watt smiles. "No, I think we're good."

CHAPTER 26

It was nearly midnight when Alex pulled into the cabin driveway and she groaned to see J.P.'s car was there. Emotionally drained, she climbed the front steps hoping she could gracefully excuse herself from their company. She wanted to be alone.

The main room lights were low, and over her grandmother's ancient stereo, the Flamingos softly crooned, "I Only Have Eyes For You." In the dim lighting, she spotted Tilly and J.P. snuggled close together on the loveseat.

Tilly sat up straight at the sight of Alex, her eyes bright. "Hello, dear!"

Alex took in her grandmother's buoyancy and J.P.'s even wider-than-usual grin and narrowed her eyes with suspicion. "What's going on?"

Now Tilly's smile looked as goofy as J.P.'s. The couple exchanged a look. Then Tilly turned back to Alex. "Come closer and we'll show you." Her grandmother was practically giddy. Very un-Tilly-like.

Alex frowned, but crossed the room to stand before them. She folded her arms. "Well?"

Tilly exchanged one more look with J.P., then pulled her left hand from his.

The diamond flashed in the low light and Alex gasped. She reached over to turn up the lamp's brightness and grabbed ahold of Tilly's wiggling fingers.

Alex dropped to the floor in front of the loveseat, still gripping Tilly's hand. "Is this what I think it is?" she managed to squeak.

"It is." Tilly smiled.

Alex tore her gaze from the glittering ring to peer into her grandmother's glowing face.

"Well, this is...this is...just awesome!" Alex said, pulling her grandmother into a bone-crushing hug. "I'm so happy for you guys!" She hugged the grinning J.P. as well. "I had no idea you guys were—well, this is just wonderful. Congratulations!" She shook her head.

"Thank you, dear. We're pretty pleased about it ourselves."

"I can barely describe how happy this little lady has made me," J.P. added, blue eyes focused on Tilly.

"No happier than you've made me." Tilly smiled back at him.

"So, what now? Have you selected a date yet?" Alex asked.

Tilly laughed, a light girlish sound. "We're still adjusting to the idea of being engaged at the moment. But probably sometime this fall."

"So soon?" Alex said.

"At our age, Miss Artist, you don't put off till tomorrow what you can do today!" J.P. said, wheezing a little as Tilly elbowed him in the ribs.

Alex smiled and rose. "Well, I suppose I should leave you two lovebirds alone now. You can go back to, er, whatever you were doing before I interrupted."

J.P. laughed as he also stood, extending a hand to Tilly. "No need to leave on my account, Miss Artist. I was just working up the will to get going myself. I've got an early morning historical society meeting tomorrow, anyway." He wrapped Tilly in his arms, kissing her full on the lips.

Alex looked away, uncomfortable, as he murmured softly to Tilly. As much as she liked J.P., it was strange seeing her grandmother in the arms of anyone besides Grandpa Joe. She went into the kitchen and made a lot of noise, filling the kettle with water and pulling out teacups.

"G'night, Alex." J.P. eventually called from the door.

"Bye, J.P."

Tilly closed the door behind him and leaned against it. "Am I a fool, Alex, or the luckiest lady on earth?" she said.

"I think the look on your face holds the answer to that question." Alex smiled.

Tilly glanced in the mirror beside the door to see shining eyes and flushed cheeks reflecting back. She turned back to Alex, grinning. "Oh, good, you're making tea. I'm too keyed up to try to sleep right now anyway."

Alex carried two steaming cups to the dining room table. The soothing fragrance of the vanilla and chamomile blend floated in the air.

"So," Alex said, settling into a chair opposite Tilly and taking a sip. "Details, please."

Tilly slowly swirled a teaspoon in her own cup. "Details, hmm...Well, if I'm being completely honest, I suspected something was up when J.P. told me our dinner reservations for tonight were at the most elegant restaurant within sixty miles." Tilly's sparkling eyes met hers. "We were having such a lovely time. You know, Alex, I haven't found anyone I could really talk to like this since, well, really since your grandfather." Her eyes grew misty. "Anyway, after dinner, the waitress came to take our dessert order. I confessed to being too full, and you should have seen the disappointed look on J.P.'s face." Tilly laughed. "Of course, I had no idea what he'd planned."

"What?"

She leaned forward confidingly. "J.P. insisted we at least look at the dessert selection. The waitress returned with the dessert tray, and right there between the chocolate mousse and a raspberry torte sat a tiny velvet box. The waitress described everything on the tray, and then pointed at the box saying, 'I believe Mr. Riley will describe this one.' J.P. lifted it from the tray, opened it, and got down on one knee."

Alex smiled, resting her chin on one palm.

"He asked me to marry him right there! I sat there in shocked silence for so long, he told me afterward, he thought I was trying to find the words to let him down easy."

Alex tried to imagine big, confident J.P. ever feeling insecure about anything.

"I hadn't realized it at the time, but the entire restaurant had become aware of what was happening. The moment I said, 'yes,' the wandering violinists came over to our table to play and everyone applauded. It couldn't have been more perfect." A tear slid down Tilly's cheek and she dabbed it with her napkin.

Alex reached over to squeeze her hand. "You seem really happy, Grandma."

"I am, sweetheart! I never thought there would be anybody for me after your grandfather. We were so happy together, and he was a wonderful husband. But as unbelievable as it is, I love J.P. too, just...differently." She shook her head slightly. "Maybe it's because I'm different now, too."

"I'll say!" Alex chuckled.

Tilly peered at her over the top of her teacup. "You think so, too?"

"Puh-leeeze, Grandma! The way you've gone about pursuing your art. How you've become so vocal at meetings, speaking your opinion with such confidence. Not to mention learning to drive."

"Oh, I forgot to tell you!" Her grandmother went to get her purse and brought it back to the table. She pulled out a folded sheet of pink paper and waved it in front of Alex. "My temporary license."

"Really?" Alex took the page and examined it.

"Really," Tilly said with pride.

"Congratulations *again*, Grandma!" Alex said, handing the paper back.

Tilly took a sip of tea, closed her eyes, and sighed. "This is just what I needed. Right now, I feel as if I'm a bundle of energy!"

Alex laughed. "No wonder!"

Tilly opened her eyes. "Okay, enough about me. What have you been up to tonight, dear? I was surprised to find you gone when J.P. brought me home. I thought you'd planned to work all evening."

Alex sighed, setting down her cup. She relayed the story of Derek's phone call and her subsequent encounter with him, as well as Jake, at the Boathouse. "I feel completely confused now," she said, massaging her temples. "I've been angry with Derek for so long. But when he apologized tonight and asked for my forgiveness...he seemed so sincere. He seemed to truly understand he has a problem and is committed to fixing it."

They sipped their tea in silence for a time, then Tilly set down her cup and looked at Alex. "You know, dear, you sort of breezed over the part with Jake. What exactly happened between you two that made Derek react the way he did?"

Alex squirmed in her chair. "There's really not much to tell. Derek took a phone call and while he was outside, Jake came over and asked me to dance. So we danced. Derek walked in, saw us dancing, and seemed jealous about it, which is ridiculous, to say the least," she added, eyes snapping.

Tilly studied Alex's face in the pale glow of the overhead chandelier. "Has Derek been jealous in the past when he's witnessed you in the company of other men?"

Alex's brows drew together. "I don't think so."

"Would you say Derek is an intelligent man?"

Alex was confused by the question. "Of course."

"And perceptive, at least as far as reading people?"

"Absolutely." Alex smiled wryly. "That's one reason he was so good at his job."

"So once again, I ask you to consider, *why* do you think he responded to Jake the way he did?"

"I don't know." Alex grew defensive. "We were just dancing."

Tilly gave Alex a knowing smile, and Alex blushed.

"Mhm." Tilly nodded with satisfaction, lifting her cup again and taking a sip. "I thought so."

"What?" Alex cried.

Tilly put her cup down again with a clink "I'm sure Derek saw what everybody who's been in the same room with you and Jake for any period of time has seen." She took Alex's hands in her own. "Darling, whether you want to hear this or not, it's quite clear that you and Jake have feelings for each other that go beyond simple friendship."

Alex snatched her hands back as if she'd been scalded. "That's not true!"

Her grandmother's face looked pained. "I don't understand why you won't let yourself be happy."

Alex surged from the table and ran into her bedroom, slamming the door shut behind her. She threw herself across the patterned quilt and lay there for a long while as her grandmother's words pinged around inside her head like a hummingbird, rushing here, flitting there.

Finally, she flopped onto her back. Tilly was wrong! Jake wasn't, could never be, more than a friend. He was a player. Cut from the same cloth as Derek. And yet, even as she acknowledged this, another part of her just as swiftly rejected it.

Moments with Jake began running like a video stream in her mind's eye. Jake holding doors for her. Helping her into her car. Comforting her as she shared her painful memories. His generosity, his kindness. And his eyes. Focused on her alone whenever they were together. Making her feel beautiful. Desirable. Treasured. And then there were his kisses...

But now, Derek was back. And he was a changed man.

Her insides twisted and she curled into a ball on her side, hugging her pillow hard against her.

She lay like that for hours, unaware of the passage of time as her thoughts churned. It was only when the darkness outside her window became edged with gold that she finally drifted into a restless sleep.

She dreamt she was walking through a lush forest and came upon a deep pool. She stepped into the dark water and immediately sank beneath its glistening depths. She struggled, trying to fight her way to the surface. But she lost track of which way was up. Confused, panicked, and suffocating, the darkness swirled around and through her, until finally, she stopped fighting and relaxed and let the current carry her away.

CHAPTER 27

A brilliant sunbeam angled across the bed, hitting Alex full in the face. Her eyes felt glued shut. Prying them open, she squinted toward the window. "Why didn't I close the stupid curtains last night," she muttered, moving away from the beam of light. She turned a bleary gaze to the bedside clock. Noon. Noon! She bolted upright and caught a glimpse of her face in the dresser mirror across the room. "Ugh!"

She'd slept in her clothes and her hair was a tangled mass, poking up at odd angles all over her head. Then the confusion from the night before came flooding back and she dropped backward onto her pillow with a groan.

There was a light tap at her door. "Alex?" Tilly said.

"Come in."

Tilly entered the room. "I'm sorry about how I behaved last night," she blurted out before Tilly could utter a word.

Tilly sat down and patted Alex's jean-clad leg. "Pish posh! I overstepped my bounds last night, sweetheart. It's I who should apologize."

"No, you shouldn't. I think I was just in sensory overload."

"I understand," Tilly said. "Between my engagement, your evening with Derek, and well...everything." She gave Alex a quick hug. "Let's start fresh. It's a new day." She rose and walked over to the mirror, smoothing her hair.

Alex flipped onto her stomach, watching Tilly's face in the reflection. "Do you and J.P. have plans today?"

"Yes." Her grandmother smiled. "We're going to start making wedding plans."

Outside, they could both hear the crunch of car tires on the driveway gravel. Tilly glanced at her watch. "He's early!"

"You seem to have an impatient fiancé," Alex said, yawning.

Tilly's smile broadened. "It appears I do."

"Tilly?" J.P.'s voice echoed seconds later from the front entrance doorway.

"Coming!" Tilly dropped a quick kiss on Alex's cheek. "I'm not sure when we'll be back, dear." She paused at the door. "Try to have a good day." Then she was gone.

Alex sighed. *Easier said than done.*

She felt somewhat refreshed after showering and eating breakfast. She carried her mug of coffee into the studio, taking fortifying swallows as she studied what she'd accomplished the day before. *Nothing like work to take your mind off your troubles,* she thought. And turning on her music, she was soon lost in her creative process.

She was immersed in painting a section of shoreline when her cell phone ring interrupted the thrumming base that had been playing. With a rush, she wondered if it was Jake, and wiping her hands on a rag, she picked it up. Derek's number glowed on the screen. She took a breath, steeling herself. "Hey."

"Hi, Alex. I missed you," his smooth voice purred into her ear.

She didn't know how to respond to that, but Derek continued. "Listen, it turns out I've got a second interview for that job tomorrow morning on the other side of the state. I'm going to have to take off in a few hours. I was wondering if I could see you before I left, maybe for coffee or something?" His voice held that same pleading note as the day before.

"Um...sure. Where were you thinking?"

"How about the Java Joint downtown?"

She agreed to meet him in half an hour. After hanging up, she changed from her paint-splattered work clothes to a pair of cutoffs and a clean white tank top. Her hair was still swept back into a clip and she wore no makeup. But she didn't care. She was no longer concerned about trying to impress Derek with what he'd lost.

She pulled into a parking space along the street and saw him waiting not far from the coffee shop entrance.

As she climbed from the car, she saw Derek's eyes widen in surprise. "What happened to Bessie?" he asked once she'd reached him.

"She suffered an unfortunate death," Alex said.

He leaned down to give her a kiss, but she angled her head so it ended up on her cheek instead of her lips.

Derek pretended not to mind, looping an arm casually across her shoulders.

"Well, it's a nice ride, Alex," he said admiringly. "You must be doing well with your art."

They walked toward the Java Joint, and she smoothly slid from beneath his arm at the door. "That's great news about your second interview," she said.

"Yeah!" He swung the door wide and walked through, holding it for Alex to follow behind. She couldn't help the mental contrast with Jake's old-fashioned manners.

"It's a really good company, bigger than the one I was with before. They handle mergers and acquisitions for a variety of businesses, not just restaurants. The downside, though, is there would be more travel." He kept up a constant chatter as they waited for their coffee orders to come up. He paid for them both, and Alex suggested they take a walk down to the waterfront marina.

Gulls swooped and circled, bawling overhead as they strolled along the walkways of the small park that bordered the deep water. Boats bobbed in the marina slips and vacationers lounged on benches or lay stretched out on the fragrant grass, enjoying the light breeze coming off the water. She and Derek wound past life-size bronze sculptures that punctuated the landscaped grounds, watching as children scampered in and out from among them. They finally reached a secluded spot overlooking the harbor and stopped to lean against a rail. Waves lapped below them and Alex drew strength from the sun's warmth. From where they stood, she could see the north end of the condominium project. She wondered if Jake was there working right now.

"So, I didn't get to ask you what you've been up to since, er, well, since we've been apart." Derek's voice broke into her thoughts.

That's a tactful way of putting it, Alex thought. But she told him about coming to help Tilly after she'd broken her arm and then about being brought into the Mural Society's project with Jake's company, pointing out the construction site.

Derek asked some superficial questions about it, but it was clear he had something else on his mind. Taking a final swallow of his coffee, he tossed his cup into a nearby trashcan and turned to face her, one arm resting on the rail. "Alex, have you thought about what I asked you?"

Alex felt his gaze upon her, but she continued looking out over the water. "I thought about it all night."

He seemed pleased with her answer and smiled. "So, we can make a fresh start then? We'll take it slow, Alex. I'll even—"

"No, Derek." She felt a stab of sympathy for him as she watched the smile fade from his lips. But she knew she needed to be straight with him. She may still be confused about Jake, but in all honesty, she now knew how she felt about Derek.

"But, Alex, why not? I told you, I'm getting help now. I've changed. I swear, I will never, ever hurt you like that again."

She took a deep, restorative breath and faced him. "I believe you."

He frowned. "Then why—"

"Because I've changed, too," she said simply. "After your betrayal, Derek, I was so angry. I hated you. I stopped painting. I stopped living." Despite the emotional context of her words, her voice was strong and clear. "Over the past several weeks, I've come to understand that the reason my anger ran so deep was partially because I was still in love with you." She sighed. "And yesterday, when I saw you, a part of me just wanted to take you back. To have things be how they used to be between us." She shook her head slowly. "But things will never be like they were."

"You're right, they won't. They'll be better!" Derek said, his eyes hot and intense. "Don't you see, Alex? We've *both* changed. I'm ready to commit to you and only you. I think I was just afraid—my parents, well, you know how it was. Their bitter divorce and my dad's philandering. They weren't exactly the best role models for me."

Derek started to say more, but she raised a hand to silence him. "Since I've been in Whispering Pines, I've done a lot of thinking. And growing. I love and care about you, Derek. I always will. But I'm not *in* love with you anymore." She turned to face him fully, tendrils of hair escaped from her clip, dancing across her face in the breeze. "I've finally begun to heal and it feels good."

As she stood looking at him, she felt no anger, only compassion. She wished she could ease his pain. But in her heart, she knew it had to be this way. It was time to say goodbye. "Derek," her gaze didn't waver. "My answer is no."

He didn't respond for a moment, just stared at her. Then, taking her by surprise, he grasped her upper arms and pulled her to him. "Please, Alex. Please give me another chance. I can't let you go." She shook her head, and his grip tightened, his upper lip curling. "It's because of *him*, isn't it?"

Alex blinked. "Who?"

"You know full well who." He pointed his chin in the direction of the construction site. "That Jake guy you were all cozy with last night."

"Jake? This has nothing to do with him," Alex said. "It has to do with me and what I want." She tried to wrench her arms from his vise-like grip, but he held firm. "Derek, you're hurting me."

"I asked around about him after you left last night," he said, ignoring her words. His voice rasped low and harsh. "He's no good for you, Alex. He'll only want one thing from you and it's the one thing you weren't even willing to give me, your fiancé." He spat out the last word. "Unless maybe you've changed your views in that area?" He pressed her back against the railing, trapping her body with his. Then he kissed her hard, the bitter taste of coffee was still on his lips. She twisted wildly, trying to get free, and her own coffee cup fell from her hand, spattering against the sidewalk. "Let go of me," she hissed, shoving both hands against his chest.

"Not until you admit what we have is worth saving," he said and crushed his mouth against hers once more.

They were far enough away from the other marina visitors that nobody noticed her struggling.

She wrenched her mouth from his. "Derek," she said, keeping her voice level in spite of the anger roiling inside her. "If you don't let go of me, in about two seconds, you're going to find yourself moaning in pain flat on the sidewalk."

She lifted her right foot, preparing to smash it onto his instep and follow it up with a knee jab to the place that hurts men most. But suddenly, he stumbled backward, and his grip on her arms released.

She blinked. Derek was lying at her feet on the sidewalk, moaning in pain.

Jake stood glaring down at him, legs braced wide, fists clenched. "I believe the lady asked you to let her go."

Derek sat up and a gush of blood flowed from his nose onto his white dress shirt and khakis. He immediately pinched his nose to staunch the flow and looked up. The nasal sound of his voice significantly reduced the impact of his next words. "What do you think you're doing?"

"I think I'm the guy who's gonna make sure you never lay a hand on her again."

"She's *my* fiancée!" Derek squeaked, stumbling to his feet.

Alex fished in the pocket of her shorts and pulled out a tissue. "No, Derek, I'm not."

Jake clearly outweighed Derek by a decent amount; his flexed biceps were visible beneath the short sleeves of his shirt. These observations were not lost on Derek either, Alex noted, as he took a step back from Jake before returning his gaze to her. "Alex, I—"

"Please go," she said, handing him the tissue.

He hesitated for a long moment. Then snatched it from her hand and strode from the park without another word.

She turned on Jake. "Hitting him wasn't necessary. I had it under control."

He looked down at her. "Not from my vantage point, angel. You looked like you could use a little backup. Were you seriously engaged to that guy?"

She picked up her coffee cup, which had become lodged against the base of the railing, and tossed it into the trashcan. "Yes, I was seriously engaged to that guy."

"Yoo-hooooo! Jakey?" They both turned and Alex saw the blond from the other day flash a dazzling smile at Jake, waving from the construction site. Even dressed in a T-shirt, jeans, and bright yellow construction hat, she managed to look incredible.

"Well," Alex said coldly. "Don't let me keep you from your...little friend." And turning on her heel, she marched off.

"Uh...you're welcome?" he called after her. She could hear the confusion and frustration in his voice, but she didn't care. She was still shaking from her encounter with Derek. And she was tired of her whole confusing relationship with Jake. She needed to go back to her original rule of no boys. Period.

CHAPTER 28

Alex found a secluded spot far removed from the other sunbathers and spread out her towel on the silky sand of the cove. She dropped her beach bag, book, and sunscreen on the corners to keep them from fluttering in the breeze. White clouds drifted lazily overhead. And beyond the cove, a sailboat tacked its way across the undulating waves of the lake, bright sail billowing.

She untied her pareo, dropping it onto the towel, and strode out into the water. Although the water in the sheltered cove was slightly warmer than that of the boundless Great Lake, when the initial chill of the water hit the bare skin of her abdomen, she sucked in her breath. To get used to the temperature quickly, she made a shallow dive beneath the surface.

Cutting through the open water, she emptied her mind of everything but the rhythm of swimming. Stroke, kick, stroke, breathe. Stroke, kick, stroke, breathe. She swam until she was breathless, arms and legs tingling with fatigue. She made another quick dive, smoothing her hair back from her face. Then, with a slow, easy breaststroke, she made her way back to shore.

Squeezing the excess water from the ends of her hair, she dripped her way back to her towel and dropped onto it, stretching out beneath the warmth of the late afternoon sun. Without opening her eyes, she stretched out her hand and patted around blindly in her bag until she located her sunglasses and jammed them onto her face. The heat permeated to her core and she willed herself to relax, letting the sound of children playing in the distance and the rhythm of lapping waves wash over her.

Derek's behavior had shocked her, leaving her with a sick feeling in the pit of her stomach. It had been a side of him she'd never seen. But then, there had been much about Derek she'd been blind to in her naïveté. And she realized belatedly that she'd rarely, if ever, seen him unable to charm his way into getting what he wanted.

By the time she'd reached home, her cell was ringing. Derek calling to apologize. Again. They'd ended up having a good talk. And although she heard the hopeful note in his voice toward the end of the conversation, Alex held firm. If she'd had any lingering doubts, she was certain now. It was over.

Jake Riley, however, was another matter. She realized it was time for her to be honest with herself. As her feelings for Derek had changed, she had to admit her feelings for Jake had changed as well. A smile tugged at the corner of her mouth as she recalled his knight-in-shining-armor act. The gallant protector. Totally uncalled for, but flattering just the same.

Now that she was in a calmer frame of mind, she realized the fury she'd directed toward him over the reappearance of the blond was the result of jealousy. Pure and simple. Between what her grandmother had said last night, and Derek's comments, she realized that, like it or not, her feelings for him did, in fact, run deeper than friendship. Much deeper. Spending so much time with him these past weeks, she'd come to appreciate the depth of his character, his sense of humor, his passion for his work, and even his chivalry. With a sense of impending doom, she finally admitted it to herself. She'd fallen for Jake Riley.

Great.

Now what was she supposed to do? She took several deep cleansing breaths. Nothing. That's what. *Let it go, Fontaine.*

She was tense again. She started working her way through a deep relaxation exercise when she suddenly felt the sun's warmth leave her face. She opened her eyes to find a large, hairy one hovering over her. She gave a shriek of surprise as Rex's wet nose bumped hers and he gave her a lick. She gently pushed at the dog's head to reveal Jake standing behind him. Sunshine blazed behind his body, giving him a flame-edged aura.

She recovered quickly. "Would you mind moving your dog, sir? He's blocking my rays."

Jake's handsome face broke into one of his dimpled grins as he spread a towel beside hers and settled onto it. He clicked his tongue once. Rex instantly returned to his side and lay down. "I never know what to expect with you," he said. "Your moods change quicker than Michigan's weather. I wasn't sure you'd even talk to me."

Alex rolled onto her side, supporting her head on her hand. "I'm sorry about how I treated you earlier," she said. "I shouldn't have been so ungrateful. I know you were only trying to help."

Jake stretched out, facing her. "I'm sorry too, Alex. I shouldn't have butted in and assumed you couldn't handle the situation. It's just that…Well, he was all over you! I remembered the stuff you'd said about him and I…" He lifted his shoulder. "I guess I just channeled my inner caveman without thinking."

She smiled, then dropped her gaze. "Jake, I have something to say and I don't want you to interrupt, okay?"

He nodded.

"Derek came to Whispering Pines because he wanted to ask my forgiveness for what he'd done to me. And he wanted us to start over."

Jake's expression hardened, but he didn't speak.

Alex plucked at the edge of her towel as she spoke. "I considered it. I mean, there's a lot to love about Derek. He's made a real effort to change and I know he genuinely cares for me." She lifted her gaze now, meeting Jake's eyes. "But I've changed, too. I'm not the same woman who came up here a month ago. Derek was my fiancé. He's not anymore."

Jake's dark eyes were steady on hers.

She cleared her throat, steeling herself for her next words. "I also wanted to apologize for my reaction to your…I mean, I won't be pestering you to hang out as much now that you're seeing someone.

"Alex, don't be, wait—what?" Jake looked confused.

"I'm just explaining I don't expect you to spend your free time with me now that you've got a girlfriend."

"What are you talking about?"

"Jake, please don't play innocent. I've seen her.

"Seen who?"

"The blond, Jake. The beautiful blond?"

He still looked confused.

She sighed, rolling her eyes. "The girl! Yellow hard hat. At the construction site today."

"The girl...ooooh!" Jake tipped back his head and laughed. "You mean Payton?"

Alex frowned. "I don't know her name, but—"

"Payton Majeski is *not* my girlfriend."

Alex snorted. "Well, you two looked awful cozy together the other day."

"When?"

Alex blushed. "I saw the two of you in town a couple of days ago. You were coming out of a restaurant together."

His features lit with understanding. "Payton is a close family friend. We grew up together, and she's like a sister to me. I'm hiring her to do a job on the site. She happens to be an expert mason specializing in historic brick and stonework restoration. She was trained by her father."

"She's a mason?" Alex said.

"You thought we were dating?" Jake said at the same time.

Alex hoped the relief washing over her wasn't visible on her face. She lifted her chin. "I think it's a perfectly reasonable misunderstanding."

"Hmmm..."

"Hmmm, what?"

He smiled, lightly touching the end of her nose with his finger. "You were jealous," he said in a singsong voice.

"I was not!"

He continued humming the nah-nah-nah-boo-boo melody.

"Knock it off!"

He didn't.

Alex let out a huff of frustration and flopped onto her back again, readjusting her sunglasses with a jab of her finger. "I was only saying that if you were involved with someone I'd understand. That's all I was saying."

A shadow passed over her closed lids and she opened them to find it was Jake's face hovering over hers this time. "If I was going to get involved with anybody right now, it would be with you, Alexandra Fontaine." He spoke so softly, his words were nearly carried off in the gentle wind. But Alex heard them. And they hung on the air between them like a tangible third party. She lifted her sunglasses, meeting the intensity of his gaze. And with their eyes still locked, Jake bent his head closer. She stopped breathing. He hesitated.

"If you're thinking about telling me to step off, now would probably be the time."

She said nothing and in less than a heartbeat, his mouth was on hers.

Like the feel of a cool wave on sun-heated skin, he took her breath away. His lips moved in a sweet dance over hers, and wave upon wave of pent-up desire washed over her. This time, she just went with it. Slipping her fingers into his soft hair, she pulled him closer. The rustle of wind in the dune grass, the rhythmic sound of gently breaking waves, all formed a blissful backdrop as she drowned in a symphony of sensation.

Moments later, he shuddered and drew back, resting his forehead against hers. "I have a confession, angel," he whispered. "Believe it or not, I had no intention of doing that."

"Neither did I," she breathed and paused a beat. "But we can do it again if you want."

He made an exasperated sound and squinted down at her. "Alex, you are anything but predictable. Not that I'm opposed to your suggestion, but why now all of a sudden?"

Her arms were still looped around his neck and she lifted her head, nipping gently at his lower lip, tasting him. He groaned, and a moment later, they were at it again until, breathless for the second time, they were forced to come up for air.

This time, though, he disentangled himself from her arms and scooted back onto his own towel. "Stop distracting me. If you don't cut it out, I'm going to forget my own name in a minute."

Alex laughed.

"You didn't answer my question."

She stopped smiling, her expression turning serious. "Tilly said something to me last night, and then Derek accused me of the same thing today. I was angry with them both, and I denied it. But I've been doing a lot of thinking and..." She trailed off, but he remained silent, waiting for her to continue.

She looked down, tracing random patterns in the sand between them. "The more I thought about it, the more I realized maybe it's been true all along, and I was just denying my feelings. A sort of self-protective mechanism because of what I'd gone through with Derek."

She peeked up at him, but he still waited expectantly. She sighed. "Oh, for crying out loud. I *like* you, Jake Riley. As in more-than-just-a-friend kind of like."

He didn't speak or move. He seemed frozen.

She continued. "I tried so hard to push you away at first. But over the past weeks, I feel we've become good friends. And um," she pressed on, despite the hot blush now staining her cheeks, "I think I'm ready to move beyond friendship with you...if you are," she added hastily, feeling suddenly insecure.

Was she being overly presumptuous? Too forward? Maybe she'd freaked him out.

She suddenly found herself in another full-blown lip lock. Moments later, his lips left hers to trail kisses across her jaw. His warm breath tickled, making her shiver as he whispered, "Alex, I don't think it's any secret I've been interested in being more than friends from the moment I first saw you walking up the beach and sent Rex over to introduce us."

Her mouth fell open. "Rex! You, you did that on purpose?" She turned an accusing look on the dog, who thumped his tail happily on the sand at the mention of his name.

Jake wore a smug grin. "One of my more suave moves, don't you think? *Oomph!*" He winced as she sucker-punched him in the abs.

"I can't believe you did that!"

"Why wouldn't you believe it, Alex? You're beautiful and interesting and..."

She pressed her fingertips to his lips to stop the embarrassing flow of words, but he only grasped them and kissed them as well.

She cleared her throat. "Just so we're clear, Jake..." She struggled for the right words. "This is...I mean I know neither of us is interested in anything long-term or permanent, right? No strings?"

"No strings. Great. Whatever you say, angel," he said as his lips returned to hers. And for a little while, she forgot her own name.

Later, Alex reveled in the feel of his arms around her as she snuggled back against him to watch the sunset. She knew this arrangement of theirs would require some mental adjustments on her part. But she had to admit it was a relief to finally acknowledge her feelings about him. And to have her feelings returned was beyond exhilarating. But, she reminded herself sternly, this was just going to be an ordinary, casual dating situation. She was always so intense about everything, like her relationship with Derek. This would be a good experience for her. A light, fun summer romance. She could do this.

CHAPTER 29

"Hey there, Tilly!" Zoe called over the music blaring in the studio. Alex turned to see her grandmother in the doorway. She reached and turned down the volume. "Are you joining us, Grandma?"

Tilly had begun creating her pottery again, and the three of them were often in the studio working together. Tilly's latest creations lined the shelves.

"Not right now," she said. "I'm just checking in on you two before Gretchen and Margot arrive for a Mural Society meeting." She walked over to examine Zoe's canvas. "I like the way you've worked the background colors on that."

Zoe looked pleased. "Thanks again for letting me work here with you both. I'm learning so much!"

Tilly patted her shoulder. "It's a pleasure having you, dear. Between the three of us, we have a regular artist's studio. Oh, and congratulations! Alex told me about your acceptance letter."

Zoe grinned. "Yup. I'm officially enrolled at the Detroit Center for Creative Studies." She indicated the canvas she was working on. "This gig I got from Jake's friend will help cover a few of my first semester expenses."

Alex nodded. "Just keep marketing yourself. You'll be amazed at how much you can earn during the summers and breaks."

"Why isn't the tea ready?" Gretchen's grumpy voice came from the doorway Tilly had just vacated. She bustled into the room with Margot close behind, her beetle-black eyes darting around, missing nothing.

"Who're you?" she asked bluntly, looking at Zoe.

Zoe put down her brush and extended her hand. "I'm Zoe Forester."

"Do you always look this weird?"

Alex bit her lip to keep from laughing. Zoe wore her usual black. Alex was amazed the girl didn't melt in the summer heat. Her spiky black hair was pulled into a ponytail on top of her head, and she sported a lime green streak in addition to her usual blue one. Her jewelry was minimalist today, though, only one eyebrow ring and an industrial in her left ear.

"Gretchen!" Margot looked mortified as usual by her friend's tactless comments.

She stepped in front of Gretchen and shook Zoe's hand. "I'm Margot Reardon and this is Gretchen Sinclair. That's a pretty scene you're painting." She fluttered a hand in the direction of the canvas. "You're obviously an artist as well."

"Thank you," Zoe said. "One day, I hope to be—"

Alex cleared her throat.

"I mean, yes. Yes, I am. It's nice meeting you, Ms. Reardon, and you too, Ms. Sinclair."

Gretchen had wandered over to the panel Alex was working on. "How's our project coming?"

"Pretty well, I think," Alex said. "The first two panels are finished." She indicated them leaning up against one studio wall. "And I'm hoping to have this one done by the end of the week."

"Nice work," Gretchen grunted.

"I'm surprised she's accomplished so much, considering how little time she's spent in the studio lately," Zoe said with a sideways glance.

"Oh, are you having trouble with your muse again, dear?" Margot asked solicitously.

"I don't believe that's the issue," Tilly smiled. "She's just been busy with...other things."

"Other things!" Zoe barked a laugh. "I'd be spending less time in here, too, if I had a hottie like Jake panting after me."

Alex felt her face flush. "Jake is *not* panting after me."

Gretchen's sharp eyes honed in on Alex's face. "What's this? You finally snagged Jake?

Alex picked up her paintbrush and sniffed. "It's nothing serious."

Gretchen smirked. "Right."

Just then, the sound of riffing guitar music filled the quiet room.

"Speak of the devil," Zoe giggled.

Alex pulled out her phone and glanced at the screen. "Excuse me a moment," she said and swept from the studio, leaving Gretchen cackling in her wake.

She waited until she was all the way into the main room before answering. "Hey!"

"Hey, yourself. You busy tonight?"

"Well," she smiled into the phone, "I was thinking about meeting up with this guy I've been seeing, but he hasn't called to ask me out yet."

"He doesn't know about us, does he?"

"No way! I'm keeping us on the down low."

"I can't believe Miss Not-Interested is dating Jake Riley!" Gretchen crowed, coming into the room followed by Tilly and Margot.

"Who's that?" Jake asked.

"Nobody. Look, are you asking me out for tonight or what?"

She could hear papers rustling in the background. "Yes, ma'am, I am. I've got a little more to finish up here. Can I pick you up around seven?"

"Terrific." She disconnected and sidled past the women as they set up their tea, cookies, and paperwork on the dining room table.

"Have fun on your hot date tonight, missy!" Gretchen called after her.

"I'm sure I will," Alex shot back.

"That's it, I'm done." Jake pushed back in his chair. "I can't fit in another bite."

Alex sipped her wine, smiling at him over the rim of the glass. "Maybe eating your entire dessert, then finishing the rest of mine might explain that."

"Hey," Jake feigned a wounded look, "it's important not to waste food. There are children starving in other countries."

Alex propped her elbows on the table, resting her chin in her hands. "And how exactly does stuffing yourself with triple chocolate mousse pie help those children?"

"Uh...no idea," Jake said. "But my mother used to say that a lot."

"Everybody's mother used to say that a lot."

Jake laughed and Alex thrilled at the sound. She loved the way his dark eyes crinkled at the corners and his dimples creased his cheeks when he smiled. She wished she could snuggle up beside him right now and kiss those dimples. Then maybe move onto that sensitive spot just beneath his ear. She especially loved how his breath caught when she kissed him there. And then...

"Ready?" He broke into her thoughts, and feeling guilty, she bent to retrieve her purse.

They left the restaurant and strolled past the closed shop windows, pausing now and then to peer at displays that caught their attention.

"This glassware is fabulous," Alex said, stopping in front of the Fire & Ice art boutique. She cupped her hands around her eyes and peered through the window into the darkened room.

"What's fabulous about it?" Jake said, sliding his arms around her waist from behind and resting his chin on her shoulder.

"Well, for starters, the color combinations the artist chose are so striking," she said. "And I love the freeform shape of the designs. For example, look at the shape of..."

She became distracted because Jake had brushed her hair aside and was busy placing soft, nibbling kisses on the side of her neck.

"The shape?"

"Yes, it's...freeform...and..."

"And?" he prompted. He blew lightly on the now moist skin, and she shivered, heat racing to her core.

"Um..."

He'd worked his way to her ear, where he was now making creative use of the tip of his tongue.

Her knees went weak and she had absolutely no idea what he'd just asked or she'd been about to say.

"You know what?" He released her ear, spinning her around to face him. "Sometimes I wonder if you really know anything about art at all?"

"What?" she said, still dazed.

"You can't even explain what's so special about a few simple pieces of glass."

"Oooh!" She lifted her hands, intending to shove him hard, but he grasped both wrists and pinioned them. Before she could speak, his lips were on hers. But just as their kiss started to heat up, a sound broke through her consciousness.

"Jake? Alex? Is that you?"

Still clinging together, they turned their heads slightly to see Keith Markham staring at them with a mixture of shock, amusement, and something Alex couldn't quite define.

"I thought it was you," Keith said, shaking his head.

He wasn't dressed in his customary suit and tie, and Alex nearly hadn't recognized him. He looked relaxed in a navy blue golf shirt and khakis. An older woman, whom Alex didn't recognize, stood beside him, her slender hand tucked into the crook of Keith's elbow.

"This is my mother, Elaine," Keith said, looking down at the woman and patting her hand. "Mom, this is Jake Riley, the man I work for." He spoke to her in a soft, pronounced manner. "And this is Alex Fontaine, his...girlfriend?" Jake grinned while Alex blushed.

Elaine blinked several times at Jake's proffered hand before finally accepting his handshake, then Alex's. Alex noted the slack grip and smooth skin of Elaine's hand. She was an elegant woman, her blue dress and white cardigan neatly fitting her delicate frame. Her silver hair was cut short in a wavy bob. The fine lines around her eyes and mouth were barely visible as she smiled at them, eyes gliding between their faces with an almost childlike wonder.

"I didn't know you two were dating." Keith smirked.

"It's a relatively new development," Jake said, throwing an arm around Alex's shoulders. "So, what are your plans on this lovely evening, sir?"

Keith glanced affectionately back at his mother. "Took my girl out for dinner at her favorite restaurant," he said.

Elaine beamed up at him.

"I didn't realize you had family nearby." Jake turned toward Elaine. "Do you live in town?"

Elaine didn't respond, her gaze still intent on Keith's face.

"She's a resident of Shady Acres," Keith said, looking back at Jake. "She's lived there for the past five years or so," he said.

Alex had heard Tilly and her friends discussing Shady Acres in the past. She knew her grandmother regularly volunteered there with a church committee. The skilled nursing facility specialized in treating patients with dementia and Alzheimer's.

"Mom's lived near Whispering Pines most of her life, though. When she was first, er, diagnosed, I tried getting her to move closer to me in Grand Rapids. But she prefers small towns." He shrugged. "That's one reason working on the condo project has been nice. I've gotten to see a lot more of her since I'm in town so often."

The two men lapsed into conversation about work issues, and Elaine seemed content to stand patiently beside Keith.

After several moments, Keith looked down at his watch. "It's getting late, I'd better get mom back." He looked at Elaine and smiled. "I wouldn't want to get in trouble for having you out past curfew." Elaine didn't speak but simply smiled back at him.

They said their farewells and Keith turned to go, then turned back, hesitating. "Hey, Farley was released this afternoon. I figured you should know."

Jake frowned. "How'd he manage that?"

Keith shrugged. "Must have come up with the bond somehow, I guess."

Jake stared thoughtfully into space as Keith and his mother walked away.

"Hellooo?" Alex waved a hand in front of his nose.

He looked down at her, frown fading. "Sorry! Let's go walk down by the lake."

At the end of Main Street, they removed their shoes and crossed the soft sand to stroll alongside the water's edge, letting the gentle waves lap at their feet.

Although there were still tourists around, the massive Fourth of July crowds had diminished. This evening, there were only a handful of people on the beach. Jake helped Alex up onto the breakwall that led to the lighthouse. Waves foamed against its steep sides as they walked along it, arms looped around each other's waists.

The sky bloomed a deep rose. The borders of the few remaining clouds flamed in the twilight, casting their blue-gray centers into deeper shadow. A trail of gold danced atop the cresting waves in a path that led from the setting sun. Their conversation flowed easily and Alex felt like the lake itself, suffused with light and peace. Not for the first time since meeting Jake, she acknowledged the joy he ignited within her. But this time, she allowed herself to bask in the warm glow it generated.

They skirted the lighthouse and came to a halt at the end of the breakwall. The pungent breeze was stronger here, whipping about them as they faced the red-gold ball that now hung just above the water's surface. "Listen," he whispered as it began its inexorable slide beneath the horizon, "and you'll hear the hiss."

She turned her face to him then and Jake kissed her tenderly. With the breathtaking Lake Michigan sunset as their backdrop, at that moment, Alex doubted Heaven could ever be sweeter.

She turned back to watch the sunset and forced herself to silently repeat the mantra that now rang hollow in her mind. But she'd been saying it each day since they'd started this no-strings-attached summer romance.

I will not fall in love. I will not fall in love. I will not fall in love...

CHAPTER 30

Alex felt boneless as she reclined in the passenger seat. Soft night air rushed through the truck's open windows as they sailed over the back roads toward Tilly's home. She didn't even mind the smooth jazz rolling from Jake's speakers. It only served to enhance her mellow mood.

He'd offered to switch the station. "Don't bother," she said. "As scary as it sounds, I think I'm starting to like this stuff."

He grinned over at her, and her heart flipped in her chest. With the fading light behind him, he looked like a dark angel.

They pulled into Tilly's driveway. The front porch light was on, but the house was dark inside.

"Looks like the lovebirds are still out," Jake said.

They walked inside and Alex started flipping on lights. She paused at the dining room table, picking up a piece of paper that lay on it.

"Hmm..."

"What?" Jake came to peer over her shoulder and she immediately flipped the page over, hiding it from his view.

"Was that my name on there? What is it?" He made a grab for it and she slipped past him to the other side of the table.

"Nothing."

"C'mon, Alex. Give it."

"I don't think so."

His hand shot across the table in an attempt to snatch it from her grasp. But she only laughed and held it away.

He circled left, and Alex mirrored his movements. "Look, it's nothing to concern yourself about," she said soothingly. "If they'd wanted you to know what they were doing, they would have told you."

Jake frowned. "What do you mean? What are they doing? They'd better not be doing anything!" He leaped to the right and Alex scurried in the opposite direction.

"As a matter of fact," she tapped her chin thoughtfully with the page, "I'm pretty sure they'd want me to destroy this evidence now that I've read it."

"Fontaine." Jake growled.

She tore off one corner, taunting him with it.

Like a striking snake, he dove across the table. She shrieked and darted away, racing into the great room, laughing.

"I wonder if it's okay to burn paper in a gas fireplace?" she mused aloud.

Jake was across from her again, but now the sofa stood between them.

She reached blindly behind her for the switch that powered the fireplace. Not finding it, she flicked her eyes to the side for just an instant, and without hesitation, Jake leaped over the sofa. He lifted her into the air and tossed her onto it. An instant later, he landed on top of her in a neat tackle, tickling her mercilessly.

She squirmed, giggling beneath him, "Cut it out! I can't breathe!"

"You wouldn't be able to talk if you couldn't breathe," he said practically, clearly enjoying himself as his fingertips dug into the sensitive area beneath her ribcage.

"Please!" She laughed, trying to simultaneously wriggle free and keep the paper away from him.

He stopped tickling her, but his body still pinned her against the cushions. "Will you give me the note?"

His face was close and she could see the playful twinkle in his eyes.

"No."

He tickled her with both hands now, and she writhed, helpless beneath a fresh spasm of giggles.

"Okay, okay!" she shouted, shoving the now crumpled paper into his chest. "Take it!"

He snatched the page but didn't release her as he read it.

"One dozen eggs, one-quart fat-free milk, three cans peaches, chamomile tea..." He looked blank. "A grocery list?"

Alex's laughter burst forth and he tossed it aside, tickling her again.

"Seriously, don't! My sides are starting to hurt," she wailed.

Jake immediately stopped. "Well, I wouldn't want to hurt you," he said, his voice husky as he looked down at her.

Her breath hitched.

He dipped his head then and teased the soft swell of her lips with the tip of his tongue, gently persuading until they parted. She melted against him from the inside out. Fingers twined into his soft curls and she drifted along the pulsing rush caused by Jake's touch, his fragrance, the heady feel of him. She no longer fought the emotions that arose in her, but let the love and passion she felt for him speak through each kiss, every caress.

He scorched a path of kisses over her eyes, her cheeks, nipping gently at her earlobe, as she trembled beneath him.

"I've never known anybody like you, Alex," he murmured against her neck. He pulled back to look at her. "You drive me crazy. You're funny and talented and sweet, and I—"

"I love you." The words came forth without conscious thought. At first, she hadn't even realized she'd spoken them aloud.

But she had. And now, Jake seemed frozen in place.

He was still gazing down at her, but the heat had gone from his eyes like a snuffed flame. They were now a flat, obsidian black. Remote.

"Jake?" Alex's voice sounded high and strained to her ears. She felt a flush rise in her cheeks. She couldn't believe what she'd just said. There was a part of her that was relieved to have finally confessed the feelings that had been building in her for weeks now. But, on another level, she knew she'd just made a fatal error.

Jake drew slowly away from her, as if she were a bomb about to explode. He sat up and turned away, elbows on his thighs, head in his hands.

"Jake?" she said again, scrambling up. Brushing the hair from her eyes, she watched him warily. "I—I'm sorry, I know we—"

He raised a palm to her, silencing her. A moment later, he was on his feet. "I've got to go."

Alex stared, lost for words.

He moved to the door without looking back.

Explanations, apologies, random excuses. A million different things to say flickered through her head and were summarily dismissed. She knew what they'd agreed. She knew how he felt about relationships. She'd felt the same way. In the beginning. But now he was leaving, and she had to say something.

"Please, Jake. Wait!" She took a step toward him, saw his back stiffen. "I need to...let me explain something." She balled her fists and, drawing in a shaky breath, she spoke quietly. "I was an emotional zombie for a long time after Derek and I broke up. I didn't think I'd ever feel..." She trailed off and started again. "Since meeting you, I've learned some things about myself. I finally realized I couldn't guard my heart forever. I couldn't avoid love out of fear over the potential pain it might someday cause. That's not living, Jake."

He kept his back to her. Unmoving.

She took a breath. "I only wanted you to know how I felt. I'm not asking you for anything in return." She knew she sounded defensive.

He reached for the door handle.

"And I'm not offering you anything," he growled, without looking at her. "Just like we agreed when we started this twisted game."

The screen door slammed shut behind him.

Alex was numb. A feeling of unreality washed over her. Why hadn't she kept her mouth shut? Things between them had been wonderful. It was as if she'd just awakened from the most amazing dream to find herself dropped into the middle of a horrible nightmare. It had changed so drastically, in an instant. Her head was still spinning.

It was only after she heard the sound of his truck peeling out of the driveway that the numbness disappeared and she collapsed to the floor, muffling anguished sobs into the pillow where she buried her face.

CHAPTER 31

Jake raced over the roads. He cursed and punched the radio off, jamming the accelerator down even harder. Why did she have to go and say that to him? She'd ruined everything! He cut around a corner with a jerk of the wheel and his tires spit gravel as he fishtailed.

Shooting forward again, he blew through a stop sign. The blare of another driver's horn snapped him into awareness. He skidded to a stop at the side of the road and, gripping the wheel with both hands, let his head fall against it.

What had happened? They'd been on the same page. In fact, the no-strings arrangement had been her idea in the first place. It's not like she hadn't had him pegged from the start. There wasn't a woman in town who didn't know Jake Riley was all about having a good time and as commitment-phobic as they come. It's not like he hid the fact.

He lifted his head to stare blindly into the darkness, his racing heartbeat beginning to slow. Now that he had some distance, he couldn't believe he'd just overreacted the way he had. He'd ended plenty of relationships in the past with his usual smooth finesse whenever he could tell it was getting too serious. What had evoked such a dramatic reaction this time?

If he was completely honest, he had to acknowledge that from the start there was something different about Alex. Something besides her beauty, intelligence, and wit. She'd intrigued him as no woman ever had. He was even willing to admit his connection with Alex was stronger than with any other woman he'd dated. But...love? He rubbed his hands roughly over his face. No. No way. Jake Riley lived by a code that had served him fine all these years. Love and commitment were two words that were not in his relationship vocabulary. He and Alex had had a good time. Now it was over.

His breathing was calm now. He did some neck and shoulder rolls to loosen the tension, then started the engine again, feeling in control of himself once more. He'd wait a couple of days and then he'd call her. Or talk to her in person to end it more...officially. He'd take the heat, let her rant at him some, get it out of her system. Because, if nothing else, Jake Riley was a gentleman.

Alex stared at her face in the bathroom mirror. Her eyes appeared sunken and lifeless, like two dark pits in her pale face. It was no surprise, of course, considering how horribly she'd slept. She still couldn't believe how wrong it had all gone with Jake the night before. Once she'd finally stopped crying, she'd lain in bed for hours, debating with herself. At first, she'd felt only regret for saying anything. But then, the more she thought about it, she knew it had been the right thing to do. It was the truth. And no matter how painful it was right now, it would've been wrong not to tell him.

She took a deep breath and exhaled, turning on the faucet and splashing her face with cold water. As she patted it dry, she suddenly heard her grandmother's voice call out, "Come in, Keith, come in!" followed by the murmur of their conversation.

Great. Alex sighed and rolled her eyes. She really didn't feel like being social right now. She'd already shared everything with her grandmother over breakfast that morning, and now she just wanted to be alone.

She waited a few more minutes but could tell they were still chatting. She sighed again. She had two choices. She could stay in here until he left—whenever that might be. Or, since there was no way to leave the bathroom without them seeing her, she'd have to at least greet him before escaping back into her room. She took a deep breath, opened the door, and stepped out into the main room just as she heard Tilly say, "I'm so sorry, Keith. But since Margo and Gretchen were already heading into town to run some errands, I just asked them to drop it off for Jake."

"No, no, it's fine," Keith said. "I'll just check with Jake when I get back to the site." His gaze fell on Alex. "Oh, hey, Alex!" he said.

"Hi, Keith," she replied. "Did your mother like the pottery you picked out for her?"

Tilly was getting such joy out of creating new ceramic pieces again. And she'd been delighted when Keith asked if he could purchase a piece as a gift for his mother. Tilly had refused to let him pay when he'd come by the day before to pick it up. And he'd been so grateful for her kindness.

"She did." He grinned at Alex. "She loves it. I put it in a safe spot directly across from her bed so she can see it every morning when she wakes up and each night before she goes to bed.

"Aww, that's sweet," Alex said.

Keith's answering smile faded a little, and a look of concern washed over his features as he looked at her. "Are you okay, Alex? You look a bit pale."

Alex waved a hand dismissively. "I'm fine, Keith. I just have some things on my mind. Some issues I need to work through."

"Ah." He nodded in understanding, then returned his attention to Tilly. "Well, I'm sorry to have bothered you. I still can't believe I left that paperwork here." He shook his head. "Hopefully, the ladies have already delivered it to Jake. Thanks again, Tilly."

"My pleasure," Tilly said warmly.

Keith turned to go and then hesitated, turning back. "Hey, Alex, whenever I'm feeling stressed or have a particularly thorny issue I'm working through, do you know what helps me most?"

"What?" Alex said, humoring him.

"A hike in the state park," he said, his eyes taking on a dreamy look. "Just being surrounded by all that beauty, breathing the fresh air, the exhilaration of climbing the dunes. I don't know, it just helps me feel like everything will be right." His gaze refocused on her and his face flushed a little. "Sorry, I'm probably overstepping. Just ignore me. It's not really any of my business."

"Actually, Keith, I love that idea," Alex said, then she looked at Tilly. "Will you be bored if I take off for a bit, Grandma?"

Tilly smiled softly at her. "I think not, dear. Just before Keith arrived I was working on an idea for a new piece. I'd like to start on it while the muse is hot."

"I've pestered both of you ladies enough," Keith said. "I need to get to the site." He bade them both farewell and hurried down the front steps to his car.

Alex headed back to her bedroom to change. She clung to Keith's suggestion like a lifeline, desperate for any distraction from the constant thoughts of Jake Riley plaguing her mind. Jake's angry words from the night before still echoed in her head like a relentless drumbeat. "I'm not offering you anything. Just like we agreed when we started this twisted game."

CHAPTER 32

The prolonged honking drew Jake's attention, and he broke off in his discussion with the electrician to see an old blue Impala pull up beside him. Gretchen was behind the wheel.

"Hi, Jake." Margot waved cheerily at him from the passenger seat.

"Hey, hot stuff." Gretchen hung out the window, her eyes roving over the site. "You're making some real progress here."

"It looks lovely," Margot said.

Jake smiled, amused. "Why, thank you, ladies. I appreciate the input. Did you come by for a tour?"

"Nope. Just dropping off something you accidentally left behind at Tilly's place last night." Gretchen waggled her brows, and Jake felt the hard ball he'd been carrying in his stomach all day drop with a sickening thud.

"Oh?"

"Yupper. Since Tilly knew Margot and I were driving into town, she asked us to deliver it. We put it on your desk in the trailer."

"Thanks."

"No problem. So, what's that guy doing over there?" Gretchen indicated a worker at the opposite end of the site.

"Gretchen, we need to get going," Margot said, pointing at the car clock. "We need to finish our errands before everything closes. Besides, I'm sure Jake has work to do."

"Nag, nag, nag." Gretchen winked at Jake, making him smile again. "Keep up the good work!" she called as they rolled out of the lot.

Later, Jake sat frowning over a report, his palm rasped over the fresh stubble on his chin. Construction prints and paperwork were strewn across the drafting table in front of him.

Payton's analysis of the mortar had led her to recommend that they shun cement in favor of a lime and sand mixture. She'd pointed out significant cracks where the brick had been previously patched. "Cement got really popular around the thirties," she'd explained. "Because it was harder and basically waterproof. Trouble is, the give-and-take balance of the brick and mortar was compromised. Cement is unyielding; it's actually ended up hurting your walls."

Her proposed mortar solution was ideal for the soft, porous nature of the older brick. Unfortunately, it set more slowly. So now he was going to have to make some adjustments to his timetable to accommodate it.

"Do you need me to submit this today, or is tomorrow all right?" Rita asked, indicating her computer screen. Rex lay snoring beside her chair, a curled-up ball of golden fur.

"Hmmm?" Jake didn't look up.

Rita sighed and turned to face him, pink bubble gum snapping. "Jake, what is your deal today? You came in late, and mentally you're still not here. This is the fourth time I've had to repeat a question."

He grunted.

"And no offense, sugar, but you look like you been chewed up and spit out. Aren't those the same clothes you had on yesterday?"

This time he did look at her, shooting her a baleful glare.

Rita stared right back, unintimidated. Her arms were crossed over a blue and silver sequined top, and her legs were crossed, too, one white stiletto bouncing up and down.

Jake broke eye contact first, turning to stack the papers on his desk into neat piles.

"Wanna talk about it?"

"Nope."

Rita's chair creaked as she rose from it, moving to stand beside him. Her ever-present Chanel No. 5 fragrance filled the space between them. She put a hand on his shoulder and squeezed. "C'mon, sugar. It can't be that bad."

He didn't say anything, so she sat down in a chair opposite him and propped her elbows on the edge of his worktable, cheek resting on one palm.

Jake's tough façade crumbled a bit as he looked at her. "I don't know why I'm so out of it today," he mumbled. "I guess I didn't sleep well last night."

"What was keeping you up?"

He shrugged.

She made a soft tsking sound and went over to the coffeemaker, filling two mugs with the steaming brew.

She handed one to Jake, then scooped generous spoonfuls of French vanilla dairy creamer into her own, stirring it vigorously with a swizzle stick. She sank down onto the old sofa cushions and patted the seat beside her.

Jake sighed. He knew she wouldn't let it go. Couldn't stand to see one of "her boys" having a tough time. So, he went to sit beside her.

"Why don't you start at the beginning?" She sipped her coffee, peering at him over the rim.

Jake leaned forward, elbows on his knees, mug cupped in his hands. He stared into it with unseeing eyes. Then, slowly, he shared the events from the night before. Once he started talking, the words flowed faster. He told her everything. And Rita never interrupted, just sipped her coffee, listening. When he finally finished, she didn't speak but studied him for a long moment in a most disconcerting way.

Finally, he couldn't take it anymore. "Well?"

"Well, what?"

"What disturbing thoughts are going on inside that fluffy red head of yours?"

Rita smiled and tapped a red lacquered fingernail against his temple. "I'm more interested in hearing the disturbing thoughts going on inside this head."

"I just told you—"

"Oh no you didn't, sugar. You just told me *what* happened. You haven't said a peep about how you feel about any of it." She gave him a pointed look.

"Geez, Rita, I dunno! I'm ticked off at Alex for ruining a perfectly good thing. I'm annoyed with myself for overreacting the way I did. I'm even more mad I didn't end it clean last night, so now I'm going to have to handle that and probably hurt her even more than I already have." He was getting himself worked up again.

"Mhm."

"That's helpful, Rita. Thanks for your incredible insight," Jake snapped.

"Shhh, I'm thinking."

The silence between them stretched until Jake thought he would explode. He considered just leaving when she finally spoke. "Jake, why did you have to end it?"

Jake's jaw fell open. "Hello? Did you listen to anything I just said? She told me she *loves* me, Rita! She actually used the 'L' word. With me. We were perfectly clear from the start of this thing that there were no strings. She can't just change the rules in the middle of the game like that. What was she thinking?"

"I suppose she was thinking that loving you qualified it as a game changer."

Jake shot her a withering look.

Rita wasn't fazed. She met his eyes and spoke carefully. "Jake, what makes you think you don't love her?"

Jake sputtered. "I think that's something I'd know, Rita! Besides, how many times have I told you I don't do 'love?'"

"'Bout a hundred thousand," Rita said mildly, then she leaned toward him. "Jake, you know I love you. But sometimes, you are dumber than a road lizard. Can't you see what's going on here?"

Jake frowned. "Please enlighten me."

"Sugar, whether you like it or not, you *are* in love."

Jake set his mug down hard. Hot coffee slopped over his hands and onto the floor. "You don't know anything, Rita McKay!"

Rita's normal attitude of calm evaporated. "I'll tell you what I do know." She jabbed a manicured finger at his chest. "I've never met anybody as bull-headed as you are, Jake Riley. I do not understand why you continue to—"

The shrill sound of the ringing office phone made them both jump.

Rita leaped from the sofa, snatching up the receiver.

"Riley Development Corporation, may I help you?" Her voice was smooth and professional as always, giving no sign of the tension from seconds before.

She frowned and plugged her open ear with her hand. "Sir, could you repeat that, please?"

Another pause.

"May I ask—" She cut off mid-sentence. "Just a moment, sir." She hit the hold button and, still frowning, looked at Jake. "I think he's asking for you?"

"Think? Who is it?"

Rita shrugged. "He wouldn't say, just wanted me to put 'the Riley kid' on the line." She frowned. "His voice sounded sort of weird, too."

Jake rose and took the phone. "Jake Riley here."

"Hello, Jakey-boy," the voice on the other end of the line twanged. It was deep with a strange mechanical quality.

The only person who called him that was J.P., but the voice clearly did not belong to his grandfather. "You're going to do something for me, Jakey-boy," the voice continued.

Jake was bewildered. "Pardon me, but who—"

"Shut up and listen!"

Caught off guard by the brusque order, Jake stopped talking in surprise.

"That's better. Now, I want you to ask your secretary if someone delivered a large envelope this morning. I'll wait."

Jake lifted his eyes to Rita's questioning gaze and said quietly, "Did somebody deliver a big envelope to you this morning?"

Rita looked confused, then her expression cleared. "She pulled a manila envelope from the top of her in-box and handed it to him. "Gretchen and Margot brought it," she whispered.

Jake cradled the phone against his cheek and took it from her. "Yeah, I've got it."

"Open it," said the voice.

"Why don't you just tell me what this is all about?"

"I said open it!"

Jake frowned. He examined the envelope carefully. Aside from his name typed on a white label stuck to the front, there were no marks or writing on it. It wasn't sealed so he peered inside, then slid out a thin sheaf of papers, laying them on top of Rita's desk. He scanned the first page, then flipped through the rest of the pages, sucking in his breath.

"What?" Rita hissed. "What is it?"

"It's a contract relinquishing all rights to the Riley Development Condominium project to another company," he said in an incredulous voice.

"You always were a bright boy, Riley," the mechanical voice mocked. "Your next steps are simple. Sign it, get it notarized, then wait for my call. You've got one hour."

"Look, buddy, I've got no idea who you are or what you think you're doing, but there's no way I'm signing this!"

He threw the pages on the desk in disgust and Rita snatched them up. Slipping on her glasses, she began reading the pages herself.

The mechanized voice chuckled. "I thought you'd react that way."

There was a rustling followed by some muffled voices coming from the receiver. Seconds later, he heard ragged breathing at the other end of the line.

"Say it," the voice hissed fiercely. There was a sharp cry, then...

"Jake?"

His gut clenched. "Alex? Where are you?"

"I can't, I'm not—" He could hear a sob choke her.

"Enough chit-chat." Mechanical voice was back. "You ever want to see your girlfriend alive again, Riley, you'll do exactly what I've just told you to do."

The room was spinning. Jake's grip tightened on the phone as he tried to comprehend what was happening.

"Oh, and I think it goes without saying, but if you involve any of your cop friends, or don't follow my instructions to the letter...she's dead. We clear, Jakey-boy?"

Jake couldn't think. Couldn't breathe.

"Are. We. Clear?" The low voice emphasized each word.

"Yeah...yeah. We're clear."

"One hour." The line disconnected.

Jake replaced the receiver in a daze.

"What's going on, Jake?" Rita touched his hand, still resting on the phone.

He was shaking as he quickly regathered the pages Rita had laid back down on her desk. "I've got to get these signed and notarized in one hour or..."

"Or what?"

"Or whoever that was on the phone is going to kill Alex."

CHAPTER 33

"Anybody home," a loud voice called from just outside the trailer entrance, and a moment later, J.P. and Tilly stepped inside. "We decided to stop in to see if anybody wanted to join us for dinner later?"

Jake and Rita, wearing identical dazed expressions, turned to the newcomers.

"What's the matter with you two?" J.P. asked, offering Tilly a chair. "You look like a couple of goldfish trapped in a fishbowl."

Jake opened his mouth, but finding no words, shoved the pages toward his grandfather.

J.P. took them and, squinting, held them at arm's length. "Forgot my reading glasses," he mumbled.

Tilly smiled and pulled her own floral-framed pair from her purse, handing them to him.

At any other time, Jake would have teased his grandfather mercilessly over the ridiculous effect he created, but the situation was too serious.

His grandfather finished quickly, then frowned at him over the top of the frames. "I don't understand?"

"You explain, Rita." Jake took the pages back and seated himself at her desk. "I have a phone call to make."

While Rita spoke quickly in a low voice, Jake picked up the phone and checked the caller ID log. "UNKOWN CALLER" glared back at him from the tiny screen. With a muffled oath, he dialed Keith Markham's cell phone.

Just before it went to voicemail, Keith came on the line. "Markham."

"Keith!"

"Jake?" he sounded surprised. "What's up?"

"Can you get over to the office right away? I've got a situation."

"I'm...I'm at Shady Acres with my mother."

"How far is Shady Acres from the site?"

"About an hour."

Jake groaned. "Never mind."

"Jake, what's going on?"

"I'll explain later." He disconnected and rose. "I thought I could have Keith come notarize this, but I'll have to run to the bank before it closes instead."

"Why aren't we calling the cops!" J.P. thundered, gunmetal brows crashing together.

"We can't." Jake snapped. "The kidnapper was clear, Pops. If we involve the police, he's going to—" He glanced sharply at Tilly's pale face.

Jake reached over to grip her icy hand. Blue-green eyes, so like Alex's, drilled into his. "I won't let anything happen to her," he said, his voice fierce with conviction.

"Wait," Rita said as he headed for the door. "Let me make a copy." She grabbed the pages from his hand and quickly ran them through the feeder before handing the originals back to him.

"Call Jon at the bank, will you, Rita? Let him know I'm coming," he said before racing down the steps.

"You got it!"

Twenty-eight minutes later, he was back, gripping the signed, stamped documents in his hand.

He'd barely registered what he was doing as he'd signed over everything to—to whom? He forced himself not to think about the fact that everything he'd fought for was going down the toilet. It didn't matter. He'd figure out how to undo it later. Right now, nothing mattered except getting Alex safely back.

J.P. paced the small space like a caged lion. Tilly, on the other hand, sat like a statue. Hands clasped tightly in her lap, translucent skin drawn taut over the bones of her face.

"Who could be doing this?" J.P. growled, dropping onto the sofa beside Tilly.

Jake shook his head. "I've been wracking my brain, but I have no idea. This hit from out of the blue."

He laid the contract down and leaned back against Rita's desk. "We've had our share of problems on this project, but nobody's shown any interest in challenging us for the property rights. It's been vacant for years. This makes no sense."

He raked a hand through his hair, then took over J.P.'s pacing. "I need to be doing something else to find Alex besides sitting here waiting for more of this psycho's orders."

"I have an idea," Rita said. She moved behind her desk and pulled her cell phone out of her purse. "Remember that guy I told you I met at the bar the other night?"

"Yeah?"

"Well, he works in the city clerk's office. I'll catch him before he leaves for the day. Have him check to see what he can find out about this Visionary Concepts Corporation named as the buyer on the contract."

"Excellent thinking, Rita!"

She punched in a phone number, and seconds later, "Hey, Cal, it's Rita. I've got a favor to ask…"

As she was finishing her conversation, the office phone jangled sharply, making them all jump.

Jake glanced at the caller ID and saw the UNKNOWN CALLER message. He picked up the phone, heart thudding in his chest. "Riley here."

"How'd it go, Jakey-boy? Does your girlfriend get to live?" the mechanical voice intoned.

Jake's stomach was a hard knot of tension as he spoke through gritted teeth, "Don't hurt her or I swear I'll—"

"Kill me? You watch too many movies, Riley," the voice chuckled. "Just answer the question."

"The contract is signed and notarized."

"Good." The speaker sounded pleased. "Here's what you're going to—"

"No," Jake cut in.

There was silence at the other end.

"Before I do anything else, I want to talk with Alex again. I want to make sure she's all right."

The silence stretched until Jake started to fear the worst.

"Jake?"

"Alex!" Relief surged through him at the sound of her voice. "Are you all right?"

He felt a gentle touch on his arm and glanced into Tilly's wide, terrified eyes staring fixedly at his face.

Jake tapped the speakerphone button so Alex's voice broadcasted through the small room.

"I'm fine. Just pissed off!"

Despite the situation, the spunk in her voice almost made him smile. "Has he...hurt you?" The ferocity of his own emotions overwhelmed him, and Jake found it difficult to get the words out.

"Not so much." Her voice quieted. "Not physically anyway. Mentally...I guess I'm no worse off than when you saw me yesterday."

Every eye in the room turned to Jake and he felt heat burn his face.

"In fact, this entire situation is like déjà vu from our second date."

Jake closed his eyes. "Alex, I—" A soft thud at the other end interrupted him.

"Time's up," the strange voice cut in. "Now you know she's fine, so pay attention. Put the contract back into the original envelope and seal it. Someone will contact you with further instructions on where to deliver it. If everything's copacetic, I'll release your little friend tomorrow."

"Tomorrow!" Jake shouted, losing control. "You can't keep her hostage all night!" Beside him, Tilly stifled a moan.

A grating chuckle filled Jake's ear. "Guess what, Riley? You're not in charge. I am. And I *will* hold her all night." There was a short hesitation before the voice added, "Don't worry, though, I'll keep her...very comfortable." The voice lingered over the last words in a way that made Jake's skin crawl. He wished he could reach through the phone and choke the life out of the stranger with his bare hands.

Without another word, the caller hung up.

Thoughts raced through Jake's head. Up until now, he'd assumed the freak was operating alone. But if someone else was going to contact them with the drop-off location, how many of them were there?

"What are we going to do?" Rita asked, her face etched with worry.

Jake punched the wall of the trailer. "I feel so helpless!"

"We all do, son," J.P. said, his voice displaying none of its usual confidence.

"At least Alex sounded feisty," Rita said.

"That's Alex for you." Tilly leaned back, holding her hands over her heart. "Even when she was a little girl, she had this core of strength about her."

That strength of spirit was one of the qualities Jake admired most in Alex. Once she made up her mind about something, there was little anyone could do to sway her from her path. He was sick at the thought of her trapped all night long, helpless against this psychotic person and who knew how many others.

"Strength is one thing, but wasn't it strange that in the middle of this crisis, Alex was blathering on about your dating life?" Rita shook her head.

Jake suddenly froze in his pacing.

"Jake?" Rita snapped her fingers in front of his eyes. "What's wrong?"

He blinked and focused on Rita's face. "That was strange. I mean, she's got to be terrified, right? Why would she start talking about our dates?"

"*Second* date," J.P. interjected.

Jake's expression cleared. "Of course! Our second date!"

"What about it?" Rita asked.

Jake ignored the question, moving quickly to the door, this time he clicked his tongue at Rex, who followed in his wake.

"Where are you going?" Tilly asked.

"To get Alex," he threw over his shoulder. "I know where she is."

CHAPTER 34

Jake barely registered the vibrant beginnings of a sunset as he shot up Lakeshore Drive. It was different but equally as breathtaking as the one he'd witnessed with Alex the evening before. He recalled how the colors of the twilight sky had reflected in the sheen of her hair. Then she'd turned, and the sky's beauty had been replaced with her dazzling smile. He clenched his jaw and his grip on the steering wheel tightened as he was forced to slow down through the resort area.

He wound his way past cyclists and dawdling sunbathers returning from a lazy day at the beach. When he finally made it past the last tourist, he cut around a slow-moving car and raced forward. He flew through the State Park entrance moments later, Alex's last words replaying in his head like the chorus of a song, "...déjà vu from our second date."

"Our second date was the hike in the woods this afternoon," he'd teased her on the first day they'd met.

Jake parked at the Beechwood Campground lot, his mind mentally mapping out the trails. He knew it would be fastest to take a shortcut straight uphill to the Lost Lake Trail. Rex bounded from the truck after him, and Jake fumbled with impatient fingers, fastening a leash to the dog's collar. Then they were running. His lungs were burning when they finally reached the northernmost point of the trail. He envisioned the stone shelter that stood at the intersection of the Lost Lake and Ridge Trails, the place he'd encountered Alex. Few hikers ever ventured to that isolated spot, certainly not at this time of day.

The trees cast long shadows over the dirt path, mingling with each other in the fading light. Rex's pink tongue lolled from the side of his mouth, but he strained at his leash, sensing Jake's urgency. Aside from a family of three making their way out of the woods at the start of the trail, they'd met nobody. Sweat soaked Jake's shirt and it clung to his back and ribs.

When the shelter was less than a quarter mile ahead, he slowed his pace. He didn't want his or Rex's heavy breathing to give any hint of their approach.

Up until now, he'd been driven by his single obsession to get to Alex. But now, he knew he needed a plan. What would he do once he found her? He had the element of surprise on his side but no weapon except the small Swiss Army knife he always carried. What if more than one person guarded her?

The jagged form of the stone structure loomed ahead, and he pulled Rex off the trail, squatting behind decaying tree trunks to consider his options. The rectangular shelter's opening faced the trail in the opposite direction. Three stone and mortar walls made up the sides and back of the structure, and there was a small open window at the rear, facing the direction he'd come. Jake squinted but saw no movement inside from his angle of view.

He tightened his hold on Rex's leash and, circling wide, he approached from the side, treading silently over sandy loam and leaf-strewn dirt. He stopped several yards away, issuing Rex a whispered command to stay. The dog obeyed.

Ducking low, Jake inched his way to the window. There was no sound except an occasional bird call and the whisper of the trees overhead. His small knife drawn, he reached the back of the shelter and held his breath, rising to peek through the lower corner of the window. He half-expected a shout. But his sudden appearance was met with only silence.

He rose higher, scanning the interior. There was a fireplace and a rough-hewn wooden bench. A dark form, unmoving, appeared to be curled up on the bench under a blanket.

He glanced at Rex, who sat panting softly but otherwise gave no indication of a presence other than their own. Jake slid around to the shelter's front and with one more quick look around, he stepped inside. Silently, he approached the bulky form on the bench. "Alex?" he touched the blanket with his fingertips.

No response.

He pressed more firmly and his fingers sank into the rough wool fabric. He snatched it up. Nothing was there. He frowned, confused. He'd been certain Alex was giving him a clue as to her whereabouts.

He threw the blanket aside in frustration, then picked it back up again, inhaling deeply. He knew that sweet, fresh fragrance anywhere. Alex.

Then he saw the blood.

Several dark red blotches stained the blanket.

Jake stepped outside, swiveling his head in all directions, but saw no one. He whistled for Rex, who galloped to his master. He pushed the blanket toward the dog's nose and gave the German command word for track. "*Such!* Where is she, boy? Where is she? Find Alex!"

Rex sniffed the blanket and then the ground, whining. Jake barely got his hands on the dog's leash before they were running up the Ridge Trail through the gradually darkening woods. After twenty minutes, the dog finally pulled him into an empty parking lot, different from the one where he'd parked.

Jake halted the dog's progress, breathing hard. "She's gone, isn't she?" He kicked a nearby tree trunk.

He was sure that Alex and her captor had left the woods, maybe even right after the phone call. There was little light from the rising moon seeping through the branches overhead as Jake stumbled over tree roots and ruts in the dirt, pulling Rex back the way they'd come.

Bats flitted overhead and the hum of the crickets was deafening by the time they reached Jake's truck. He pulled out a water bottle and drank huge swallows from it before filling the dog's water dish with the rest.

There was no mistaking that Alex had been in the shelter at some point. But where had she gone? Nothing made sense, and he had no more leads. Just as he put his key into the ignition, a rhythmic buzz filled the interior. His cell phone! He'd been in such a hurry to get to Alex, he'd left it behind without thinking. He snatched it up.

"Jake!" Rita shouted into his ear. "Where in blazes have you been?"

"I—"

"Never mind. Look, I've got to tell you what I found out," she said. "Cal called right after you left. He did some digging and found out who is behind that Visionary Concepts Corporation."

"Who?" Jake demanded.

"Elaine Weston."

"Is that name supposed to mean something to me?" Jake asked.

"Well, it didn't to me either. But when I mentioned the name in front of Tilly and J.P., Tilly recognized it because she volunteers at the place where this woman lives. She's a resident of Shady Acres Nursing Home."

"Shady Acres? That's where Keith's mother lives. I just met her a few days ago. In fact, her name is Elaine."

Rita made a choked sound. "In the information Cal gave me, Elaine Weston is named as owner, but there's a *Keith* Weston listed as the CEO."

No way was this a coincidence. In shock, Jake tried reasoning through these revelations. Keith Markham was Keith Weston? But why would Keith be using a different last name? And what was his mother's involvement? It didn't seem plausible that his friend and loyal attorney for the past three years could be behind this. There had to be something he was missing.

"Jake, you still there?" Rita's voice broke into his thoughts.

"Yes, I'm leaving now." He turned on the speakerphone and started the engine.

"There's more," Rita said.

"Keep talking." He pulled out of the lot.

"A kid showed up at the trailer with an envelope for you. It held a computer-generated satellite map. The city park is circled on it."

Jake felt his stomach drop. "A kid?"

"He was about fifteen. I drilled him with questions, but he didn't know anything. Just said some guy paid him $20 to deliver it. The guy was wearing a hat and sunglasses, and the kid couldn't tell me more than about how tall he was. Anyway, there's a note typed underneath the map. The signed contract is supposed to be placed under the park pavilion's garbage can by ten o'clock."

Jake's eyes flicked to his truck's clock. It was nine-fifty. He punched the steering wheel. "I'll be there as fast as I can!"

"Um..."

Jake shot through the park exit and up the empty dune-swept road. "Spit it out, Rita!"

She sighed. "J.P. and Tilly already left to deliver it."

"What?" Jake shouted. "Why didn't you stop them?"

"I tried, Jake!" she shouted back. "But you know J.P.! Tilly had worked herself into a frenzy thinking you wouldn't get back in time, which you didn't!" she added accusingly. "And when we couldn't get ahold of you, J.P. took matters into his own hands."

Jake swore under his breath.

"J.P. put on a Riley Development windbreaker and baseball cap to hide his face some. He figured you two are built enough alike that from a distance nobody would know the difference. And Jake..." She hesitated. "They're hiding nearby to see if they can catch whoever comes to pick it up."

Jake ground his teeth. That's all he needed! To have his grandfather and Tilly hurt on top of everything else.

He took a deep breath. "All right, Rita, here's what I need you to do. First, call J.P. Tell him what we suspect, and tell him to stop playing spy. Then try calling Keith."

"This late?"

"Yes. If he answers, tell him we're having some sort of an emergency situation with legal ramifications at the site, and we need him there right away. Be vague. I'll be there in five minutes."

Jake roared through the blackness toward town. It was clear the kidnapper's motivation was to take over the watchcase factory property. It was also clear that as psychotic as the guy sounded, he was intelligent. The kidnapping, the prepared contract, everything had been carefully orchestrated. But by the calculating mind of his lawyer and friend? His phone buzzed again.

"J.P. and Tilly are leaving the park, but they said nobody's shown up yet. And Keith didn't answer his..." Rita stopped speaking.

"What's wrong?"

"I just decided to do a quick online public records search for Elaine or Keith Weston. I found an address for Elaine Weston just outside of town."

"Great thinking, Rita!"

She continued. "It looks like it might be owned by the city now. According to the satellite view I'm looking at, there are a few acres with one small building on it."

"What's the address?"

He punched it into his telephone's map app as Rita dictated. "I'm going to drive out there," he said. "It may amount to nothing, but it beats sitting around waiting all night. While I'm doing that, call J.P. back. Since he's so anxious to help, maybe he and Tilly could drive by Keith's condo just to see if his car is there. Tell them to call me if it is. And tell him not to talk with Keith. Not until we have more facts."

"Okay."

They disconnected and he drove back through town. He hoped he wasn't wasting his time, but if there was any chance of finding Alex tonight, he'd take it.

Thoughts roiled inside his head. Why had Alex been moved from the shelter? Had it been her blood on that blanket? Had the psycho gotten angry and hurt her? As the phone's GPS directed him toward the outskirts of town, the nasty mechanized laugh and insinuating words about making Alex comfortable replayed in his mind. The thought of any harm coming to her froze his blood. Jake took deep breaths, calming the fear and rage that swept over him. He needed to keep a level head.

He was shocked at the power of his emotions regarding Alex. Of course, he'd be just as concerned over anyone he cared about being placed in such a frightening situation. Especially if that person was merely being used as a pawn due to their association with him.

Even as he reasoned with himself, the voice of his subconscious mocked him. For all his advice to Alex about overcoming her fears, in the end, it was she who'd been the brave one. She'd confessed her feelings for him without reservation, and without knowing whether those feelings would be returned. She'd told him she loved him. This incredible, talented, gorgeous woman loved him.

And what had he done? Run. Just as he always did. Too afraid to admit to her what he now knew was the truth.

He pressed the accelerator harder, traveling several miles along the dark pavement before the app directed him onto a dirt road, which soon became more path than road. Tall weeds brushed his windows as he bounced over the rough terrain, and he prayed he wouldn't get stuck.

He was nearing his destination, and as a precaution, he shut off the headlights. Squinting, he relied instead on the rising moonlight.

A shadowy mass grew from the landscape and Jake rolled to a stop. This had to be the building Rita saw. There were no cars or signs of life, but Rex whined softly beside him.

"I know it, boy." Jake scratched the dog behind one floppy ear. "Something doesn't feel right to me either."

He shut off the engine and got out, the dog trotting obediently at his side. As Jake drew closer to the darkened structure, he realized it was an old abandoned house. He could just make out the brick wall and porch, which wrapped around one side and the front of the home. Jake walked the perimeter. He suspected the sprawling old farmhouse might have been beautiful once. But now, the front porch sagged with rotting wood. The glass on the windows was gone leaving yawning black holes.

Moonlight bathed the landscape in silver as Jake paused, listening. Above the steady hum of innumerable crickets, the only sound came from a lone pine tree at the far side of the house, its needles scouring the brick in the light breeze. The structure seemed completely empty. Jake started to turn away when he heard a faint scrape. He could almost believe he'd imagined it, except that Rex's ears pricked, a low growl forming deep in his throat.

"Shhh...*Nein.*" Jake leaned close, speaking low into the dog's ear.

Not his imagination, then. Someone was here. Was it Alex? And if so, was anybody with her?

Jake moved soundlessly up the front steps, Rex still at his side.

They moved past the doorless entry into the shadowed darkness of a spacious interior. Squares of moonlight from each empty window frame created a pattern across the old wooden floor, now warped and rotted where rainwater had wreaked its damage over the years.

Stepping cautiously, Jake made it several feet into the room before there was a sudden creak above him to his left. Rex growled low, and an instant later, Jake instinctively shut his eyes as a blaze of light hit him full in the face.

A familiar voice mocked, "Well, hello there, Jakey-boy."

CHAPTER 35

Jake squinted, raising a hand to block the source of the light.

Keith Markham's ordinarily genial expression was absent, and his brown eyes were hard. He stood on the lower step of a staircase, one hand resting on the battery-powered construction lamp now flooding the room with light. In his other hand, he held a gun, which was now trained on Jake.

"Surprised?" Keith's tone was smug.

Jake's eyes adjusted, his gaze flicking over the room. A battered La-Z-Boy chair was shoved into one corner and a sunken sofa stood in the center of the room. There was a broken end table beside it. The walls were covered in the peeling remains of some type of floral wallpaper, which was now dark with splotches of mold. But no Alex. He looked back at Keith and, for the first time, noted deep, raw scratches down one side of his face.

"Where is she, Markham? Or should I say, Weston?"

Keith smiled, unperturbed. "Safe. For now." He descended the remaining steps. "I confess, I'm surprised you found me." He tilted his head, looking thoughtful. "But this works out even better for me."

Jake forced his voice to remain calm and repeated, "Where. Is. She?"

Keith's smile disappeared. "Perhaps you'd like to join her?" He swept a hand toward the staircase and, stepping back, indicated Jake should precede him. When Jake hesitated, he moved forward, jabbing the gun against Jake's ribs. "Upstairs, Jakey-boy. Now."

Puppet-like, Jake moved forward, and Rex padded out of the shadows to join the entourage.

Keith started but recovered quickly. "Not the dog."

"He stays with me," Jake said.

Keith's eyes narrowed for a moment, then he lifted one shoulder. "Suit yourself." He reached down and patted Rex's head.

Traitorously, Rex wagged his tail and nuzzled Keith's palm. Keith laughed, then stepped behind Jake. "Nice watchdog." Waving the gun in the direction of the steps, he said, "Move."

They filed up the rickety staircase. At the top, Rex turned left and trotted down the hallway while Keith shoved Jake in the same direction. He tripped but caught himself, noting the floors and walls here were in worse condition than the lower level.

Rex entered a room on the right at the end of the hall. A sudden sound came from inside as Jake reached the doorway.

"No point sitting in darkness anymore, I suppose," Keith said. Seconds later, light from another battery-powered lamp lit the room.

A stuffed rocker that may once have been yellow sat beneath the window and a rusted bed frame sagged beside the far wall. Alex sat in a battered wooden chair in the center of the room. Her ankles were bound, and her hands were tied behind her with rope. Rex's front paws were on her lap as he ecstatically greeted her.

As she avoided the dog's questing nose, Alex's dark hair hid her face and the sounds she made were strangely muffled. The moment Jake entered the room, Rex trotted back to him, tail wagging, as if to announce his discovery.

Freed from Rex's exuberant greeting, Alex flipped her glossy hair back, and Jake could see her clearly. His anger boiled as he rounded on Keith. "You gagged her!" He crossed the room in two strides, gently prying the duct tape from her mouth. He noted some dried blood on the tape and a faint blue tinge on Alex's jaw.

Keith made no move to stop him. Lounging against the doorframe, he smirked as he watched.

Alex spat several times, then licked her lips, pursing and releasing them to regain mobility. Rex circled three times, then lay at her feet, head on his paws, as if this were an ordinary visit. Jake moved behind her, intending to free her wrists next, but the soft click of the gun's safety being released arrested his progress.

"That's enough, Jakey-boy," Keith said in an easygoing tone. "Step away from your lady now, please."

Jake gritted his teeth and slowly obliged, eyes fixed on Alex. "Are you all right?"

She smiled wanly, her golden skin pale in the harsh light. "I've been better." Her voice was rough from lack of use and she cleared her throat. "I could use a glass of water."

Jake looked at Keith. "How about a glass of water for the innocent victim, you psychotic piece of—"

"Shut it, Riley!" Like a cloud passing over the sun, Keith's bemused expression turned murderous, his nostrils flaring. "You're not in charge here. I am." His voice rose, emphasizing the final two words in an echo of their earlier phone conversation. "I'm not giving her a drink or anything else until I get what I want." He crossed to the window and looked outside. "Which should be any time now." He looked back at Jake, eyes narrowed. "Since you apparently didn't follow my partner, how did you find me?"

"A hunch."

"You'd better not have involved the cops, Jake." Keith's tone was vicious. "If I catch even a hint you didn't obey my instructions to the letter, not only are you two dead, but J.P. will be joining you as well."

Alex sucked in her breath, but Jake studied Keith, trying to think. No matter what he thought he knew of Keith, the man standing before him was not mentally stable. And in his present agitated state, Jake had no doubt he was capable of anything. "Take it easy, Keith. I didn't call the cops," he soothed. "Pops was at the trailer when you called. And when your instructions arrived, I wasn't there. So Pops took it upon himself to deliver your package. You know how Pops is."

"I know exactly how your grandfather is, and he better not have screwed this up," Keith spat.

"He put it right where you told me to," Jake said. "I'm sure your partner will be here soon."

Keith pulled a cell phone from his pocket and looked at it. "The deadline was over an hour ago. He should be here by now." He shoved the phone back into the pocket of his jeans and swore, muttering, "I should never have used him."

Jake knew the only reason Keith hadn't killed them already was that his plan wasn't yet complete. Once he had the signed and notarized contract in his hands, however, they would become liabilities. They knew too much. Keith's mysterious partner could arrive at any moment. Jake needed to act.

Now. As Keith peered out the window, Jake took an experimental step toward him. The man's eyes were icy as they shot back toward Jake. "Get back where you were. And don't move again."

Jake lifted his hands in surrender and eased back a step.

Keith glanced at his phone again. Holding the gun steady on Jake, he punched a button and held it to his ear. Jake could hear the line ringing in the silent room. It went to voicemail. Keith swore again and disconnected.

Jake looked down at Alex. She shifted uncomfortably in the hard wooden chair. In addition to the bruise on her jaw, her lips were cracked and dry, but she gave him a small smile. Jake tried to smile in return. He ached to free her, to hold her in his arms.

And yet, although her eyes were a shadowed green right now, there was a ferocity in their depths, which gave no doubt as to her true feelings. Keith had been wise to confine her, Jake thought ruefully. No shrinking violet here. If he'd given Alex the slightest opening, she would have ripped him apart.

He was frustrated he was unable to ease her physical discomfort, so he focused on distracting Keith. Maybe he could talk him down from the precarious psychological ledge he was on.

"Why are you doing this?" Jake asked.

"When did you figure out it was me?" Keith countered. Jake didn't answer right away, and Keith laughed. "There's no way you've known for long. I was too careful." He sobered. "In all fairness though, this," he waved the gun in a lazy circle, "wasn't my original plan. I didn't intend to involve the girl." He jerked his chin at Alex. "But circumstances changed," he sighed. "And you're just so stubborn, Riley. It's completely your fault it's come to this."

"You're not making sense, Keith."

"I'm making perfect sense!"

Jake controlled his frustration, trying a different tact. "Why do you want me to give you the condo project?"

Keith sneered. "I couldn't care less about your stupid condo project. And I'm fed up with your brownfield renovation and all that green nonsense. It's the property I want."

"Why?"

"Because it's rightfully mine."

"Rightfully yours?" Jake felt his anger rise. "It's only yours because you forced me to sign some bogus contract—"

"NO!" Keith thundered, taking a menacing step toward Jake. "That contract merely corrects a wrong that should have been corrected decades ago."

"What are you talking about?"

"That property was my father's. It belongs to me." Keith emphasized each word, the cords of his neck bulging.

"Your father's? Who's your father?"

Keith straightened. "Peter Weston."

A faint memory stirred. Jake looked at Keith. "I remember reading about this. Peter Weston attempted to buy the factory and property back in the late eighties. But he lost his rights to the place."

Keith shook his head slowly, a disturbing light glowed in his eyes. "That never should have happened. But thanks to the good people of Whispering Pines and their stupid red tape, he lost everything, including his life."

Out of the corner of his eye, Jake noticed Alex's fingers working on the ties that bound her. Raw cuts marked her wrists as she strained to loosen the knot.

Keith was looking out the window into the darkness with a frown. Jake needed to keep him talking, get his attention away from his missing partner. "That's unfortunate about your dad, Keith. How did he lose the property?"

Keith turned from the window and paced in front of them. "My father was the first person to recognize the potential of that property. Twenty-five years ago, he bought the rights for it with a plan to resell it to a developer for a huge profit.

"He was an honest man. When he discovered the contamination, he did what he was supposed to do. Reported it to the authorities. But then he spent years battling bureaucrats and the DaviSmit Corporation. He used money out of his own pocket trying to get everybody to do what they should have done in the first place: clean up that blasted site.

"It took so many years to straighten everything out, real estate prices skyrocketed. Dad tried to renegotiate the original terms of the deal, but the developer wouldn't go for it, especially after they learned his idea to put up a luxury hotel wasn't well received by this ignorant community. The developer had no interest in fighting Farley and his shortsighted cronies, so he backed out." Keith stopped pacing. His eyes glittered. "Dad was trapped. He had everything wrapped up in that watchcase factory deal, and he'd neglected all his other ventures. When he lost it, he lost everything. He was bankrupt."

Keith looked directly at Jake, his voice bitter. "He died of a heart attack less than a year later, the same year I graduated from college. There was no life insurance. My mother and I were forced to sell everything just to survive." He stretched his arms wide to encompass the room. "And we lost our home."

"This was your home?" Alex said.

"That's right. And this was *my* room." He spoke with a strange note of pride in his voice.

As he turned to peer out the window again, Jake exchanged a glance with Alex. She said nothing but gave him a look that said, "Yeah, the guy was a nut all right, but a dangerous one."

"You overcame your situation, though, Keith," Jake said. "You made a success of yourself."

"I did," Keith said smugly. "I was determined to get that property back, so I worked my way through law school. By the time I graduated, though, Mom's mental health had begun to deteriorate." He started pacing again, growing more agitated. "What should have belonged to my mother and me reverted back to DaviSmit. But I promised Mother I would find a way to get back what was ours. I was making progress, too." He turned blazing eyes on Jake. "Then Riley Development swooped in and stole it out from under us."

Jake crossed his arms. "You can't blame us for that. We came along well after the fact. And we had no idea how the history of the site personally affected your family."

Keith shrugged, sneering. "Like you'd care. You're just a spoiled rich kid, Riley. Your career was handed to you on a silver platter. You have no idea what it's like for the rest of society. What it's like to struggle."

"I never said—"

"Shut up!" he screamed. Jake jerked back in surprise, and Alex's eyes went wide, whether from fear or surprise, he couldn't tell.

Keith was working himself into a frenzy, which was the last thing Jake wanted. As he searched his mind for a way to calm him, Keith's tone suddenly softened, holding an almost dreamy quality. "I tried getting it back from you the easy way first, you know."

"What?" Jake said.

"Did you really think Farley came up with all his claims and lawsuits against you on his own? Or that the missing shipments and messed up orders were just bad luck?" Keith's lip curled. "Of course you did. Because that's precisely what I wanted you to believe. But instead of abandoning ship and selling the property so I could buy it in a nice, neat sale, you held on. Worked harder. Had to prove yourself to Daddy," he spat. "I was forced to create bigger problems. But between the two of you," he shot a meaningful glance in Alex's direction, "you even managed to mess that up!"

Jake frowned. "You mean—"

Keith rolled his eyes. "The falling bricks, the car accident, those were all to get you out of the picture, Jake." He glared at Alex. "But *she* kept getting in the way."

Jake felt his mouth go dry as the implication behind Keith's words hit him.

"You caused those accidents that nearly killed me!" Alex's voice was choked with fury.

Rage welled up inside Jake, and he clenched his fists in anger. With everything in him, he wanted to choke the life out of the man with his bare hands. But he wouldn't be able to take a single step before Keith got off a shot. And then what would happen to Alex?

"The accidents were such good ideas," Keith mused. "I knew your father wasn't as into this project as you were, Jakey-boy. If you'd gotten seriously hurt or killed," he shrugged, "he'd want nothing more to do with that property. He'd have sold it and I would have gotten it back. But that didn't happen, did it?" He turned a quizzical gaze on Jake. "By the way, what was Alex doing driving your car that day?"

"I loaned it to her when hers died," Jake muttered through clenched teeth.

"Ah." Keith nodded in understanding. "Anyway, I got sick of waiting and drew up the contract. I hadn't quite decided how to handle your signature. Should I forge it or force you to do it before I killed you?" He spoke matter of fact, as if discussing an ordinary business deal. "But as it turned out, Tilly decided it for me."

"Tilly?" Alex stopped working on her bonds and frowned. "What's she got to do with it?"

Keith turned his hard brown eyes on Alex. "She's a lot like you. She butted in and messed up my plan."

Alex looked confused as Keith continued. "I'm sure you recall my visit yesterday?" he drawled. "When I'd picked out the pottery piece for my mother the day before, I inadvertently left behind the envelope with the contract inside it. When I went back to retrieve it, your buttinski grandmother had already sent it off with her friends to take it to Jake since she'd noticed his name on the envelope. I realized once Jake read the contract inside, he'd know something was up, so I had to act fast. I must say, my brainstorm suggestion that you take a hike alone in the woods was pure genius. You went for the idea so easily!" he said with a laugh. "I knew you'd provide the perfect leverage I needed, so I followed you."

Keith's expression grew maniacal as he turned his gaze back to Jake. "But then, true to form, Alex once again spoiled everything by giving you her little clue. Did you really think I wouldn't notice your random second date reference?" He scoffed. "Because of her little stunt, we were forced to abandon the shelter. That's how we ended up here."

Jake's head was spinning as the puzzle pieces fell into place. Keith had been behind...everything. Every annoying complication Jake had endured, the situations which had endangered Alex's life, even the life-threatening circumstance they were now in. He needed to be stopped. But how? Jake risked a sidelong glance at Alex. Was the knot loosening?

"Where is that idiot, Farley!" Keith's anxiety was growing and he began to pace again.

"Farley!" Jake was shocked. "Why team up with him? He caused as much trouble for your dad as he has for us." Jake said.

Keith gave a wry smile. "No doubt you're familiar with the 'kill two birds with one stone' philosophy? He was the perfect choice. He's as guilty as anyone for the stress my father was under. On top of that, he's a stupid, bitter old man who's hated your family for years. Some ancient love triangle with your grandmother. Apparently, he even proposed to her. But she shot him down and chose J.P. instead." He waved the gun dismissively. "All I had to do was fan the flames a little, and voilà, the perfect partner. And scapegoat." Keith's eyes burned. "It will be so easy for everyone to believe he's been behind everything when you're all found dead up here.

"Dead?" Alex's voice cracked."

Keith tilted his head, reminding Jake of how Rex looked when hearing a strange sound. "Poor naïve little Alex. It's unfortunate I had to bring you into it. But surely you didn't think I could let you go after all this?"

"You're being ridiculous, Keith," Jake said. "You'll get caught."

Keith shook his head, a patronizing smile played at his lips. "Jakey, Jakey, Jakey." He made tsking sounds. "I'm just the poor, befuddled contracted attorney for Riley Development. What possible motive would I have? No, no. Frank Farley has a well-documented history of causing trouble for you and that property. Why, he was even arrested for planting a bomb on the site." Keith shrugged. "He finally must have gone over the edge."

"You freak! You're the one who's gone over the edge!" Alex burst out. Her face was flushed with fury.

Keith sneered and drew close to her. "No, my dear. If anybody is suffering from mental illness, it's you." He caressed her cheek with his free hand and she jerked her head back. "Getting involved with this Casanova was your first mistake." He nodded toward Jake. "Though I must say, I was surprised to realize he'd fallen in love with you."

Jake felt the blood rush to his face as Alex's eyes shot to his.

Keith stepped back, letting his amused gaze swing between them. "You didn't know?" He laughed out loud. "Ah, Alex. Your naïveté truly knows no bounds."

Alex stared at Jake, her blue-green eyes wide. He stared back, willing her to see the truth in his own eyes, but also wishing he could pound Keith to a pulp for saying what he had, the way he had.

He wished he could have explained everything himself. Put the depth of emotion that he'd kept in check for so long into his own words. Tell her how he'd been a stubborn fool. How he hadn't been willing to admit his love for her even to himself. But now, he was ready to confess it all to her. Breathe her in. Kiss her. Protect her.

Although, judging by the homicidal look on her face at the moment, perhaps she wouldn't appreciate his protection just now.

Keith was pacing again, and Jake saw Alex begin working her bonds with renewed vigor.

"That's what inspired me to use you, Alex," Keith said, as if Jake had just commented on his revelation. "I knew he'd do anything to save you." He smiled smugly. "And I was right. It's all coming together. You two will be out of the picture, Farley will get blamed, and ownership of the property will go to Visionary Concepts Corporation."

"Meaning you," Jake said flatly.

"Meaning me," Keith agreed with a satisfied smile. "It's a perfect plan, with the exception of..." He frowned and stepped back to the window, Jake's eyes tracking him. He yanked out his cell phone and dialed as he had before, waiting with the phone pressed to his ear. With a growl, he shoved it back into his pocket. "As usual, it appears I'm going to have to handle everything myself."

He faced Jake. "Well, buddy, it looks like I'm going to have to shoot you both now. A lover's quarrel," he grinned.

"Not bad," Jake agreed. "I have another idea, though. Why don't you give me the gun? I'll stay and guard Alex while you go check on Farley."

"You're a funny guy, Jake." He sighed. "I'd really have preferred the nice murder-suicide, but there's no help for it." He shrugged. "I'll figure out what to do with Farley later."

He eyed the dog, who still slept at the foot of Alex's chair. "Get him out of here," he said to Jake. "I don't need any more complications."

"What do you want me to do with him?"

"Get him out of the house and tell him to stay put, otherwise I'll shoot him, too."

Under Keith's watchful eye, Jake led Rex back outside and issued the command to stay. Keith trailed far behind Jake as they slowly climbed the stairs.

Jake clenched and unclenched his fists as his thoughts whirred. They were out of options.

He re-entered the room and Alex turned those amazing opalescent eyes to his. The burning rage he'd seen sparking in them earlier had been replaced with dark fear. Keith directed him to stand beside Alex as he stood close and raised the revolver to point at Jake's head.

"You don't want to do this, Keith!" Alex cried out.

"I believe I do, my dear."

"Keith," Jake's voice sounded remarkably calm to his ears, "let us go and I'll give you the property, no challenges, nothing. I'll just walk away."

Keith lowered the gun slightly. "Promise?"

"Promise."

For a moment, everything stopped. As if time itself seemed to hold its breath.

Then Keith said, "Nah," and he once again leveled the weapon at Jake's head. "I think my way is better."

There was the click of the hammer.

Then everything happened at once. A split second before Jake started to move, Alex, ankles still bound, launched herself at Keith. They crashed to the floor in a heap. Body parts flailing.

Kicking the chair aside, Jake lunged for the gun in Keith's hand. He missed when Keith used it to hit Alex squarely across the face.

Her head snapped and she clutched at her face with both hands, looking dazed. Jake hauled her off Keith, who quickly regained his feet. With a guttural roar of rage, he barreled headfirst into Jake's abdomen, slamming him hard against the wall.

They crashed to the floor at an awkward angle, and a sharp crack of pain shot through Jake's left wrist as he caught himself.

Keith was on top of him then, punching at Jake's face and torso. Through a blood-red haze, Jake managed two solid kidney jabs with his right fist, then shouted, "Rex, *Hier!*"

The scrabble of the dog's claws on the wood floor was audible as he bounded back into the house.

Keith stumbled up, and Jake followed him with an uppercut to the jaw.

Keith staggered backward, trying to aim the gun, but Alex swung her bound feet directly into his path and he thudded to the floor again.

Jake dove after him, left hand useless as he reached for the gun with his right. Keith rolled to one side and leaped up just as Rex entered the room.

"Fassen!" Jake shouted to the dog, pointing at Keith.

The dog sprang at Keith's extended forearm just as he lifted the gun and fired.

CHAPTER 36

Keith cried out as he fell backward. The gun dropped from nerveless fingers as Rex's sharp teeth sank into the soft flesh of his arm.

Jake stooped and retrieved the weapon. Then he immediately crouched beside Alex and used his small pocketknife to cut through the rope binding her ankles.

A large welt had risen on her cheekbone with a small cut oozing blood. His right hand still held the gun, but he pulled her against his chest with his left arm, ignoring the pain in his wrist as he held her close. Adrenalin was coursing through his body, and he could feel Alex quivering against him.

Gone was the playful, Frisbee-toting dog. Rex growled viciously, maintaining a tight hold on Keith's arm.

"Call him off!" Keith shouted. "He's hurting me!"

Jake shook his head. "Nah. I think my way is better." Then added, "Impressive, isn't it? How old police dogs never lose their training?" He frowned, pretending to think. "Hmm, now what was the German command for 'kill?' You don't think it's something as obvious as 'Kill,' do you?"

"Murder?" Alex said helpfully.

"Nooo, maybe it's..."

A second later, the dog released Keith's wrist and instantly latched onto a more sensitive part of his anatomy. His screams echoed across the moonlit fields only to be carried away on the night wind.

"That should do it, Jake," the doctor said as he finished inspecting the fiberglass cast that encased Jake's left wrist and forearm. "The break was a clean one, so it should heal well. I'll remove the cast in about six weeks."

Jake hopped down from the exam table, aware of the muscle aches throughout his entire body. "How's Alex?"

"Fine," came a voice from the doorway. The smiling doctor retreated through it and Alex stepped into the room. "I like the color." She indicated Jake's brilliant blue cast.

"Is it the right blue?"

She laughed. "It's perfect." The bruises on her jaw and cheekbone were already deepening, shading one side of her lovely face a dark purple. A butterfly bandage covered the cut caused by Keith's ring when he'd punched her.

"Are you really okay?" Jake said, laying his good hand on her shoulder and studying her.

"You're definitely the one lookin' worse for wear in this scenario," she said, taking in his own cuts and bruises.

The nurse entered then with a sheaf of papers and gave Jake his release instructions. He barely heard her, lost in the ocean of Alex's eyes.

The nurse left and they were alone again, standing side by side, leaning against the exam table. "I'm so sorry, Alex." Jake spoke barely above a whisper. He reached for her hand and pulled her around to face him. "You would never have even been in this situation if it weren't for me. Can you forgive me?"

She took a deep breath. "From the day I met you, Jake Riley, I knew you'd be nothing but trouble. That's why I told you I had no intention of—"

Her next words were cut off as he bent his head and captured her mouth with his own. His lips were soft and tender, lingering over hers as if sampling a fine ambrosia.

When he finally released her, her eyes were unfocused. "Okay, you're forgiven."

"Do you even know what I'm sorry for?"

"If you kiss me like that again, I really don't care."

He smiled down at her. "I was an idiot, Alex."

She snorted lightly. "What else is new?"

"I'm serious."

"You couldn't possibly have known you were employing a psychotic lunatic."

"That's not what I meant."

"I know."

He sighed, pulling her closer and resting his chin on her head. "As much as I hate that it was the psychotic lunatic who said it first, I have to admit he was right about one thing."

"What's that?"

"I do love you, Alex Fontaine."

She didn't reply, but he felt her become suddenly still within his embrace. He drew back. "Did you hear me?"

Those bottomless blue-green eyes rose to meet his, and the emotion he saw there squeezed his heart.

"Yes," she whispered. "I heard you. Say it again."

"I love you. I love you. I love you. I—" She rose onto her toes and took the words from his lips, making them her own. He crushed her against him and they were soon lost in another kiss.

"Ahem!"

They broke apart guiltily as the nurse stood in the doorway, one brow lifted.

"I would say 'get a room,' but you're in one, and we need it."

A crimson blush glowed beneath the purple bruise on Alex's cheeks.

Jake grinned. "Sorry."

He slipped his good arm around her waist and they walked down the sterile white hallway, floating dream-like through the automatic doors that led to the waiting room. Once through, they were summarily attacked by Tilly, J.P., Rita, Zoe, Gretchen, and Margot.

"What happened?"

"Oh no, your arm is broken!"

"Alex, sweetheart, are you all right?"

"Was Keith Markham really behind everything?"

Jake kept his grip firm around Alex's waist, unwilling to release her or the euphoric feelings he was experiencing since his confession.

Finally, J.P. gave a loud whistle, silencing the group. They all agreed to conduct the remainder of the reunion back at Tilly's house.

Three-quarters of an hour later, they were clustered around Tilly's dining room table. A nearly empty teapot stood in the center and a plate of crumbs was all that remained of the heaping pile of Margot's cookies that once sat there.

"So," Gretchen said, washing down her last bite of cookie with a swallow of tea. "Keith Markham's father was Peter Weston. I never noticed the resemblance."

"The fact that Keith had a different last name probably didn't help," Rita said.

"So strange," Margot said wonderingly. "We all knew Peter had a family, but they never lived in the village. Then, of course, Keith and his mother moved away soon after Peter died."

"Why did Keith change his last name?" Zoe asked.

"Markham was his mother's maiden name," Gretchen said. "He probably wanted to keep his real name secret to ensure there was no connection between his family and that property."

"Speaking of secrets, Pops," Jake said, turning an accusing gaze onto his grandfather. "You could have told me Farley was once *engaged* to Nana!"

J.P. laughed. "That was ages ago, Jakey-boy. We always considered it a brief moment of insanity on your grandmother's part. Cleared up the day she met me, of course." He guffawed and ducked as Jake threw a wadded up napkin at him from across the table.

"I hope Keith doesn't get off on some insanity plea!" Zoe said.

"I just hope he gets the help he needs," Tilly said. "Do you think Elaine Weston ever knew how bitter and obsessed her son was?"

"I doubt it," J.P. said.

Jake saw Alex suppress a grin. He followed her line of sight and smirked at the picture J.P. made, sipping tea out of the dainty floral teacup Tilly had just handed him.

"She was a sweet lady even back in the day," J.P. continued. "I don't think that woman had a bitter bone in her body. Never was the type to carry a grudge. Peter wasn't like that either. He's probably rolling over in his grave to know what Keith was up to."

"Now that he's locked up, will his mom lose her place at Shady Acres?" Alex asked.

"No," Jake said firmly. "She won't. I'll make certain of it."

J.P. beamed with pride at his grandson.

Jake smiled back, then frowned slightly, his gaze taking in the group. "Not that I'm complaining, but does anybody know why Farley never showed up?"

"I know why," Gretchen said with satisfaction. "Because Margot flattened him!"

"What?"

Margot waved her hands dismissively. "I did not flatten him," she said over Gretchen's raucous cackling.

"C'mon, sugar, give it up. What happened?" Rita said, leaning in expectantly along with the rest of the group.

"Well," Margot looked down, smoothing her skirt. "After we saw Jake at the site and delivered that, er, dreaded envelope. We had several errands to run. One of them was to pick out a thank you card for our friend Evelyn. You remember, she's the one who—"

"Get to the good stuff!" Gretchen cut in.

Margot pursed her lips. "Anyway, we were outside the Hallmark store when Frank Farley walked by."

"You shoulda' seen Margot's face." Gretchen cackled again. "She lifted her prissy little nose in the air, straightened her sweater—just like she's doin' now." Gretchen pointed at Margot, who stopped abruptly at being caught in the act.

Margot shifted uncomfortably. "I fully intended to ignore that nasty little man."

"But then he started in on us," Gretchen said with a shake of her head. "You know how he is. Wouldn't let it go. Why does Whispering Pines need a stupid Mural Society? And what exactly have we beautified? Then he starts in on his usual rant about how we need to stop trying to change this town. How we don't need condominiums or any more bloomin' tourists."

"He just would not shut up!" Margot said, pale eyes wide. "He's such an…an ignoramus!"

Jake saw his own surprise mirrored around the table at the hot anger coming from mild-mannered Margot.

"If he'd just stopped there, maybe I could have let it go." She drew herself up in her chair. "But then, he started in on Jake and J.P. Saying such horrid things." She shook her head. "He can rant all he wants in his letters to the editor, but I was *not* going to let him disrespect my friends that way."

"So Margot here gets right in his face." Gretchen picked up the story. "Tells him as sweet as you please that if he needs any help, she'd be happy to recommend someone to pull that stick out of his yahoo."

Jake pinched his lips together to stop from laughing, and Alex covered her mouth with her hand.

"Then the big baby starts shoutin' how he's gonna sue us both for defamation or something," Gretchen continued. "So, I tell him he'll probably have just as much luck with that case as he has with all the rest of his lame lawsuits. He yells some more nasty stuff, I yell stuff back. Then he takes a step toward me, looking like he might hit me or something. And that's when..."

Alex was on the edge of her seat. "What?"

Gretchen grinned wide and jerked a thumb in Margot's direction. "She tackled him."

Five gaping mouths turned in Margot's direction. She still sat primly, avoiding eye contact with anyone, and took a sip from her steaming cup.

"You...she..." Jake sputtered.

Margot set the cup delicately on its saucer and dabbed the corner of her mouth with her napkin. "That's right. I tackled him."

Everyone at the table burst into laughter, and Margot's face turned brilliant red, but her lips quivered. "Well, I'd had it with that horse's rear end!" she said. "He's caused so much trouble for this community; I just sort of lost it."

"I'll say!" Gretchen guffawed. "Boy, did she give it to him. You should have seen her hitting him with that massive handbag of hers and kicking at his shins. You can just guess how hard those clunky orthopedic shoes are that she always wears. Well, she must have packed a pretty hard wallop because ol' Farley starts hopping around, holding onto his leg and hollering like she just broke it or something. And that's when one of Whispering Pines' finest comes around the corner."

Gretchen leaned back in her chair looking smug, both palms flat on the table. "The officer naturally assumed we poor, frail, little old ladies must be fighting off an attack."

"Frail?" Rita snorted.

Gretchen clasped her hands together, attempting to appear helpless. "Why yes, officer, we were just finishing our shopping when this evil man started making inappropriate overtures to us!" She batted her eyes, creating such a ridiculous visual that the group laughed even harder.

"So, that nice police officer arrested him on the spot and took him away," Margot said, then leaned forward. "But we had no idea about the kidnapping or anything!"

After the laughter died down, Jake shook his head. "Well, Alex and I need to thank you, ladies. Farley's failure to show up bought us time. Time that ultimately saved our lives."

"Farley should thank you, too!" Alex added. "The minute he showed up with that signed contract, he would have been framed for our murder and killed himself." She shuddered, and Jake slipped his arm around her, pulling her close.

"What if everything hadn't turned out as it did?" Tilly's voice quavered, and J.P., mimicking Jake's move, placed his big arm around Tilly.

"But it did, Grandma!" Alex reached across the table to grasp Tilly's hand. Then she slid a sidelong glance at Jake. "Besides, you know Rex adores me. He would never have let anything happen to me."

Jake poked her in the ribs, and she jerked aside, laughing. Rex, hearing his name, snuck under the table, tail wagging, to place his shaggy head in Alex's lap.

Eventually, the animated discussion of the group waned. Jake couldn't stop yawning, and shadows darkened Alex's eyes.

He pushed away from the table and rose. "Well, folks, I'm whipped. And I'm going to have a boatload of work tomorrow." He glanced at the wall clock. "Er, today."

"I guess that means me, too," Rita groaned, rising as well.

Gretchen, Margot, and Zoe cleared the dishes as everyone prepared to leave.

Jake took Alex by the hand and pulled her through the door with him.

Bird song floated in the early morning air as they descended the front porch steps. Feathery pines were silhouetted against the horizon's pale glow and the sky was clear, holding the promise of a beautiful day.

When they reached Jake's truck, he swung her around and placed a kiss on her upturned lips. She tasted like cinnamon tea, and snickerdoodles, and Alex. His heart flipped in his chest as the foreign but powerful feeling of deep joy suffused his body.

Releasing her mouth, he rested his forehead against hers and whispered, "Miss Fontaine, I was wondering if you were busy tonight?"

She pulled back to gaze up at him. Delicate brows arched over eyes shining a deep sea green in the shadowy light. "Do you seriously think you can ask me out last minute like this, Riley?"

"No, ma'am," he said, shaking his head. "I was merely inquiring as to your plans for the evening in the slightest hope that you might possibly be available to meet me for a sunset stroll on the beach."

"This is not a date though, right?"

"Well…"

She laughed and, rising on tiptoe, planted a light kiss on his cheek. "I'll see if I can rearrange my schedule."

The front door of the house swung wide and the rest of the group clattered out. The women were all talking at once, looking and sounding to Jake like a brood of hens. J.P. met Jake's eyes over the top of ladies' heads and he rolled them heavenward with a grin. Rex galloped past everyone, and Alex opened the truck door so he could leap into Jake's passenger seat.

She shut it and reached through the open window to scratch him behind his ears. Then she planted a kiss on his shaggy golden head. "Rex, I don't think we ever thanked you for what you did for us today. You're my hero!" The retriever wriggled excitedly, trying to lick her face in return. She laughed and backed away from the truck as Jake climbed in and started the engine. He yawned widely, and she yawned in return.

"See you tonight," he said with a smile.

"Tonight," she echoed.

CHAPTER 37

Alex scanned the beach. It was nearly empty and she quickly spotted Jake at the water's edge. He stood facing the horizon, hands in his pockets, dark curls ruffling in the breeze coming off the lake. He'd rolled his cargo pants to his knees, letting the dark blue waves wash over his legs and feet.

She made her way barefoot across the sand to where he stood. He couldn't have heard her approach over the rush of the waves and cries of swooping gulls, but somehow he knew she was there. He smiled even before he turned to face her. His dimples flashed and then those incredible midnight eyes locked onto hers.

"Hey." He reached out to take her hand.

"Hey," she answered, feeling uncharacteristically shy for some reason.

"I've got a surprise for you," he said and led her up the shoreline, guiding her to a large blanket spread over the still sun-warmed sand. It was secured at each corner with a picnic basket, cooler, small backpack, and two water bottles.

"No Rex?"

"I didn't want to have to fight for your attention." He grinned, falling onto the blanket and pulling her down with him.

They sat side by side on the blanket in companionable silence, watching the play of light on the water as the sun sank lower in the sky.

Finally, she tilted her head toward the picnic basket. "What's all that?"

With an enigmatic smile, he pulled items from inside: a hunk of Brie, a spreading knife, a small package of wheat crackers, fresh strawberries, and two plates.

"Honey, you baked!"

"Not exactly," he laughed, spreading the feast before them. Then he faced her, stretching out his long legs.

She opened the water bottles, handed him one, and took a sip from the other. "How was your day?"

"Informative," he said after a moment's contemplation. He explained he'd met with Frank Farley after his release earlier that afternoon. "Apparently, he had no idea who Keith really was or what he had planned. He was genuinely shocked."

Alex sat with her legs tucked beneath her. She swallowed a bite of cracker with Brie and shook her head. "He isn't completely innocent though, he was willing to put a bomb on your site after all."

"That wasn't the case either," Jake said, placing a large strawberry on her plate.

"We saw him, Jake!"

"Apparently, Farley was trying to *remove* the bomb."

"What?"

"When Keith first approached him about working together to stop the condo project, Farley thought it was a good thing. Keith was an attorney and smart. But over the past couple of months, he could tell things with Keith were escalating out of control, and Farley started getting nervous. The day Keith got hurt at the site, Farley had been arguing with him about taking things too far. Keith started boasting about the bomb. Farley figured he couldn't go to the police since he'd been working with Keith all along. So, he tried handling it himself."

"Wow, I wonder what he thinks now that Keith's been arrested?"

"I think knowing what happened to us has really affected him. I doubt he'll be causing any more trouble for us or the rest of Whispering Pines anytime in the near future."

Alex grinned. "The butt-kicking he got from Margot probably didn't hurt the cause any either."

They laughed together.

Their picnic finished, Jake cleared up the remains. Then he reached into the cooler and withdrew two champagne flutes, along with a chilled bottle of sparkling white grape juice. His cast made it difficult, but with her help, he popped the cork and quickly filled the two glasses with the fizzing liquid.

"What's the occasion?" Alex said as he handed her a glass. "Because we defied death yesterday?"

He smiled. "Partly."

She lifted her glass. "To life!" she said with a smile.

Their glasses clinked and they each took a sip.

"I have a toast of my own I'd like to propose," he said.

"And what might that be?"

He pulled his gaze from hers, silent for a long moment. When he finally spoke, his words carried softly on the twilight breeze. "I was really young when I lost my mom. A lot of people thought that being so young, I probably wasn't as affected by the loss as my older brothers were." His head dipped low. "All I know is, the gaping hole it left in my life was a palpable thing. The best way I can describe it is that it felt as if someone had literally turned off the sun in our lives. Everything warm and good and light was replaced with this dark empty space. My father and my brothers, we all went through the motions of living. But it was only when I was here in Whispering Pines, with Pops and Nana, that I felt happy again."

He raised his head and looked out over the water. "Pops was always great, but Nana Ellen," a small smile tugged at his lips, "she was really the one who..." His voice choked off, and Alex saw liquid pool in his eyes. "When she died, I just shut down. I *knew* then that real love only led to pain. I still had my brothers, Pops, my dad, Rita—but I refused to add anyone else to the list of people I loved. Nobody would ever hurt me that way again. And I locked my heart up inside a protective shell." His gaze swung back to Alex. "You shattered that shell, Alex. You turned your own dazzling light on it, and you made it disappear like the mist from these waves."

He took a breath. "You're so brave. You faced your fear and you won. You told me that living in fear is no way to live. And you were right. You made me realize it really is possible for me to love again."

He stood and drew her to her feet. The sunset encircled them with its rich tapestry of flaming color as Jake pulled a silky drawstring bag from his pocket and tipped its contents into his open palm.

Her breath caught as a pear-shaped diamond winked up at her in the transforming light.

"This was my grandmother's ring," he said.

She looked up and met his unwavering gaze. "The toast I'd like to propose is to love that was lost and found...and to love that lasts a lifetime."

He dropped to one knee, never taking his eyes from hers. "Alexandra Fontaine, will you marry me?"

"I—you..." She felt herself swirling, spinning. "But we agreed nothing permanent. No strings," she finished weakly.

"I'd been living for too long no strings, Alex. And then I met you."

It was as if they were taking turns being brave. First her, with her confession. Now him, daring her to take the next step with him. But marriage?

Brushing away the tendrils of hair that danced around her face in the wind, she gazed down at him. And she saw doubt flicker in the depths of his dark eyes.

He cleared his throat, "Look, um..."

"Yes." The word came out in a rush of air. She took a deep breath, steadied herself, and let go. "Yes, Jake Riley. I will marry you!"

He jumped to his feet, lifting her off the ground in one move. He let out a whoop of joy as he twirled her around and around, making the fuchsia, orange, and purple of the sky blend in a dizzying kaleidoscope of colors.

She threw her head back and laughed. Feeling lighter and happier than she had ever felt in her life. And then his lips found hers and they melted together against the backdrop of the setting sun.

A Note from Holly...

Reviews...they're critical! Reviews help authors more than you may realize. If you enjoyed *Whispers in the Dark,* I'd be grateful if you'd consider leaving a review on Amazon. Thank you!

Ready for the next book in *The Secrets of Whispering Pines* series? Enjoy this summary of Book 2 in the series, *Whispers of Redemption,* along with a sneak peek bonus scene.

Whispers of Redemption (Book 2)

Wade Riley is a dedicated police officer, committed to upholding the law. Cassie Sherwin is a woman who wrestles with authority issues. When a mysterious art theft draws Cassie and Wade closer together, they find themselves caught between their convictions and an undeniable attraction.

This second book in the Secrets of Whispering Pines series is an enemies to lovers small town romance with a guaranteed HEA, and a mystery that will keep you turning pages long into the night.

Whispers of Redemption
Sneak peek bonus scene:

Hugo Garcia parked the patrol car outside of the manufacturing company's main entrance. It was a sprawling building with tall, faded brick walls. The two officers got out and walked beneath the portico to the front door that had a security pad beside it. There was a faint beep as Hugo pressed the intercom button.

A feminine voice came over the speaker. "Yes?"

"We're officers Hugo Garcia and Wade Riley from the Whispering Pines Police Department," Hugo said. "We need to speak with the manager in charge of this facility."

Seconds later, the door buzzed and they opened it, stepping inside the building reception area. The young woman who'd let them in sat behind a sleek, curved reception desk. A door behind her popped open to emit a rotund, perspiring man with wire-rimmed glasses. He had an anxious expression on his face as he hurried toward them. "Good afternoon, officers. I'm Jeff Greenway, the general manager. What can I help you with?"

Hugo said, "Good afternoon, Mr. Greenway. We're investigating a robbery that occurred yesterday. We suspect that one of the vehicles involved was a black Ford pickup truck registered to your business."

Wade watched the man closely. His eyes widened at Hugo's words, and his jaw dropped slightly, telltale signs of legitimate surprise.

"We do have a black pickup truck," Jeff said. "It's parked out back. But as far as I know, nobody has driven it for weeks."

"May we take a look at it?" Hugo asked.

"Certainly," Jeff said. "Follow me."

He led them through the building and out a door leading to the back. Wood pallets lay stacked up all along the back exterior wall, and beyond the lot, an unkempt open field stretched out before them. Off to one side was a small parking lot with a few cars in it, including a mud-spattered, black pickup truck.

Wade and Hugo walked slowly around the exterior of the truck, examining it closely.

"The license plate is right," Hugo said, standing at the back end. "And mud is covering the last three characters, just like Cassie described."

"That window wasn't like that before," Jeff commented.

Wade looked at the driver's side window. The glass was slightly lowered and sat at an angle, indicating it had somehow been rocked off its track. "Do you have a key?"

Jeff fumbled in his pocket and pulled out a ring of multiple keys. He flipped through them until he found the one he wanted, then handed it to Wade, who pulled a pair of rubber gloves from his duty belt and put them on, using the key to unlock the driver's side door.

"Does anyone else have a key?" Wade asked, handing it back to him.

Jeff shook his head. "I keep both keys with me on this key ring," he said, jangling it. "Unless I give one to someone who's going to drive it. But like I said, nobody's driven it for weeks."

Hugo also put on gloves and opened the passenger side. Then he and Wade carefully examined the floor and interior of the truck.

"We'll arrange for our evidence tech to come dust for prints," Wade said, pulling his head out from inside the truck to address Jeff. Just then, a movement and brief flash of color at the side of the manufacturing building caught his eye.

"Hang on," he said quietly to Hugo. Wade strode swiftly to the back of the building, then edged along the brick wall before suddenly stepping around the corner and surprising Cassie.

She gave a startled cry and put a hand over her heart. "You scared me!" she said in an accusatory tone. She stood there with Angel beside her on her pink leash. The fluffy white dog immediately trotted over and began sniffing Wade's shoes. He took a step back.

"What are you doing here?" he said.

Cassie's heart-shaped face blushed a deep red.

"Wait a minute. Are you following us?" he asked, incredulous.

"Maybe," she said, quickly regaining her composure. "Why, is that a problem?"

"Yes, it's a problem!" Wade said.

"Why? It's not illegal," Cassie said quickly.

For a moment, Wade was at a loss for words. She was right. It wasn't illegal. But somehow, it still felt wrong.

"Besides," she added, lifting her chin, "I just wanted to make sure you followed up on the clues I gave you guys." She stepped away from the building to look into the parking lot where Hugo and Jeff Greenway stood. "It looks like you found the truck. You're welcome," she added.

He was annoyed at how smug she sounded, and he could feel himself beginning to lose it again. Her attitude toward him, combined with her complete disregard for following any kind of rules, was making him crazy.

Wade took a deep breath, fighting to master his emotions. "Look, Cassie, you need to stop this. Just let us do our job."

She smiled.

"What are you smiling about?"

"You finally called me Cassie."

He just stared at her for a long moment, then without another word, he turned on his heel and walked back toward the truck. But he could hear her footsteps crunching on the gravel behind him.

"Yup, that's definitely the truck I saw in the robbery," Cassie said, coming up to stand beside him. Angel sat down next to her.

Jeff Greenway looked worried. "I don't understand!"

"Was the key ever out of your possession yesterday?" asked Wade.

"No, the keys are always with me. But I have an alibi," he said in a rush. "I was here at work until about three-thirty yesterday, then I left to go watch my oldest son's baseball game."

"Nobody is accusing you of anything, sir," Hugo said. "Do you keep a record of the vehicle's mileage?"

"Yes, it's in my office."

"Can you please get it for us?" Hugo said.

While Jeff Greenway hurried off, Cassie poked her head inside the van on the passenger side.

"Don't touch anything!" Wade said.

"I just want to check something. Do you have an extra pair of gloves?" Cassie asked.

"What do you want to check?" Hugo said.

"I was just wondering if there was a spare key inside the car."

"Mr. Greenway already told us he has the only keys," Wade said, annoyed.

Suddenly, Angel hopped up into the cab of the truck and began sniffing around the floor mats.

"Get her out of there!" Wade commanded. "She's interfering with potential evidence."

Angel began pawing at the passenger-side floor mat. Her little paws worked in rapid succession until she suddenly pushed her tiny snout down and came up with a small, black object gripped between her teeth.

"What is that?" Wade asked.

"Release!" Cassie said, mimicking Hugo from the other day.

Angel immediately dropped the item and Hugo reached over to pick it up. The object was rectangular with a hard, plastic loop at one end. He pulled on it and a thin object slid out from the outer casing. "It's a plastic key," he said, holding it up.

"Sometimes cars have a valet key that car owners don't even know they have," Cassie said. "They're a common way for car thieves to steal cars. It might have originally been in the glove box, or maybe inside the owner's manual."

"We know all about valet keys," Wade said, sounding huffy. In truth, he had forgotten about that possibility. What was it about this woman that flustered him so completely?

Hugo turned the key over between his gloved fingers. "Maybe we can get a print off it," he said.

"Doubtful," Cassie said, and they both looked at her. "Oh, um...I may have forgotten to mention that the thief was wearing gloves."

Wade rolled his eyes and Hugo sighed. But he still zipped the key up in a small evidence bag.

Jeff returned with the mileage records, and Wade looked at them. They showed a thirty-one-mile discrepancy between the last recorded mileage and the odometer reading.

"I don't understand," Jeff said again. "How is that possible?"

"I suspect someone stole your truck yesterday afternoon, used it for the theft, and then returned it," Wade said, making notes in his notebook. Out of the corner of his eye, he noticed Cassie typing into her cell phone.

Jeff's face went pale.

"You may want to consider installing a steering wheel lock or ignition immobilizer so this can't happen again," Cassie said. "By the way, do you have any cameras covering your lot?"

Wade shot her a look, but she just grinned back at him, amusement gleaming in the depths of her eyes.

"Uh...no, I'm sorry we don't," he replied.

"Sir, would it be possible for us to speak to any of your staff who were here between three thirty and when you close up shop?" Hugo asked. "Just to see if anybody saw anything."

"Yes, yes, of course," he said, and led the way back toward the building. At the door, Jeff and Hugo passed through, but Wade paused, turning to block Cassie. "I need to ask you to leave now."

"Are you sure you don't want more of my help?" Cassie asked, arching a delicate brow at him. She was sassy. And beautiful, as she stood there boldly meeting his gaze. Aside from some of the criminals he'd arrested, he'd never met anyone with so little regard for authority.

"Admit it," she added, "you wouldn't be nearly as far in your investigation if it wasn't for me."

"That may be true," he said. "But as I said before, it's not appropriate for you to be involved in this case. Hugo and I will take it from here. Have a nice day." And he let the door close in her face.

When Wade and Hugo eventually exited the building, Cassie was waiting.

Ugh. The woman was relentless. Could he arrest her for unnecessary butting in?

"What did they say? Did anyone see anything?" Cassie asked as she and Angel fell into step beside them.

"Unfortunately, no," Hugo said.

"Hmmm..." she mused, walking with them toward their patrol car. "So, I'm guessing this was clearly premeditated then. I mean, the thief took the time to steal a vehicle and then return it. No ordinary car thief would do that."

"Really? Are you speaking from personal experience?" Wade shot her a suspicious look.

Cassie ignored his comment and continued. "And this place is so close to PCS." She waved her hand in the direction of the courier service that was only a block up the road. "That made it easy for him to follow me to Olga's." The reality of her last statement appeared to strike her. She stopped walking and shivered.

Wade noticed, and regardless of how annoying she'd been up to that moment, the expression on her face gave him a strong urge to wrap a protective arm around her.

He turned to face her then. Her rich, auburn hair glowed like flame in the sunlight, her teeth gnawed unconsciously at her full lower lip. He realized he was staring at it and cleared his throat, pulling himself up straight. "Listen, Cassie," he said, his voice more gentle than it had been, "I understand how important this is to you, and we promise to keep you posted on our progress. But you need to go home now."

She met his eyes and held them. And rather than making her usual argument, she nodded slowly. "All right," she said quietly. She turned to walk back toward her own car, Angel trotting alongside. She was a few paces away when, without stopping, she called back over her shoulder, "At least for now."

Plan to read them all!

Other books in the Secrets of Whispering Pines series:
Forbidden Whispers (Book 3)

Maggie Milena is a professional matchmaker who can match up anyone but herself. Noah Riley can't manage to get a second date...with anyone. When Maggie applies her trademark skills, the results do not go as planned. And now both of their lives are in jeopardy.

Whispers of the Heart (FREE series prequel)

How would you like a free novella? *Whispers of the Heart* (a prequel to Alex and Jake's story) is available here: hollybownebooks.com/free-book. Along with your free book, you'll also begin receiving my occasional newsletter offering exclusive content, sneak peeks on new releases, and information on special giveaways.

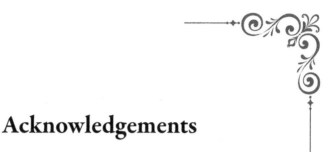

Acknowledgements

First and foremost, I want to thank God for blessing me with a passion and gift for writing. Glory to him!

I want to thank my beloved, beautiful, and favoritest daughter in the whole wide world, Ashleigh, for being my very first reader and editor, and for constantly encouraging me along the way.

I want to acknowledge my incredible husband Chris, who never read a romance novel in his life – until now. I'm grateful that you were so happy to read mine. I appreciated your helpful editing notes, patience with my many questions regarding story details, and your endless encouragement.

I want to thank my son Josh, for always telling me that "everything will be fine."

I'm deeply grateful for my late mother and father who always believed in me and never doubted that I could do this.

I owe a special shoutout to a most talented muralist, Tom Colaluca, for allowing me to invade your home and interrogate you for hours on end with my questions about your work.

My sincere appreciation to Kavita Borsum and Sarah Bednarcik, for your help in getting my facts straight regarding construction and development.

I would also like to express my gratitude for my mother-in-law Mary, sister-in-law Traci, and my BUNCO Babes for being my beta readers, spotting plot holes, and encouraging me by sharing how much you each enjoyed the story.

A special thanks to Alicia Thrams for giving me great feedback on the story and a great starting point for the book cover.

And last but absolutely not least, I want to extend thanks to my amazing editor, Cameron Yeager, for your efficiency, professionalism, and kindness in pointing out my penchant for "head hopping."

Holly

Meet the Author

Holly Bowne is the author of the Secrets of Whispering Pines romantic suspense series. She's worked in advertising, journalism and as a freelance writer. And she finds inspiration everywhere, from movies, TV series, the news, conversations with her friends and conversations she's eavesdropped on (shhh!). She currently lives on a beautiful lake in southeast Michigan where she dreams up new stories, falls down research rabbit holes, and witnesses the beauty and song of God's creation every single day. She's happily married to her college sweetheart, mother of two grown children along with a daughter- and son-in-love, and passionate Gigi to three adorable grandchildren. And she's not biased about this at all.

You can learn more about Holly and her books at www.hollybownebooks.com

Printed in the USA
CPSIA information can be obtained
at www.ICGtesting.com
LVHW092334010524
779101LV00031B/660